A Masked Earl

by

Kathleen Buckley

This is a work of fiction. Names, characters, places, and incidents are either the product of the author's imagination or are used fictitiously, and any resemblance to actual persons living or dead, business establishments, events, or locales, is entirely coincidental.

A Masked Earl

COPYRIGHT © 2019 by Kathleen Gail Buckley

Cover Art by *Abigail Owen*

The Wild Rose Press, Inc.
PO Box 708
Adams Basin, NY 14410-0708
Visit us at www.thewildrosepress.com

Publishing History
First Tea Rose Edition, 2019
Print ISBN 978-1-5092-2837-9
Digital ISBN 978-1-5092-2838-6

Published in the United States of America

Praise for Kathleen Buckley

Kathleen Buckley's second novel, *MOST SECRET*, was a finalist in the 2018 Oklahoma Romance Writers of America (OKRWA) International Digital Awards, historical category, and in the 2019 Next Generation Indie Book Awards Romance category.

"It's easy enough to find a murderer—"

The door to the library opened, and a female peered in, saying, "My lord, your mother would—" The thick and tightly fitting doors in Barlyon House and a Turkey rug carpeting the corridor had muffled her approaching footsteps. Before Barlyon could speak, she hurried into further speech. "I beg your pardon. I didn't realize you had a guest with you. Excuse me." She began to pull the door shut.

"Wait, Mistress Aurelia!"

She froze.

"May I introduce my friend, Ambrose Hawkins?"

Hawkins sprang up and executed his best bow. Aurie cautiously entered and curtsied.

"This is Mistress Aurelia Kennet, Viscount Pennyroyal's daughter, who has come up to town to bear my mother company."

They exchanged pleasantries before she murmured, "I did not mean to intrude. Your mother only wished to know if you will dine at home tonight?"

Receiving an answer in the affirmative, she made her escape as quickly as possible.

Hawkins stared at the closed door. "Do you think she heard anything?"

"Almost certainly."

"Will she have hysterics or vapors and blab?"

"I don't think it. Mistress Aurelia's a sensible young lady, not like the heroine in some over-heated novel."

Chapter 1

Advertisement, *London Gazette*, 1 November 1740:

Recently died at Barlyon Manor, Kent: Abel Cornell, eleventh Earl of Barlyon, well known in those parts for his upright character. Three of his four sons having died before him, anyone possessing knowledge of the fourth, John Davenant Cornell, long missing from his home, whether that same be living or dead, is earnestly solicited to contact William Reeves, Attorney at Law, Maidstone.

****

The Honorable Aurelia Kennet sat straight-backed and uncomfortable in the drawing room of Barlyon Manor. Her father, Viscount Pennyroyal, had dispatched her on a condolence call to Lady Barlyon, the eleventh Earl of Barlyon having fallen down dead of an apoplexy some three weeks since. The footman present at the time of the seizure reported his lordship had read some article in the *Gentleman's Magazine* that caused him to exclaim, "Hang the scoundrels!" He then collapsed and was dead before he could be carried up to his bedchamber and the doctor summoned.

"Being a female, Aurie, you will do a better job than I could do," her papa said, "and, having a great deal of composure, will be a better choice than your mama, who can weep over no more than a dead mouse.

She would only make the widow feel worse."

Although his phrase "a great deal of composure" actually signified "phlegmatic"—for which, read "stolid"—she did not consider it insulting. Heaven knew what would have become of her during the last eight years if she had been delicate-minded. She obliged her parents in any way she could, as they had supported her decision and never alluded to the reason she was an old maid. Even had they been less understanding, guilt for the humiliation and difficulties she had caused them would have impelled her to do anything she could to please them.

He went on. "Though the poor woman must find it a blessed release. I couldn't stick the fellow for five minutes at a time. There's no harm in a man being moral if he don't carry it to extremes. I had the greatest difficulty at the funeral listening to the parson mouth pious balderdash about Barlyon."

Aurelia suspected him of two motives. The first would be to distract her. The viscount would have gone himself, whatever his feelings about Barlyon, and so would her mother, who would sternly have maintained a dry-eyed but sympathetic face, had they not had arrangements to make. They thought the sight of the great travelling coach being inspected for needed repairs, cleaning, and furbishing up would remind her of her one visit to London. As those activities did, of course. How fortunate she had no feelings to speak of, or her life would be quite depressing.

The second motive would be to encourage her to venture outside her limited circle. Once she had been of a gregarious nature, though since her return from London, she did not visit anyone she had not known for years. Lady Barlyon was a neighbor, certainly, but one with whom she had seldom spoken and then merely at the weekly ordeal of church. The conversations had been little more than the necessary greetings with a colorless, timid female with nothing to say. Had her mother and father thought the visit to Lady Barlyon would make a change in her routine?

At least, it was not as though the widow could be prostrated by grief. Aurie would have had difficulty concealing her glee if she had been Barlyon's widow. The man's ways must have been insupportable. Lady Barlyon would enjoy company, and very likely they would talk of parish matters. Such a condolence call would not be unpleasant.

However, when she was shown into Lady Barlyon's boudoir, a gentleman was sitting beside the widow, patting one of her hands, while she employed the other to blot her eyes with a handkerchief. Had the man been another neighbor, she would have been surprised but not discomfited. Instead, he was a stranger of no more than thirty years, if as much. In a suit of gray silk, laced with silver, with very fine lace at his cuffs and neck, he was dressed too fine for the country. A black armband completed his costume.

Only good manners prevented her from gabbling out some excuse to withdraw immediately. Could he be some relation come to support the countess in her bereavement? He rose very quickly when she entered the room and executed a bow more suitable for court than for a country house. He appeared to be the complete London beau.

Lady Barlyon looked up, smiling, eyes still shining with tears. "Aurelia, my dear, such good news!"

After a polite curtsy to both, Aurelia came forward to take her hands, having to detour slightly around the gentleman.

"Aurelia, my prayers have been answered. May I present my son, John, who was lost to us so many years ago?"

"Oh! Certainly, my lady." The local gentry spoke of the lost youngest son as a slightly scandalous mystery, though the subject had evidently been forbidden in the Cornell family, as discussion of her own situation was banned among her family and their friends.

"John, this is Aurelia Kennet, Viscount Pennyroyal's daughter."

She saw him look at her appraisingly and attempted to be less obvious about her own study of him. He was pleasant in appearance though nothing about him stood out. He was average in height and weight, with eyes of a light brown. His fashionable powdered wig was more memorable than he was.

"I believe I recall Mistress Aurelia," he murmured.

"I don't know how we could have met, Lord Barlyon. I must have been a child of no more than eight or nine, and I suppose you spent your time climbing trees and swimming and…and doing whatever boys do." From her own brother, she had a fair notion of how boys spent their time. Would the previous Lord Barlyon have permitted such boyishness? Not if he knew of it, she thought.

"Perhaps I saw you at church? Or the midsummer festival?"

Only if he'd slipped out of the house to attend the latter. Perhaps he had. Judging from occasional comments by older people, John Cornell must have been rather wild.

"John, tell the footman to have a tea tray sent up, please."

"You must only have arrived, my lord. We had not heard a word of your arrival."

"I came the day before yesterday. Given that my mother is in mourning, we thought it best to wait for a while before creating a nine days' wonder." He opened the door and called a brusque order to the footman stationed in the passage.

It should have been impossible to keep such news secret. Then she reconsidered. The late Lord Barlyon had been a strict master. His servants never questioned his orders or gossiped about the family. If they did, they were turned off without a character and could not expect to get work or even remain in the village.

She did not stay long, excusing herself on the grounds that Lady Barlyon and her son, so miraculously restored to her, had years of catching up to do. Her hostess did not press her to stay. However, an additional inducement to leave was the new Lord Barlyon's manner. She found it embarrassing. His compliments were a little fulsome, better suited for a ball—or no, a masquerade, where strict propricty was not always observed—than for a visit, particularly when the family was theoretically in mourning. It would be blatant hypocrisy to pretend to grief in this instance, but a certain level of decorum should be observed. Though perhaps wild boys grew into rakish men. If he had heard of her in London, he might suppose she would not be offended by his manner.

Oh, her miserable London season! Her parents had

expected to find her a husband easily; instead she had made a disaster of it and ensured that she was unlikely ever to marry. Certainly she could never return to London.

****

When she related the news of John Cornell's near-miraculous return, her mother was all exclamations.

"How wonderful that poor boy has now inherited the title. I vow I always felt sorry for him in particular, as he was quite different from his papa and badly treated. It was much talked of when he ran away, and only thirteen, too, though no one wondered at it. "

"Boys of that age are all wild," her father remarked. "I suppose I must call upon him, but I'll wait a few days or a week, until we hear it announced. It's very odd that it hasn't already been made known."

"We should not wait too long," Aurelia's mother said. "Barlyon will be looking about him for a wife, even during mourning, for what a terrible thing it would be if some accident befell him, ending their line."

"We'll not rush in. He will hardly find any girl in the neighborhood as well-bred and suitable as Aurelia. He must be thirty; he will not want a chit out of the schoolroom."

Even if she was six-and-twenty and almost an ape-leader, which would be bad enough, without the other thing. The memory of her contretemps in London had not been forgotten. Her brother Philip's betrothed and her family had declined an invitation to visit on an obvious pretext. Her fault, no doubt, like his very infrequent visits to King's Penny. Now her parents had been invited to stay over Christmas at the Merriatts' country home. The invitation had not mentioned

Aurelia, but a letter from Philip made it clear she was not welcome and would not be invited when he and Charlotte married in London in the spring.

She did not mind. If she was not happy with her circumscribed life in the country, going where people would whisper about her would be worse. Her future loomed bleak, however. When her brother Philip succeeded her father, she would have to leave home, a daunting thought. Her papa clearly cherished hopes that the new Lord Barlyon might offer for her, overlooking the fact that he would surely hear the talk, if he had not heard it before.

"It would be delightful if he formed a partiality for Aurelia," her mother agreed, though even her usual optimism must be tempered by the knowledge that the new Lord Barlyon would be aware of Aurelia's history. Or if he were not aware now, someone would tell him, for his own good.

However, only two days after Aurelia's call, a more startling development than the sudden reappearance of the heir caused Viscount Pennyroyal to alter his intention to visit Barlyon Manor.

The viscount came into the breakfast parlor and hurriedly dismissed the footman, saying, "We'll serve ourselves." He must have been agitated, for he and her mother seldom scrupled to discuss any but the most private matters before the servants.

He proceeded to pile meat, eggs, and bread on his plate absentmindedly and poured out coffee. "There's a second claimant to the Barlyon title. I heard it from Bradley when he came in with my chocolate. He heard it from Cook, who heard it from the carrier who brought the groceries from Maidstone. The second fellow came with old Barlyon's attorney yesterday afternoon."

"A second claimant?" Lady Pennyroyal uttered. "How can that be, when there was only one son left?"

"One of them is an imposter."

"But Lady Barlyon accepted the one who came, didn't she, Aurelia? A mother would recognize her son."

Her father looked momentarily struck by the statement, and admitted, "You would think so, certainly. Did she appear to be in any doubt, Aurelia?"

She chewed on her lower lip, a bad habit acquired during her visit to London. "It's been many years since she saw him, hasn't it? If he went away at the age of thirteen, that's seventeen years. He looked to be about the right age. People do change as they grow up."

"But still…"

"I wonder if there might not be an element of wishful thinking in her recognition of him, Mama. She hoped her son would see the obituary and return, because if he did not, some distant relative would inherit the title and manor, and Lady Barlyon would lose her home."

"That's very true," her mother agreed, much impressed.

"Hmmf. I own I have never found Edith Barlyon remarkable for character or understanding. But there must be a servant or two who would be able to recognize the first claimant if he were genuine."

"If they were not afraid to speak, Papa. After all, even if they were not fearful of offending Lady Barlyon, if any doubt existed about the heir, they might fear to offend him. He might replace them." She privately thought servants so cowed as to be able to keep secret the arrival of the heir (or claimant!) for as much as five minutes would probably keep any doubts to themselves.

Her father patted his lips with his napkin and rose, leaving no more than a scrap of ham fat and a smear of egg upon his plate. "My dear, it is a pity you were not born male. I would have had you trained up in the law."

She wished she had been born male. It would have saved her family shame and allowed her a future.

"Would that your brother had your sense. We will not call upon the family until this business has been sorted out, which I have no doubt Attorney Reeves will do."

Chapter 2

London, 1 November 1740

The man who called himself John Barlicorn blinked and glanced around the coffee house, hoping his eyes deceived him. The light in the corner where he sat was not ideal for reading. No one had come to consult him yet today, else he would not have picked up the *London Gazette*. Only one of his associates or petitioners would join him at the table reserved for his use on Tuesdays and Thursdays.

The words remained unchanged. Alack.

How could it come to this? He had heard of Matthew Cornell's death some six years past, for it had taken place in London, although word of it reached him by roundabout means. The only news of the nobility to which he paid attention came by word of mouth and concerned those active in London. The late Earl of Barlyon had spent time in town only to attend the House of Lords. He had not been dissolute nor run up debts. From that description, one might take him for an estimable man. The rest of the family, if they left Kent for London, made no stir either. Or not one that had come to Barlicorn's attention, except for Matthew.

He gazed around the coffee house, aware again of the sound of conversation, the haze of pipe smoke, the plain wooden tables and benches. Job's was neither famous nor large, but it was convenient as to location and in its range of customers. It had not attracted any particular group, like actors and playwrights, or lawyers, or the fashionable, or those in the shipping industry, like Lloyd's. Anyone might wander into Job's—soldier, sailor, tinker, tailor, as well as merchants, craftsmen, professional men, and the occasional lord or rogue—making it easy to conduct business that could not discreetly be done at his office at the back of the Saracen Queen tavern.

His heart pounded as if he had been running, and the room felt too warm, sensations he recalled all too well from his boyhood. One of the lads who went around with pots of coffee veered away from his corner, warned by his expression, like enough. He would have been happy never to hear the name Barlyon again. The notice brought all the memories back and, with them, seething rage. He made an effort to breathe slowly and deeply. Someone might come to request his assistance at any moment, making it necessary that he be clear-headed.

If only this Tuesday had brought as many to his table as usual, he need never have picked up the curst newssheet and never known of the earl's death and the problem of the succession. How in the Devil's name could the others be dead?

Strike him dead! What's to do?

The answer was unavoidable. He had been content here for seventeen years. Not happy, perhaps, when at first the challenge of surviving was all that occupied him. Now he had a place and work to do. Some days, he felt he was accomplishing something.

He no longer saw the notice before him. Good

God, what was to be done? Who would inherit the title and the manor? Wasn't there a cousin who was a parson in Cornwall? Not the hard-riding, hard-drinking sort of cleric, either, judging by the fact that Lord Barlyon had approved of him. If Tamar or Lady Barlyon were still alive, they would either live as the cousin's dependents or be turned out of their home. Whatever the marriage settlement had been, it would mean a substantial change in the countess's circumstances, and not for the better, financially. Tamar would no doubt still be living at home, poor girl.

He couldn't do it. Most would say, grab the opportunity. Carpe diem. He sighed. He could ignore the chance. He had never been trained to take on the duties of the estate, had not even seen the place since he was thirteen, when he had sworn a solemn oath he would never return. He had responsibilities here in London. He did not give a damn what became of Lady Barlyon. What was she to him? But he could not ignore Tamar's plight, whatever the cost to himself. If he were not accepted, he could not come back to Job's and the Saracen Queen. His position here would not wait for him. Not that he needed to work, but what would he do with nothing to occupy his time, trapped between two worlds? He could start again somewhere else, under a different name, in better circumstances. As a merchant in Bristol, perhaps, or the American colonies.

Going back was a risk. Yet he really had no choice. The realization made him feel sick. Damnation! What were the odds of it coming to this? He sipped coffee that had grown as cold and bitter as his life in the same few minutes.

He caught a waiter's eye and beckoned him.

"More coffee, sir?"

"Ay. But I will leave presently and see no one today. I will be here on Thursday."

"Very good, sir."

Thursday he would come here for the last time to do business, negotiate agreements, and adjudicate disputes when necessary. Dickson would not be able to take over this part of his business, though he would try. He would make bad decisions and would lose the trust Barlicorn had earned over ten years or more. Gentlemen would not deal with him, not once they'd met him, cutting off a valuable source of revenue and information. Whatever Barlicorn did, he would be abdicating his responsibility to someone. But one responsibility was slightly more compelling than the other…and brought with it a golden opportunity, a fact he realized only now. Being golden, it was also weighty.

His fresh coffee arrived. Between sips, he began to make a mental inventory of things to be done.

See the green bag to arrange an annuity for Lem Grigson.

Transfer his share of Job's to Gwen. She had come to him from a coffee house, after all. The income would make her secure and get her a husband if she wanted one.

Turn the Saracen Queen over to…well, he'd think about who would be best.

Visit his business agent.

Visit Monmouth Street for secondhand gentleman's suits and haberdashery. It wouldn't do to arrive with all new clothing. Grigson could dispose of his old clothing and most of his other belongings for a little more gelt.

Pack the possessions he would take with him, apart from his new clothing. Those would not amount to much: shaving gear and the like, a few books, the portfolio.

Order a travelling coach for Friday.

Speak with Hawkins and Easterday. They were almost friends and should be apprised of the change. Hawkins could pass the word discreetly to anyone in his circle who should know.

Visit Solomon, who was a friend. Rot him, he was more a brother than those three damned dead men.

Two days should be enough for what he must accomplish. At least travel would be swift. The weather having turned cold, though without snow, the roads would be hard as iron.

The last thing would be to break the news to Dickson. He'd been loyal thus far, but there was no reason to give him a chance to think things over.

Damnation.

****

As the coach lumbered up the lane from the gatehouse, Barlicorn tried to fight down the sick feeling in his stomach. The attorney facing him remarked, "It's a fine house, not more than a century old."

The attempted deceit steadied him. "The most recent parts were built shortly before Queen Mary ascended the throne. Bits from the original house were incorporated, like the undercroft. It's used, or was when last I lived here, for storing wine and other supplies. There's a tower left, but it's totally enclosed in the newer construction. It provides an extra, if rather inconvenient, stairway for the servants."

Barlyon Manor gave the impression of a large, fine house from the outside. Of brick and ragstone, it was studded with many chimneys and a number of gables, and the mullioned windows shone like diamonds in the sunlight, each lozenge-shaped pane reflecting at a minutely different angle. In some old houses, the casements had been replaced with double-hung windows. He was glad it was not so at Barlyon Manor; the sight of the windows catching the light like the facets of a gem was one of the few memories he treasured. He found the rest as appealing as Newgate, not that he had ever lived in Newgate. But he had visited acquaintances there.

The chimneys might lead one to believe the manor would be cozy. One would be mistaken. The house surrounded a great inner court connected to the outside by two narrow passages, one to the kitchen garden, the other to the grounds behind the house. Where the wings were only one room wide, the rooms had possessed two exterior walls, which must have made them chilly and drafty. In places two small rooms occupied the width of the wing as in the nursery area, where the space had been cut in half to form a bedchamber and a second room, making it possible to keep almost warm. Cornell children grew up hardy or not at all. The Cornell family seat had gone virtually unchanged for almost two hundred years, except for the addition of passageways along the courtyard side and two or three formerly large chambers peculiarly divided. The alterations made some improvement on the original plan in which each room had led into the next, a circumstance which did not allow for much privacy. How could one possibly enjoy one's wife if a servant or other inmate of the house could pass through one's bedchamber on his or her way to some other room? Granted, the bed curtains would be drawn, but still it would be nearly as bad as the poor families living in one room who wapped, gave birth, lived, and died surrounded by others.

Chapter 3

Viscount Pennyroyal's sensible resolution was overset within hours by the delivery of a letter from Barlyon Manor. His eyes fairly bulged as he read it.

"Whatever is the matter, Pen?" her mother asked, startled into using the nickname they preferred in private, though it was an open secret that she called Papa by his title only in public.

"Reeves writes us, acting as executor of the estate, inviting us to dine at Barlyon tomorrow evening, with three other couples."

"How very odd! How should he issue an invitation to Barlyon Manor, and during the first month of mourning, too?"

"Perhaps not surprising, though it is presented as a social event. He writes that 'those invited are longtime friends'—" Here he snorted. "—'of the Cornell family.' He implies there may be future dinners or house parties with far-flung friends and connections." He shot a glance at Aurelia. "What would you gather from that, my girl?"

"It sounds as if he doesn't know which man is the real John Cornell, sir."

"But how could we or other acquaintances know, if his mama doesn't, Pen?"

Pennyroyal raised his bushy eyebrows. "I expect she's taken to her bed with a megrim."

"Having thought she recognized the first, it must be a little difficult now to admit she may have been wrong," Aurie said.

"She has always dithered over any decision she had to make," the viscountess agreed. "Barlyon did not let her make many, which may have been why. Poor lady. I have always sincerely pitied her."

"Who would you think most likely to detect the real Lord Barlyon, Aurie?"

"As his mother apparently cannot, in the absence of other close relatives, I would look for boys he had played with, or his and his brothers' nurse."

"Most of them have moved away." Her mother's brow furrowed. "If the attorney intends to request those who have moved away to come and…er…view the possible Lords Barlyon, that must be why he speaks of house parties."

"Have they moved away, though, my dear? Our boy did not play with the Cornells much. I believe he was only two years younger than John Cornell, but I don't recall they spent time together. I seldom saw young John, except in church. He must have stayed near home, or played by himself. The other three…Matthew was a miniature of his father and a nasty little bully. I saw him beating a younger child in the village once, because the poor little boy objected to Matthew kicking his dog. I boxed his ears for him. Mark and Luke I don't recall particularly."

"I do. Mark bore tales about anyone who committed a fault. Luke was Mark's shadow, but sometimes I received the impression he was rather a sad little boy. I remember hearing John was wild, but he was not much in evidence, and I can't call to mind any particular misdeed of his."

Papa grunted. "I suppose we must accept the invitation, as a civic duty, though I don't see what help we can be."

"Oh, good. I am agog to see the other claimant. Who else is invited?"

"Sir William and Lady Neville and their son—"

"Ah, of course! He is of an age to have known John Cornell."

"The Ashleys, and Dr. and Mrs. Simmons.

Her mother's fingers twitched, one after another. "But that will be thirteen at table! Awkward, even if not unlucky."

"Not at all. You've forgotten to count Reeves."

"No, I added him. The three Nevilles, Ashleys, the doctor and his wife, and us are nine. Then there is Attorney Reeves, Lady B., and the two claimants, which is four."

"Did I not make it clear that Aurelia is also to come?"

"I, Papa? What can I contribute?" She did not attend entertainments where strangers would be present, not if she knew of them in advance.

"Reeves, who has a head on his shoulders, first consulted Dr. Simmons, hoping to hear of some physical peculiarity or scar that would indicate which man was the Barlyon heir. He knew of none but suggested you should attend, as you are very observant. That's certainly true." Her fond papa grinned. "He said you had a mind like a…a what-do-ye-call-it?…one of those devices that magnifies tiny things, but with people rather than grains of sand or insects."

"Somehow, it hardly seems like a compliment,"

Lady Pennyroyal complained.

Aurelia laughed but hugged the doctor's good opinion to her guiltily. The habit of studying those around her as if they were under a microscope dated to her lost London spring. Until then, she had thought herself the kind of young lady to whom young men confided their troubles and their broken hearts. It had been astonishing to acquire two suitors in her only season, in spite of her inability to flutter or flirt or charm because she could not pretend to be something she was not. She had been innocently gratified to find herself admired.

Kit Hastings had paid her court almost from the first. He was a good-looking young man, several years older than she, and his parents came of good families, though his father had no title. Kit, the only son, would inherit his father's wealth and house. Her own father regretted that Hastings owned no country property, but it was a minor flaw.

A greater problem emerged over the weeks, that warm, lovely spring. While Kit was her first suitor, he was not the only one. Robert Sedgewick, as eligible as Kit Hastings and the second son of a viscount, began to show her marked attentions. Initially, she felt a partiality for Kit, flattered because he was the first to pay her court, and the most ardent.

Then disaster struck, and compliments, except from her parents, were few. She reverted to being the sympathetic listener, the sensible daughter, the helpful one. Their neighbors and friends were as friendly as previously, but eligible men were cautious and made no overtures. One could hardly wonder at it. Even if they did not believe the gossip, they would not wish to court a lady who had been the center of a tragic scandal. She was happy to take what she could get, even if it were no more than the good opinion of the local doctor. That one of the qualities he praised was the direct result of the experiences that destroyed her reputation was ironic.

"There would be almost no one present at the dinner you do not know, Aurie," her mother ventured, drawing her attention back to the present. "Only the second claimant and Reeves. And if Dr. Simmons thinks you can be of assistance, and Reeves particularly asked for you, I think you should attend."

She left the vicinity of Barfield infrequently, a trip to Maidstone perhaps twice a year being the limit of her travels. Even within the area, she seldom went anyplace where she would encounter strangers: how embarrassing for her parents if someone gave her the cut or started up the old talk again. Her own humiliation hardly weighed with her now, after several hundred Sundays. The Earl of Barlyon appointed the vicar of the Barfield living, and his lordship's preference being for hellfire and damnation, nearly every sermon felt like an arrow in Aurelia's flesh. The current incumbent disapproved mightily of females. St. Paul's strictures on women were a frequent topic, as was immorality in all its forms.

"Under the circumstances, if Mr. Reeves wishes me to be present, I do not mind accepting the invitation." She could not turn down a request for her assistance, and as there would only be two persons she had not met, she would make the sacrifice. Actually, she was quite curious, both about the new claimant and as to why it had not been possible for anyone else in the neighborhood to identify the real heir.

****

They were all assembled in the drawing room. Lady Barlyon drooped like a wilting flower on the settee, with Aurelia's mother on one side and Lady Neville on the other. As Aurelia knew everyone present except Attorney Reeves and the new claimant, she was able to take part in the desultory conversation as they waited for dinner. It was difficult to keep her mind on it, however, when much of her attention was on the second John Cornell. The first looked decidedly disgruntled. The second sat at his ease and listened to talk of the last harvest and the price of hops—as much as eight guineas the hundredweight for the best quality! which, alas, was in short supply—without comment. Aurelia found her eyes drawn to his lean length. He did not look like a fashionable gentleman, though his suit was in quiet good taste. He was quite different from the John Cornell she had met first. He lacked "bounce," and his heavy-lidded eyes gave nothing away.

When the last of the guests had arrived, Mr. Reeves addressed them briefly.

"This is an unconventional situation, my lords, my ladies, ladies and gentlemen. I cannot call to memory a similar one, in all my years of practice. Lady Barlyon and I are hopeful that by consulting with those who knew John Cornell before his disappearance, it will be possible to determine which of these gentlemen"—here he nodded to the opposite corners of the room in which the two had taken seats—"is the eleventh Lord Barlyon's heir. This is the first gathering in what may be a series of several. I have also written to those no longer in this neighborhood who may be able to assist in the matter."

Aurelia found herself glancing between the John Cornell she had already met and the new claimant. The man she now thought of as "John I" had burst forth in teal silk and old-gold brocade. John II was dressed plainly in brown velvet with a cream-colored waistcoat. He lacked his rival's fashionable lightness of complexion, wore no wig, and had left his own reddish-brown hair unpowdered. His hands, though manicured, appeared to have done work, though his manners were those of a well-bred gentleman.

"I realize this may seem an odd way to make the determination, but who should know the facts and background better than those who knew the fourth Cornell boy? Further, no one knows better than an attorney that a court proceeding can take years, cost many thousands of pounds, and expose the parties to notoriety. Better to settle it quietly, if it can be done. First, however, let us enjoy the dinner Lady Barlyon has provided."

Talk was general, though Reeves managed to steer it to old times, before young John had run off. The attorney might have primed the older gentlemen beforehand to reminisce in the hope that something useful would come out. Aurelia knew he had cautioned them not to divulge any information that might assist a false claimant. Whether they would remember the warning remained to be seen.

Mr. Ashley said, "I remember the lad disappearing as if it were yesterday. We spent two or three days searching the woods in case John had suffered an accident but found nothing. Inquiries along the roads turned up a carter who had seen a boy, but he'd taken no particular notice. All he could say for sure was that the boy was going north."

"Had the carter been going north, I might have begged a ride with him." John I sighed. "Though I can't claim I recall such a person. My brain was too full of plans for a life of adventure."

"I'd hazard a guess you did not run away to sea." The speaker was the Nevilles' son, Tom. Aurie met his eyes and suppressed a smile. Their parents had once hoped—before that terrible season in London—they would make a match, but she and Tom had already known they would not suit, though they shared a similar sense of humor.

"Good God, no! What a horrid idea!"

Her papa addressed John II. "And you, sir, do you remember the carter?"

"No, my lord. But I avoided the roads, thinking that if I were sought for, it would be there. And the roads were very muddy anyway, it having rained heavily the previous night and the morning of the day I set out."

It might be revealing to go through the claimants' belongings. Had the attorney thought of that? Probably not. Who was acting as their valet? Who would be better placed to find some incriminating thing among their possessions?

Mrs. Simmons, a forthright woman, even surrounded by those of higher standing, inquired, "Were you, too, in search of adventure?"

He gazed at her for a moment, apparently taken aback. "No, ma'am. I was not willing to wait to escape my father's rule."

"But…school?" Mrs. Ashley asked hesitantly.

"When you went to school, you'd have been away from home much of the year."

"Oh," Lady Barlyon replied, speaking for almost the first time, "you did not marry Mr. Ashley until after my son vanished, did you? My husband did not believe in sending our sons to school, where they might meet boys who were not as strictly brought up and might teach them bad habits. Our oldest son was at Cambridge, the second was studying with a classics tutor before his first year at university, and Luke and John still had Tate to instruct them here."

"I will ask you for his name and direction later, my lady," Reeves said. "He might be a very helpful source, if he is still alive."

The talk was more discreet at table because of the servants, and the number of guests made it impossible for conversation to be general. The table arrangement too was awkward. Both claimants were seated toward the foot of the table, across from each other, and not far from Reeves. John I spoke freely with Mrs. Simmons and Lady Neville, on either side of him, though Aurie's own attention was taken up by following John II's conversation, first with Mrs. Ashley, then with herself. John II answered questions readily but did not expand upon them, as John I did. However, what he said was to the point and without flummery, a point in his favor. John I's fond glances at Lady Barlyon struck her as mawkish.

Eventually, the ladies withdrew. Over the port, the men would no doubt continue the inquisition.

"They both seem gentlemanly in quite different ways," Lady Neville observed. "The one is elegantly clad, a veritable beau, such as one might find in St.

James's Square. His clothing and wig were prodigious fine for a simple dinner in the country! He must have a very good valet. The other has the manner and appearance of a plain gentleman. I can find no fault with that, for my own husband was dressed much the same," she said merrily.

"I do like to see a man well dressed." Mrs. Ashley sighed. "I wish I had a gown the color of his coat." No one doubted she was referring to John I.

"As to his valet," Lady Barlyon said, "he did not bring one. His man refused flatly to take up residence in the country. Fortunately, Huggins had volunteered to stay and clear out Barlyon's chamber, which I could not face. He has been attending..." Her voice trailed away. Now that there were two claimants, knowing what to call them evidently defeated her. Led by Mr. Reeves, most had addressed both of them as "Cornell."

Aurie ventured, "I have been thinking of them as John I and John II."

"What a good idea, Aurelia. As I was saying, Huggins has been attending John I."

No one could be surprised that Barlyon's valet had stayed on to pack up his late master's clothing, cast-off garments typically being the perquisite of one's maid or valet.

Lady Barlyon resumed. "I am very glad he stayed, for Barlyon left him only a small bequest, which I must say seems quite inadequate, considering he served Barlyon for a good fifteen years. The other gentleman—John II, as Aurelia would have it—did not bring a valet, either. He said he had left his man behind, having been accustomed to doing for himself when he was younger. Huggins offered his services but was refused."

"It is fortunate for Huggins that his services are still required here for a time. It gives him an opportunity to seek a new position."

"If the first gentleman is proven to be the twelfth Lord Barlyon, he may retain Huggins. He seems very pleased with him, though I confess I have never cared greatly for Huggins in spite of his having shared the late Lord Barlyon's views in all matters."

Perhaps it was because he shared his master's views that she did not care for him. Aurelia certainly wouldn't. After her disgrace, Lord Barlyon made no secret of his contempt, which led to the relations between her family and his going from cool to icy. "Lady Barlyon," Aurelia began hesitantly, "can you not tell which is your son?"

Edith Cornell, Lady Barlyon, who had a little recovered her spirits, such as they ever were, threw up her hands in dismay. "I am quite overset by the shame of it, for the fact is, I can't! Poor little John was only thirteen when he ran away, still almost a child. He did not particularly favor his papa though of course children do change in appearance as they grow. His brothers were sturdy as boys and grew to be burly men, like my brothers. Barlyon was between slender and stocky, but his face was square, like the three oldest boys. They all had brown hair. John had red hair like my mother's and such a trial it was to her! Neither of the gentlemen has red hair...at least, the second does have a reddish cast to his hair, though nothing like John's was. His was like polished copper. The other...I really don't know, for he wears a wig and I haven't seen him without it, of course. But he doesn't seem like a redhead, and his brows are brown. He is not above average in height, either, but then, John was rather small. Barlyon called him 'the runt of the litter.' "

None of the other ladies seemed likely to say anything. She knew she should not pursue the matter, but she could not help wanting to know, and as her father had once remarked, she hunted facts the way French pigs were said to hunt truffles. "I could not help but notice that the second gentleman, John II, has teeth that are not quite straight."

"My dear, I myself saw that they are positively crooked, though it does not make him unattractive. Although he is such a quiet, serious man, when he smiles, they give him a charmingly roguish look. If you mean to ask whether my son had such teeth, I cannot say." She pulled a handkerchief out of her pocket and dabbed at her eyes. "I fear I was an unnatural mother."

How could one not recall whether one's child had crooked teeth?

Mrs. Simmons moved to the settee and put her arm around Lady Barlyon, without speaking. Minerva Neville said, "People do change as they age, and it has been the years when they change most, since you saw him. No one thinks you unnatural, I vow."

"But I was. Barlyon was always harsh to him, and I did not try to protect my son, as I should have."

"What could you have done? Lord Barlyon was your husband. You had to obey him," Aurelia's mother said. It was perhaps a little hypocritical, for Mama did not hesitate to argue with Papa when she thought it right and won as often as not. But Papa was not Barlyon and would never strike a woman. She suspected the same was not true of the late earl.

"I could have let John know I loved him. I could have spent time with him when his father was out of the house. I never made the attempt because I was afraid to defy my husband. He said it was enough for me to see him for half an hour in the evening as many ladies saw their children. He said the boy should not be cosseted. But Barlyon was always there when I saw John, which meant John scarcely spoke except to answer questions, and that briefly. He was afraid of Barlyon, too. He could have had fangs like a cat's, and I might not have known."

In the light of the last Cornell son not resembling the three older boys, and Barlyon's greater harshness to that son, whispers Aurie had heard came back to her.

"His high-and-mightiness thought he had a cuckoo in the nest," someone had said, not knowing Aurelia, age ten, was in the barn's loft, cuddling the tamest of the barn cats, out of sight but not out of earshot. She had wondered about the significance of a cuckoo in the nest. Where else would you expect to find a cuckoo, except flying or perching on a branch?

Only a few years ago she had overheard two old men talking quietly in the village churchyard as they tended graves.

"I allus wondered about that lad going the way he did. He'd plenty o' reason to go, but never a trace of him seen or heard of again. Often boys come back from the sea or wherever they go to, once they've grown too big to beat. Not him."

"I believe Barlyon reckoned he'd got horns and figured to take away the shame any way he could," the other replied. "I don't believe it was true, his lady being such a mouse, but there! Some take an idea and won't let loose of it." By then she understood the reference, though she had dismissed it as ridiculous. No one had ever suggested Lady Barlyon had betrayed her marriage vows—if there had ever been a suspicion of it, the rumor would have run through the neighborhood women.

Poor Lady Barlyon. Poor John, whoever he was.

Chapter 4

The port made its way around the table, and any semblance of a social evening was abandoned, with the gentlemen in full cry in pursuit of the fox. Or the heir.

Ashley asked if they would be good enough to say where they had gone after leaving Barlyon Manor.

Beau Cornell, as Barlicorn thought of the other claimant since first seeing him, replied, "London, of course!"

When Ashley looked at him, he repeated, "London."

"Neither of you having gone to sea, how did you survive?"

Again Beau Cornell spoke first. "I had a very thin time of it on the way, I assure you. I fear I was guilty of raiding both orchards and gardens to stave off starvation." He smiled deprecatingly. "Having been a boy, it never occurred to me to wonder how I would support myself in the city. Once there, I spent a very miserable first night in a shed. The next day I was almost fainting with hunger, when I was rescued by an angel of mercy. Rather an elderly angel, and the widow of a Huguenot instrument maker, but quite well-off. She took me in."

"Pray, what is her name and direction?" Reeves inquired.

"Mistress Barray, in Princes Street, Spitalfields,

near Christ's Church. She has been dead a number of years now. Twelve, I think, or a little less."

No one pressed for more details, though no doubt Reeves would be writing to his legal brethren in London to learn what he could of Mistress Barray.

"And you, sir?" Ashley inquired.

"My journey to London was much the same. But when I arrived, I offered to do any chore a shopkeeper or householder had for a farthing or a ha'penny or a place to sleep or food. Sometimes if they didn't have work for me, they gave me a farthing or food anyway. I held horses for their owners, hawked broadside ballads, ran errands, loaded and unloaded wagons. " And steered visitors to gaming hells and schools of Venus and gave the hells warning of impending raids. "Once I was hired to wash a dog. Nasty, yappy little brute. He nipped me, too. Then I was a printer's errand boy. He discovered I could write a fair hand, cipher, and knew French and Latin. Eventually, those skills brought me work as a clerk and then a jobber and a sort of business agent."

"Jobber, hey? What did you buy and sell?" That was Sir William Neville.

Ah, the gentry of England: hard-riding, hard-drinking, with weathered features, blunt or aquiline. Men who stood little nonsense, in his experience. Some were stupid except about horses, hounds, and crops, but few were easily cozened.

"Whatever I could buy cheap and sell for a profit, Neville. The stock of a dealer in hardware who had died. I sent that lot to the American colonies, shipping costs being cheap. The draperies and bed hangings discarded from a house on Grosvenor Square when the new bride replaced them. There's a buyer for anything. It's only a question of finding him." He would not mention the silks that the Chinese silk packers compressed very tightly for ease of smuggling. The East India Company imported thousands of yards of Chinese silk exclusively for re-export to Europe and the colonies in order to protect the English silk industry. Nevertheless, the law was often broken, as would be obvious to anyone who actually inspected the silk used in many wealthy homes for clothing and furnishings.

"What sort of business agent?" Ashley asked.

"I sometimes acted as a go-between in negotiations between two parties."

"Is there anyone who can confirm any part of your history?" Reeves, naturally.

"The latter part, at least, is known to Ambrose Hawkins, of Hawkins & Company, Cinnamon Street, Wapping. I believe Captain Marcus Easterday, a ship owner and importer, Leadenhall Street by East India House, will answer for my character."

The viscount harrumphed. "It's vulgar to talk of money, but under the circumstances, someone has to ask how you prospered. You both present yourselves as gentlemen and dress the part—"

"Sir! I am a gentleman!" the other claimant interrupted, outraged.

"You at least"—he directed a level stare at Barlicorn—"have told us something about how you earned your livelihood. You, sir"—here Pennyroyal glowered at the other—"have not."

He seemed the sort to dislike men who dressed too well.

"My dear Mistress Barray gave me some money

and advised me how to invest it. She could not leave me anything in her will, as she feared her surviving relatives, a pair of nephews, would contest it. They never visited her during the period I lived with her, and I never met them. I doubt they knew of my existence. Through her generosity and some wise investments, I have no need to work at any occupation."

"My lord, the heir to a title and property is the heir, whether he is wealthy or a tradesman or a beggar," Barlicorn said softly.

Pennyroyal grinned rather savagely and inclined his leonine head, conceding the point.

Eventually, they joined the ladies in the drawing room to socialize and drink tea. The females were far cleverer about their interrogation, probably because they spent more time thinking about the people they met. Men, less dependent upon others, tended to be somewhat self-centered. On the other hand, ladies had no experience of wide swaths of life, rendering them selectively blind. Though mayhap most people suffered the same affliction regarding the unfamiliar.

Barlicorn toyed with the idea of ending the game at once; he could see the tension in Lady Barlyon. Having it over would be a relief for her. But he was curious to see how it all played out, and why worry about her comfort? It would be a pity to break off too soon.

"I suppose you have not been in the country since you went to London," Lady Neville said, addressing a place between Beau Cornell and himself. Somehow they had found themselves in adjacent chairs.

"No," Barlicorn replied. "Those who work are seldom able to let their business attend to itself while they take a holiday."

Before the Beau could respond, Pennyroyal growled, "Are tradesmen and laborers the only ones who work?"

"No, sir. Management of an estate is also labor, but a property owner usually has an estate steward or another employee who can oversee matters while the owner visits London or friends in other parts of the country."

"You, sir—John I, as I think we're calling you. What do you know of estate management?"

The popinjay sighed. "I fear I was an irresponsible lad and took no interest in such things. It was not as if I were the heir, with three older brothers. And no, I have not visited the country since I departed from the home of my forefathers. I enjoy the stimulation of London life. "

"A point," Neville muttered under his breath.

Home of his forefathers, indeed! As if an unbroken line of Barlyons, father to son, had dwelt at Barlyon since the Conquest, when the tenth earl was only a second cousin or some such connection to the ninth earl, who had died without issue.

When no one spoke immediately, a soft voice inquired, "I wonder why one of you came directly here, while the other sought out Mr. Reeves?"

It was the only young lady present, who had sat to his right at dinner. She was very pretty, though already past her youth, with classic features, a handsome figure, honey-colored hair, and eyes of golden-brown, like bingo. Brandy, that was. They were also keenly observant. Yet she had somehow learned the art of being inconspicuous, not only because she was quiet but because she did not fidget.

His rival, as usual, spoke first. "As my father's heir, I naturally came home to support my dear mother in her bereavement. There was no need to go through a lawyer."

"As the late Lord Barlyon's heir, I presented myself to Reeves because it seemed to me that after so long an absence, it would be a shock to Lady Barlyon to find me unexpectedly at the door. It was clear from the obituary that little hope was held of my being alive."

Ashley proposed a game of whist. Enough agreed to play, including Beau Cornell, that two tables were set up. The others gathered at the far end of the drawing room to talk. As he chatted with Tom Neville and Dr. Simmons about the relative merits of country life and London life, Barlicorn kept a discreet eye on his rival. John I had unusually graceful, well-kept hands, noticeable in the way he handled the cards. Supple wrists, too. The man kept up a flow of London gossip and banter unconnected to his play. He won a little, lost a little more, and judging by certain remarks at his table, made a beginner's mistake or two, apparently through inattention. He avowed that he was not much of a card player.

The gathering broke up early: country hours. Barlicorn found himself in his bedchamber soon after ten; he had been allotted the one customarily occupied by the heir. Beau Cornell had been given the earl's chamber, having been accepted unquestioningly when he arrived. His rival's continued occupation of that room was not a sign the Beau was the favored claimant. It must have seemed awkward to move the fellow out when he himself appeared.

The amenities in the room included paper, pens,

ink, and both wafers and sealing wax. Wondering if Attorney Reeves would be scrutinizing outgoing correspondence, he sat down to write a letter. It would be well to stroll to the village and send it from there. He would have to find someone reliable who was going to Maidstone to carry it to the postmaster there for a fee. With luck, he might receive an answer in five or six days. It would travel quickly to London, but the reply would suffer the delay usual to mail going to small country towns. If it arrived at all; scarcely an issue of the *London Gazette* appeared without a notice of some post boy being robbed of the mail. He must simply hope that his message got through.

Chapter 5

Their coach rattled along toward King's Penny by starlight, a wedge of moon, and the horses' instinct. Aurie wished she might have been present with the gentlemen in the dining room when they drank and questioned the claimants.

The women's questions of Johns I and II had not been probing enough, apart from her own, and she wondered if the men had done better. They were supposed to be more direct, but they were also all gentlemen and might have been restrained by good manners. Neither claimant was obviously impossible as the heir. Were the gentlemen observant enough to see subtle clues in the claimants' replies and behavior? She had asked Papa as soon as Mama lapsed into silence. But his brief account of what they had learned by questioning the claimants undoubtedly left out a good many details and included his own opinions.

The challenge of working out which man was the heir began to interest her mightily. Had either man betrayed himself by his manner or speech, the mystery would be easy to solve…assuming that one of them was the Barlyon heir. Once those who had known the real John Cornell well arrived, they should be able to determine which was Barlyon. But if both were impostors, both would fail to convince. On the other hand, those who had known John Cornell and had already met the claimants plainly were not sure, unless they were too timid to voice an opinion. Would any of the expected guests recognize him?

Her mother said, "The first claimant has the same elegance as the late Lord Barlyon."

"You mean he's a fop," her father snorted. "A man don't dress so finicking fine in the country unless it's for a grand entertainment. A wedding or a ball or some such thing."

"You never voiced such an objection before, Pen, not even when—"

The sudden silence betokened some reference to her disgrace.

"Barlyon possessed so many faults, what was the point of mentioning the least of them?"

" 'Not even when—'?" Aurelia inquired.

Her father cleared his throat. "You may as well know. He wrote to me suggesting that you and either Mark or Luke marry. I declined. He wanted your dowry for one of them."

"My dear, you make it sound as if her dowry was the only reason the earl would seek a marriage with Aurelia for his son."

"It was. Supporting two sons in the grand manner was expensive. Most men would settle a younger son in a profession if they hadn't the estates to provide for all of them. Not he! None of his sons should go into the army or church or any other profession. Our girl might have been hunchbacked and walleyed for all he cared. I would not have had her part of that family for anything. He would not have asked, for we never liked each other, if 'twere not for that nonsense in London."

"Thank you, Papa. I would not have been willing to

marry either of them."

"Ay, I thought not."

Sophia Kennet dragged the conversation back to its starting place, or close to it. "What I never understood was why the earl dressed as he did, when gentlemen ordinarily cannot wait to change their town clothes for country wear. And the boys, too. The older three, I mean."

"As to that, it goes back to the late earl's father. He was a country gentleman in the West Country, until he came into his cousin's title. I do not know if he always aspired to ape the London beaus, but when he inherited, he arrived dressed very rich, and his son followed his habit."

"I wonder who he was trying to convince?"

"I believe you have hit the mark, Aurie. No doubt he felt he had to prove he was an earl by getting himself up as he imagined an earl would. Acting as he thought an earl would, too. He outranked everyone else for some miles around, so there was no need for him to be always demanding deference and a mort of bowing and scraping. My father did not much like the new man, who came of a family with Dissenter tendencies, and I could never stomach the son. Don't think much of this new one, either."

"Which new one do you mean, Pen? The newest new one or the first new one?"

"The popinjay, Sophia. We were speaking of him."

"Oh, of course. Did you form an opinion of the newer one—John II as Aurie has dubbed him?"

Aurelia smiled: the viscount's opinions were never held in secrecy.

"Not a bad sort. Plainspoken. His manner may be

accounted for by having been in trade. Too bad he don't favor Barlyon. I'd rather he was the heir. He'd be more convincing if he had carroty hair. You mightn't recall it, Aurie, but everyone knows John Cornell had a head like flame. Hair turning gray or white with age is understandable. Hair as red as new copper turning brown isn't."

"His hair is a reddish sort of brown," Aurie pointed out.

"I can't agree, Pen. My little brother, Godfrey, had hair as pale as the finest combed flax when he was a baby. My mother had a miniature painted of him when he was three or four, I think. He was sickly as a child, and she wanted something to remember him by. As it happened, he outgrew his frailness, and by the time he was grown, his hair was brown."

"Hmmm. Well, Reeves expects to learn the truth of it. Too bad Lady Barlyon can't recognize her own son, however."

****

Aurelia looked up as her father entered the boudoir where she and her mother sat near the fire, sewing. Mama was embroidering a set of handkerchiefs while pretending they had nothing to do with the forthcoming visit to the home of Charlotte Merriall's family. Aurelia pretended to believe the pretense, while she replaced the braid on the jacket of her riding habit, the original trim having frayed badly.

"There are messages from Lady Barlyon," he announced. "One for Aurelia and one for us, my dear." Sophia Kennet immediately set aside her embroidery frame. He presented an opened sheet of creamy paper to her, and another, still sealed with a black wafer, to

Aurelia.

She had not broken the wafer before her mother exclaimed, "What a good thing! Aurie, Lady Barlyon invites you to her house party. In fact, she wishes you to come early, to help her prepare for it."

Aurelia read her own letter. It begged she would agree, as Lady Barlyon felt in need of female companionship, and also of her assistance. *For as you must know, my late husband did not care for house parties, and in my entire married life, I have never planned one. Do say you will come, and I hope you will call upon me in a day or two so we may discuss what preparations are needed.*

Her parents were eying her hopefully.

"Aurie," her mother murmured, "I really think you should agree, out of Christian charity if not inclination. It is certainly unconventional in a house of what should be mourning, but it will give the widow something to do."

But who else would be present? If any fashionable people from London attended, she ran the risk of being ostracized, even of spoiling the house party. She dreaded the thought.

"The question of who is the heir takes precedence over convention—and no one would think a display of sorrow convincing anyway," her papa stated.

His brusque common sense jerked her back to reality. The purpose of the gathering was the investigation of the rival claimants, not pleasure. The guests would be those who might recognize the real John Cornell and his searching out must come before not only convention but also her own comfort. Besides, her mama and papa would be able to attend the

Merriatts' house party without worrying about her, if they were convinced she would not be moping at home by herself. Duty as well as kindness to her parents and Lady Barlyon required she accept, whatever her misgivings. She forced herself to smile.

"I will be happy to give Lady Barlyon my company. She must feel quite overwhelmed with two gentlemen and no companion. I will enjoy helping with her house party." She was also curious. The problem of the rival heirs was the most interesting neighborhood occurrence she could recall.

"Very good," her father rumbled. "You'll have a fine time."

"It will be such good practice for you, Aurie, dear."

In case she should ever have a home where she might hold house parties?

"That's settled, then. I am pleased that you will be at Barlyon Manor. Your mama did not like the idea of your being here on your own, over Christmas, too. Neither did I, come to that."

"I wonder who else will be present? The daughter, I suppose, if she is able to leave her own home. Reeves meant to locate John Cornell's boyhood friends, too. I wonder if he found any."

"I don't think any of Barlyon's boys had many friends, although Matthew may have made a few at university," her father said, missing her mother's meaning. Mama would be hoping that one or two of the friends who came—if any did!—might be unmarried. Even if they were, they would have to be men who lived in the country and never went to London, where they might have heard about her. Not that she could accept any proposal without informing the gentleman of her history.

"Pen, I think Aurie and I must visit the mantua-maker. We have just time to order a new gown or two. Aurie's are quite out of fashion and not really becoming. I can't think why I let you select such dull colors last time."

"My dear Sophia, I had nothing to do with the choice of colors."

"My last remark was intended for Aurie," her mother said with awful dignity.

Her father only grinned.

"A spinster of my age should not be dressing to attract attention, Mama."

"Your age! You are six-and-twenty. You should not be dressing like a poor relation or a lady of fifty."

The veiled allusion to Aurelia's generous dowry did not escape her notice. Her mother now evidently hoped that if Aurelia were exposed to some unmarried gentleman, he would consider her dowry adequate to offset her reputation. Had Philip's imminent marriage reminded her that someday he would inherit King's Penny, necessitating Aurelia's departure? Her father could live for many years yet, but as matters stood, whether his end came soon or late, Aurelia would still be living at home. Her mother had given up hoping for a miracle and now planned to bring one about. Aurelia suppressed a sigh.

****

Her female friends in London had envied her Kit's devotion: like something out of a romance, like Lancelot and Guinevere, one of them sighed, forgetting that theirs had been an illicit affair. He called upon her almost every day and always had some suggestion for an outing she might enjoy. He sent little gifts: flowers or a book or some amusing trifle.

At balls, he could not flout the rules of etiquette by asking her to dance more than twice—and her mother forbade her to dance twice with any gentleman, saying it was too soon to show such partiality, when Aurelia had so recently come to town. Kit tried to keep to her side whenever she was not dancing. Aurelia felt uncomfortably conspicuous until her mother told him bluntly that his behavior, while no doubt affecting, was gauche, and he must dance with other girls and not haunt her daughter. He obeyed, though he danced less often than the balls' hostesses would have liked, and whether he danced or stood on the periphery, his eyes followed her.

Her mother confided that Kit's mother had approached her to plead his case. His fond parent claimed his heart was sincerely engaged, and she looked forward to welcoming Aurelia into the Hastings family.

"I replied that I thought it too early for you or her son to commit yourselves. Young people fall into love or what they think is love, very readily, only to fall out again. The season has just begun."

Sometimes when she went out with friends to shop or walk in one of London's parks, they would come unexpectedly upon Kit, who would then escort them. One young lady commented on how often these chance meetings occurred. Kit charmingly claimed it could only be fate.

Once, Kit sent a poem he had written, rolled up and tied with a ribbon, with a red rosebud. Aurelia found it touching, and surprisingly good poetry. Months later, reading an old volume in the King's Penny library, she found Kit's poem was identical to one written by Robert Herrick. Only the title had been changed, from "To Anthea, who may Command him Anything," to "To Aurelia."

Perhaps she had permitted herself to be too obviously charmed by his attentions. When he called upon them, the presence of other unmarried men caused him annoyance. If she chanced to be out when he came, the next time he saw her, he asked where she had gone and whom she had seen. Robert's staid behavior began to seem more appealing.

On 7 June 1732, her life ended.

Chapter 6

Barlicorn crossed the lawn at the front of the house as he ended his morning stroll. Surprisingly, a travelling coach was rumbling up the drive. Guests arriving a week before they were expected? It drew up before the entrance, and a greatcoated footman clambered down from the seat beside the driver and ran to rap on the door, then returned to open the coach door and let down the steps. A lady alighted with his assistance, and a Barlyon footman emerged from the house to help unload trunks and portmanteaux. The lady remained by the coach, evidently speaking with someone within as the footmen carried in a trunk, portmanteau, and a pair of bandboxes. The Barlyon servant did not reemerge, and the lady turned away and entered the house. The first footman climbed back up to his seat, and the coach began to move, its roof still piled with luggage.

Ah. Viscount Pennyroyal's daughter had arrived. He recalled hearing that she would be coming to stay before the others, while her parents went somewhere else. Surely she was too young to have any useful memory of John Cornell. While no excuse was necessary for including a lovely lady in any gathering, he had found her odd watchfulness at the dinner disquieting. No one else seemed to notice. In a group of country gentlefolk, who would be as sensitive as he was to others' scrutiny? Well...Beau Cornell should be.

When he walked into the hall, the only remaining sign of an arrival was a footman carrying away a portmanteau and a bandbox.

"Are Lady Barlyon and her guest in the drawing room?" he asked the footman on duty in the hall.

"No, sir. Her ladyship has ordered tea in her boudoir for them." The man hesitated.

"And her ladyship and her guest wish to enjoy it without further company?"

"Mmmm…ay, sir. Lady Barlyon wished me to convey that she will see you and the other Mr. Cornell in the small parlor at five o'clock."

"Thank you." It was out of character to thank a servant; the eleventh earl would never have done so. The attitude of the late Lord Barlyon and the rum culls he had met over the years brought to mind a saying Tate had once quoted: "When Adam delved and Eve span, who was then the gentleman?"

****

"I cannot thank you enough for accepting." Lady Barlyon came forward to take Aurie's chilly hands as she was shown into her hostess's boudoir. "Paul, we want tea." The footman bowed and retreated. "Come, sit here at the table."

She did not know Lady Barlyon well because of the strained relations between the two families. Possibly few of the neighbors knew her better, as Lord Barlyon's character tended to keep others at a distance. No, to be honest, most of the surrounding gentry found his rigidity, lack of humor, and harshness obnoxious. They had met at church, certainly, and at gatherings of ladies to discuss parish projects. She was bland and timid, with large eyes and a rather weak chin, like a mouse.

However, a change had come over her since Barlyon's death. Edith Barlyon showed flashes of animation and even some decision.

A maid bore in a tray heavy with everything necessary to brew tea: a pot of hot water, a silver tea caddy, cups, a pitcher of milk. Lady Barlyon opened the caddy with a key she took from her pocket, measured out the tea, and relocked the caddy. "Barlyon used to insist I keep the key locked in my jewelry box. It was quite inconvenient. Since Barlyon died, I keep it with me and leave it in my escritoire drawer at night. If anyone is creeping in to borrow the key at night to steal tea, I will know it soon enough by the household accounts. Even with Bohea selling at twenty shillings a pound, I cannot worry about a little pilfering. Now we must wait a little while it brews."

Aurelia admired the creamy porcelain before her, painted in blue with an austerely simple Chinese scene. "What an elegant set."

"It was a gift from my brother some years ago. It is rather plain, but I like to think it is more in the Chinese taste than the highly colored wares." She poured tea into Aurelia's tea bowl and offered her the milk jug. "Do take a Shrewsbury cake. Cook does them very well, with plenty of nutmeg, and has made a good supply of them to have on hand. "

After Aurelia had sampled the sweet biscuit, Lady Barlyon said, "I know the entire house needs furbishing, but not much can be done this late in the year. I have set the servants to take down the bed hangings and draperies and shake them out thoroughly—isn't it fortunate that the weather has been dry in spite of the cold? As for food, things will keep in the pantry. I've sent for additional beeswax candles, tea, coffee, chocolate, and all sorts of things that we don't make ourselves. Oh, and I've called in the sweep to make sure the chimneys in all the guest rooms are clear and drawing as they should. It's how to keep everyone amused that daunts me."

"How many are expected?"

"Between five and nine, I think. I arranged for them to come over several days, as having them all arrive at once would mean the servants were run off their feet bringing in the trunks and portmanteaux, showing everyone to his or her chamber, fetching washing water and refreshments, organizing the visiting servants and assigning them places to sleep. You are the first to come. Tamar will arrive on the nineteenth, then the boys' old tutor, and their nurse, over the next several days. She's an old woman now and moved away almost twelve years ago. Oh, and Jemima Wilson, the old vicar's sister. As she lives by herself, and a good three miles away, I have invited her to stay. Hugh Langston and Clement Pettigrew, boyhood friends of John's, will be the last to come.

"There are two or three others who have not yet replied. You know how slow the country mail can be. It may not all work out quite as planned. Travel is chancy, and weather or a broken wheel or an accident may delay someone. Besides, some may celebrate Advent as Barlyon chose to, very solemnly. He would not have travelled during the month, and if that is the case, some guests will set out later than expected. Still, unless they encounter difficulties, they should all be here by Christmas Eve. When they are here, in addition to myself and…er…"

"The two Johns?"

"Yes, in addition to them, we have Mr. Reeves, and possibly his clerk, who has been going back and forth from Maidstone, which means nine or ten house guests, which is not a great number, but so many of them being male will make things awkward. On the other hand, they will find things to occupy themselves: they can play cards, ride, or take the muskets out and shoot."

"Perhaps that last would best be avoided, my lady."

Lady Barlyon gazed at her blankly.

"Because of the risk of accidents, you know."

"I had not thought of that. Surely any who go out shooting would be unlikely to have an accident. It's not as if any of them are young men, who tend to be careless."

Perhaps she should simply agree and let the subject die. So to speak. No. Shocking her hostess now might prevent a worse catastrophe befalling her. Lady Barlyon had certainly had enough disaster in her life already. "I was thinking of, er, an intentional accident, my lady."

Edith Barlyon stared at her. "An intentional…Would anyone…?"

"To gain a fine estate and a title? Everyone knows fortune hunters will seduce heiresses or entice them to elope, and girls scheme to be compromised by a rich or titled man. It shows me lacking in delicacy, I'm sure, but I do not see how this situation is much different."

"But murder?"

"It's certainly more extreme than seduction, but men are sometimes shot while hunting with friends. Would it not be quite easy to make an accident happen?"

"But the survivor's identity would still be in

doubt."

Aurelia looked down at her clasped hands. "True. But with one dead, it would be harder to prove or disprove the identity of the survivor. And he might be tacitly accepted as the heir rather than let the estate pass to some other branch of the family."

"Faith, Aurelia…" She did not finish. Quite likely she realized that if she were faced with one surviving claimant, she would accept him. Even a counterfeit coin might be preferable to no coin at all. Finally she continued, "I hope someone recognizes my son."

"Someone must remember something about him."

"John spent time with our previous gamekeeper, I think—you understand, Barlyon was strict with the boys and did not encourage them to make friends of the servants and staff. But in any event, old Perkins is dead. We must hope that one of the house guests remembers something. I keep thinking some detail may come back to me, when I'm not nervous. But it hasn't, although I'm almost never overanxious now. It's the strangest thing."

Aurelia smiled at her. She was sure Lady Barlyon knew the reason for her new calm was the permanent absence of the late Lord Barlyon. Now if they could but determine which John Cornell was her son (if either of them was!), she could be completely at ease.

"If hunting is discouraged, the guests can still get their exercise by gathering greenery to decorate the house. Holly and ivy must be growing somewhere nearby, and I am sure you have bay and rosemary in your kitchen garden. Oh, and mistletoe. You must have some in your apple orchard, but if not, we can get it from ours. The yule log must be brought in."

"I had almost forgotten those traditions." Lady Barlyon's voice was wistful. "My family always had a yule log and great garlands at home when I was a girl. I missed them after I married. I don't suppose it is wrong to have them again, as we are having guests for Christmas, even though Barlyon died so recently."

"Not at all," Aurelia said resolutely. "Then there are the traditional games and the usual house party amusements. We will have plenty to do."

It might not be as bad as she feared. Her hostess had shown her to a pleasant room. From her fluttering manner, she expected Aurie not to be favorably impressed.

"The door to the left connects to a little room that is not really a dressing room, as they apparently did not have such conveniences when this house was built. I was told that some of the bedchambers included a little room called a closet, where one could retreat to be alone or pray or read. There is a cot where your maid can sleep."

"I'm sure I will be comfortable here, my lady. It has such a welcoming air, and a pretty view, too."

The room was cozy, not by reason of size, because it was big enough to serve as a boudoir as well as bedchamber. The bed, its canopy supported by heavy posts carved with spiraling foliage and fruit, was hung with faded red velvet draperies. They were rather moth-eaten but would certainly keep drafts out. Large as it was, the bed did not take up a significant portion of the space. In addition, the chamber contained a small table meant to serve as a dressing table, with a straight chair, two armchairs probably dating to the reign of Charles II, one upholstered in moss green, the other in brown, and a high-backed settee of similar vintage, covered in cheerful but amateurish crewel work.

Many in the beau monde would assume shabby, mismatched furnishings indicated a family fallen on hard times. Knowing a good deal about the Cornells, Aurie did not make that mistake, or suppose she had been given an inferior room. The Barlyon lands were profitable, and the eleventh earl had not been a spendthrift. By common report, however, the tenth earl for all his airs had not been secure in his late-acquired title, having been mere gentry down in Devon. He had himself fitted with a splendid wardrobe and took his seat in the House of Lords but made no effort to court society with house parties at the manor or entertainments in town. The late earl had not entertained either, being both unsociable and disapproving of enjoyment in general. If one need not impress society, why buy new furniture? Her own family's home was not fashionable. The newest pieces in it were a pretty dressing table her mama had received as a wedding gift and a wingback armchair, bought to replace one Phillip had broken when he was a boy, by clambering on it to reach an upper shelf in the bookroom.

Chapter 7

Barlicorn was the first to arrive in the small parlor, the most cheerful of the public areas at Barlyon Manor. Lady Barlyon had often sat in it to embroider, he thought, as the mullioned windows faced west and provided good light as well as some warmth in the afternoons. A fire warmed it pleasantly today.

Lady Barlyon and Mistress Aurelia entered together, followed by Beau Cornell. Barlicorn could have dispensed with the Beau's presence; he would have liked a chance to study the mysterious and fascinating Aurelia Kennet uninterrupted. Why did she make him think of a mouser crouched before a hole in the wainscoting? Would her rump twitch before pouncing as the cat's did? Rot him, it had been too long since he had left London and Gwen's bed. How had the lovely Aurelia escaped matrimony to such an age?

The other John Cornell devoted himself to charming Lady Barlyon. Wasted effort, when she had as good as admitted she had no idea which of them was her son. John I's attentions drew no response from her beyond a polite smile. A rather troubled smile, if he himself were any judge. Lady Barlyon might be asking herself how a son with whom she had had so slight a relationship could be so very fond of her. Well might she wonder!

Exerting himself to draw Aurelia out was wasted

effort on his own part. He learned that she had spent two or three months in London eight years ago, which suggested she was five- or six-and-twenty. She had come home and seemed not to have stirred since. No, she had never visited Bath. Occasionally she shopped in Maidstone. An unwary word from Lady Barlyon explained the laden travelling coach, which was bearing Mistress Aurelia's parents to stay with her brother's betrothed's family. Why had she not gone with them?

The Beau inquired jovially of Aurelia, "Good old Philip, marrying? I trust his bride-to-be is pretty and lively."

Aurelia smiled in a manner that might be either cool or meaningless. "She is said to be pretty. I cannot judge of her personality, having never met her."

Beau Cornell did not miss her reaction. John I— Barlicorn admired the mind which had come up with the designations for the claimants—was observant.

"I regret Philip is not here, though his absence is understandable, under the circumstances. As we are of an age, we might have traded boyhood memories."

What memories? He supposed he had seen Philip Kennet at church, but they had never played together; Philip was two or three years younger, and their families had had little contact even if they had lived close enough to make it possible for the boys to meet often.

Beau Cornell said, "It was kind of you to lend your assistance to my mother when you might have spent Christmas with your family and soon-to-be new relations."

"It was no sacrifice. I do not enjoy travel."

The fellow could not have missed the surprising

flatness in her response. Had she spoken lightly, her words might have meant no more than that she tended to travel sickness in a coach, explaining why she did not visit London again, or Bath, or, apparently, anyplace except Maidstone. Instead it hinted at some greater objection. Lady Barlyon showed no surprise at the curt reply, leading him to sense a secret. Had he been in London…but he was at Barlyon Manor and possessed no friend in London of whom he might seek information about a member of the aristocracy.

****

Vauxhall Gardens, 7 June 1732

Robert Sedgewick had invited her family to the grand reopening of Vauxhall Gardens. Aurie was thrilled, most especially since the event was the first ridotto al fresco, an Italian masquerade, to be held there. It had been eagerly awaited by all, throngs of people even visiting the Gardens in advance to see the decorations that had been installed. All manner of people could afford the usual admission price of a shilling, but tickets for the ridotto sold at a guinea apiece, a vast sum that would keep out the lower orders. It was claimed two thousand tickets had already been purchased. Her family's party consisted of her parents, herself, her brother and a young lady he had been courting and her mother and father, and Robert Sedgewick.

As they arrived, they smelled roasting meat and chicken and baking bread, promising treats at supper. Friends had described Vauxhall Gardens as magical, romantic, and enchanting. Those words paled in the presence of the actuality.

Part of the magic was merely that of strolling

outdoors at night in a seemingly limitless garden to the strains of soft music and the nightingales' song. Part of it was strolling with an attractive gentleman. When the older members of the party stopped near the orchestra to listen, Philip suggested that the two young couples might walk around the paths. They would be each other's chaperons, and in any case, the Gardens were thronged with pairs and groups of people.

She and Robert were in the lead, a little way in advance of Philip and Mistress Louise Whitten, Aurie leaning on Robert's arm and laughing at some remark of his—afterwards she could not have said what it was to save her soul—when several gentlemen approached from the opposite direction. They were on one of the lighted walks, enabling her to recognize Kit Hastings even as he exclaimed, "Sir! What are you about with my betrothed? Stand away from her. Come, my dear, I will escort you back to your party."

"Mr. Hastings," she managed to utter in spite of wanting to die of embarrassment at his gauche attempt to rescue her from a stranger—as if she would be so imprudent as to go walking with one! Surely he recognized Sedgewick? "My family and I are Mr. Sedgewick's guests here, and my brother is a few steps behind. Thank you for your offer of escort, but I do not need it. You and I are not betrothed."

"How's this? Can you disavow your betrothal to me when you have permitted me every liberty, Aurelia?"

Philip and his young lady had caught up by then. "What?" he demanded.

Aurelia stood speechless. The two gentlemen who had been walking with Hastings muttered something to him and continued on their way.

The blonde sylph on Philip's arm murmured distressfully in his ear.

"Good evening, Kennet. I am surprised to see Aurelia, who is promised to here, here with another man…ah, Sedgewick. You'll forgive me if I relieve you of my intended bride."

"Aurelia?" Philip asked.

"Mistress Aurelia?" Sedgewick gazed at her inquiringly.

"I am not betrothed to Mr. Hastings. What he said…it's not true." She wanted to cry, How could you say such a thing? but could not choke out the words.

"Under the circumstances, my dear, you cannot marry anyone else. I will call upon Lord Pennyroyal tomorrow."

Anger overtook shock. "You need not bother, Mr. Hastings, for I assuredly will not marry you when you have traduced me and lied about me."

Philip burst out, "For God's sake, Aurie!"

Sedgewick said, "Kennet, will you escort your sister back to our party?"

Thin-lipped, Philip offered her the arm to which Louise Whitten was not clinging like a drowning woman. "Come along."

"I will follow in a few minutes," Sedgewick said.

Philip led her away past two or three other couples who had come to a halt on the walk. Whatever they had heard, they recognized a delicious scandal; she could see it in their faces. She stumbled along, wishing the earth would swallow her, oblivious to Louise Whitten's distress and Philip's attempts to soothe her.

****

Tamar, the only Cornell daughter, arrived five days after Aurelia Kennet. Barlicorn gathered she was now the wife of a squire in Rutland. The poor girl had been a homely child, and probably had little dowry—raising four boys was expensive—but Leavitt might have been pleased to get a wife who was the daughter of an earl. Not much of a basis for marriage! Unless one considers marriage for a connection to a titled family preferable to marriage to gain a well-dowered bride.

She arrived accompanied by a chit too countrified to be a true lady's maid. "I left Leavitt at home," she explained. "He has his manor to run, and his duties as a magistrate, and his amusements. 'Tis hunting season, after all, and we could not both leave the children behind, with Christmas coming. I will miss them, but Leavitt and I agreed that if I were needed here, it was my duty to come, as I am not currently increasing. 'Tis not as if we cannot bear to be parted." But she said the last with a smile. Beau Cornell for once had nothing to say. Too plainspoken for his finical taste. John Barlicorn grinned at her. If there were more to her marriage than status-seeking by her husband, so much the better.

Chapter 8

The following morning at breakfast, Tamar announced that she meant to walk to the village. Beau Cornell offered to accompany her. If offered were the correct word; his suggestion made it impossible for Tamar to refuse without rudeness. However, she did say, "Aurelia, would you like to come?"

Aurelia Kennet fairly leapt at it. "I would very much enjoy a walk. I need a few things from the shop in any case."

"May I accompany you? Three is an awkward number for a walking party," Barlicorn said. He would like to keep the Beau under his eye.

"Please do," Tamar said. The Beau added heartily, "The more, the merrier," but his eyes belied the sentiment. Aurelia appeared to approve; did she want to keep both of them under observation?

If Beau Cornell had meant to extract information from Tamar, he postponed the attempt. Either he did not want his rival learning anything more about the family or feared that his fishing would show he was an impostor. Their excursion might have been any two couples taking a walk during a house party, with nothing but inanities exchanged. Except that each of them was studying at least one of the others intently. Barlicorn paid careful attention to his rival's words and expressions, and the Beau repaid the compliment.

Tamar and the Kennet girl watched both of them.

John I recounted to Tamar tidbits of beau monde gossip interspersed with descriptions of entertainments he had attended and the latest quirks of fashion. The man's manner was notably different from that he displayed at Barlyon Manor. In the presence of Lady Barlyon and Reeves, he acted the part of a stickler for rectitude. Very like the late earl, in fact. Yet in the present group, he was the complete fashionable fop.

Mistress Aurelia seemed not to find it necessary to fill the silence between them. If he was correct, she was busy watching John I. Barlicorn tendered an occasional comment as to simply stroll without speaking would seem peculiar.

"How do you occupy your time, ma'am? Some ladies find the country boring, unless they play an active part in the running of a household."

She did not look at him as she answered. The path they were taking was somewhat uneven, but the way was shorter than following the carriage drive and the road. Still, she might have glanced up at him.

"Parish activities take up a good deal of my time. Even in a village, some people are terribly poor, particularly widows and orphans and the elderly who have no family left. Sometimes they are ill and need help."

"To take the trouble to help is a very fine thing," he said. "I hope you do something purely for amusement, however."

"I enjoy preparing cordials and preserves from a collection of receipts made by my grandmother. Remedies, too. The ones that do not involve disgusting things like horse droppings, you know. There was one in Grandmama's book that called for binding a frog to an afflicted member until it healed. But her note said she had never tried it, as the source from which she copied it did not specify whether the frog should be living or dead, and in the first case both the frog and the patient would be uncomfortable, and in the second, having a dead frog bandaged to one's body would be nasty."

He heard the humor in her voice and laughed, stealing a glance at her face. "I should think it would, indeed. Particularly depending upon what member was afflicted."

She choked back laughter. Aurelia Kennet was delightful when she was not watching as intently as a thieftaker. Who would have guessed she had a sense of humor?

Tamar and Beau Cornell were ahead of them and walking a little faster. A few phrases drifted back. Tamar was talking about her home near Hambleton in Rutland. Her voice was not animated, suggesting that she was making polite conversation. The Beau's careful questions hinted at a lack of familiarity with even those things he should have learned as a boy growing up in the country.

Mistress Aurelia was silent. He wondered whether she was straining to follow John I's conversation or simply was not one for idle speech. She was biting her lip, looking very grave. He was trying to think of something he could say to make her laugh, when she murmured, "I cannot but feel pained for Lady Barlyon. Imagine the shame of having to admit you cannot recognize your own child."

He made a noncommittal sound in his throat.

"And yet I found it quite understandable, when she explained it to us."

"She did?" He had not meant to say it. A mildly interrogative "Oh?" would have been better.

"After dinner that night, in the withdrawing room, while the gentlemen were drinking port and—I am sure—discussing horses or sport or, or other gentlemanly amusements."

"We weren't, you know. John I and I were being thoroughly sifted for evidence."

"How vexing that we ladies did not hear any of it."

"Would you have been interested in the boring, vulgar details of how we fared in London before we…er…made our fortunes?"

"Of course, Mr. Cornell. I was hoping someone would sufficiently overcome his good breeding to ask. Knowing how you and John I made your money would be very revealing. Somehow both of you survived."

"Beau Cornell—"

She snickered. It was oddly endearing. Aurelia Kennet did not titter. A titter was ladylike; hearty laughter was considered coarse. The women he knew in London did not hesitate to laugh out loud or to scold like fishwives, either. Neither offended him. Open hilarity or anger were preferable to vapid propriety or sullen silence.

"What a perfect description!" she exclaimed.

"He alleges that he was fostered by a well-to-do merchant's widow, who gave him money that he invested with her advice, and thus never needed to work. You should ask him directly, however. I did what orphaned boys in London do to avoid starving: ran errands, did chores, begged occasionally. I was fortunate to get permanent work with a printer who made me his assistant on finding I could read and write French and Latin as well as English. Eventually, I began buying and selling odd lots of merchandise and mediating commercial disputes."

"That is not at all boring. Did you think of yourself as an orphan?" she inquired.

No. Yes. Both and neither. Perceptive of her to pick up on the one unwary thing he had said. "It's what I told those who asked about my background. You were telling me how you came to understand why Lady Barlyon does not recognize her own son."

"Yes. I must work up to it in a roundabout way, however. How much contact did you have with your mother? Assuming Lady Barlyon is your mother?"

"My brothers and sister and I were on display every evening for a few minutes before we were sent back to the nursery for supper. She asked each of us about our day's activities."

Mistress Aurelia turned her head to look up at him and stumbled when her foot came down on a rock she had failed to observe in the path. He steadied her.

"And that was all?"

"We attended church together on Sunday. As we reached the age of twelve, we were permitted to eat Sunday dinner with our parents, if we had committed no sins or errors during the week."

"She saw you no more than that, even when you were very young?"

"We had a nurse and a pair of nursery maids, and eventually a tutor."

She mumbled something under her breath that sounded like "Good God!" "Then she hardly knew you, did she, Mr. Cornell?"

"I suppose not."

"Will it come as a surprise to you that the late Lord Barlyon was not well liked hereabouts?"

"Was he not?" He had not often observed the earl with other adults, except the servants, who were fearful of offending him. On Sunday, the villagers truckled to him. The neighboring gentry and the Cornell family…he could not recall their contacts with the eleventh earl. Why would he? As children, they had not been present at adult gatherings. Before and after church, if not under Lord Barlyon's eye, his attention had been on his only two friends.

"Were you and your brothers afraid of him? Lady Barlyon was."

He did not answer immediately. Of course he'd feared him. "He found me unsatisfactory in many ways. My brothers were more to his liking." Though they were certainly beaten often enough. He swallowed something in his throat. "Lady Barlyon feared him?"

"A man who is harsh with his servants and children usually treats his wife badly, too."

He had often noticed the same since he had been of an age to pay attention. Certainly examples of hard, violent men abounded where he lived in London.

"She told us her husband was always there when she saw her children in the evening, and that the youngest boy scarce opened his mouth."

A bitter laugh boiled up, taking him by surprise. "Quite often our audiences with Lady Barlyon were followed by visits to Lord Barlyon's study," for caning as a result of some word or action to which he had taken exception. The only way to avoid giving offense was to say as little as one could. Even that did not always serve.

If Lady Barlyon did not know her own son sufficiently well to recognize him, how could her son know anything about her?

"She is much less timid now that the earl is dead."

Barlicorn understood the message in the apparent non sequitur.

The day was sunny and crisp, less cold than it had been, and with no wind. His favorite part of the autumn had been kicking the fallen leaves. Aurelia paused to pick up and admire a perfect oak leaf. "This one is just the color of your hair." Then she blushed and dropped it.

They reached the outskirts of Barfield and were catching up with Tamar and the Beau, ending their tête-à-tête, a profound relief. The conversation with Aurelia Kennet had opened wounds he believed had healed years ago. Instead they were only scabbed over, and she had ripped the scab off. He preferred not to think about her brutal surgery.

Yet he also regretted they could not speak at greater length on some other subject. He would not willingly have missed hearing Aurelia Kennet laugh and liken the red-brown of a leaf to his hair.

Well enough! They had taken some pleasant exercise and the discovery of John I's dual character was useful. As he himself knew, acting a part consistently before different people was difficult. Neither Hawkins nor Easterday had shown any surprise on learning why he intended to leave London. Solomon de Toledo had known about his origins for years.

Barfield seemed smaller than he remembered. A

younger man was working in the smithy now, the son of the previous smith. The shop and its proprietress had not changed at all. Mistress Beck must be seventeen years older yet to his eye, she had not altered. To a boy of twelve, she had looked as old as Methuselah; she still did. Even the merchandise appeared to be the same—including the barley sugar twists that had been so popular with the children.

The people they met greeted them cautiously, calling both him and the other claimant only "sir." They would not show any favoritism, in case they offended whichever was eventually determined to be the new earl. Very sensible, given the character of the eleventh earl.

Before they started back, Mistress Aurelia attached herself to the other John, and Tamar took his own arm. However, conversation did not come. He remembered her as a little girl, timid and longing for someone's affection. Tamar seemed content now. Marriage to a decent man and a home of her own must have given her confidence. Beau Cornell had made much of her the previous evening, and called her his dearest little sister, which she accepted placidly, though her gaze often rested on one or the other of them in a puzzled way.

He should try to prove to her that he was her brother. He could not stoop to it.

"You have not told me how your son and daughter do." Her children, at least, were bound to be an acceptable topic.

"I know men find a mother's bibble-babble about her children boring."

He had not intended to say, "Tamar, they are my niece and nephew," but the words spoke themselves.

"And it is pleasant to hear a woman speak of her children, or to them."

She looked stricken and swallowed several times before replying. "Mother…sometimes it's difficult for a woman…" She addressed the thought he had not consciously uttered.

"It's all right, Tamar. It doesn't matter now. Tell me about little James and Frances. Do I understand he is the elder? Has his papa thrown him up on his first pony yet?"

She laughed. "No, silly! He is only three. Though Leavitt does take him up before him for short rides. And Francie is still learning to stand."

This subject occupied almost all of the rest of the walk back to the manor. They were in sight of the entrance when in a pause after Tamar declared that never had a woman been as happy as she, Barlicorn found himself asking, "Do you always call your husband by his surname? Indeed, I do not think I have heard his given name. Of course, it's common among…" Our class? He no longer belonged to it.

"Yes. I never liked the practice until I met Leavitt, but he hates his given names—both of them. His beast of a father—who is a delightful man, but wrong-headed about naming children, and Leavitt's mother was besotted and allowed it—called him 'Barnabas Ulysses.' Can you imagine such cruelty? There is no way to shorten either satisfactorily, for Leavitt refuses to be called either 'Barney' or 'Uly.' "

They entered the house together laughing. John I glanced back at the sound, a sour expression fleeting across his countenance. It passed in a heartbeat, and he hailed them, "We have all had a jolly time, I perceive."

"We have," Tamar agreed cheerfully. Aurelia smiled blandly.

****

To Aurelia's surprise, Tamar visited her in her bedchamber on their return from the village.

"This is lovely. We never used to have a fire in the bedrooms except in the coldest weather." Tamar curled up on the settee near the fire. "Aurie, what do you think of the two Johns?"

Aurie sat at the dressing table, massaging a paste of milk, almonds, oil, and egg yolks into her hands. "Today was the first time I have really talked with either. Before, when we've been in company, the talk has been merely social."

"I don't feel that my conversation with John I today went any deeper than polite chit-chat. He was affectionate, which was almost as I remember my brother being, yet we did not really talk about the past except in general terms. I know Mr. Reeves expressed a desire that we should make note of anything a claimant says which supports his claim without supplying any information to him, but it's difficult. You cannot draw reminiscences out without raising the subject in the first place, if you see what I mean. When I talked with John II, it was all about my children. He asked about them and seemed interested. I like him. Had you any success?"

"I learned nothing from John I except what fashions are now seen in town, and a vast amount of society gossip. John II told me something that I think may be revealing, but I need to confirm its truth. Would you tell me how often you and your brothers saw Lady Barlyon when you were a child?"

"We were taken down to the drawing room before our supper and 'the troops were reviewed' as Leavitt phrases it. We bowed or curtsied to our father and mother, and Father asked us questions. What new thing we had learned that day or whether we had completed the lessons we had been assigned. He let Mother ask us questions, too, but hers were more likely to be easy. Whether we had been out to take exercise in the fresh air, or how we had amused ourselves indoors if it were raining or too cold to play outside. The formal visit did not last long, thank goodness. It was better when she and I were alone. She taught me what I suppose a governess teaches in some other households—embroidery, how to conduct myself, how to dance, and the frivolities: reading, writing, arithmetic, history." Her inflection was decidedly tart.

She continued, "The boys spent more time with Father but not a great deal more. He did not possess much patience with them. He mostly ignored me. Being a girl, I was unimportant as long as I did not disgrace the family."

Another razor cut to her soul. "How would you describe your and your brothers' childhood?"

After a significant pause, Tamar said, "We were not carefree children, like the ones we saw before and after church. I'm sure we would have been worse off in an orphanage because we always had enough to eat unless we were being punished for some mistake."

"You were never caned?"

"I wasn't, usually. Being sent to our rooms with nothing but bread and water or hasty pudding was the penalty for a simple mistake. Deliberate mischief or defiance earned a caning. The boys were caned quite often. Especially John, for less reason than the others. I didn't realize how dreary our upbringing was until I came to know Leavitt's people."

Aurie hadn't known how badly the children were treated, although Barlyon was assumed to be a stern parent, based on the way he treated grown men and women.

"Did you eat dinner with your parents? I would guess that would be trying."

"Father did not approve of the presence of children at the table. Until we were sixteen, we ate in the nursery, apart from Sunday dinner, after we were old enough to use good table manners. And not then, if there were guests. Oh, and Christmas. I positively dreaded such occasions. We did not speak unless spoken to. A fault in table manners led to dismissal from the dining room. Now I have observed other people, I realize what a harsh man my father was and how impossible to please."

"Tamar, when you talk with John II, how does he refer to your mother and the late Lord Barlyon?"

Her brow furrowed. "We have not talked much, not about our childhood. Previously, I suppose we mostly talked about Leavitt and our home. He asked about my life, and I do run on about it. Somehow he turned off my questions about what he had been doing. Today he referred to 'Lady Barlyon.' I don't think he has spoken of our father at all."

"I wondered, because I have heard him speak of Lady Barlyon but never 'Mother' or 'my mother,' whereas John I calls her mother at every opportunity."

"He does," Tamar agreed. "It's rather maudlin. Odd, too, because we never addressed our parents as

'Father' or 'Mother.' It was always 'my lord' or 'sir,' 'my lady' or 'madam.' I was closer to my mother than my brothers were, but I never addressed her so familiarly until my wedding day—and not in my father's hearing then."

How many would know such details of life in the Barlyon home?

"Has neither said anything that might tend to prove or disprove he was the true heir? Can you think of no test to settle the matter?"

After a long pause, Tamar said, "I'm a goose. John can—could—draw. He made me a pencil sketch of my cat. I still have it. Not with me—at home in my parlor. Leavitt had it framed for me."

"A good many gentlemen learn to draw, if not as many as ladies."

"I know, and I would guess that, like most ladies, most of them do not draw particularly well, for whatever one's instructor may say, a certain talent is required. John had it. My cat's portrait has been much admired by people who remark in tones of amazement that they had no notion I could draw so well, and why did I not do it more?"

"Then if the claimants can be induced to draw, the results might be an indication."

Acrostics, anagrams, and charades and all such puzzles paled in comparison to this problem. Had the Barlyon son been absent for only a few years, certainly someone would recognize him. Seventeen years, and those from childhood to full maturity, made a significant difference when no one thus far had known him well. How many mothers would fail to recognize their child even after such a lapse of time? Yet if matters had been as Lady Barlyon claimed, her inability to identify her son might be understandable. She was a dry well.

Even Tamar, who had apparently been close to John Cornell, had failed to think of an identifying feature until pressed. Then she had provided two bits of useful information. One, her brother had some artistic ability, and two, she had confirmed what John II had told her about the children's treatment.

Simply questioning the claimants was not adequate. One would have to confirm their statements with the people who had known the boy John Cornell and question them for details about him. It was too bad that the only one who had known him well and was available at the moment was Tamar. Still, she might dredge up more useful memories. Talking with those who came for the house party should be illuminating.

She had not felt so alive in years.

Chapter 9

The tutor and the Cornells' old nurse arrived together the next day, Mr. Reeves having arranged a hired coach to bring them both, as they both lived near the main route to Barfield.

"I trust they will be able to provide incontrovertible evidence of my identity," John I muttered to Reeves. "Otherwise, the money spent in bringing them here is tossed away."

Aurelia overheard this, despite the claimant having kept his voice low. They were in the reception room, the entrance hall being full of the newcomers, their valises, the butler, a footman, and Lady Barlyon, who was hugging a thin little old woman.

"Nurse Redding, it is good to see you again. I hope your niece's family is well? And your journey not too uncomfortable? This cold weather may be seasonable, but it makes one long to stay inside, by the fire."

"My girl and her man and children are all well and prosperous, m'lady. He's a saddler with a very good trade. They were fair amazed to see me off in a coach and four!"

This cheerful remark covered from all but Aurie the attorney's reply to John I. "The estate can easily bear the charge. Who should know the true John Cornell better than the woman who supervised him from infancy and the man who taught him?"

Lady Barlyon turned to the elderly gentleman. "Mr. Tate, you are looking well. I hope you are not bored now that you no longer teach? Dare, you will have hot drinks sent up to Redding and Tate while they get settled upstairs."

"I have been writing little articles for a magazine, my lady, on Anglo-Saxon remains."

Aurelia, paying more attention to John I than to Lady Barlyon's reception of the tutor and nurse, thought he disapproved of the warm welcome shown them. Did he think they should enter through the servants' door? Or be assigned to their old chambers on an upper floor, the tutor near the schoolroom, the nurse to the little room adjoining the nursery, as if they were still employees? Many would agree, but given the peculiar circumstances that made their presence necessary and that they had agreed to come with no benefit to themselves (and some inconvenience), Lady Barlyon's reception of them as if they were valued guests seemed fair.

"Old Tate and his antiquarian interests! My father thought them frivolous."

John II had ghosted into the hall, probably from the library. "Reddy!" The pleasure in his voice was unmistakable.

"John? How you have grown! And you are as brown in the face as a heathen."

Reeves moved to the door of the parlor and cleared his throat. "Mistress Redding, this is one of the claimants. For convenience, we call him John II. The other, John I, is here." He beckoned the first claimant forward.

"Reddy. It's been a long time since I have eaten

hasty pudding."

The elderly man, a scholar if ever Aurelia had seen one, moved to speak to John II, who shook his hand warmly.

Mistress Redding peered at him. "I couldn't blame a child for refusing it, as his lordship forbade Cook to use as much butter as hasty pudding needs. Not but what I think it a very mean, poor dish for a growing child, no matter how much butter's in it."

John I laughed. "I suppose one's memories of childhood are overlain with a rosy glow." He turned to the tutor, interrupting something John II was saying. "Tate, good to see you again."

Tate inclined his head, smiled slightly, and said something. In Latin, at a guess. John I chuckled uncertainly.

"Once a schoolmaster, hey? Haven't had any use for the language, myself, since I left. Nobody speaks it anymore. Not like French, *n'est-ce pas*? Not that I would ever claim to have been much of a scholar, anyhow."

"Some gentlemen find it useful for making epigrams," Tate replied. "I admit it is less useful for laying a wager or ordering dinner."

John II's eyes sparked with amusement. Had Mr. Tate tested his understanding of Latin, too? Or had there not been time before John I broke in?

Then Tate and Mrs. Redding were led upstairs by a footman and the housekeeper, ending her observations for the moment.

Nothing of substance had come from the arrival of Redding and Tate, although what she had observed reinforced her impressions of John I and John II. The first claimant's behavior toward his (alleged) former nurse and tutor rang false without being proof. Arrogance toward servants, tenants, and the common folk in general was ungentlemanly: her father was courteous to all—except close friends, with whom he might be rude in the peculiar way of men, who thought nothing of jeering at each other's horses or skill with a gun.

The aristocracy did take their rank seriously, she knew from her two months in London. They maintained a distance between themselves and those of lower birth, which accounted for all the intricate rules about precedence, who curtsies or bows to whom and how low. On the other hand, members of the nobility often treated long-time servants with the fondness they would use with a favorite dog or horse. She could not imagine regarding Nan, once her nurse and now her maid, with anything but affection.

Matthew or Mark Cornell might have been capable of slighting Reddy or Tate, but everyone agreed the boy John Cornell was as different from his brothers as chalk from cheese. John II's spontaneous greeting of Mistress Redding seemed more consistent with Tamar's account of her brother.

Last, she simply disliked John I's manner: caressing with those he wished to impress, on his dignity with anyone lower in the social scale, and embracing all of the late Lord Barlyon's least endearing traits. In London, she had seen jumped-up cits hold themselves aloof from their less successful fellows and servants, aping gentlemen. Did she detect a whiff of the same behavior in John I? John II seemed comfortable with everyone, as if he had been born to his position.

The Barlyons' old nurse and the tutor knew their former charge far better than his mother had. Given the opportunity to talk with the men, they might identify the heir. She inclined to believe John II was the missing earl. Was it merely because she liked him or because she did not like John I?

Could her partiality be influencing her judgement? For real proof, Tamar's recollection of her brother's artistic ability might be useful. Mayhap he had less skill than his fond little sister believed, but if one could sketch and the other could not, it would be another bit of evidence.

****

Barlicorn found the evening meal amusing. The Barlyon servants' shoulders twitched at the presence of Mrs. Redding, rather like a horse troubled by a fly. Reddy was serene in spite of the situation's lack of decorum. Tate, of course, was a gentleman born and bred, however poor, and therefore acceptable at the table. Beau Cornell seemed to be all on edge and drank more than he had at previous meals, while eating less. As there were guests, the meal was more elaborate than an ordinary supper, though less heavy than a formal dinner. Though even a family supper among the gentry would offer more variety than the panam and cash he and many others in Wapping and Shadwell would think thoroughly satisfactory. Bread and cheese! It was proving difficult to forget the idioms of his past life.

Even with so few at table, conversation should have been limited to those on either side. Lady Barlyon had buried social conventions with the eleventh earl, so talk was general.

Reeves fixed his gimlet eyes on John I. "Do you

find the village and Barlyon Manor much changed?" Barlicorn could well imagine the attorney as a barrister in black robe and wig, interrogating a witness in court. Beau Cornell showed no discomfort, however. One would need sangfroid to be an imposter.

"In essentials, no. In details, I am not sure. It's long since I left, and I was a boy. Like most boys, I ignored things that did not directly affect me. Some of the older folks must have died, and a few new families moved into the neighborhood, though I confess what I chiefly recall is playing in the wood, swimming in the stream, and being disciplined for lack of decorum."

Then the gimlet eyes turned to him.

"I remember old Potter, the smith. I used to sit in the oak on the other side of the street and watch him work." He did not glance at Beau Cornell but sensed his unease. The tree had been lightning-struck, and its remains chopped down. The addition to the inn was under construction, taking the oak's place even before he ran away.

"I swam in the stream—and caught fish there, too. Sometimes I visited the previous vicar's sister—"

Interest flared in the attorney's cold gray eyes.

"—when I knew he was out. Mostly I wandered in the woods, or found a place to sit and read where my brothers would not find me."

Tate was nodding slightly. Reeves shot him a warning glance.

Barlicorn had grown accustomed to Mistress Aurelia Kennet. He had been comfortable with Tamar from the first. The addition of Reddy and Tate, both of them keenly observant as nurses and tutors must be, bothered him not at all, but still their presence had introduced the kind of tension Barlicorn associated with alcohol-fueled gatherings involving fists and chives. Knives. Neither the nurse nor the tutor asked any questions. Reddy was watching him and the Beau like a hawk. Tate would be biding his time. He would wait until he had one of them alone and then turn out the contents of the Beau's or Barlicorn's brain, looking for traces of his own lessons. He might drop the phrase *pons asinorum* and wait to see the result. No one who had studied geometry with Tate was likely to forget that the phrase referred both to Euclid's proposition that the angles opposite equal sides of an isosceles triangle are equal, and as a metaphor for any problem that separated the intelligent student from the dunce. Tate's test of the Beau's Latin had gone well: his rival did not know Marcus Aurelius from a pickled eel.

It was not until they assembled in the drawing room after supper to drink tea that Reddy struck in one of those moments when silence falls over a group, no matter how lively the conversation has been to that point. Not that it had been.

"Will you gentlemen tell me about the time John Cornell broke his ankle falling out of the apple tree?"

A shadow of disapproval passed over Reeves's face. Barlicorn sat back and waited for the Beau's answer.

"Why…Between the shock of falling and the pain, I don't recall much about it. It wasn't the first time I'd climbed a tree and come down faster than I went up, nor the last time, neither. I do remember my activities were curtailed for some time afterward, and I was bored with staying in."

"How old were you?" Reddy asked.

"It's been years since I thought of it. Ten or eleven, I suppose."

Barlicorn let the silence draw out before saying, "I was nine. My noble sire thrashed me when I was brought home. You, Reddy, smuggled treats to me while I was confined to my chamber. I especially appreciated the gingerbread."

Someone sighed. Reddy gave a curt nod that somehow only acknowledged that they had both responded. Beau Cornell's relaxed posture seemed not to change. Impossible to survive as a criminal if your nerves gave you away. Impossible to survive among rogues if you could not read the signs of tamped down fear or anger. Then Tamar asked Reddy what she advised to treat costiveness in children, and the moment passed.

The Barlyon carriage fetched Jemima Wilson the next day. Lady Barlyon had ordered the coach sent as Mistress Wilson had moved a few miles away after her brother's death. Barlicorn wondered at her ladyship's temerity; had she ever given an order about anything more important than the week's menus and housecleaning? Mayhap the order came from Reeves, filtered through the lady of the house.

"I am thankful the vicar left his money to her, being a widower with no surviving children. It cannot have been a great deal, but it was enough to purchase a tiny cottage and hire a woman to cook and clean. She remains active in parish affairs—a different parish, now, alas—though she maintains ties also with Barfield."

As it happened, when the coach rattled to a halt before the door, only Barlicorn and a footman were on hand to meet it. Lady Barlyon was consulting the housekeeper and cook, and Tamar and Aurelia were taking soup and some other comforts to the elderly, arthritic father of a laborer on the home farm. Beau Cornell was upstairs, prinking with the valet's help, at a guess. Attorney Reeves in his little improvised office at the back of the house could not have heard the coach's arrival.

Barlicorn smiled unrestrainedly as Mistress Wilson stepped down from the coach with the footman's assistance and went to offer her an arm. She searched his face, then smiled and accepted his assistance up the steps. Mistress Wilson appeared to be the very pattern of an unsentimental, strict old maid, devoted to caring for her brother, who never guessed she overflowed with kindness, or he would undoubtedly have curtailed some of her activities, to the detriment of his parish. She had been Barlicorn's first friend, after Tamar and Mrs. Redding.

"You look well," she said.

"I am. You do not age, ma'am."

"I do, but I keep busy and that staves off the worst of old age."

He had been five or six, just old enough to escape the house and wander on his own, when she found him sheltering from the rain in the vicarage garden shed. Where would he be now if she had not found him? He could guess, having seen his share of men dead by violence or hanged at Tyburn. Almost everything he knew of trust and compassion he had learned from Jemima Wilson, bless her forever.

Then Lady Barlyon was at the door, and their few minutes of privacy were ended.

Chapter 10

Lady Barlyon was writing letters, and Tamar had ridden over to call upon a neighboring family. Feeling somewhat shy of the other guests, Aurie sought solitude in the music room. She was picking out "Sally in Our Alley" on an elderly harpsichord, the only instrument available, apart from a battered lute missing half its strings. She had never been more than an adequate performer, and this relic was sadly out of tune. John I's arrival startled her into stopping in mid-phrase.

"What a pretty picture is a lovely lady sitting at a harpsichord!"

"Particularly if she is not playing it, Mr. Cornell?"

Her tart rejoinder made his smile falter. "It sounded very sweet. I regret I never learned to play an instrument. I limit my participation in the musical art to appreciating those who can."

She rose and closed the lid. If she were not uncomfortable with him, she might have taken the opportunity to learn something about the first claimant. Not in a chamber so far from the presence of others, however. She felt cornered.

"If you will excuse me, I must see if Lady Barlyon—"

"Stay a moment, please. I have been hoping to become better acquainted with you, Mistress Aurelia. It's difficult to converse in the drawing room with everyone else claiming your attention or talking about farming or colicky infants or the news from abroad. You cannot be unaware of my admiration for you."

She evaded his hand, which would have stayed her, and made for the door. "I may be ruined, but I am not immoral, sir."

He caught up with her and stopped with his hand on the door handle. "I never believed you to be immoral. Ruin? A young lady can be ruined by no more than a kiss or being alone with a man." He opened the door and bowed her through it. "My intentions are honorable, I assure you."

"How can they be honorable, Mr. Cornell? The earl, whoever he proves to be, cannot marry a lady who cannot return to London for fear of an old scandal being revived."

"As the earl, I can marry whom I please. Who will question an earl's choice? Obviously that other fellow is a jumped-up tradesman of some sort. He has scrambled to educate himself, perhaps, for by his speech, he might be mistaken for a gentleman, but he has no understanding of a nobleman's dignity. He has worked with his hands—he has calluses! Spent as much time in the sun as a ploughman or a sailor or such, too, judging by his complexion."

"He has admitted to manual labor. One can scarcely blame him for working rather than starving." Thank heaven, they were nearing the front of the house where at least there would be a footman on duty. Someone was certain to be in the drawing room. The footman in the hall sprang to open the door for her at her hasty approach, mumbling something under his breath. Aurie erupted into the safety of Lady Barlyon's presence.

Who, unfortunately, was entertaining—if that were the word—the Reverend Mr. Griffin, incumbent of St. Ethelburga. The footman had tried to warn her, but his hurried, low-voiced, "…vicar's here," had failed to penetrate her preoccupation. No: her panic.

"Aurie, Mr. Griffin has come to call. How delightful you could join us, and…er…the first Mr. Cornell, too."

One might charitably suppose the vicar had come to comfort the widow. However, John II was present, as well, face bland, eyes veiled. She distrusted that expression. Both men rose at her entrance, and John II smiled. Mr. Griffin inclined his head in her direction but came forward to shake John I's hand. By his effusive greeting, she concluded his real purpose was to ingratiate himself with the claimants, in the hope of keeping his living. The only mercy was that his narrow, dour wife was not present.

Having entered the drawing room, there was no escape. She seated herself in a chair near Lady Barlyon; John I might have joined her if she had chosen one of the settees.

To her relief, Mr. Griffin was disposed to ignore her, after a brief inquiry about the health and whereabouts of her parents. He had noted their absence on Sunday but had not heard they had gone away for a house party. She was amused rather than surprised: his parishioners did not gossip with Mistress Griffin, who performed her parish duties with vinegary efficiency. They certainly did not confide in Mr. Griffin, whose interest was entirely in their spiritual welfare. Their bodies were of no concern to him.

He proceeded to address his comments about his parish to John I: not a single misbegotten child born since his arrival—

Aurie had taken up her knotting on sitting down. She paused in her work on a simple trim and exchanged a glance with Lady Barlyon, who might not have expressed an opinion or opposed the eleventh earl in anything, but assuredly did hear the neighborhood news. Girls sometimes made mistakes during harvest. Quite often the error was followed by marriage quickly enough that even Mr. Griffin and his wife would not notice if a child came a bit early. Poor little Bertha Dawkins, having made her mistake with a married man, had left Barfield with none the wiser except her mother and Jemima Wilson, who put it out that she had gone into service with a friend of Mistress Wilson's in Norfolk, and Lady Barlyon, who supplied the necessary money for travel, clothing, and a cheap wedding ring. The friend in Norfolk, cut from the same cloth as Mistress Wilson, would see the girl eased into some suitable situation in some other part of the country after the baby was born, where she would be accepted as a poor widow. Aurie had learned of it when she came upon Lady Barlyon sewing infant clothing not long after her arrival. She had been so flustered that when Aurie had inquired who the gown was meant for, the truth burst forth.

"—though some are lax about attending my Wednesday prayer meeting, particularly in harvest and in inclement weather. Their immortal souls must take precedence over agricultural matters and mere comfort, I tell them. Devotion has declined sorely since the reign of Queen Anne. Her Majesty did a great deal for the church and churchmen. Yet now some clergymen hold no more than the two Sunday services and administer communion but three or perhaps four times a year. I hear of some who see no harm in playing cards on Sunday."

"Most improper." John I, sitting primly upright, shook his head at such doings.

John II, lounging in his chair, asked, "Do you blame our German royal family for the decline?"

What a pleasure to see Mr. Griffin disconcerted.

"Why…no, certainly not. I am at a loss to account for it, sir. King George I was chosen by Parliament for his unquestioned Protestantism, and no one can doubt our present monarch's religious beliefs."

Aurie concentrated on her knotting so she could keep her face down and conceal her quirking lips. After all, being uncouth, bad-tempered, and having a bevy of mistresses did not mean the king was not sincerely devout. She dared not glance at John II, lest one or the other of them betray amusement. She was sure he would be amused. While His Majesty, like the Whigs, supported religious toleration to a degree Mr. Griffin was unlikely to endorse, the vicar dared not seem to criticize their sovereign.

The Reverend Mr. Griffin excused himself soon thereafter, on the ground he had other pastoral calls to make, and Jemima Wilson joined them.

Aurelia liked the briskly practical Mistress Wilson, who had been very kind on her own return from London after that terrible spring. It was impossible to guess what she thought of either of the two John Cornells. John I made a great play of seeing to her comfort, offering her a seat nearer the fire, and inquiring after her health. His attentions struck Aurelia as being overdone, like the solicitude of a nephew who hopes to inherit from his wealthy spinster aunt. John II asked about her new home in Longlea, eliciting a list of activities that would have exhausted Aurie, at less than half Mistress Wilson's age.

At supper, informality continued to reign. It was useful for the attorney's purposes, however. Reeves wanted to follow all the conversations, an impossibility for one person. He had sought her out earlier to ask that she listen to those around her as much as she could without being obvious and without trying to direct the conversation. She suspected that he had also enlisted Jemima Wilson and Tate.

Tate asked Mistress Wilson about the school she had begun in Longlea, and she described its curriculum. Unlike the dame schools found in some places, it taught more than reading and perhaps sewing and household tasks.

"I laid my plans when I first moved to the village, but I could not open my little children's academy until the woman who kept the dame school died. I could hardly have lured away her students and deprived her of their fees, though she taught them little enough. I announced the opening of my school with unseemly haste, once she was in the ground. Few laborers' children fail to learn the usual chores, so we concentrate on academic studies."

"We? Do you have another teacher?" Tate asked. He would naturally be interested.

"As luck would have it, the curate is interested in natural philosophy and thus can teach the students about astronomy, rocks and minerals, the physiology of people and animals, and botany. I fear those are not as interesting to the children as his lectures on new inventions, such as Newcomen's atmospheric steam engine. It's used to pump water out of coal mines," she added, seeing some of her audience look blank. "One day, he brought his microscope and let the children see what a variety of tiny things looked like when enlarged."

"What need can laborers' brats have of such knowledge?" John I inquired. "If they can read and do their sums, that is more than enough to plough or thatch or tend animals."

"Ignorance is not admirable, and knowledge is never wasted," Mistress Wilson replied.

"It's like to turn their heads and give them ideas above their station. It's God's will the king should rule us all, and the aristocracy rule over clodhoppers. What would become of us if ploughmen thought themselves as good as lords?"

"This is England. Our standards are higher than in those countries where serfdom is still the rule. Nor did Jesus scorn the common folk. Indeed, he was born among them, and they, not the noblemen of the time, were the first Christians." Jemima Wilson showed no reluctance to disagree with any man now her brother was dead and not dependent upon the carl's favor to keep his place. The Reverend Mr. Wilson had been the late Lord Barlyon's choice, as the living was his to grant. A thin, tight-lipped man, quick to preach hellfire, his ways failed to endear him to his flock. His sister was another matter entirely. She had been the spiritual guide and consolation for most of the parish, and a fount of good sense. It was to her they took their earthly and moral problems without her brother or his lordship realizing it. No doubt they would have agreed with John Knox's opinion of "the monstrous regiment of women."

"It is not at all the same thing." His tone was repressive. Mistress Wilson was serenely unaffected by it, though Lady Barlyon was biting her lip.

Tamar leapt into the breach. "It must surely be to your students' benefit to learn about Tull's inventions. My husband is a great admirer of his seed drill, which prevents much wastage of seed."

"Which is certainly a benefit," Tate said.

"The late Lord Barlyon cannot have been opposed to education," Reeves observed, "as he employed Tate, whom I know from recent conversations to be knowledgeable in many fields of learning."

Tate gave a brief nod and half smile to acknowledge the compliment. "I wish I could think he hired me for that reason. But he wished the boys to be educated as gentlemen and did not care for the idea of sending them to school. His notion of what they should learn did not extend much beyond acquiring enough arithmetical ability to understand the household and property accounts, some Latin, literature, history, and geography. I included some natural philosophy and the elements of logic, but…" He shrugged.

"Mr. Cornell and Mr. Cornell." Reeves's dry, dusty voice commanded immediate attention. It must be something attorneys learned. "What are your recollections of your lessons?"

"I was, as I have admitted, not a scholar. I spent as much of my time as possible running loose on the estate." John I smiled deprecatingly.

John Cornell was said often to be found—or not

found—in the wooded part of the Barlyon lands.

"I enjoyed my lessons and usually had a book with me when I went wandering. Mr. Tate told us fascinating stories about the Romans and Anglo-Saxons. Those tales held Luke's interest as well as mine. He no more dared admit to it than I did." John II and Tate exchanged slight smiles.

Brushing her hair that night, she reflected on the conversation at the table. It had provided food for thought, which she would digest at leisure. She had hardly had to speak at all.

Nan finished putting away her clothing and silently began to braid Aurelia's hair for the night. She was not given to idle chatter. Thus it came as a surprise when she said, "Huggins—the valet here?—is certain That Fop is the heir and tries to convince the other servants."

Aurelia had no difficulty in guessing who Nan meant. "Does he? I imagine John I is likely to retain his services if he is declared to be Lord Barlyon."

"More to it than that, I'd say. The laundry maid says he's as thick with your John I as if he had served him for years. Bess says the third footman came upon them speaking together very earnestly in the Long Gallery. That Fop was monstrous put out. He demanded to know why the footman was in the Gallery, which he had every right to be, as he was on an errand for her ladyship."

"I thought the Barlyon servants were a close-mouthed set?"

"Used to be, right enough. They've loosened up a good bit since the Old Devil died. They don't talk before Huggins, in case Mr. Reeves decides it's John I is the new earl. Huggins is That Fop's man, and That

Fop is too much like the Old Devil."

"Good God, Nan!"

"I didn't raise you to use such expressions, Miss Aurie."

"No, indeed. I had a very genteel nurse—except when she was depressing the under-footman's pretensions! I apologize. I should have rapped out, 'Zounds!' instead."

"No, you should not. Her ladyship your mother never says worse than 'Lud!' "

"Oh, but I am a ruined woman and need not guard my tongue."

"You most certainly are not ruined, no matter what anyone thinks."

"Tarnished, then. And you know, Nan, that 'tis not what's true that counts but only what people believe."

Nan had no answer but a sigh.

Chapter 11

After going to his chamber, he sat up with his sketch pad. Supper that night had been…interesting. The more guests who arrived (Barlicorn almost thought of them as jurors), the more revelations should ensue. More yeast, more rise in the dough?

In response to Tate's remark concerning what he had hoped to teach the Cornell sons, Tamar had surprised him by saying tartly, "Knowing Matthew, Mark, and Luke, I conclude it was an unrewarding chore."

"Tamar," Lady Barlyon murmured in reproach.

"Mama, you know as well as I that the three of them were more like the coarsest sort of squires rather than the sons of an earl. Leavitt and I are acquainted with a few of the old hard-riding, hard-drinking gentry, but most of them, at least, are well-intentioned."

As Matthew, Mark, and Luke were not. Though Luke, poor fellow, might have been all right, given a better example.

"I never thought the earl's notion of caning them for the slightest fault was good policy," Tate had said.

This went too far for Beau Cornell. "My father had a proper understanding of his place and of holding to a high standard. I was a wild, undisciplined lad, and I suppose my brothers committed their share of faults. He was a good, if strict, father."

Tamar stared at him, eyes narrowed, lips a thin, flat line. Such an expression on the face of women he knew in Wapping would mean *the fuse is lit*.

"How many times were you caned? No, better I ask, how often, for you cannot have kept count."

The Beau laughed and replied, "As often as I needed it, I expect."

She looked at Barlicorn, her expression softening. "And you?"

"There was seldom a week I wasn't beaten for some offense or other. That last day I was caned and confined to my chamber after we returned from church, for having grinned at something the vicar said. I was not the only one to find it amusing, but it did not suit my lord's notions of propriety."

"I remember," she said.

"My brother muddled his words on that occasion," Jemima Wilson remarked. "He was quite offended at the laughter, and when I explained later why it seemed droll to the congregation, he told me they should have understood what he meant to say and not mocked him."

"He was correct, though I suffered for it at the time. My father kept to an older, more formal standard. He did not take the slackness of others for his guide. He may sometimes have been a more exacting taskmaster than we would have liked, but his sternness sprang from a desire to mold us into decent, God-fearing men." At that speech, Barlicorn decided he despised Beau Cornell.

Tamar said, "My three older brothers were not decent and God-fearing. I'm sorry, Mother, but you know it is true. No decent person who knew them would say otherwise. And I cannot imagine my brother

John, who was the kindest boy, growing up to mouth such pious pap."

The Beau ducked his head, as if in embarrassment. "Sister, it is not thought right to speak ill of the dead, who cannot defend themselves. I put the best interpretation I can upon our papa's actions."

" 'Tis hypocrisy to pretend he was not harsh and unloving."

Lady Barlyon twisted her fine handkerchief and uttered a soft protest. It was ignored.

"If our brothers were here—"

"If they were here, we would not be having this conversation. I blame my father for the deaths of all three. If I believed in his harsh God, I would say it was God's judgment upon him."

"Oh, Tamar." Lady Barlyon's voice broke.

"I cannot agree. Mark drowned, and Matthew took some ailment in London and died of it."

Reeves pursed his lips. The cause of Mark's death came as news to Barlicorn. He knew Matthew had died, but it had been the result of a brawl in a school of Venus. It had been cause for rejoicing in those circles. And what of Luke?

Tamar was no longer the timid little sister he recalled. But then, she had only been seven or eight when he last saw her. How had she turned out so well? Was it no more than maturity, or was it her marriage? She had clearly made a happy marriage in spite of everything. Watching her, it occurred to him that her lack of beauty had benefitted her. Barlyon would have married her to the suitor with the highest title, whatever her preference. Mr. Leavitt must have been the only aspirant to her hand. Well, good for her.

"Mark was drunk to insensibility when he fell in the mill pond. The whole village knew it, though the fact was suppressed at the coroner's inquest. My father's doing, needless to say." Tamar's lips compressed.

"Father was not to blame that Mark could not hold his liquor," John I said.

"Sometimes men drink because they are unhappy or afraid. Mark was both."

Tamar's statement took Barlicorn by surprise. It might be true, but how perceptive of his little sister to realize it.

"Afraid? I cannot agree. He was a man's man. He would set his horse at any fence."

Beau Cornell might have been the late earl, come back to life, damn him.

"He rode as he did and got into fights because he feared our father and Matthew would think him hen-hearted. You know—no, you don't know, do you?—" she interrupted herself, looking very directly at John I, "how Father derided anything that smacked of timidity. Except in females, where he considered it mandatory."

"Well...you cannot believe that Father was responsible for Matthew's death—unless you believe he used witchcraft to make him ill with cholera morbus."

"I can believe it. Matthew was in London, and I suppose had been disporting himself in a very poor area, as was his habit."

"You cannot know that." Beau Cornell looked scandalized.

"Once Father let him go to London, he would boast after he came home to Mark and Luke, even in my hearing. He visited brothels—"

"Tamar!"

"I'm sorry, Mother, but he said he did, and often they were in very mean, poor parts of town. They were cheaper, and no one cared if he used the women hard."

The company was struck silent. Even Barlicorn, who knew the truth.

"It's not appropriate for a lady to speak of such things. Even if he did, anyone might fall ill with cholera morbus."

Beau Cornell was more scandalized by her bluntness than by Matthew's habits. Appearance matters more than substance.

As Lady Barlyon had already heard the worst, Barlicorn spoke. "It was not cholera morbus that killed him. No doubt the late earl felt that an illness was a more acceptable cause of death than the brawl that actually did for him. I am sorry, ma'am, but I believe my little sister is correct in thinking that we need plain speaking."

The Beau opened his mouth, but Tamar rounded on him. "Do not say it was not Father's fault. I cannot help but wonder if Matthew's...habits...were learned from him. If so, they took him to parts of town where footpads and fights are likely to be found."

"Dear, Barlyon did not patronize places like that," Lady Barlyon protested.

"Mayhap he did not. I do think he enjoyed beating us. When he was younger, Matthew treated the village boys badly. I expect he did the same at university, too. And as I said, he boasted of mistreating women of the town." She delivered these statements in a matter-of-fact voice, as though it were perfectly acceptable for a lady to express them. Barlicorn thought he would like to meet her husband. He must be quite unusual.

"We should not air our dirty laundry in public," Lady Barlyon protested.

"Don't you think a good many things will likely come out before we arrive at the truth?" Tamar inquired.

"I think they must," Tate agreed. Barlicorn did not find it surprising. If Tate believed in a deity, it would be Truth. As a tutor and therefore hardly better than an upper servant, he must sometimes have had to practice tact in presenting the truth as he saw it. Now he was free to express himself without fear of dismissal.

He hoped everything did not come out! His past in London at the Saracen Queen and Job's were certainly disreputable, though not as bad as Matthew's, at least, though Matthew's might be considered the sins of a "gentleman." And Matthew was dead.

"Let us put such a distressing subject behind us now." Lady Barlyon rose, signaling the ladies to withdraw.

Before they could do so, Barlicorn asked, "How did Luke die?" Tamar seemed the most likely to give an unvarnished account. But if Tamar had been able to lay his death at their father's door, surely she would have done so, as she blamed him for both Matthew's and Mark's deaths. It must have been only accident or some common ailment. But he would like to know; of his three older brothers, Luke had been the least valued by their father.

Dead silence greeted his question except for the rustling of a napkin, the creak of a chair, the scrape of a heel against the floor. Lady Barlyon sank back onto her chair. Glancing around the table, he saw that her face and those of John I, Tamar, Jemima Wilson, and Aurelia Kennet were frozen. Reeves was impassive. Tate radiated curiosity. The good-humored lines around Reddy's mouth turned down. He read sadness in her eyes.

"I beg your pardon if it causes you distress, ma'am, but I know how two of my brothers died. Luke has not been mentioned."

Lady Barlyon looked beseechingly at Attorney Reeves. He gave a slight shake of his head, declining to answer. Her lips trembled, and Tamar said, "Have you noticed the old gamekeeper's cottage is gone?"

"I have. I used to play there"—well, hide there and read—"after the gamekeeper married and moved closer to the village. What happened to the old one? I was surprised to see a lilac and rosemary growing where it used to be."

"It burned down," she replied through stiff lips.

"With Luke inside, asleep?" Drunk, probably, but why say it? Their mother and Tamar were already upset.

"So I understand," Beau Cornell volunteered when neither lady answered. "That is what I have been told."

"By one of the servants? They were instructed not to supply either claimant with information," Reeves said.

"Oh, please don't blame Huggins. Naturally, I wondered what had become of my poor brother—the nearest to me in age, after all—and I did not recall seeing any mention of his death in the papers. I fear I overpersuaded him."

"We will have no dishonesty." Tamar, of course. She swallowed visibly. "The coroner's inquest called it an accident to spare our family the shame and so there could be no difficulty about the burial."

"I see." Difficulty about burial meant a suicide. Usually a coroner's jury would bring in a verdict of accidental death in such a case, and most parsons would hold the decedent had not been in his right mind, permitting burial by the Church. Certainly any suggestion of suicide would have been rejected by the eleventh Earl Barlyon.

"Sister, there is no reason to think it was anything but an accident."

If Beau Cornell had not addressed her as sister, would she have continued? Mayhap she would; she had already spoken out about things never acknowledged in the family. Or in mixed company. Or even in all male company, as a rule. Pretending something out of existence is an easy way to avoid having to fix a problem.

She did not bother looking at John I. Instead, she turned to him.

"When the debris was cold, Father had the outdoor servants search it. Luke hadn't been seen since before the fire."

"Tamar, please." Lady Barlyon pressed her handkerchief to her lips.

"They recognized Luke's body by his ring. A pistol was beside him. The butt had burned, but the metal parts survived."

"No testimony at the inquest mentioned a pistol," Reeves said.

"Mr. Reeves, do you suppose that my father would have permitted it to come out?"

He smiled sadly. "No."

"After, he had all the cinders and charred beams removed and buried, so that in a year or two, no trace of the cottage would remain. I planted rosemary. I think Mother planted the lilac; I can't think how. Father never found out."

"I paid the under-gardener thirty shillings out of my pin money. I knew Lord Barlyon would avoid the place."

After that, the ladies left the table in silence to take tea in the drawing room. The gentlemen drank their port, and no more was said about the deaths. Still, the knowledge cast a pall over the gathering, leaving no one with any interest in idle conversation or cards. Awkwardly, the group began to break up early. Tate would likely sit up in his bedchamber, to read by the luxury of a branch of candles. If Barlicorn recalled anything of Reddy, she would sit by the fire in her chamber, knitting. He wondered what the others would do.

He himself went to the library, hoping to find a book to read. As he reached the stair with a copy of *Observations upon Experimental Philosophy* by Margaret Cavendish, Duchess of Newcastle (the ninth Lord Barlyon's choice, surely, having been published some seventy years before—he wondered the last Lord Barlyon did not burn it!), he came face to face with Tamar.

He whispered close to her ear, "Did Stripes the cat have her kittens safely?"

She stared at him. "Yes! I would never have known how to hide and feed her without your help. Papa and Mark and Luke never found out, and I found homes for all the kittens, that litter and the others. I had Stripes until I was near as old as you were when you left. Thank you, John. I still have a cat—well, cats—for my dear Leavitt says why should I not have cats when he has dogs? Too, he cannot abide mice and rats, and I dare say there is not a home in the county as free of vermin as ours. To think you should recall such a thing!"

"It's good to have happy memories, Tamar."

"You did not have many of those, John. I hope you may make some now you are home."

"Attorney Reeves will decide whether it is my home or not."

She laughed. "Of course it is. I believed so almost from the first, and Reddy knew instantly." Then she grew serious. "John, how did you know Matthew died in a brawl? Was it published in the paper in London?"

"No. I learned of it from an acquaintance, as my office was not far from where it happened."

"Was it not investigated?"

"Had it occurred in Westminster, I am sure it would have been—though perhaps the details would still have been covered up. But it happened in a very poor part of town. Not far from a street named 'Cutthroat Lane,' in fact. Violent death is not uncommon in such areas. It's fortunate that he was not simply tipped into the Thames."

"I see."

Obviously she did not.

"No one who was present reported it, for fear of being charged with murder. Someone provided a coffin for the body and had it delivered to Matthew's rooms. His manservant arranged for it to be transported to Barlyon Manor. I expect he wrote Lord Barlyon to explain, which would have prevented Barlyon from insisting on an investigation. God forbid Matthew's behavior in a seaman's brothel should come out."

"Then it was not a drunken brawl," Tamar said.

"I don't think his death was intended. The brothel keeper and the ruffian who sees the shot is paid and incidentally protects the women viewed it as an act of God. Or so I was told."

"I suppose he had hurt one of the women more than even they considered permissible." His little sister had grown up tough-minded.

"He killed her accidentally, they thought."

"Then 'act of God' seems a reasonable verdict. You won't tell Mother?"

"No."

"Thank you for not lying to me. Good night, John."

He found he had no particular desire to read natural philosophy that night. Instead, he sketched Tamar laughing at some remark of Mrs. Redding's, and the anxious face of Lady Barlyon. Ay, an interesting evening. Informative, too. He drew Aurelia Kennet, eyes intent. He did not know what Reeves's plan entailed, but Tamar and Reddy, at least, believed him to be the heir. Probably Tate did.

The sketch was not quite right. After a moment, he added a suggestion of a cat's pricked ears and whiskers. Sighing, he concealed the pad in the false bottom of his trunk before beginning to undress.

Chapter 12

As the winter twilight set in, the coachman and a footman returned from Maidstone with additional supplies and the mail. Since Attorney Reeves had taken up residence at the manor, he had arranged for footmen to make regular visits to his office in Maidstone. He was carrying on his practice and supervising his clerks by post, determining the real heir being his highest priority, and Lady Barlyon had the footman call at the post office as well, to collect the mail intended for Barlyon Manor.

The butler presented the mail bag to Lady Barlyon, where they had gathered in the drawing room to await supper. She glanced at Reeves and instructed Dare to give it to him. The attorney opened the bag and briskly sorted its contents: three to Lady Barlyon, two for the estate steward, which Reeves would put in the steward's office, as the man lived in a cottage on the property, one for Aurelia Kennet, one for Barlicorn, and half a dozen for Reeves.

With a moment's misgiving, Barlicorn wondered if Reeves would insist on reading his letter. He had warned Hawkins to be circumspect, but it might have been difficult to be obscure while conveying the information.

"Were you expecting a letter, sir?" the green bag—attorney—inquired. Hard to be subtle and still elicit information!

"A friend was to send me news of an acquaintance about whose welfare I was concerned. If you wish to read it, I have no objection."

"I misdoubt it's necessary," Reeves replied, to Barlicorn's relief.

Lady Barlyon slipped her own letters into the pocket under her gown. "Mr. Cornell, if you and Mistress Aurelia would care to read your letters, I am sure no one would be offended. I expect yours is from your parents, Aurelia, and you will like to know they arrived safely."

"Thank you, ma'am. I confess I had hoped to hear they have not had difficulties. On a previous journey, an axle broke and they were stranded in a terrible inn for two days while it was being replaced." She broke the seal, unfolded the sheet, her expression apprehensive as she skimmed over it. Understandably, as travel could be dangerous.

Barlicorn thanked Lady Barlyon for the permission and broke the seal.

"Did the viscount and your mama reach their destination without difficulty?" Lady Barlyon asked.

"They did, ma'am. The roads were good all the way and the inns tolerable. Mama writes that the Merriatt house and property are very fine." She made no further comment on her letter.

Hawkins had written:

I have heard from Sol and others who recognized him from your description and sketch that your friend is in no danger of being clapped up in debtors' prison at the moment, at least. You may wonder that he practices a profession, but his income from it keeps him adequately if not richly, and not being a gentleman born, he must make money as he can. He is usually in Tunbridge Wells and Bath, London not being to his taste, nor the reverse. He is no needle-sharp London practitioner, though well enough for most. Also he avoids it because some know him to have begun as a valet, like his father before him. I understand his uncle still is employed as such in your part of the country.

A. Hawkins

"You must have had good news," Reeves remarked as Barlicorn folded the letter and stowed it in his pocket.

"Indeed it was. My friend is not in desperate straits, as I feared he might be." Was Huggins the uncle Hawkins mentioned in his letter? Their lack of resemblance to each other proved nothing, as he and his brothers had looked nothing alike.

****

Barlicorn was in the library when he heard the front door open and the voice of the footman on duty in the front hall. Drawn by curiosity, he ventured out into the passage. Ahead of him, Lady Barlyon popped out of the parlor. As he came up behind her, through the open door he glimpsed a carrier's wagon drawn up before the entrance. Clement Pettigrew was already in the hall, and the footman and a roughly-clad man were carrying in his trunk and valise.

The surprise came near to stopping him in midstep. Reeves had not told them who had been invited to the house party. How had he known of his and Clement's friendship? Ah. Attorney Reeves was no fool. He must have determined that the old vicar's sister knew everything that went on in her vicinity and questioned her to learn who might best recall the lost Barlyon son. Mistress Wilson might well remember the time she had dried his clothing after he had slipped off the bank into the river while fishing with Clement. If he had gone home with wet clothes—no, he would not think about the likely outcome.

"Mr. Pettigrew! Did your coach suffer a mishap?" Lady Barlyon peered out at the wagon. Surely no such plebeian a vehicle had ever been seen at the front of the house.

Clement Pettigrew had arrived without commotion, as he always had. One might be sitting still, fishing, and then he would simply be there, unheralded by the rustling of brush or grass or whistling. Many, many years ago, Barlicorn had thought him a good height. But John was the "runt of the litter" as his father put it. He was surprised to find Clement a head shorter than himself. It's as if he'd only started to grow when he left here. Otherwise, Clement was little changed: stocky, round-faced, and beaming. He wore a plain black suit of good cloth, neither new nor shabby, with his own rather rumpled fair hair tied back. What had he been doing all these years, to arrive in a carrier's wagon? He had been the third son of a squire with limited resources, but surely there was money enough to train him to a profession?

"No, indeed, Lady Barlyon. I travelled as far as Maidstone by the stage, and a friend there arranged for one of his parishioners, a carrier, to bring me here." He shook the freight man's hand and slipped something into it. The fellow grinned and bobbed a bow, mumbling a farewell, and piked off as fast as he could. Like enough he'd tell his family and friends for years to come how he'd entered the front door of an earl's house, in the presence of her ladyship the countess and all.

The Beau entered the hall ahead of Barlicorn. Clement smiled vaguely at John I, then caught sight of Barlicorn over the Beau's shoulder. His smile widened.

Lady Barlyon, flustered by the absence of Reeves, murmured, "Mr. Pettigrew, here are our two claimants. To save confusion, we call this gentleman John I"—she gracefully indicated the Beau—"and the other is John II."

Reeves came down the stairs briskly, no doubt anxious to repeat his caution to the newcomer not to reveal anything of the past.

"Mr. Reeves, this is the Reverend Mr. Pettigrew. Mr. Pettigrew, Mr. Reeves is our attorney and the executor of the eleventh Lord Barlyon's will."

Reeves administered his usual speech, ending, "I know you will not be led to impart any details of the past to either of the Messrs. Cornell."

Clement Pettigrew turned parson? Barlicorn's London associates would laugh to think of having a black-coat as friend.

"My dear fellow." Beau Cornell clapped him on the shoulder. "Good to see you again. How does your family do?"

"All well, I thank you."

John I smiled graciously. "I trust a servant will show you to your chamber soon. You must be feeling the effects of a cold, bone-rattling ride in that wagon. You should have hired a coach."

"It was refreshing to be in the open air rather than mewed up in a coach. The seat was no harder than a pew, though somewhat more active."

Lady Barlyon completed her instructions to the footman and dispatched Pettigrew to his assigned bedchamber, telling him that she would have refreshments brought to the drawing room, if he cared to refresh the inner man after he had freshened the outer one.

Any private talk with Clement must wait; the drawing room, surrounded by others, would be no place for it.

****

In the drawing room after dinner, Barlicorn settled to talk with Tate and Reddy. Tamar and Jemima Wilson were engaged in a lively discussion about many farmers' resistance to Tull's inventions. Reeves conversed quietly with Pettigrew while Lady Barlyon sat working at her embroidery. Beau Cornell had contrived to draw Aurelia Kennet into a corner apart from the rest and to be speaking to her earnestly. It would be interesting to know what he was saying. She was not a lady to be convinced by flummery.

As will happen sometimes, the other groups all fell silent at once, allowing them to hear John I's soft-voiced remark, "…subject which must distress you. I would I had been here eight years ago to console you, or better yet, so that you need never have visited London in the first place."

The silence lasted a frozen moment. Lady Barlyon's head came up abruptly. Her gaze went to Aurelia. Clement studied Beau Cornell as if he were an insect under a magnifying glass. Tate and Redding appeared to understand the allusion no more than Barlicorn did. Let no one begin speaking in the scrambling way that indicates a desire to cover an embarrassing moment. By the devil's spiked tail, he would dearly love to know what had happened eight years ago in Miss Kennet's life. He, Tate, and Reddy had all left the area before that time. Clement Pettigrew must also have gone, but his family's seat being nearby, he would likely have heard of any scandal concerning a neighbor.

John I was evidently taken aback to have been overheard.

Aurelia Kennet suffered from no discomposure. Her voice was clear even over Lady Barlyon's hurried question to Pettigrew about activities in his parish. "My friends in this neighborhood are kind enough never to speak of the matter."

"I do most sincerely apologize. Huggins—who is acting as my valet—spoke of it only to warn me to avoid giving offense. I risked it to assure you of my respect and support, and so you need not feel any concern about my hearing of it."

It might have been a masterstroke if he had spoken privately with the lady, demonstrating both that he had been ignorant of something he should not have known and had been enough of a friend of the Kennet girl's that he would be sympathetic. If it had worked, his implied courtship must be balm to a spinster with some sort of blot on her past and might make her overlook the fact that John and she could hardly have been friends at the time he ran away. The distance between their homes made it virtually impossible for a boy of thirteen and a girl of eight or nine to see each other except perhaps at church. Given the relations between the Cornells and the Kennets, closer acquaintance would have been impossible. The complexity of it brought back the favorite perplexed oath of an elderly man he had known years ago, "by the cross of the mouse foot." Whatever it meant, it exactly expressed his bafflement.

Now, if he'd had his servant with him, he might have learned all sorts of interesting things that had occurred in the last seventeen years, which would not be helpful, as he would have to remember he was not supposed to know them. Then the thought of Lem Grigson in the servants' hall provoked a smile, though it could only be internal, given that Tamar had started describing her son's terrifying bout of measles.

After a time, Reeves excused himself to deal with some correspondence. The females repaired to the countess's boudoir to discuss whatever matters they thought might embarrass the gentlemen, who tended to be shielded from many of the earthier aspects of women's lives. Barlicorn would have liked to know what they discussed. It was probably as revealing as men's conversation over port. Mayhap more so.

With their numbers reduced to himself, Tate, Clement, and the Beau, talk turned to the recent act granting an aid to the king by a land tax. Judging from the household provisioning and a dozen other clues, it was evident the thrifty habits and wise investments by the tenth and eleventh earls made the tax a matter of little concern, though the Barlyon lands could produce more revenue than they currently did. Tate disapproved of it, not because of the burden on landowners but because, as he pointed out, the king would not need additional funds if he had not embroiled the country in a war which had very little to do with England's interests. Clement wished that it might be so easy to pry out funds for relief of orphans and the indigent. Beau Cornell seemed to have no opinion at all. He sat silent, turning the claret glass in his hand.

"I'm not used to late hours, gentlemen, and I say unto you, I will drink no more of the fruit of the vine— tonight. A good evening to you all."

When the tutor had closed the door behind him, John I guffawed. "Old Tate's bowsy on only three or four glasses! He can't often have the chance to drink deep. No wonder he's sucky."

"I would not say he was overcome with drink."

All through dinner Clement had been studying the Beau. Clement, for all his kindness and lack of guile, was sharply perceptive.

"He always was abstemious," Barlicorn said.

"I suppose he had to be, being a tutor. What a miserable thing, to be beating Latin and the like into boys." If someone had been drinking deep, it was the Beau. He poured himself another glass. "Life's devilish hard."

"It often is," Clement agreed.

John I looked up to see Barlicorn and Clement staring at him.

"Ah…I'd better retire. I've drunk more than usual, I fear. Damnably early hours people keep in the country." He drained his glass, stood awkwardly, and with a vague nod in their direction, shambled out.

When he'd gone, Barlicorn closed the door.

"I would never have guessed you would take orders, Clement, in spite of not being a hell-born babe like me."

"You never were that, whatever your father may

have called you." He said it without a smile, sounding very much as he had spoken of things which disturbed him as a lad: a carter basting a tired horse or a family thrown on the parish because the man had died or could no longer work by reason of injury. Clement had always seethed at injustice. Perhaps he should have realized Clement would choose the Church, in spite of the Church's faults.

"Welcome home, John."

"It doesn't seem like home. It never did."

"I know. But now you have come back, you must try to make it your home."

The fire burned down to nothing as they finished the bottle in near silence.

Chapter 13

8 June 1732

The day after the disastrous events at Vauxhall, Aurelia and her mother had attended a musical evening at the home of her mother's cousin, though neither wanted to go. Failing to appear, her mother pointed out dispiritedly, would look worse than facing down the gossip. Conversation hushed as they approached, then turned into a wave of whispers that followed them. Aurelia felt ready to die. She shook with reaction for an hour after reaching their house. "It might be best to go home," her mother said. "Next year, or the year after, we can visit London again. You are only eighteen. You have plenty of time." Her smile was unconvincing.

The second day after Vauxhall was far worse. They did not go out, until her father returned from White's in the late morning, ashen-faced. "Aurie, you must come with me. I gave my word I would bring you and let you choose. But 'tis a bad business."

"What, Pen?" her mother asked. "Where are we going?"

"I will explain later. It's best you not come with us."

"I am not dressed for visiting," Aurelia protested.

"It will not matter. Come."

In the coach, he said, "Hastings and Sedgewick

met this morning at Barn Elms."

"Which one is dead?"

"Neither. Yet. Hastings's father asked me to bring you to their home. I did not feel I could refuse."

Eight years later, she still recalled her horror. They were shown into Kit's mother's boudoir, where his father explained with stiff lips that Kit was dying and that his last wish was to marry her to save her reputation. "If there should be a child, he does not want it to be a bastard. And if a son, he would be my heir, of course."

"There cannot be a child, because nothing of that sort happened between us, sir."

Mr. Hastings did not believe her denial. "Marriage will save your reputation."

"And oh, if there were a baby, it would be such a consolation," his mother sniffed into her handkerchief.

"It's impossible anyway, even if…The banns must be read." Even if I were willing, she almost said.

"I have sent for a parson. My son had already secured a special license. He still lives and can make his responses."

Somehow she found herself in Kit's bedchamber. The sight of his gray, drawn face convinced her of his mortal wound. There was a doctor beside the bed, and a minister sat nearby, prayer book in hand.

Kit's eyes turned toward them as they came in, focusing on her.

Her own eyes wandered around the chamber, rather than linger on Kit or his parents. The scent of the coals in the fireplace and the burning beeswax candles, necessary with the heavy velvet draperies drawn against the daylight, dizzied her. Why did they always shut out the light in sickrooms? Surely brighter surroundings would encourage the patient, unless he suffered from a megrim. The candles gave hints that the chamber was large and elegantly furnished, though little was clearly visible beyond the bed. Oddly, a pair of candles burned on a cabinet in one corner, serving little purpose.

When did Kit apply for a special license? Would there have been time in the day before the duel?

All she could think was, Why should she marry him, when it was all based on a lie? Even if her reputation was somewhat damaged by the talk, it would be better to take her mother's advice than to marry Kit and then be a widow.

Her father spoke neither to persuade nor oppose, leaving the decision to her. He would surely prevent them from attempting to force the matter.

"My love." The word ended on a cough. "…want to make things right before…"

"Save your strength, my dear," his mother murmured. "For the vows." The parson stood and moved closer.

Aurie shook her head. "There's nothing to make right." Except Kit's appalling aspersions on her virtue, for which she could not demand an apology from a dying man. As his mother held a glass of some cordial to his lips, Aurie drifted toward the corner, as if drawn by a tether. The candles stood at either side of a cabinet about the height of a console table. Between the candlesticks stood a watercolor sketch of herself, clad in the jonquil-yellow closed gown that was her favorite for strolling in the park or the Mall. Before it lay a glove, one she had thought lost. At one side a small vase held a rose, and at the other lay a handkerchief.

She recognized the embroidered initial in the corner.

"My dear boy is devoted to you, and such a sentimentalist." Kit's mother must have seen her staring at the display. At the shrine.

"…my dying wish…marry you…"

Aurelia turned to face the bed.

"You surely cannot refuse my son's last request?" Mr. Hastings asked, on a pleading note. "When it will make you a respectable married lady?"

Aurie licked dry lips. "I swear there is no need. I will not enter into a marriage under false pretenses, even for a good reason." As she spoke, she wondered why she was certain it would be a bad, a terrible, idea. She had liked Kit's parents…though it sometimes seemed to her that they doted on him too uncritically. Anything Kit said must be true; anything he did must be justified. Whatever he wanted, they had given him. Now they wanted to give him his last wish. Her. And what if he did not die?

Dear God, what sort of female was she to think he and his family might pretend he was dying, merely to trap her into marriage? Even if it were not a deception, they would be waiting hopefully for Kit's posthumous child. They would expect her to mourn Kit, a monument to the tragedy of his great love. It would give solace to his parents, but she would be trapped in a pretense. She looked desperately to her father.

"If my daughter feels she cannot agree, there is no more to be said. We will leave now."

Later, Aurelia could not recall how they had got out, in the face of Kit's gasped protestations of love, his father's anger, and Mistress Hastings, who clung weeping to Aurelia.

****

The last to arrive was Hugh Langston, who came at midafternoon the next day, borne in on an icy wind, with clouds blowing up. He shrugged off his greatcoat in the hall and accepted Lady Barlyon's suggestion that he warm himself before the fire in the drawing room and drink a cup of punch before going to his chamber. Unless he preferred to wash his hands and face first, as she delicately phrased it.

Grinning, he agreed to the first proposal. "For I think my hands and face are clean enough until I have refreshed myself with a hot drink."

It came as no surprise that Hugh had been summoned, though his family no longer lived in the area. They had moved to a Hertfordshire manor his father had inherited a few years after Barlicorn left. But Jemima Wilson knew they had been friends in spite of Abel Cornell barely tolerating Hugh's people, whom he considered the next thing to Papists.

A bowl of steaming punch was brought in almost before they seated themselves. Hugh wrapped his hands around the punch cup with a happy sigh and explained he had married the heiress to a small property after attending Cambridge. He and his wife raised horses.

"I did not like to leave her and our three boys at Christmas, but she said it was my duty, and I could not have refused to come, under the circumstances. As it must be so, she will see to our stable, and an impoverished cousin of hers is come to visit over Christmas and we hope she will stay.

"Cecilia has suggested Cousin Eulalia might make her home with us. She is very fond of Eulalia, and it would benefit all of us. Particularly as Cecilia is better at stable management than household matters."

He stared at both claimants in an absentminded way as Reeves ladled him another cup of punch. Finally, he said, "I can't think of anything to ask you to prove who you are. But I expect I'll know after I've talked with each of you."

"I'm sure you will," Beau Cornell said. "All those boyhood memories will come back."

Barlicorn merely smiled.

Aurelia, with a glance out the window, murmured, "I fear it's coming on to snow."

Lady Barlyon peered at the gray landscape beyond the panes. "How lovely, Aurelia! I do like a dusting of snow at Christmas, don't you? What a pity it will melt by tomorrow or the next day." And indeed it was only a few flakes drifting down. It seemed no great thing. They were indoors with a good fire, making it easy to enjoy the gusts of wind that shook the windows.

But between the time they sat down to sup and the ladies' withdrawing perhaps an hour and a half later, six inches of snow fell, with the wind blowing it into drifts. If Lady Barlyon had not intended to have a house party, she would have had one forced upon her by the weather. No one could have left that night.

Reeves was in no way disconcerted by the snow. He had both of them and several people who might identify the true Earl of Barlyon mewed up in the house. No one now believed Lady Barlyon would identify the real John Cornell.

When they joined the ladies, Tamar, Reddy, and Lady Barlyon were sitting close together on a settee at a distance from everyone else, their heads together. Tamar had not come home to visit since her marriage.

The implied reason was the distance and the birth of her two children. John might guess at the real reason.

Hugh could still not think of a way to test them. Barlicorn's mind wandered while listening to Hugh describe his horse-breeding endeavor, a topic in which few English gentlemen could be uninterested. Hugh had never been quick of wits, his appeal resting in his cheerful disposition. He did know horses, however. He had been horse-mad as a boy.

Clement, Tate, and Reeves were discussing, of all things, canon law.

Aurelia Kennet and Jemima Wilson were too far away for him to catch even the sense of their discussion. Something serious and satisfying; with a last brisk nod, they separated. Attorney Reeves excused himself and drifted over to Mistress Wilson to address her. Impossible to tell whether it was purely social or whether he was questioning her about her memories from all those years ago. He would surely have met with her before to discover if she was a credible witness. She was the only one who lived close enough for him to interview before the house party.

Aurelia, followed by Tamar, joined Clement and Tate.

Lady Barlyon and Reddy appeared to have settled to a comfortable discussion. The young ladies, Tate, and Clement were soon laughing over something. Beau Cornell had managed to shift his position to be nearer them. Was he intent again on exercising his charm upon the Kennet girl? Rather the Kennet lady, as she was past girlhood. A little older than Tamar, who had followed her around like a duckling trailing after its mother, whenever she could.

Aurelia Kennet possessed a keen intelligence, as he'd noticed before. He'd cap downright—No. He dared say or he'd wager—she was little impressed by Beau Cornell's inanities.

"…by my Barb stallion. I'm trying to retain the Barbary stamina and agility while improving the gait. The Barbs are a bit short in the back…" Hugh was saying.

"The Arabians are a handsomer breed," Beau Cornell offered. "A man is a laughingstock on an ugly nag. Is that not the case, Mistress Aurelia?" he called across the few feet that divided the two groups.

Mistress Aurelia's patience must have worn thin; she said pleasantly, "I believe the Scots have a saying, 'Better a good kind of cow than a cow of a good kind.' "

Hugh Langston chuckled. "It's true for horses, as well. A man's a laughingstock on a stumbler or a horse with no paces nor stamina, no matter what its looks or pedigree."

"I prefer agility to beauty, myself," Barlicorn said.

At intervals, someone would rise, go to one of the windows, and part the draperies, which had been drawn to keep out the chill and dark. The report did not vary. "Still snowing, and blowing fierce. There will be branches down, and trees, too, I shouldn't wonder."

"It would be a kindness to let the poor gather the fallen limbs. It's hard to keep the cottages warm in winter," Mistress Wilson said.

Lady Barlyon looked first at Beau Cornell, who said, "Do we want the villagers free to prowl through our property and take what belongs to us? Next they would be snaring rabbits or fishing in the stream."

She looked at John Barlicorn. "I would take Mistress Wilson's recommendation. Lord Barlyon would never have permitted it—"

"Exactly!" the Beau interpolated. "And the law forbids it."

"—which seems to me an excellent reason to let the poor have the wood. As for the law, if the property owner permits, has the law anything to say in the matter?"

Reeves said judiciously, "Tenants have lost their rights in common land, such as gathering wood, grazing their own animals, and so forth where the common has been enclosed, as it was here, by the eleventh earl. It is a criminal offense to damage a tree, fire a hayrick, or poach, among other things, or even merely to be present in a wood, field, chase, or down while wearing a mask, or with one's face blackened, in any way disguised, or with a firearm."

Langston added, "My father stood out against the Black Act that made those and half a hundred other offenses capital crimes, though they had often been traditional rights of the common folk."

"Attorney Reeves has informed us it is a crime," Beau Cornell began.

"Sir, few legal opinions are so plain and without exception. The law is meant to protect landowners from the depredations of poachers or disgruntled tenants. If the landowner chooses to give permission for tenants and villagers to collect the fallen wood on his property on this occasion, the law has nothing to say about it. Indeed, there is reason to do so, as someone must clear away the debris, and tenants or others would have to be hired for the work, if there is much damage from the storm. The said tenants and villagers should of course be warned that they must not wear masks, blacken their features, or carry weapons. Or cut down trees or fire hayricks, of course." This bit of dry legal humor amused everyone except John I.

Lady Barlyon glanced at Tamar, who said, "I think they should be permitted to gather the wood."

"Mayhap nothing should be decided until the identity of the twelfth Lord Barlyon is determined. One would not wish to set a precedent." That from the Beau.

Lady Barlyon glanced at Reeves, who said blandly, "In such a circumstance, I think it not unreasonable to deal with the matter now. You would not hesitate to order needed food or household supplies, after all."

Lady Barlyon looked to Aurelia Kennet appealingly.

"It's now they need the wood," she said. "At least, once it's daylight and the wind dies down."

"Then I say, let them collect it." Lady Barlyon looked momentarily terrified when she realized she had made a decision, but her mouth firmed and her chin came up slightly. "I will inform the servants and send a message to the vicar in the morning."

"I will write a document to that effect to be signed by the interested parties, to wit, both claimants and your ladyship, and witnessed by those present here. Doing so will prevent any claim later that a crime was committed. Indeed, the branches would have to be removed, and letting the common people do it for their benefit will save your forester work, and you would not burn branches in your fireplaces. In the case of a fallen tree, you may wish to let the folk remove its limbs, leaving the trunk to your use."

"Please do so, Mr. Reeves. You will copy it out several times? I should like one, as well as one for the steward."

So proof of the permission will be available even if the steward were instructed by the new earl to lose it? Rumly done, Lady Barlyon.

The Beau shrugged delicately. Barlicorn smiled at Lady Barlyon, which seemed to startle her. After a moment, she smiled back timidly.

Aurelia observed, lightening the mood, "Do you realize tomorrow is Christmas Eve? What a pity the snow is too deep to gather greens to decorate the house."

Tamar said, "We could still bring in ivy. There is some growing behind the stable. It would not be far to walk even in the snow, and the grooms going back and forth will have made a path from the stable to the kitchen. And there's bay and rosemary in the kitchen garden."

"Can we do no better than that? The ladies might bring in the ivy, rosemary, and bay"—Hugh Langston bowed slightly in their direction—"while we brave the snow to find some holly and mistletoe."

"But not if the wind continues to blow," Lady Barlyon protested. "Or if it continues to snow tonight."

Chapter 14

The day dawned cloudy. The snow and wind having stopped, the men went out to gather greens, but they did not linger in the bitter cold. Pettigrew commented with a sigh, "When I was a boy if we had snow, we would have had a snowball battle. Someone would have been tossed into a drift. The courting couples might have become lost in the trees for a few minutes. It's not the same without the ladies, bless them. It's too cold anyway."

"I remember kissing my intended bride on such an occasion," Reeves remarked. "It was our family tradition to drink lambswool after we brought in the yule log and greens, not only on Twelfth Night. Lambswool and gingerbread. And we played foolish games."

In the few minutes his family had lingered after church while Lord Barlyon spoke with the parson to compliment him for the sermon or tell him what his next sermon should address, Barlicorn recalled hearing others speak of bringing in bay leaves, holly, mistletoe, and ivy. The Reverend Mr. Wilson, like the earl, believed in observing the birth of Christ solemnly. Neither had succeeded in imposing their views on the village, tenants, or local gentry, although those who depended on Barlyon for their livelihood were careful to be discreet about their celebrations. But he himself had never had a clear notion of what those festivities entailed, beyond what Hugh or Clement had mentioned. Among his London acquaintances, the celebration centered around drink and food. Mostly drink, for some.

This excursion might have seemed more a chore than an occasion for merriment, given the cold, the absence of children, and the recent death. Tamar and Lady Barlyon clearly did not agree, as they had insisted on the house being decorated. Reeves, Langston, Tate, and Clement showed no sign of finding the cheer unseemly. Barlicorn watched like a traveler studying the customs of a foreign land. The Beau was quiet.

"The wind is coming up again." Langston paused in binding up a bundle of holly as a gust shook the tree limbs, causing clumps of snow to fall. One branch creaked ominously.

Reeves frowned. "It might be best to start back. If there is a gale like last night's—" A blast of wind swept through the wood, moaning through the trees and bringing down more snow.

"Best to go back," Tate agreed. "We have enough holly and ivy to satisfy the ladies, surely."

"It seems a little warmer," Clement observed as they trudged back through the drifts. By the time they reached the house, the wind was blowing steadily.

The rest of the day was taken up with decorating at the direction of the ladies, until the mantels and balusters were wreathed in greenery, and mistletoe hung in various places in the public rooms. At intervals, they were plied with treats: mincemeat pies, gingerbread, hot drinks, and a rich cake. It was indeed very rich, full of currants, raisins, citron, and candied peel, iced with a snow-white glaze of sugar.

Barlicorn was—with some embarrassment—eating a second slice. "Ma'am, I can identify nutmeg and cinnamon, but there is some other flavor I do not recognize."

"There is orange-flower water, of course, and sack, and musk and ambergris. Do they not make such cakes in London? I'm sure they used to do so."

"I do not recall seeing anything similar sold in the bakeshops." In my neighborhood. "It is usually only plum cake, seed cake, and pound cake they offer. Mayhap the musk and ambergris make it unprofitable for common bakeshops."

"Oh! I suppose it would be expensive." Lady Barlyon appeared to realize that a boy on his own in London, who supported himself by odd jobs and decidedly ungenteel trade, would not shop in Fortnum & Mason's.

What would it have been like to grow up celebrating Christmas? He had sometimes been a guest of Solomon's family for dinner over the years; what little he knew of family celebrations was learned at their table. But the holidays they observed did not include Christmas.

Later in the afternoon, when they were surfeited with food and drink and sat conversing desultorily or playing cards or tric-trac in the drawing room, Langston went to the windows and peered out. "The weather is changing. I think it means to rain."

"It feels warmer. But if the snow begins to melt, the road will be deep in mud," Aurelia observed.

Rain it did.

They had planned to attend the service in the

village church in spite of the cold and snow. The thaw having begun, the three-quarters of a mile to the village became first a matter for concern, then simply impossible as the rain ate away at the snow.

"I fear we will find the brook over its banks and the road running with streams or deep in mud by the time we should leave for the service," Tamar said.

Lady Barlyon sighed. "I do not think I have missed a Christmas Eve service since I was a girl. I attended even when I was recovering from Luke's birth. I would have had to be on my deathbed before Lord Barlyon permitted me to stay home. The servants will be sorry to miss going to church, too. I suppose if someone will read from Matthew and Luke, and we sing, that is as much as we can do."

"We can do a little better. You have a serviceable parson in your midst—"

"My goodness! I beg your pardon, Mr. Pettigrew. I tend to think of you as the lad who spent an afternoon trapped in a tree with John after the bull chased you."

"I am relieved that your memories of me are no worse, my lady," Clement said with a smile.

"We also still have a chapel, I assume. Unless it was struck by lightning." Barlicorn meant the comment to be humorous. Instead it rang flat.

"It has not been used since…since Lord Barlyon's death."

"Still, it can hardly have fallen down or even acquired a layer of dust in that space of time. What say you, Clement? Will you preside?"

"I do not suppose you brought your cassock, but if you would be willing to lead the service, we would so much appreciate it," Lady Barlyon ventured.

"My lady, I have my cassock and bands with me. Of course I will officiate."

"Well! 'Tis good to have that settled and not to have to trudge through snow and rain. After, we might have some light refreshment." This was John I's sole contribution to the question.

"The staff will prepare a cold collation to await us after the service, and punch will need only the hot poker when we are ready."

The chapel, oddly enough, was one of the warmer areas, as whether by foresight or by accident, the architect had positioned the chimneys of the rooms on either side in the walls adjacent to the chapel. The eleventh earl might have disapproved of its being comparatively warm, but even he would not have thought it reasonable to tear down the chimneys or block off the fireplaces. Lady Barlyon had ordered fires lit in those rooms in spite of their being unused.

With candles in all the many-branched candle stands, tall as a man, ivy wrapping the slim, graceful pillars, and the entire household in attendance, the chapel was actually cheerful. As they waited for Clement Pettigrew to take his place in the pulpit, Lady Barlyon said, "How strange life is. I was married here during the great storm of 1703. It was in November rather than December, yet this seems a sort of anniversary." She became absorbed in her Book of Common Prayer.

Then Pettigrew, unusually impressive in his black cassock with pristine white Geneva bands falling from the collar, ascended to the pulpit.

****

No one was up very early on Christmas Day. It was

ten in the morning when Aurelia was ready for Nan to assist her in dressing, and near half an hour later when Nan came in with a jug.

"Huggins!" Nan uttered as she poured hot water into the wash bowl.

"What's he done to annoy you?"

"I filled your jug with water and turned away to ask the kitchen maid if the chocolate was ready, and Huggins sidles in and pours it into That Fop's jug. Then there wasn't enough hot water left for a full jug, as others' wash water had gone up too, so I had to wait while more heated. And the cook and the kitchen maid both feeling put upon because Huggins had complained there was no coffee ready and wanting buns to take up to That Fop with it."

"Do I gather Huggins is not much liked below stairs?"

"Well…he was his lordship's man and had a right to hold himself up and demand service first in everything. But stiff-necked! Agreed with his master on every point, too, they tell me. When he found out Mary was courting, he told the old lord, and she was let go without a reference. Like master, like man."

As she washed her face and hands, she recalled Lady Barlyon saying Huggins had been employed at Barlyon for fifteen years. While Nan tied her corset strings, Aurelia did mental arithmetic. Huggins must have arrived well after John Cornell ran away. He could never have known John, and if he had made himself immediately unpopular with the other servants, probably heard little of the fourth Cornell son from them, even if they had been willing to talk to him. Huggins would understandably hope to serve the new earl when the first claimant made his appearance. When a second unexpectedly arrived, the valet might be anxious to insure that the first claimant was accepted and be willing to feed him information to achieve that end.

****

Lady Barlyon showed her household management, surprising even Aurelia, who had been assisting her. The meals had always been good, but she had had no notion of the orders her hostess had given and the prodigies performed by the kitchen in secret. Several sorts of candied fruit, marchpane, and ratafia puffs eked out the dinner of turkey and sausages, ham, pickled salmon, cheese cakes, and other good things.

There was even a chocolate cream, a novelty to Aurie.

"It's easy to make, though expensive," Lady Barlyon admitted. "Break a quarter pound of chocolate into a quarter pint of boiling water and beat and boil it until it be dissolved. Then add a pint of cream and two beaten eggs, and beat it while it boils. When you take it off the fire and 'tis cool, beat it again to make it froth. Those quantities will make enough for eight, so Cook increased them by half."

Somewhat fatigued from the previous day's exertions and attendance at the midnight service, they passed Christmas Day quietly. Gusty wind and rain discouraged outdoor amusements, and the investigation into the two John Cornells proceeded no further. Mr. Reeves did look very like a mouser waiting outside a promising hole. Wherever she went, Aurie found him: he prowled from the breakfast table to the parlor to the library to the long gallery to the small drawing room.

He had been interviewing every servant who had worked at Barlyon Manor before John Cornell's disappearance, of whom, unfortunately, most had not known the boy well.

The following day, which was still unpleasantly wet, Huggins came to the small drawing room where the females had assembled to chat while Lady Barlyon and Tamar embroidered, Reddy knitted, and Aurelia knotted an edging. Someone was always in expectation of a blessed event and knotted edging dressed up an infant's cap or gown prettily, with less effort and concentration than embroidery required. And unlike embroidery, one could easily carry the shuttle and thread with one, and even work on it during a coach journey.

"Lady Barlyon, Lady Tamar, Mistress Aurelia." He bowed to them, ignoring Mistress Redding. "Mr. Reeves requests the presence of Mistress Aurelia in the west parlor."

"If you will excuse me, my lady, Tamar, Reddy, I will attend upon Mr. Reeves." Aurie tucked her knotting shuttle into the pouch at her wrist with the length already knotted, nodded, and preceded Huggins out the door.

A sour man, well suited to be the late earl's valet. However did he and John I go on? Many men were given to pious mouthings, even when they did not live a rigorously moral life. It was hypocrisy, and worse than the nonsensical convention about not speaking ill of the dead, even when they deserved it. When she and John I had been tête-à-tête, his conversation reminded her of fashionable, fribbling young men met in London, though mayhap with an element of calculation: he seemed to be courting her.

Huggins accompanied her to the parlor and opened the door for her. The room had been given over to Reeves to use as an office, and an old-fashioned desk moved into it—from the attics, no doubt. He rose, bowed, and invited her to take a chair near the desk.

He was not a man to waste time. "Good morning, Mistress Aurelia. We have not spoken except socially"—his tone making his opinion of social exchanges clear—"but the time is now ripe to consult with you as Dr. Simmons advised."

"Will the others not think it very odd that you are speaking with me?"

"Not at all, Mistress Aurelia. I have already called most of the servants in and will speak with all of them as they are available, to ask what they remember of young John if they were employed here then, and even if they were not, whether they have observed anything of the two men that they think worth mentioning."

"Gossip, in other words."

"Indeed. It's often helpful." He dipped his quill in the standish and wrote her name at the top of the blank sheet before him. "However, from you I anticipate more than mere gossip. Dr. Simmons told me you notice details others overlook. I have some skill at weighing men's characters from forty years' experience as an attorney." He smiled faintly. "I wanted a second pair of eyes, someone keenly discerning, preferably belonging to someone—forgive me, Mistress Aurelia—who would not be suspected of acting as my informant. Your being a female was an added advantage. A woman often sees things a man would miss."

"My father did say I was invited to the dinner after

the second claimant's arrival at Dr. Simmons's suggestion. Thank you for explaining the reason, sir. It puzzled me, as I did not know John Cornell. I was too young, and the only time I could have seen him was at church. I have been watching the two John Cornells like a hawk."

"I will ask your deductions about them later. At the moment, I am interested in what you think of the other members of the house party, and the staff, too, if you have any impressions of them. Pray begin by telling me what you think of Lady Barlyon, forgetting ladylike reticence and good manners, if you will."

"I hope I can be of assistance. If you had given me notice, I would have written out my thoughts and perceptions."

"It is a mistake to overthink one's first impression. If you later recall some detail, tell me then."

Describing her reactions to her hostess and the other guests—and why did he want that, unless to aid him in evaluating their evidence?—she had to agree that speaking spontaneously she might be giving a fuller and less restrained sketch of each person than she could have done if she had written it out.

She told him why Lady Barlyon did not remember whether John had crooked teeth, and that Tamar had confirmed the boys' limited contact with their mother and said her youngest brother possessed some artistic talent.

She lost track of time. She talked about her conversations with both John Cornells, how John I fawned over Lady Barlyon and John II never spoke of her as his mother. She mentioned, with embarrassment and an apology for sounding vain, that John I seemed almost to be courting her.

"I would not be at all surprised," Mr. Reeves remarked. "If he is not identified as the twelfth earl, marrying a well-connected young lady with a good dowry would be almost as satisfactory. I trust, however, that you are too sensible to accept an offer from an unsuccessful claimant, as a fraudulent attempt would indicate bad character."

"There is no chance of my accepting an offer from either one," she replied.

He nodded his understanding. He could scarcely help being aware of her history. "Thank you, Mistress Aurelia. If you would ask Mistress Redding to join me?"

When Aurie returned to the small drawing room, she was startled to discover she had been with Reeves for nigh upon two hours. Through the rest of the day, she watched the comings and goings. The attorney must be close to completing his investigation.

****

At supper, John I contrived to sit beside her. He maintained a steady flow of inconsequent remarks, the only one at table who seemed to be in spirits. Aurie suspected it was desperation rather than insouciance. He frequently smiled at her with a caressing intimacy, which was embarrassing. Lady Barlyon did her best to encourage conversation, with Tamar's assistance. John II stared unblinking at John I, and Mr. Pettigrew stared down at his plate as if in a brown study. Mr. Langston assisted Lady Barlyon's efforts when he could, while seeming puzzled at the party's mood.

The end of the meal came as a relief. But before Lady Barlyon could rise to lead the females to the drawing room, Reeves spoke.

"I believe all of you have had sufficient time to study the two claimants." He drew a stack of slips from his pocket. "I would be obliged if you would each ponder carefully tonight, and set down the name—the designation, that is, either John I or John II—of the man you believe to be the late Lord Barlyon's heir. Give me your vote by tomorrow afternoon, and I trust we will have determined the true heir. It will be unnecessary for the two Mr. Cornells to cast ballots."

The men did not linger over their port, but Lady Barlyon had already gone to her chamber before the gentlemen made their appearance in the drawing room. Aurie wished she too could hide in her chamber to escape the feeling of tension, but duty required her to help fill in for her hostess. Several points struck her forcibly. Tamar and Nurse Redding chatted amicably while Tamar embroidered a baptismal gown and Reddy knitted another stocking. Pettigrew and Jemima Wilson discussed the difficulties of teaching, laughing occasionally over some pedagogical anecdote. Hugh Langston chewed his lower lip and talked first with John II and then with the other claimant—Beau Cornell, as John II called him. After Langston's departure to find a book to read in the library, John I shot out comments and remarks seemingly at random and fidgeted. Tate kept up a gentle patter about a visit to the Ashmolean Museum at Oxford, which required few responses from Aurie. Reeves watched everyone.

Chapter 15

The hours dragged the next day until Attorney Reeves summoned them to the library after their midday meal. Barlicorn wished the whole business done. A curious mixture of gloom and tension affected everyone, including the servants, resulting in raised voices, and the dropping of a jug of wash water by a maid.

The attorney opened the slips of paper one at a time, smoothing each and making a tidy pile. He dipped his quill in the ink bottle and wrote something on a sheet of paper. Presumably "John I" and "John II." Then he scrutinized the slips one at a time and made a mark on the sheet for each. Beau Cornell was sitting by the fireplace, legs stretched out and crossed at the ankle, arms crossed on his chest. No wonder he was only moderately successful as a cardsharper. Dexterous but not clever at concealing his emotions.

At last Reeves gave a brisk nod and turned to them.

"Of eight ballots cast, one is an abstention and seven believe John II is the rightful twelfth Earl of Barlyon."

"The devil!" John I burst out. "Their opinions are no proof!"

"It would have been better to have a larger group," Reeves remarked, "but it was impossible to find anyone else. I suggest you listen to their reasons for voting as they did. Lady Barlyon, will you begin?"

Her hands clasped in her lap, the knuckles white, she spoke in a thread of a voice. "I abstained. To my shame, I simply cannot be sure. What I believe is based solely on female intuition." She burst out, "I feel such a fool for assuming the first claimant was my son, based on nothing at all except wishful thinking…"

The attorney inclined his head. "Mr. Langston?"

Hugh frowned. "I never was good at puzzles or charades. John I is clearly a gentleman and his opinions are very like what I recall of old Barlyon, begging your pardon, my lady. Keep the rabble in their place, sneer at cits and men of business, hold himself better than neighboring gentlemen of good family, even if their lineage was as ancient as his. The thing is, it's as if John I has turned into old Barlyon. I can't see how the John Cornell I knew could have changed that much. John liked people, all kinds of people, and they liked him. I believe John II is my old friend."

"Reverend Pettigrew?"

"I cast my ballot for John II because I've dealt with men—ay, and women, too—who were brutally treated by a parent. Some turned out well and some ill, but none of them forgot."

"Greater maturity and Christian forgiveness —" the impostor began, piously.

"Christian forgiveness? The best of them told me they had put their feelings of betrayal behind them and forgave. But they never thought the treatment meted out to them showed love. And John was a good friend of mine. Even though he's grown from an undersized boy to a man, I could not mistake his features."

"Thank you, sir. Mistress Leavitt?"

"I know John II is my brother. He always listened to me when I was upset. He smuggled food to me once when I was locked in my room on bread and water. I forget why I had been punished, but he climbed the ivy outside with some cheese and an apple, and a slice of mutton. I've never forgotten it. Nothing since has tasted as good. Matthew ignored me, and Mark broke the doll Aunt Susan brought back from France." Evidently, it still rankled. "Luke called me 'Fat Fub,' even in front of our father. Of course, it only meant a small, plump child, and I was, but he didn't mean it kindly."

Oh, Tamar.

Tamar continued, "He remembers my cat, Stripes. My brother could draw. The other couldn't draw a floor plan when I asked his opinion for a design for the greenhouse we plan to build."

"My failure, for which I apologize, resulted from my lack of acquaintance with such things. I have never paid much attention to glass houses, though some of my friends and acquaintances who have gardens have them."

"You could not even sketch a rectangle half as wide as long, which was the first step. My brother drew the outline and how the framing should be done, too."

"I have not kept up my sketching. I was too busy in London."

Reeves cleared his throat. "Mr. Tate?"

They all looked expectantly at the tutor.

"In my opinion, John II was my student. He has not forgot the Latin I taught him, or a dozen other things. He was attentive and possessed an inquiring mind. You, sir"—he looked directly at Beau Cornell—"are oddly forgetful of your lessons. John Cornell read more than merely the lessons I assigned him. He read whenever he could get away with it. Your education is oddly deficient in those things any man of education should know, certainly any lad I taught: geography, natural philosophy, history, and books I know John Cornell read because I lent them to him and we discussed them. He liked to read and draw, activities Lord Barlyon did not encourage. But in the schoolroom John concealed those tastes from his brothers, who would have told his father. I believe only his sister and I were aware of his artistic ability."

"Mistress Wilson, may we hear your reasons?"

"Certainly, sir. I knew John Cornell well, I believe, from the time he was seven or eight years old until he disappeared. We all know how the late earl treated him, and his brothers were not kind, either. Except for the schoolroom, he spent as little time at home as he could. Sometimes he played with boys from the houses nearby—Mr. Hugh Langston and the Reverend Mr. Pettigrew, mostly, but usually he wandered by himself. Sometimes he visited me at the parsonage, particularly when the weather was inclement. He talked to me. Not about his family—except Tamar. He worried about her. He told me about the cat he helped her save, after swearing me to secrecy. He told me about books he had read and places he wanted to visit, as soon as he was old enough to leave Barfield.

"He was a serious boy. I rather hoped he would decide to go into the church, although how it could have been managed, I do not know. Certainly his father would not send him to university, and there would be no question of giving him the living here even if he did. I worried what was to become of him. I hoped to

141

interest one of my acquaintances in him, to train him up in some genteel business. Then he vanished. I have spoken with him at some length since his return, and he has mentioned things we spoke of and events no one else would recall. Our old cook knew him well, too, and treated him like a favorite nephew, but she was laid in the churchyard years ago, as I told Mr. Reeves when we first spoke of witnesses. But John II remembered in detail the treats she gave him, which is telling, as she was from Cornwall originally. Once she made him a stargazy pie, though she had to use fish from the stream—poached, I'm sorry to say!—rather than pilchards. She made a particular sort of bun, too. He was always hungry, poor lad. The other claimant, with whom I have also spoken as much as possible, speaks only in generalities. He obviously recalls nothing of John Cornell's life here.

"I can't imagine my John Cornell ever speaking in the mealy-mouthed way the other affects. It goes against nature that a boy treated as John was could speak well of his father, unless he was a hypocrite. There is no question in my mind that your 'John II' is the true heir."

"Thank you for a very full explanation. Now, Mistress Redding?"

She had been sitting placidly, knitting. "John Cornell, who's sitting over there by the bookshelves."

"But on what do you base that opinion, mistress?"

"I knew him when he greeted me. If you know the child well, you can see the child in the grown man or woman. He was a dear, sweet boy, too, and I don't think he could have turned into that other gentleman"— she tipped her head toward John I—"no matter what happened to him later. And his poor teeth could not have grown straight. He had not got all his adult teeth when he left, but the ones he did have at the front were crooked. It's a thing I have seen before, in a child that's undergrown for his age, as Master John was."

"Then in your opinion, which claimant is the real John Cornell, Mrs. Redding?" Reeves inquired. "If you would use John I or John II to indicate your choice."

"Why, the one you call John II," Mrs. Redding said. She continued knitting.

"One last person remains to be heard from. Mistress Aurelia, being several years younger than John Cornell, is unlikely to have known him well. I asked her to take part in this investigation not for her memories—though if she has any to share, I welcome them—but because I was informed by more than one local that she is exceptionally perceptive and observant. Ma'am, may we hear your reasons for voting as you did?"

She showed signs of being disconcerted by the attention focused on her. Still, she spoke clearly. "It's true I had no acquaintance with John Cornell when I was a child. I don't recall seeing him except in church. I don't think we ever spoke. However, during the course of Lady Barlyon's house party, I have noticed several things. Some you may perhaps have already taken note of, sir.

"First, John I has portrayed the doting son of Lady Barlyon. I saw this the day after he arrived when I paid a call upon her. Lady Barlyon herself has said she hardly ever saw her youngest son: the children were brought to her once a day to be…mmmm, inspected. Little conversation was involved. I find it impossible to believe John Cornell could grow very fond of his

143

mother under those circumstances. John II has been cool to Lady Barlyon, which seems a much more believable reaction. Second, John II obviously recognized his old nurse when she arrived and greeted her affectionately. John I did not. In my experience, those of us who had nurses commonly are very fond of them."

Langston and Pettigrew both nodded agreement.

"Third, I have clear memories of the late Lord Barlyon, though our families were not close. John I shares many of his attitudes, when he remembers to do so. At other times, he appears to be the typical man of fashion. John Cornell left home seventeen years ago. By all accounts, he was nothing like Lord Barlyon at that time. This is all a guess on my part, and I don't wish to cast any aspersion on someone who may be innocent. I recall hearing that Lord Barlyon's valet was hired about two years after John Cornell's departure and therefore never met him. John I knows some details about John Cornell, which he must have learned somehow, probably from Huggins, who has been acting as John I's valet. I do not believe he would have heard them from the other servants, who seem not to have known the young John well. Most of what Huggins knew of the missing Cornell son must therefore have come from Lord Barlyon, who cannot have known his son any better than Lady Barlyon did. If in an unguarded moment Huggins mentioned anything about John Cornell, it would have been based on what he had heard from Lord Barlyon, which would not necessarily be an accurate portrayal of reality. If you see what I mean?"

Reeves appeared struck. "Ay, thank you, Mistress

Aurelia. If I follow your reasoning, you mean John I would have learned the eleventh earl's opinions relating to John but few if any details about his activities."

"Yes, sir, that is the point I was trying to make."

Jemima Wilson sat, hands clasped in her lap, her face that of a judge. Barlicorn fancied he could hear the echo of the words "and may God have mercy upon your soul" hanging in the air. Tamar smiled at him, blinking to hold back tears. Aurelia was pale and stared down at her own clasped—no, clenched—hands. Reddy was turning the heel of the stocking she was knitting. Tate studied Beau Cornell, frowning slightly. Lady Barlyon was visibly choking back her own tears.

"You have heard the opinions of those who knew John Cornell that this," Reeves addressed the Beau, and made a little bow toward Barlicorn, "is the twelfth Earl of Barlyon. Do you have anything to say, sir?"

The Beau sprang to his feet. "I won't be cheated. I'll take it to law. You can't choose an heir by vote, even if Parliament chose a king."

"The opinions of those who knew John Cornell are as much proof as would be available to judge and jury," Reeves said. "This is not some fantastical play in which the lost heir can conveniently be identified by a birthmark attested to by his devoted old nurse."

"This fellow doesn't even look like my father or brothers. He doesn't look like my mother. He doesn't even look like a gentleman! From his complexion you might take him for a sailor or farm laborer. Look at the calluses on his hands! He has acquired a little polish somehow, but he's no nobleman or even a gentleman. To decide he is the heir merely because he has insinuating ways—"

Several of the listeners were looking uncomfortable. Lady Barlyon smoothed her quilted silken petticoat, ignoring unpleasantness as she had hundreds of times before.

Tamar interrupted in a most unladylike manner. "He doesn't. If anyone has insinuating ways, it's you."

John I's nostrils flared. Before he could retort, Barlicorn said, "While I don't have a birthmark, I think I have proof as good." He turned to Lady Barlyon. "Ma'am, I see the family Bible is no longer kept on the table between the windows. May I ask where it is?"

"I put it away after Lord Barlyon's death." She sat very straight, her shoulders back. "I did not care to continue the morning and evening readings and prayers myself. Do you want it?"

"Please."

She went to a glass-doored bookcase and, opening one of the lower doors, took out a thick tome. She set the leather-bound volume on the table, then stood to one side. Barlicorn approached it slowly and placed his hand on the front cover.

"Do you mean to try to convince us by swearing on the Bible?" John I sneered.

Barlicorn stood with his fingers on the cover for a long moment. Everyone but Reddy and Jemima Wilson drifted over to crowd around.

"This is not the family Bible. Not the one my father read from twice a day every day of my life here. It's not as worn, and it is somewhat smaller in size."

"What? Nonsense." Beau Cornell opened it and flipped to the pages on which three generations of the Cornell family were listed with their dates of birth and death and names of spouses and children. "Look, my grandfather's name is the first entry."

Barlicorn did not notice that Aurelia had come up to stand beside him until he heard her dispassionate voice by his shoulder.

"All the entries are in the same hand, which is not the case when one enters births and deaths as they occur in different generations, and the ink is the same. I have seen inscriptions that have faded to brown in old books. Mr. Reeves, have you not examined many old documents and seen how ink fades?"

"I have. But even if the earlier entries had not faded, there is no question that the handwriting is identical for all, and if I am not mistaken, it is the late Lord Barlyon's. It will be possible to prove by the many letters and documents in my possession that he wrote. I suppose he might have replaced the Bible and re-written the births and deaths to exclude his fourth son." The attorney leaned closer. "No, here is John Cornell, born 1 May, 1710, with a single line through it."

"What became of the original Bible?" Barlicorn asked, then held up his hand. "No. Let me guess. Before I left that night, I cut my name and birthdate out of the page with my penknife. I would hazard a guess that it sent him into a fury and he wrote our family history afresh in a new Bible, before he destroyed the old one." He should have expected something of the sort, given the kind of man his father was.

"Easy to claim, impossible to prove. It's as likely he made an unsightly blot when he lined out your name and replaced it for that reason. Even if you had the part you say you cut out, who's to say it came from the family record when the page is not available for comparison?"

"Perhaps my sister or Lady Barlyon recalls seeing it?"

Tamar shook her head mutely. Not surprising, considering her age at the time he ran away.

Lady Barlyon said, "Lord Barlyon told our butler to burn it even though it had been his grandfather's gift. I took it instead. If you will excuse me for a few minutes, I will bring it."

"Mama, why not send Dare or a footman for it? Or I will go," Tamar offered.

"I know where I put it. It would be difficult to describe its location to anyone. I had to hide it, you see, lest my husband find it." She walked out, petticoats rustling.

Silence reigned.

Beau Cornell stalked over to the window, where he stood like a man tried to the limit of his patience. Barlicorn patted his sister's hand. No one made any pretense of unconcern. Aurelia Kennet did sit down again, apparently tranquil, though from certain faint movements, he gathered her nerves were a-twitch.

Lady Barlyon returned, bearing a book of larger size and greater age than the one on the table. She pushed the first aside to make room. No one spoke as she opened it to the page on which the generations of Cornells were listed in two different hands and several shades of ink.

"There." Lady Barlyon pointed to where a long, narrow rectangle had been excised.

The Beau grated through thin lips, "And yet you do not have the slip, do you? I suppose you learned of this from a servant and thought to make use of it."

"I carried it with me until it was stolen along with my purse—and all of three shillings—and one or two other things. I had been in London almost a week, I think."

"Faugh! I will not listen to this any longer. I shall retain an attorney and take my case to court."

"It would be a very bad idea. The fact that you are a former valet and current cardsharper, and the nephew of Huggins, would certainly come out."

At Barlicorn's words, the color drained from the fellow's face. "That is a pack of lies." His denial came too slow. "I will not stay and be slandered." He strode out stiff-backed.

Lady Barlyon followed him to the door of the drawing room and watched as he ascended the stairs. "George." She addressed the footman when Beau Cornell was out of sight. "Tell Dare that man is an imposter. Make sure that he doesn't steal anything when he leaves. Huggins will be going, too. The same instruction applies to him." She turned back to the drawing room. Her hands were clenched under her bosom. "I beg your pardon, Barlyon. I should have let you give the order."

"Ma'am…I hope you will not insist on calling me 'Barlyon.' It reminds me of my father."

"John, I am so glad you are home. I was not a good mother to you, but I hope to do better."

He went to her and took her hand. She clasped it with an audible sob.

After a moment, Reeves said, "It is unfortunate that we cannot expect the false claimant to depart until the stream subsides and the roads dry enough for the carriage. He cannot carry his trunks and portmanteaux, and he will not wish to leave them behind," he added with a dry legal chuckle.

Lady Barlyon whispered, "Excuse me, please," and contrived to reach the door without anyone seeing her face.

"How did you know he was a cardsharper and related to Huggins?" Aurelia asked.

"The way he played whist put me in mind of certain behaviors I have noticed in men who cheat at cards. I wrote to a friend in London and asked him to learn what he could of a cardsharper of his description."

"How fortunate that you knew someone who could find out," Tamar said.

He smiled wryly. "Scraping a living as I did, I met a great many people, very few of them from good society."

"Thank goodness! But we knew you were our John anyway." Tamar beamed at him, a look he recalled from her childhood.

"Your information has prevented a drawn-out, expensive legal battle, however," Reeves said. "I will begin proceedings to confirm you as the twelfth Earl of Barlyon. Do you wish to lay an information before the magistrate, my lord?"

"What do you advise, Reeves?" He barely managed to suppress a start at being addressed as "my lord."

"I urge you to do so, if only for the record. Though Squire Neville, the nearest magistrate now that your father is dead, is away at the moment, and I am sure Huggins and John I—whatever his real name might be—will have vanished by the time it is feasible to reach the next nearest magistrate."

Lady Barlyon swept in, followed by the butler bearing a tray with bottles of champagne and glasses. She must have had a great deal of experience in concealing the signs of weeping: her eyelids were a trifle puffy, but her face was not blotchy, as most women's became after a bout of tears.

"We will drink to my son's return. How fortunate that I ordered champagne for the dinner I meant to hold. And how very lucky I had not yet composed myself to send out invitations by the time he arrived." A smile appeared, slight at first, growing until she was beaming at them. It increased the resemblance between Lady Barlyon and her daughter.

Dare passed around the room with glasses.

"Ladies do not offer toasts," she continued. "I have always been careful to behave as I was told a lady ought to do, no matter how disagreeable or how at war with the teachings of our religion. Today I am too happy to care. To John Cornell, twelfth Lord Barlyon."

"Hear, hear!" the others exclaimed, as they raised their glasses and drank.

Restraint vanished.

"What are your plans now that you are Earl of Barlyon?" Pettigrew inquired. "You were always the best at planning mischief. Although I suppose it's been many years since you have been guilty of any devilry."

Aurelia saw the faintest check in the motion of Barlyon's glass toward his lips.

"Indeed. I've been a responsible businessman for many years now. As for my plans as Lord Barlyon...I suppose my first tasks are to study the estate accounts and to see what repairs my tenants' cottages need. When I was a boy, they were always in need of work. I misdoubt that has changed."

"I hope you will consider starting a school for your tenants' and laborers' children," Jemima Wilson said. The suggestion verged upon being a command. "The only reason the late earl could see for it was to enable the laborers and domestic servants to read the Bible, and he felt attending church rendered it unnecessary for the lower folk to read Holy Writ. His own servants received the benefit of his leading morning and evening devotions. He actually told me that reading might lead the common folk into the sort of extreme religious fervor one finds among the Dissenters. Far better the Established Church should tell them what to believe."

Barlicorn laughed. "As long as the minister represented the more Puritan end of the church. Will you assist me in setting up the school?"

One by one, the others drifted out until only Tamar remained, sewing something small and white. Mayhap she and her husband were expecting an addition to their family. He stared at the glowing coals in the fireplace, not sure how he felt about his victory. That he had done what he had to do was small consolation for accepting a burden of responsibilities greater than those he had borne in London and requiring him to change as thoroughly as he had done when he first left Barlyon. He had been content in London for the most part, once he had learned to survive. Perhaps he would eventually settle to his new position here.

He should speak to Tamar but did not know what to say. She set aside her sewing and joined him where he stood near the hearth. He glanced at her and met her eyes.

"I'm glad you're home, John." She patted his arm.

"I suppose it feels strange. When I married Leavitt and went to live at Bramble Hall, everything was as different as if I had been transported to a foreign country. The servants were cheerful. Leavitt joked with them. When we visit his family, no one minds if children act like children. I knew when I married him that Leavitt was quite different from our father, but I did not really understand how different until I was away from Barlyon. Then I found that most people I met were nothing like our sire. I gradually ceased to act like a mouse. It will be the same for you, I expect."

"Am I a mouse?"

"No. You are more like a starved cat, wary of kicks and thrown stones."

"Really?" What an appalling notion!

"Perhaps most would not perceive it. You are affable in company, but you are also watchful and not quite at ease. I see it because I was the same, always waiting for the next chastisement. You will grow accustomed and be a wonderful Lord Barlyon."

"I will strive to do my duty."

She barely suppressed a snort. "I hope you'll find it no great hardship, as you need not turn into our father. You always were the best of the family."

Chapter 16

Aurie wished John I and Huggins could leave at once. Their continued presence made things awkward even though John I kept to his rooms. The earl's rooms, actually, but Lady Barlyon said there was no point in moving him because the flooding and the mud must soon abate, leaving the roads dry enough for traveling. Huggins would leave also.

"Huggins is taking his meals with That Fop, which is an annoyance in the servants' hall, as it means two trays to prepare, but at least Huggins carries up the second tray. Dare forbade anyone else to do it though they don't want him sitting at table in the hall, where like as not he'd still take his old place as the earl's valet," Nan confided, "which he hasn't no right to, the old lord being dead and him not the new earl's man. But he's not airing his notions as free since his new lordship was discovered. Well! No need to think about either of those rapscallions again."

Nan did not know that the impostor had approached Aurie the day after his exposure. She had woken early, found the sun shining, and scrambled into her clothing, with jumps rather than corset. The rain having kept everyone inside for two days, she craved fresh air. The earth was still saturated, but she could at least stroll through the parterre and along the paved coach way before the house.

She was idling along a row of rose bushes, wondering what they would look like in the summer, when a voice behind her spoke.

"My dear Mistress Aurelia—"

She started, and the thorn of a sweetbriar rose pricked her even through her glove.

"Some difficulty has attached to speaking with you until this morning, when I spied you out walking. I shall be leaving once the roads have dried, but I will not go without expressing to you my ardent admiration." He took her hand, the one with a spot of blood marring her glove, and pressed his lips to it before she could pull away.

"Sir!"

"You must think me a scoundrel, but you will understand if you only let me explain. I was found wandering as a boy with no memory of who I was or where I came from—"

"No explanation is necessary. If you will excuse me, I must return to the house."

"Aurelia, my darling, I have been entranced by your face and your goodness and deeply saddened by your plight. Your circumstances make it impossible for you to find a mate here, but while my upbringing since my boyhood may be thought to make me ineligible, I have one advantage. I care nothing for your past, only for your future. Be my wife. We can live quietly either in town or on a small manor. You will be a married lady, which will silence the whispers—"

She lengthened her stride. "I thank you for your gracious offer, but I must refuse." She reached the door and tugged it open before he could do it and found herself precipitated into the presence of Tamar, Tate, and Jemima Wilson, evidently on their way to breakfast.

John I stopped short, made a jerky bow in their direction, and hurried up the stairs. A moment's uncomfortable silence reigned. Did they think she had been willingly in his company? Then Mistress Wilson said, "I hope that man was not persecuting you."

"He was, but you were here, and so I am rescued."

Tamar smiled and asked if she would join them in the dining room.

****

The sun and warmer weather finally vanquished the mud. Five days after Christmas, the Barlyon coachman judged the roads were, if not dry, at least not muddy enough to make travel hazardous, and Barlicorn ordered the travelling coach to be readied for early the following morning. He informed the false claimant and Huggins that it would deliver them to the nearest coaching inn. They all behaved with punctilious civility, the only way to make the meeting endurable to any of them. Lady Barlyon having written a reference for Huggins before Barlicorn's arrival on the scene, no question arose of the new Lord Barlyon either providing one or refusing to do so. As his mother assured him that Huggins had never been known to be dishonest during the fifteen years he served the late Lord Barlyon, it seemed unnecessary to raise the issue of his recent attempt to elevate his nephew to the peerage. He was unlikely ever to be employed in another household with a missing heir. Nor could either of them be making off with Barlyon treasures: the silver was locked up in the butler's pantry when not in use, and Dare and the footmen had been keeping a sharp eye on the various small valuables.

When the coach drew away, loaded with Beau Cornell's trunks and valises and Huggins's smaller collection, Langston suggested riding out on a tour of the Barlyon lands. The females either had not yet risen or had kept to their chambers to avoid seeing John I. They all sat down to a late, rather festive breakfast on the riding party's return.

"You might consider planting box trees on the western side of your property," Hugh Langston said.

"Why? I admit that part is not scenic, but does it really need planting?"

Langston laughed. "Apart from considerations of beauty, box trees are a valuable crop and should do well on that soil. Don't build a boat of it; it won't float. It's useful for all manner of other things and commands a high price. You may be glad of the income when you have sons to educate and daughters to marry off. And once the trees are of some size, they may screen the fields to the east of them from the wind. They can be started from slips in March."

The idea of having sons and daughters came near to displacing the subject of box trees from Barlicorn's mind. "Children? I'm not even married."

"Now that you are Barlyon, you must plan for the future," Tamar remarked. She and her mother traded meaningful glances. Barlicorn was struck speechless, not at the thought of his hypothetical marriage but at the realization that he now was Barlyon. Somehow it had not seemed real even when his identity had been confirmed. Recovering his wits, he responded, "Box trees seem a good beginning. My thanks, Hugh. I fear I have a great deal to learn."

"I'll give you the name and direction of a plantsman who can supply the slips."

His mother and Tamar left the breakfast table together. Probably they would adjourn to Lady Barlyon's boudoir to plot his marriage. Mistress Wilson and Reddy were agreed on visiting several old friends in the village, and Aurelia meant to take brisk walk in the park, having avoided going out when the Beau was yet in residence. He wished he might offer to accompany her.

Marriage would present problems. How could he court a lady? His background would horrify her if she found out—as she might well do. Impossible to conceal his secrets within the married state. Or was that the thinking of his former life in the crowded, squalid streets of Little Barbary? Wapping. A part of London his present company would never have seen or perhaps even heard of. The couples he had known there could hide nothing from each other, living in a single room or in lodgings. Aristocratic husbands and wives had separate bedrooms; the wife had her boudoir for a private sitting room, the man had a study, and they would spend much of their day apart. Probably they never knew each other as well as friends would. If he married and his countess discovered the kind of life he had led, how could it not poison their marriage?

He had never considered wedding during his years in London, although not because he somehow foresaw he would one day return to the ranks of the aristocracy. Who could have imagined such a thing? He had kept carefully selected mistresses. Marriage had seemed impossible, given the chance of unexpected death, living as he did on the margins of the criminal world, or so he told himself. This was nonsense, when everyone faced early death by accident or disease or childbirth. He had never found himself attracted to decent—or indecent—women of the lower classes as potential wives. He momentarily enjoyed the thought of Billingsgate Betty as a countess. A handsome young woman and not unkind, her obscenity-laced conversation could make hardened rogues blush like maidens.

Given the character he had created for himself, he could not have aspired as high as a merchant's or successful tradesman's daughter. He had not needed a wife, in any case, having no land or title to pass on. His will provided for Gwen, who had been his mistress for six or seven years, bequeathed large sums to several charities, and left the balance to Sol. He would have to change his will now he had a mother. Gwen had her interest in Job's. He would still fund the charities. Sol was not in need of more money, though he would put it to good use.

He had come back to save Lady Barlyon and Tamar from being dispossessed of their home by the next heir after himself. He need not marry; he could will a substantial sum to his mother to protect her if he died before her. Still, if he did not marry and produce a son, the next earl would be that distant cousin who might not deal well with the estate and its tenants. Or the distant cousin's son, who might or might not be better.

He had a duty to marry to pass Barlyon to a son. He could not expect a woman to love him, which should matter not at all. No one among the nobility married for love. Respect and toleration were as much as one could expect. The trouble was, he could not hope even for that much.

If he were worthy of anyone's regard, he would court Aurelia. But he did not want to see contempt or outright hatred in her eyes. In time, he might find some lady desperate enough to be grateful for marriage even to him. The first thing he must see to was the making of a new will to protect his mother's interests. Then he must become comfortable with his new position and responsibilities. When he had settled into his new role, he might be resigned to seeking a wife.

****

Only Tamar and Lady Barlyon were at the breakfast table when Aurie entered, most of the guests having departed. Reeves had gone back to Maidstone, the better to prepare documents to confirm John Cornell as Earl of Barlyon. Tate and Mrs. Redding were to be taken to their homes in the Barlyon traveling coach, delivering Clement Pettigrew to Maidstone on the way. Clement needed to return to his parish, the tutor wanted to get back to his work, and Reddy missed her niece's family. Jemima Wilson had been driven to Longlea in the chaise. Hugh Langston meant to leave tomorrow.

Her hostess exclaimed, "Aurelia! The very one we want."

"You find us immersed in plotting. But do not let my mama dragoon you into helping unless you would enjoy it." Tamar grinned in an unladylike manner.

"We are planning the dinner to celebrate John's return. Do help yourself to food first, however."

"Am I very late coming down?" Aurelia asked as she filled her plate with kippered herring, an egg, a bit of ham, and one of the rolls Lady Barlyon's cook did so well.

"The men ate early. John is meeting with his steward and Langston to discuss what improvements are necessary."

"My goodness! It's a beehive of activity, my lady."

"Yes, my son is wasting no time. He is quite different from how he was as a child. Or as I remember him, anyway."

"He must have acquired confidence, being on his own."

"I am glad he intends to make changes. They are sorely needed. You've changed, too, Mama. Since my last visit."

Abel Cornell, the last Lord Barlyon, had died. What a pity that anyone's death should be a good thing. Having known the man, however slightly, Aurie could not feel sorry for regarding his departure as a benefit to his family, his tenants, the village, and the entire neighborhood.

When she was settled, Lady Barlyon said briskly, "Now, the dinner should not be held until the weather improves, for I mean to invite friends and family who must travel some distance. However, it has been a very long time since I have planned a large entertainment, so I wish to arrange everything well in advance, and it will be helpful to have your and my daughter's suggestions. And your mother's, too, Aurelia, once she and your papa are back from their visit."

Tamar said, "I have been telling my mother that Leavitt and I have not held any house party of more than half a dozen couples and only informal dances. I fear I am not of much help in this matter, and must go home soon in any case. But you have been to London,

Aurelia, and I am sure attended a number of grand entertainments."

"I did, though it was years ago." Before she left London in disgrace.

After Aurelia finished her breakfast, they repaired to Lady Barlyon's boudoir to make lists: who to invite, what dishes could be made in advance, what renovations must be made to the house in preparation for guests.

"I am not quite sure how much we can do, apart from ordinary spring cleaning. I fear a number of improvements are necessary to the property and the tenants' cottages, and those must take precedence. John did say he had made some money in business, although I suppose it cannot be a great deal."

Looking ahead to the dinner and even better, helping plan for it, was more enjoyable than Aurelia expected. She was not likely to marry and have a home of her own. If she did marry, her husband would be some country squire with no social pretensions beyond dinners for a few neighbors. She would be lucky to find a husband of any sort. Certainly there were none in this area—and she would not want to live near King's Penny once her brother inherited it.

Lady Barlyon's little writing desk was awash in sheets of paper covered with closely written lists when they finished.

"I like your suggestion that we use wildflowers to decorate the table, Aurelia. By March, I hope we can count on at least some being in bloom—wood anemones, dog violet, red campion, bluebells, speedwell, and dog's mercury, and who knows what else? They would be a charming change from the usual greenhouse flowers. Some greenery, perhaps. I will speak with our gardener. Once the snow melts, it might be possible for him to dig up some to grow in pots, too. With careful management, they might be made to flower at the right time to assure we have some, whatever the weather. He will grumble, I suppose, but it will be worth it. We should write the invitations to have them ready to send, leaving only the date blank, but this will not be as elaborate an entertainment as a ball: only about thirty couples, and a neat dinner of two courses, with herb soup, fricassee of chickens, forced lamb, collops of mutton, fish of some sort, peas, creamed morels, tartlets and cheese cakes, and just a few other things as we think of them. As soon as the weather improves a little more, John—I cannot call him Barlyon; he will always be my son, John—will pay calls on the local gentry, and then we will send out the invitations."

Chapter 17

Aurelia was the last to leave, when her parents returned from their visit to the Merriatts' country home. They arrived at midafternoon on a chilly day and being pressed to stay overnight, agreed.

"We could continue on," the viscount said.

Lady Pennyroyal added, "I don't like to impose when you've had company. You will be glad to have the house to yourselves again."

But the light was failing, and they had set out early that morning. Barlyon and his mother persuaded them to stay.

"I confess to some curiosity about how matters played out with the impostor," Lord Pennyroyal admitted.

"And I am interested to hear about your son and his betrothed and her family," Lady Barlyon said.

When the subject of the false claimant's unmasking had been exhausted and talk moved on to the Merriatt family, Lady Barlyon said, "I am very grateful to you for letting Aurelia stay with me. She has been so much help with the house party, and under such peculiar circumstances, too, and in planning the dinner we mean to hold in the spring—have I mentioned that? The invitations are ready to go out, closer to the date. She also supported my spirits while the issue of who was the true heir was still unsettled. I was overset to think I did not recognize my own son."

"It had been many years since you saw him," Lady Pennyroyal pointed out.

"But still! John might have ended the charade as soon as he arrived had he chosen to bring up the matter of the family Bible. Although I cannot say he was wrong to wait. The judgments of his old friends, tutor, nanny, and Tamar lent great weight. And…" Her lip trembled.

The viscount and Lady Pennyroyal waited for her to speak. Barlyon wondered what she would say, if she said anything at all.

Aurelia Kennet spoke instead. "I think when there are bad memories that have been suppressed for many years, it may be helpful to speak of them, rather like lancing an abscess. There must be a feeling of relief."

Barlyon gazed at her in surprise, though he believed he concealed it well. She was correct, even if he had delayed out of anger. Speaking of things he had pushed to the back of his mind for seventeen years, expressing his rage against his father for hating him and against his mother for not loving him, had indeed released some of the pain he had not realized he still felt. How had Aurelia Kennet understood? Once or twice over the past weeks he had thought she possessed unexpected depths. Why was she a spinster? A gentleman could not ask such personal questions, not on such brief acquaintance. And John Barlicorn would not ask because in his world men and women did not share their dangerous secrets. Although one might ferret around to discover what others preferred to keep hidden, because knowledge is power.

"That is very true," his mother said. "Until we

began to think about the time when John disappeared, I never realized how much I disliked my husband. No. I actually hated him. The Church and the Bible would say I should forgive him. If God wishes to forgive him, He may. No doubt I'm wrong to feel Abel Cornell did not deserve my forgiveness, but I can't forgive him for the way he treated John and the way he ruined the other three by trying to make them like himself." She ended on a horrified gasp of laughter. "I shouldn't have spoken. It seems blasphemous to say such things."

"I understand perfectly, Edith, and most who knew the late Lord Barlyon would probably feel the same." Lady Pennyroyal was a kindly woman and also honest.

"I have never agreed with the convention of not speaking ill of the dead. How is it worse than speaking ill of the living? When a man's neighbors agree he was a bad landlord, treated his family and servants cruelly, and promoted unjust laws in Parliament, to pretend he was a decent man is pure hypocrisy," Pennyroyal said.

He would enjoy having the Pennyroyals as neighbors.

****

The next month passed like a dream. With the last guests gone, he came to pity his mother more than he had ever pitied himself. She had endured his father longer and with no chance of escape. The ineffectual creature he remembered turned into a woman with opinions, who was concerned for the tenants' welfare, was torn between pity and distaste for his older brothers (though she never said so), and wanted to build a relationship with him. It was too bad that marriages among the aristocracy were usually made by the parties' parents to make alliances between great families or to secure a rich dowry. It had been even more common in his mother's youth.

He had forgotten, living over half his life where men and women married for lust or love or lived together without benefit of clergy. Economics sometimes played a role, but he could recall few instances where the girl or woman was forced into an unwelcome marriage, as his mother had been. Or so he deduced; once when he raised the subject, she mentioned that she had never met her husband-to-be until her family arrived at Barlyon Manor two days before the wedding. The tone of her voice and a faint sigh revealed her feelings.

He visited all their neighbors whether gentry or tenants, stopped in at the village shops, reminisced with the blacksmith, drank a pint in the alehouse occasionally, and ordered box tree slips to be delivered in March. He spent hours with his father's downtrodden steward planning necessary improvements. He found it easier than expected: Langston and Tamar (to his surprise) had talked to him about estate management during their visit. When he suggested planting box trees, Fox, the steward, showed real enthusiasm.

"Ay, the very thing for that thin, chalky soil. Granted, they grow slow, which is what makes the wood dense. 'Tis what makes good axle trees. Furniture inlay, scientific instruments, and wheels for blocks and pulleys, too. You might plant holly in that low-lying place in the southwest. It's near as useful as box, for many of the same things and others as well, and it likes a damp ground. We can take the seeds or sets to plant from your holly near the stables, my lord. September is the time to plant those."

Being addressed as "my lord" still gave him pause, although he had begun to feel less like an impostor and more as though he could perform his duties adequately. They were not really much different from what he had been doing in London, except for the agricultural matters.

When he sat in Job's reading his father's obituary, he had dreaded, no, actually feared, returning to Barlyon. He'd cap—swear!—he hated the place. But when he rode out, he rediscovered his pleasure in the fields and woodland: a tree whose branches had hidden him, the stretch of stream where he'd fished, the hedgerow that often sheltered him. A tenant's thatched cot reminded him of Granny Goodale who'd lived there with her son and his family. She always had a kind word for him and sometimes an apple or a bit of cheese. Her grandson was the tenant now, a young man Barlyon recalled as a child younger than he.

He was glad to be home. He had not fled from Kent, or the estate, or even the house—though he had not appreciated it as a boy—but from his father. With the eleventh earl gone, the bad memories were only memories. His mother was gently eradicating the ones connected with the house by changing a painting here, adding a vase of flowers there, or rearranging furniture to make the rooms less formal.

Barlyon was only peripherally aware of her ongoing plans until he appointed one of the younger footmen to be his valet. He had been able to get along without one when he first came home, but it rapidly became clear that a gentleman's wardrobe required a good deal of effort to maintain. Grigson, Barlicorn's all-purpose servant, had done far more than Barlyon had known. When he asked the housekeeper who could sew on a button come loose from one of his coats, she hesitantly suggested Bartholomew Holm, who aspired to be a valet. Barlyon took him on trial and soon found him indispensable.

A week after being confirmed in his new position, Holm remarked while laying out his shirt and suit for the day, "My lord, your formal suit requires replacement."

When Holm paused to scrutinize disapprovingly the handkerchief he had taken from Barlyon's meager supply, Barlyon said, "I do not have a formal suit."

"Precisely, sir. You will need one for the dinner."

The dinner. How had he forgotten or lost sight of the fact that such an event would call for suitable clothing?

"You will wish to visit your tailor, my lord. I am sure he can produce something appropriate within three or four days to spare you having to make two trips to London, or"—here he primmed up his mouth—"have the garments sent to you without a final fitting."

Barlyon had finished shaving. Holm patted Barlyon's face with a damp towel to remove any lingering traces of shaving soap.

"I really have not the time to visit London at the moment," he said. It was too soon. After a longer interval, he might feel more confident. He needed time to work on his manner. If one of his acquaintances hailed him as Barlicorn now, he might revert to that identity.

"I know you have been busy settling in, my lord. It occurs to me that you might send that brown suit to your tailor to use for a fitting guide. It fits you excellently, but if you will pardon me for saying so, it is past its prime."

"And not à la mode when it was new," Barlyon conceded. "Holm, I did not lead a fashionable life in London. I don't think my former tailor would meet with your approval." He had never had a tailor. He had bought his coats and breeches secondhand, with alterations being done by the dealer. His shirts—he'd noticed Holm eying them dubiously—had been made by a seamstress near Job's.

"As it happens, my sister married into a tailor's family in Canterbury, my lord. Beckwith supplies garments to many gentlemen, some of them titled, though none of the foppish sort, as you might say. If you wish, I could take your lordship's old suit to Beckwith."

"Bearing in mind that I am no beau. What would you suggest for color and fabric?"

"A deep red velvet, with a gold-embroidered waistcoat. The buttons should be gold—" Seeing Barlyon's raised eyebrows, he went on, "Gilt, I mean, my lord. The lace on the shirt must be of the best quality. Your shoes must have red heels."

"You may take the brown shoes as an example of size. They're comfortable. I don't want the heels too high, Holm."

"Certainly not, sir. Your silk stockings are decent. I see no need to replace them yet. Now had it been for a ball in town…"

"Thank you for that concession. Very well. You may leave tomorrow."

"I see you have no powder. Shall I buy some? As I believe you do not care for wigs."

"I suppose I must powder my hair?" He would have to powder it when he finally went to London. He might as well become used to it.

"Of course, sir."

"I may consider a wig sometime." A wig would substantially alter his appearance. "Yes, buy powder."

After his conversation with Holm, the prospect of a dinner for the gentry from as much as forty miles around took on reality. Some of the guests would be staying over for several nights, as those coming from more than ten or twelve miles or so would certainly not leave until the following day, and many would have to stay the night before as well. When he broached the subject with his mother, she assured him that not everyone would stay at Barlyon Manor. Quite a number of those coming some distance would stay with friends in the immediate neighborhood.

"Aurelia tells me that the Duke and Duchess of Camber, Viscount and Lady Hayward, Baron and Lady Moorfield, and the Ruskins will be staying with them. The duke was at school with Viscount Pennyroyal. They will be bringing their daughter, and the Ruskins will bring their two girls, and Lady Moorfield has a niece who has been staying with her. We must have enough young people to enliven the evening."

"I trust some of the guests will bring their sons or nephews, or the young ladies will have a thin time of it."

Lady Barlyon suffered a relapse to the nervous, dithery manner he recalled from childhood. "Why...I'm sure...no doubt some young gentlemen will attend. Some, of course, will be at university and unable to come. Of course there will be unmarried men: Sir

Stephen Satterfield, for one, and William Ruthven."

"If that's the Ruthven I remember from years ago, he must be sixty. Had he not lost three wives by the time I ran off?"

"He will do his duty by the ladies," his mother stated. "He is still active and in very good health. He's an important landowner, you know, and influential. We could not fail to invite him."

"I'm sure the ladies will be thrilled." The dinner concealed a hidden agenda. He preferred not to think what it might be.

Chapter 18

By London standards, Lady Barlyon's dinner party was small and undistinguished. By local standards, the dinner was a nine days' wonder. She had provided delicacies seldom seen in country houses, the most startling of which were cups of lemon ice, made from a receipt in Mrs. Eales's fascinating *Complete Confectioner*, using ice made from snow packed hard in barrels swathed in straw and stored in the coldest part of the cellar. She had been on tenterhooks since Christmas, hoping it would stay frozen, and that Cook would be able to duplicate the ice she had enjoyed once in London shortly before her marriage. Ices were largely limited to Italian and French confectioners' shops in the larger towns. Barlyon had never eaten one. Never attended a society event either, though one might rub shoulders with the aristocracy at Vauxhall Gardens and masquerades at the Haymarket Opera House, open to anyone with the admission price.

He hoped his manners were up to the challenge and that he would remember the dances Aurelia and Tamar had taught him. When he mentioned his concerns to Lady Barlyon—his mother!—she asked Aurelia to assist him with additional lessons. He wanted to impress her with his aptitude. He also wanted the delightful series of encounters to continue.

He had paid visits to the gentry for some miles

around, sometimes with his mother, but also with Viscount Pennyroyal, who introduced him to several of his cronies, crusty old squires with whom the viscount hunted or played cards. These were a relief from calls at houses harboring young ladies. The marriageable ones always appeared in the drawing room or parlor in gowns a little too ornate for daily country wear and sat blushing and smiling shyly. The younger ones peeped between the stair balusters or were strolling outside when he departed. A man would be corky-brained not to realize he had become prey. He could not imagine bedding any of the girls he met. They were too young and too innocent.

However, the excruciating round of visits and introductions did serve to prepare him for the dinner. His mother had decided that it should be followed by dancing "so that you get some practice in a ballroom setting."

At table, he had only to deal with the ladies to his left and right, both of them young, unmarried, and silly. Afterward, he spent as much time as possible talking with the gentlemen and married ladies, though most of them were anxious to further the chances of some young female relative. Even those who had no niece, granddaughter, sister, or cousin present would praise the absent chit's beauty, accomplishments, and sweet disposition.

"Your property is over by Sevenoaks, I think, Mr. Bell." Bell was happy to discuss hop growing, oasthouses, and related matters, which suited Barlyon very well. Mistress Bell hinted gently that the earl had now probably heard as much on the subject as any reasonable man would care to do. He was rescued from her description of her eldest daughter's charms by a lady who proved to be an old friend of Lady Barlyon's and lived near Canterbury. She was a widow and—thank God—had no daughter nor even a niece for whom she was seeking a husband.

For the first dance, he led out the duchess, the highest-ranking lady present. She had no unmarried daughters, and if she possessed other unmarried female relatives, did not mention them. Too, the movements of dance made sustained conversation impossible. One was usually limited to a few words at a time. As soon as he had led out the ladies whose rank made it necessary, he meant to ask Aurelia to dance. She was amusing and sensible, rather like Gwen, his former mistress.

She was partnered in the third dance by Ruthven (old goat that he was), the first unmarried man with whom she had danced, as best he could tell. Good God, she must be desperate indeed if she considered Ruthven a suitor. Why the devil didn't she dance with better prospects?

She could not dance with men who did not ask her. The thought made him miss a step. A lady could not courteously refuse to dance with one man and agree to dance with another. Therefore, no suitable bachelors were asking her to dance. Both ladies and men talked to her with every evidence of pleasure. She was not shunned; she must merely be regarded as unmarriageable. It could not be her age. Or solely her age.

When he led Aurelia Kennet onto the floor, he said, "That salmon-pink suits you very well. Are you enjoying yourself? You should, having done so much of the planning for tonight."

"Thank you, both for the compliment and for the thought. I am having a wonderful time, and I was happy to lend my help to Lady Barlyon. It has turned out well, has it not? Although I note that you have sometimes appeared a trifle apprehensive, my lord."

Her tone and the twinkle in her eyes told him that she knew perfectly well that part of the festivity's purpose was to expose him to future countesses.

He lowered his voice. "If my mother expects me to marry a girl straight from the schoolroom, she will be disappointed. They chatter and titter too much. And are too innocent." He had meant only inexperienced in society. Aurelia evidently took it otherwise for she blushed to match her gown. Ah! She had a discreditable secret. As she did not respond, he decided to try to reassure her, at the risk of making it worse.

"They are timid and their minds are as yet mostly unformed, being taken up with romantical dreams rather than life as it is. The idea that a man should marry a young girl and train her up strikes me as a mistake: what if she proves to have no potential for development?"

"I have heard ladies point out the possible drawbacks, but never a gentleman. Never ladies with young daughters, either."

Good, he had restored her composure and humor.

"I hope you will not blame your mama too much for being concerned about securing the succession, my lord."

"No. The heir presumptive is a Nonconformist parson from Wales."

She was a restful female, easy to converse with, witty, and well-informed. He might have had more

176

difficulty proving his identity without her help. He had not noticed it at the time, until the scene with the Bible, when she pointed out the discrepancy of the ink not having faded. In retrospect, she had on several occasions asked questions that had steered the conversation in his favor. He did not know how to thank her without awkwardness. He would like to know what her past concealed, but he could not ask. Not yet. To fill the silence, he said, "One of the chits I danced with obviously thought me too old for a husband."

"Good God," she burst out, fortunately not in a loud voice, "is she blind?" Then she blushed again and fixed her gaze on one of his waistcoat buttons.

He laughed, which did draw attention to them. If he blushed for it, no one would know, given his complexion. "They are nice buttons, aren't they? My valet chose them."

Startled, she looked up at his face. She gave a choke of laughter; he grinned.

"What will people think, sir?"

"Only that we are having an amusing conversation."

The music ended, and he walked with her toward the chairs around the edge of the floor.

His mother approached, beaming. "John, how convenient! The duchess was talking about their summer festival for the laborers and tenants, and it occurred to me that we ought to hold one. It's never been done since I came to live here, but many large property owners do host such events. My father did, certainly. It was always looked forward to. This year it would be a celebration in honor of your return, too."

"If you can plan it, I think it would be a fine idea."

"Aurelia, may I count on your help again? Your family holds a tenant day, don't they?"

"They do. As long as yours is not the same day as ours, I would be delighted to help. Ours is after harvest."

"We might hold ours before harvest begins. Come, let us sit for a few minutes and discuss it. My feet need a rest."

He left them to it and strolled around the room, stopping to chat with those he had not yet had time to speak with at length, and casting around for a safely married woman with whom to dance. As he was between groups, Lady Delacorte waved him to her side. She had no young lady with her at the moment. He had already danced once with her daughter, so he need not be apprehensive on that account.

She drew him apart, and said in the ghost of a voice, "Lord Barlyon, I could not but notice you were monstrous friendly with poor Aurelia Kennet, and of course, your dear mother is very fond of her..."

Barlyon raised his eyebrows inquiringly.

"You have been away, and perhaps no one has mentioned it, for we are all used to Mistress Aurelia's situation...but I do think you should know."

"What, my lady?"

She heaved a sigh to show she was reluctant to be the bearer of bad news. "She ruined herself years ago in London. She has never been back since, for it was a shocking scandal and will never be forgot."

"Is a young lady able to ruin herself?" he inquired jovially. "Does it not usually require a man's assistance?"

Lady Delacorte plied her fan before her face with

vigor. "My lord!"

"Please explain, ma'am. I assure you I am all ears."

The lady tutted. "Lud, I suppose I must. Two aspirants to her hand dueled over her, and the one she had been expected to marry was mortally injured. He had ruined her and sent for a special license that they might be married to save her reputation."

"The least he could do, I would say."

"She refused! His poor parents begged her to accept...in case there should be a posthumous child, you understand. They had only the one son...and even then she would not. Then when the first died, the other man nobly offered to marry her and she would not have him either. The talk it caused! She has lived here very quietly since, and I am sure has no thought of marriage, for what decent man would ask, under the circumstances? Though I think it is quite a settled thing that Ruthven will offer for her, not that he is not decent, but he lives year 'round on his manor, and already has two healthy, grown sons with sons of their own."

"Thank you for telling me. Lady Delacorte. I confess I wondered why she was not drawing men as bees are attracted to lavender."

She favored him with a sweet, sad smile. "All your neighbors and friends have your interests at heart, after your miraculous return." She inclined her head and drifted away.

Later he requested Aurelia honor him with a second dance as much because of Lady Delacorte's feigned reluctance to blacken her name as because he enjoyed her company. Barlyon contrived to intercept the Kennets after they took their leave of his mother and started for the entrance hall.

"I wanted to bid you a safe trip home, and thank Mistress Aurelia again for helping my mother arrange tonight's festivity." He took her hand and pressed a kiss upon it. Let anyone who saw make what they would of it. To lend the weight of his title to rehabilitate her reputation was the least he could do.

He and his mother sat alone in the dining room early the next morning. He was accustomed to rising early but was surprised she was already up after such a late night.

"I did not feel I could be abed when one of our guests might come down early. And I could hardly sleep for thinking how well it has gone."

He had finished his cold beef, ale, and a bun, and was now drinking coffee. Odd to drink it at home, rather than at Job's. He could not get used to taking it with his meal; hence the ale.

His mother had eaten her egg and toast. "I will leave you to the enjoyment of your coffee, John."

"Ma'am, I have a question to ask about one of the guests last night. Shall we talk in the library or in your sitting room?"

The keenness in her look befitted a hawk sighting a field mouse. "Upstairs in my boudoir, by all means. I cannot like the library."

"Nor can I: it reminds me of my father. I mean to make changes there."

"Oh, what kind?"

"I will dispose of the desk—too many canings while bent over it—and install comfortable chairs to make it less like the lair of a Spanish inquisitor. As I get the chance, I'll buy books." He opened the door to Lady Barlyon's suite. "You may wish to buy new furnishings, too. These heavy, dark pieces may be of historic interest, but do you not find them ponderous for a lady's boudoir?"

"My dear, they are horrid. I'm sure they have been here since before your grandfather inherited the title." She seated herself in an uncompromisingly upright oaken chair meagerly upholstered on the back and seat, and he made himself as comfortable as possible in a similar one.

"You wished to ask me about a guest." Her tone was encouraging. She was fairly eaten up with curiosity.

"Lady Delacorte referred to some scandal—"

"That viper! I wish I might have left her off the invitation list. I could not do it without provoking ill-feeling. I hope you were not smitten with that coquettish girl of hers. No matter how suitable she might be, and she isn't, I assure you, Frances Delacorte would be a dreadful affliction as a mother-in-law."

"Rot my guts! I'd sooner hang!" He eyed his startled mother guiltily.

"What a...colorful oath."

"I beg your pardon! It slipped out. I should have said 'zounds.' "

"He would have hated either."

"He would have caned me for either, too."

"Well, he's gone, for which I am duly grateful. How lovely to be able to say so! Now, Frances poured some poison into your ear. She is usually quite sly about passing on destructive gossip. I make no doubt it was about some young lady to whom you showed partiality, for she is determined to marry her foxy-faced Mirabel to a nobleman. Whose reputation has she cut up?"

"She spun me some nonsense about Mistress Aurelia."

Her face fell. "Oh."

"Then there is something in it, after all?" It was no more than he had suspected, though Lady Delacorte's account seemed unlikely.

"I do hope it has not given you a disgust for the poor girl."

"Not at all. I danced with her a second time by way of snapping my fingers at Lady Delacorte's attempt at character assassination. She pretended to be reluctant to tell me."

"Shall I send for refreshments, John? Claret or ale? Some biscuits? Brandy?"

"We rose from breakfast minutes ago. Why not simply tell me about the scandal? Surely it cannot be so bad I will need to be fortified with spirits. I assume the Delacorte woman made it sound worse than it was."

"I don't think it would be possible to exaggerate." She proceeded to tell as much as she knew of the matter.

"I was not in London, needless to say, but I heard from friends who were and even saw a terrible account in the St. James's *Evening Post* and a broadside ballad about it, both sent me by my sister."

"Did Father permit you to receive correspondence without reading it?"

"No. Your aunt Adele knew his ways and sent me a pair of gloves with an unexceptionable letter. Her real letter and the enclosures were folded carefully inside the gloves. The ballad was scurrilous as those things always are, and the newspaper clipping was no better, though it only implied instead of stating anything as a fact. Some things were known, however." She proceeded to recount the events of Aurelia Kennet's London season very much as Lady Delacorte had. She ended by saying, "The pitiful thing is that no one would have thought twice about it if only she had married one or the other suitor. At least, the talk would have died a natural death in a few weeks. After a year, if anyone mentioned Aurelia or Kit Hastings or Robert Sedgewick, his or her hearer would have yawned and wondered that anyone cared about such stale stuff."

"Why didn't she marry one of them? Do you know?"

"My sister heard from a friend of hers who knew the family that Aurelia denied being ruined and claimed she therefore had no need of marriage to save her reputation."

"How original of her."

"How deluded, is more to the point. Pennyroyal brought the family home and because Aurelia had always been popular, no one cut her acquaintance. No one would have wanted to offend Pennyroyal or Lady Pennyroyal, either, which helped. I vow I felt sorry for her eight years ago, when I hardly knew the family. I've come to have a great affection for her since knowing her better. She has very good sense now and is kind besides, but I know from my own youth that no girl of eighteen has any sense at all."

"It's a wonder her parents did not force her to marry."

"That is because not all fathers are like my late husband, and not all mothers are like Frances Delacorte. Pennyroyal let her have her way. If she had agreed to wed Hastings, she would have been a widow within a day and could have married again in a year if she chose. I can only guess she loved some unknown man who was not one of her recognized suitors and believed he would marry her despite the talk. If she counted on it, he failed her and she lost her chance of marriage."

"Surely, with her beauty, all her virtues, and a dowry—I assume there is a dowry—some man would be happy to take her."

"Unfortunately, what is known of her character even here among her family's friends is outweighed by the scandal. Men hope for beauty and goodness, but they always insist on purity. The ones who would not care as long as her dowry was large enough are rakehells or spendthrifts, neither of which would be acceptable to Pennyroyal nor to Aurelia either. You must know this, dear. Is it not the same in your London circle?"

In his former circle, few would bother to ask if a woman as desirable as Aurelia was a virgin, even without a dowry, though Ambrose Hawkins and Captain Easterday might agree with his mother. No, now he thought on it, Hawkins might not care, particularly given his recent disappointment. In fact, Aurelia would fulfill most of his requirements for a wife: family connections and the ability to move comfortably in the upper ranks of society. No, mayhap not the latter in London, unless the scandal were forgotten. Those were the things he had mentioned as important, but Barlyon suspected Hawkins was assuming they would be accompanied by a good appearance and intelligence. In return his bride would get Hawkins. Who apparently was attractive to women and was as rich as anyone could wish. And Easterday had married a lady with what some would consider ungenteel connections to business and no interest at all in the beau monde.

Would a six- or eight-year-old scandal prevent Aurelia from being accepted again in London once she was married? It might depend on her husband. Hawkins wanted entry into the upper levels of society. His origins in county gentry and his fortune were acceptable; his business interests in the shipping trade and his air of danger were not. The daughter of a viscount would be helpful to him if she were acceptable. No, Hawkins would need a lady of spotless reputation and excellent connections. He would have to shift for himself in the matter of marriage.

Barlyon's own connection with the beau monde was nonexistent, except that as an earl, he would certainly be accepted. A title made up for a great deal. Even the worst rake with a sufficiently high rank would be accepted by most.

"You are very quiet, John." His mother's voice recalled him from his reflections.

"I'm sorry, ma'am. I was in a brown study. In answer to your question, I know men who would not hold her past against her. Someone should make a push to find Aurelia Kennet a husband." Why was he trying to matchmake for Mistress Aurelia? Could it be because in some way, her situation reminded him of his own before he came back to claim the earldom?

His mother laughed. "It's a rarity for a man to think of such a thing. If you have a turn for matchmaking, we should look about for a wife for you. It is necessary to secure the succession," Lady Barlyon stated with unusual bluntness. "Though I should in theory be in mourning for another six months, I am out of black, and in any event, your marriage is a duty we cannot postpone. I have spent little time in London the past few years—as you know, your father did not enjoy the social life—but I correspond with friends there. I will inquire as to suitable young ladies."

This pronouncement was met by a long silence. Finally Lord Barlyon said, "Ma'am, I prefer to choose my own wife."

"I would never expect you to wed someone you disliked, but surely from a list of ladies of appropriate birth, you will find one to your liking. You cannot be acquainted with many ladies of good family, and while you will meet many girls in town, you will not know their family's background: whether there is a history of insanity, or a tendency to gamble or infertility."

He smiled. "I have not lived in genteel society for more than half my life, yet I am not unaware of how marriages are arranged among the aristocracy. A selection of chits fresh from the schoolroom are trotted out, the gentleman's female relatives decide which will suit him, and before he knows it he has been manipulated into offering for her. Was Tamar's marriage arranged?"

"No, thank goodness! Even I thought she would never marry, poor child, unless the curate made her an offer. And your father would never have permitted such a mésalliance. He meant she should stay home and take care of us in our old age. Then she met Leavitt at the Pettigrews' when he was staying with them. He proposed to her the day before he was to leave, as she had come of age. When Tamar refused to let Barlyon bully her into refusing, he gave in, though with a bad grace. It helped that the Pettigrews invited her to come and stay with them until she and Leavitt could marry."

"Mother, I think your marriage was arranged by my grandfather?"

"It was the rule rather than the exception when I was a girl." She blinked, perhaps to clear away a tear. "How will you proceed then? You will go to London and attend the various entertainments, of course. As an earl, you will have no difficulty obtaining invitations. The problem will be avoiding females who are on the scramble for a rich, titled husband. Not that there's anything wrong in seeking a man with a title and the money to support it. It's the way of the world, after all, but not all of them would be suitable countesses or agreeable wives, which is why I suggested making a list of suitable candidates."

"Not every family would consider me suitable, Mother. As my rival pointed out, I don't look like a gentleman. I have lost many of the attitudes of gentlemen, too."

"Your title and fortune are sure to make you acceptable, John, and you are good-natured and attractive in what my father would have called a sort of go-to-hell way."

"Mother! Such language!"

"Shocking, I know. But I don't know how else to describe the way in which you are attractive to ladies."

"According to one chit, I'm too old."

"If she thought so, she's too young to think of marrying and has no discrimination, besides. Any number of ladies indicated that they found you appealing. And not only those looking for a wealthy husband. I know! Piratical! The duchess said it of you. You have the look of a pirate."

"She meant it as a compliment?" He wondered what Hawkins would think, given that Hawkins had met real pirates and held no great opinion of them.

"Perhaps she meant a privateer instead. Privateers are respectable. Like Sir Francis Drake, you know." She appeared to reflect on privateers in general or possibly Sir Francis Drake in particular before proceeding. "I hope you will find a lady who will like you for yourself, as you did not marry while you were lost to us. Which I must say I think a fortunate thing, as you might have wed some cit's daughter or someone even less acceptable. Though if you had, I hope I would accept her cheerfully and help her become accustomed to her state."

Barlyon suppressed a smile, thinking of Billingsgate Betty. His mother might have made something of Gwen, however. "I will marry a woman who is acceptable to me, whether or not she is an acceptable countess, and trust to you to supply the polish." He grinned at Lady Barlyon. "As it happens, a wealthy ship owner I know married a lady who manages her own shipping company. They appeared well matched, and I suspect them of loving each other."

"Upon my soul," she uttered faintly. "Things must have changed beyond recognition since I was familiar with the beau monde."

"I will not claim they belong to the highest levels of society though both are of decent birth. Nor do I have any ambition to enter those circles myself. Apart from doing my duty in the House of Lords, I will spend most of the year here. It's clear to me that the estate could be improved somewhat."

"Well, I do not mean to make you uncomfortable about marriage. Meanwhile, if you should think of someone who might be interested in Aurelia, let us put him on the guest list for our entertainments. She needs to marry, too."

Chapter 19

They bade farewell to the last of the overnight guests early that afternoon. When the final coach rolled down the drive and the footman shut the door, his mother turned to him, glowing, and said, "Wasn't it delightful, John? I can't call to memory when we last had guests here. Everyone expects you will be a fine earl and a valuable addition to the neighborhood and the county."

"Pray, spare my blushes, Mother."

"No, really! You might have been training for the earldom since childhood. I can't think how you became such an adept in society when, if I understood correctly, you were in business in London. Though I suppose men of business have their own gatherings and assemblies and the like," she remarked doubtfully.

With the departure of their guests, Barlyon Manor settled into a routine, which suited him very well. Ride the property, talk with tenants, visit and be visited by neighbors, learn country ways, get to know his mother.

The butler presented the post at the breakfast table. As usual, his mother had two or three letters. As he had not spent his adult years writing to friends and acquaintances, he was unaccustomed to receiving letters or at least, letters not relating to his business. Today, he had two. One was from the earl's man of business. It could wait. The direction on the other was inscribed in an unfamiliar hand. Out of curiosity, because it had not been impressed by a signet, he broke its seal first.

How will it be when it is known Yr Ldship is no more than a common felon? In return for a moderate payment, no one need learn of John Barlicorn. Deposit five thousand Pounds to the account of Mr. Charles Wilmott, Hoare's Bank, Fleet Street. Advise of the deposit by letter to Mr. Augustus Otley, Simon's Coffee House, Fleet Street.

Yr well-wisher,

A. O.

"Bad news, John?" his mother inquired. "You are frowning."

He refolded the sheet and stuffed it into his coat's deep pocket. "Say rather, annoying news. 'Tis nothing of import."

He ate abstractedly. Fortunately, Lady Barlyon was absorbed in her own correspondence and did not demand his attention, apart from an occasional comment on what she was reading.

He was drinking another cup of coffee when she ventured, "Lady Hortense Angwin has written me. We were good friends when we were girls. I have seldom heard from her since."

"Ah?" Barlyon raised his eyes from contemplation of his coffee bowl.

"Not because we stopped being friends but…I suspect your father did not pass on to me any of her letters, which he considered to contain improper matter."

"Improper?" What the devil would a lady be writing to a female friend that could be considered

191

improper?

"Hortense was a lively girl. If she included gossip about affairs or made some critical remark about the Church or the government or a man, Barlyon would have thought it unsuitable. From the letters I did receive, it was clear there had been others I had not seen."

"I'm glad you are able to reestablish your friendship."

"I wondered if I might invite Lady Hortense to visit. I have not seen her since my marriage."

"Of course you may, Mother." He heard something in her voice. He continued to gaze at her.

"Her daughter would accompany her. I promised not to interfere in your choice of a bride, and I don't mean to do it. I will make it plain that there can be no presumptions made and no matchmaking."

"With that understanding, I certainly have no objection to her daughter accompanying her."

"But you are not pleased."

"I am not displeased. However, I wouldn't wish the girl to be hurt if she has any expectations that the visit will be more than what it is."

"I would not endorse a young lady I had not met, for though Hortense was a dear friend, there's no saying I would necessarily like her daughter. All I know of the girl is that she is one-and-twenty and unmarried." She added, "From what her mother says, I gather she is not lively. I suppose that means she is shy."

Or bland or stolid or possibly only placid.

"Do you have plans for the day, John?"

"I'll visit some of the tenant farms and perhaps look at that low-lying ground Fox thought suitable for holly trees." A leisurely ride on a pleasant day would give him time to think. He also needed the practice, as he had hardly been astride a horse between the time he ran away and his return to Barlyon Manor. In town, men like him—men like Barlicorn—did not ride unless they were pads. Highway robbers. Though, like swimming, riding was a skill never forgotten, the muscles did grow unaccustomed. He would be sore tomorrow and likely for days to come.

During his ride, he contemplated the letter. Who would know he had left London to take up his life as John Cornell, twelfth Lord Barlyon? Hawkins and Easterday, of course. Hawkins would not blackmail him. While his morals and ethics might be irregular, cheating a friend would be against his code, and he was already as rich as Croesus. Could someone have learned of it from him? Unlikely; a secret lodged with Hawkins was as good as buried. Better.

Easterday? Barlyon thought not. The captain was painfully honest. He would not have told anyone intentionally…except perhaps his wife. Barlyon had not met Olivia Cantarell Easterday, but she was said to be a sensible woman whose chief interest (presumably after Easterday) was her shipping business. He could not imagine her gossiping with lady friends. He was not sure she had lady friends.

Might one of Easterday's clerks have seen Barlyon's letter? Impossible to know without inquiring.

His own circle in Shadwell and Wapping seemed likelier, though few of them could have written the letter.

The writer was not uneducated: the hand was elegant, the phrasing fluent, and yet it sounded not quite like a gentleman's. A clerk or tradesman might have written it, or a forger, any of them on behalf of someone less literate. A forger might be trustworthy and not peach on his customer. But an honest man would likely not betray a relative who belonged to the canting crew, not only from family loyalty but also from a desire not to be implicated in the crime.

He had no enemies to speak of. True, a few men might have resented his decisions in matters he had mediated for them, but none could say he had not been fair. And how would any of them know he had metamorphosed into Lord Barlyon, like a caterpillar into a butterfly? Coincidence would be strained to breaking if one of them had somehow learned who he was.

Nodding intelligently—he hoped!—while a tenant talked about the need for a purpose-built oasthouse with a better flow of air through the drying floor, he gave up puzzling over the identity of the blackmailer. He had several threads that would lead to the fellow. Augustus Otley must be an assumed name, but if he or "Charles Wilmott" had set up an account, Hoare's Bank might be able to tell him something about their client. Someone could be posted at the coffee house to wait for him to pick up Barlyon's letter; mayhap the coffee house staff could be bribed to let the watcher know when he came in.

It would take a little time to set it up. He would write—

"...hops'ud dry better, mark you, my lord. Steward said he couldn't do nothing 'til there was a new earl, then 'twas winter. Now's time to build." The tenant waited expectantly.

"I will talk to Fox and find out how much it will cost. It could mean a rise in your rent."

"Could be worth it, my lord."

No, he wouldn't write. He would visit London. He should have done so sooner, but it had seemed unwise. If he went in a country gentleman's town suit, with his hair powdered, and avoided his former haunts, it should be safe enough. Most of those he encountered in London would never have seen him in his previous life. He need not worry about Hawkins, who might attend some of the same events he did, or Easterday. The prospect of meeting Viscount Ardrey again, however, did cause him concern. Ardrey might well recognize him even in a different setting and gentleman's attire; Barlicorn had given him some reason to remember.

As proud as Ardrey was, he likely attended only the most exclusive entertainments. No, he need not worry overmuch. Even if they found themselves at the same gathering, it should not matter.

He would talk directly with Hawkins about the blackmail. But when he left, he would send a letter to Otley, explaining he could not raise such a large sum immediately.

At supper, he mentioned his intention. His mother looked up from her olive of veal.

"Going to London? What a good idea. You could inspect the town house, meet with your banker, and attend some social events. Your father was not sociable, as I'm sure you remember. I expect the house will need some repairs or at least refurbishing. I haven't been there in years."

"Would you like to come with me? You could order new clothes. Besides, you'd know better than I what the house needed."

"May I?"

"Why not? You could renew your friendship with Lady Hortense at the same time." Visiting her old friend Hortense in town would make it easier for him to avoid the daughter.

She tilted her head thoughtfully. "I don't know why not. I've been in a cage for so long, I haven't yet grasped the fact the door is open. The only reason I can think of is that, in town, it might be thought odd I've put off my mourning after only six months."

"Not by anyone who knew my father. Our neighbors here understand."

"Well…I would like to come with you. It would be delightful to visit old friends and see their children. Lud! I suppose it would be their grandchildren by now. Let us have another glass of the Haut Brion and drink to what you will. "

He poured the wine: with only two of them at table for a simple supper, they had no footman in attendance, which made conversation easier. "To an adventure, perhaps? I would like to leave on Wednesday, if that's convenient. I find I have some business there which will not wait long."

"You should give the staff at Barlyon House notice of our arrival."

"If a groom leaves early in the morning, he could change horses along the way and be there in the afternoon. A day should be adequate to make the place habitable, I hope." Barlyon strode to the dining room door and gave orders to the footman in the hall.

When he sat down again, Lady Barlyon began hesitantly, "John, may I bring someone with me?"

"In addition to your maid, ma'am? Certainly, if you wish. I will likely be out on business much of the time. Having a companion with you would provide company and be more interesting than going about only with your maid or a footman."

"Then if it is agreeable to you, I should like to invite Aurelia Kennet."

"I have no objection, if you think the scandal is forgotten. Or even if it isn't." No, he had no objection at all. In fact, he would like to see her again. "Would she be willing to visit London?"

"If the embers are still warm, they should be extinguished, and we can do that much for her. I am indebted to her and her parents for her stay here over Christmas, and it would be fitting to reestablish her in society."

He regarded her with raised eyebrows. "Why has her family not done so before now?"

"In spite of his title, Pennyroyal is essentially a country squire with no taste for fashionable life. He and Lady Pennyroyal spend little time in town and are not of the beau monde. Their friends are mostly those of similar habits. Though I have been immured here, I do have connections in the highest circles both from family and from before my marriage. I am sure many of them will oblige me by accepting Aurelia."

"She is a pleasant young lady. Invite her, by all means." He would enjoy having her stay with them in London. Aurelia Kennet fascinated him.

****

When Aurie and her father came in from an invigorating ride to inspect the leaking roof of a tenant's barn, her mother intercepted them before she could go upstairs to change out of her habit and her papa could slip away to his study.

"Pen, Aurie, please join me in the drawing room. I have the most wonderful news."

"Will it not wait until dinner, my dear?" He tossed his crop and hat onto a side table, with a wry glance at her mother.

"No…James, you may take the hats, gloves, and crops upstairs."

She did not wish to speak in front of the footman.

Once he had departed, her papa remarked, "So it is a problem rather than wonderful news."

"No, not at all. Not precisely."

"I am filled with apprehension." After Mama took her accustomed chair by the fire and Aurie perched on an upholstered bench, her father settled into his own armchair.

"Lady Barlyon called upon me," Mama began.

"The neighbors will come calling, whether you want 'em or not."

"Only listen. She and Lord Barlyon mean to visit London—"

"Well, you'd expect him to do that. There must be legal matters to attend to, and naturally she would want to go, too. The poor lady hasn't been farther than Maidstone in years."

"You are being deliberately provocative, Pen. She invited Aurie to accompany her."

A long pause. "I see."

Aurie, making a little pleat in the skirt of her habit, could feel them looking at her. "How…how kind of her," she managed to stammer at last.

"Lord Barlyon will be busy with various matters

and she has not been to London in ages, just as you said, Pen, and she will be quite lonely without a companion, and she enjoyed your company so much over Christmas…" Her mother's voice trailed off.

"What do you think, Aurie?" her father asked.

"I…" She had meant to say she could not possibly return to London. "I really don't know." The prospect seemed strangely attractive. She had enjoyed the house party and not merely the fascinating puzzle of which claimant was the new earl. The dinner and informal dance at Barlyon Manor had not been an ordeal, even though some of the guests were strangers to her. And the earl had asked her to dance twice. The memory of the warmth in his eyes as he gazed down at her sent a quiver down her spine.

"It is a surprise. There's no need for Aurie to decide immediately, Sophia."

"They plan to leave in two days, so she should give Lady Barlyon her answer tomorrow at the latest. I think you should go, dear."

"If I went, my presence might be an embarrassment."

"I believe Lady Barlyon is well-connected. Her reputation will survive having a guest who was slightly touched by a foolish scandal years ago."

Papa said, "If I'm any judge, my love, Barlyon will be much in vogue, partly because his father was so seldom seen and partly because he reappeared after being thought dead. Good society will flock to the Barlyons and, if you are with them, to you, Aurie. The unfortunate events have surely been forgotten, given that Hastings and his wife have been rusticating in the country for the last half-dozen years and never come to town. And, errr, the embarrassed flee when no man pursueth. You should not forfeit this opportunity and live out your life buried in the country."

Their concern for her was evident in their faces. She had never really understood before how they must have worried for her ever since her return from London. She had known her parents were sufficiently concerned for her future that her father had made provision for her support in his will. They had been happy when she had agreed to attend Lady Barlyon's house party. Perhaps if the earl and his mother could ease her back into society, Philip would recover from his anger at the humiliation she had caused him. Their estrangement was yet another cause of sorrow for her family.

And she would like to see Lord Barlyon again. She had looked forward to their dancing lessons. Since Lady Barlyon's dinner, they had only exchanged a few words after church on Sundays. Once her family had invited the Barlyons to dinner. She hacked out most days in the hope of encountering him, and how pitiful was that? None of these occasions provided the opportunity for talking as they had done during the house party.

He would be looking around him in London for a countess. If her reputation could be repaired, and she were present in the Barlyons' home, familiarity might give her a slight advantage over younger, more beautiful ladies. If she were not utterly ineligible by reason of being ruined…She might as well wish for the moon and stars or for a royal suitor! On second thought, given the House of Hanover, perhaps not. Far as she was from the court, rumors of their family discord would give any sensible lady pause. She almost laughed at the thought. The moon and stars, then. She surprised a faint, hopeful expression in her mama's eyes.

How bad could her reception in town be? "I think you are both correct. I've hidden in the country long enough. I will write to Lady Barlyon to accept and send it by a groom immediately."

Chapter 20

Barlyon House, off Hatton Garden, had replaced the family's earlier London residence, destroyed in the Great Fire in 1666. That structure had already been ancient. According to his mother, his paternal grandmother claimed that at her betrothal, her mother had congratulated her on the newly acquired Barlyon house. By all accounts, the old one had been cramped, inconvenient, and situated in an area no longer genteel. "Sad as it is to admit, the Great Fire did us a favor," his mother said.

Barlyon House's surroundings were no longer fashionable, the beau monde having moved westward. However, the house was spacious by modern London standards, as it had been built for a wealthy merchant some eighty years ago. Soon thereafter, his fortunes declined, and the property came into Barlyon hands. Barlyon did not think he had ever visited it as a child. Built of brick with a somewhat high-pitched roof, it formed a squared U around a courtyard large enough to accommodate a coach. Graceful shallow steps led up to the door, raising expectations that the interior dashed. The rooms' proportions and woodwork were handsome, but he should have anticipated the air of dreariness. The furniture and draperies were worn, as he had expected. What bothered him the feeling of a house long unoccupied and lifeless. At the manor, his mother's influence gave a degree of warmth—greater since his father's death—but her rare stays in the townhouse had provided no scope for her homemaking talents. For the most part, his father had visited London alone to attend Parliament. His unalloyed presence would have chilled any place he stayed. By comparison, Barlicorn's lodgings in Shadwell had been cheerful, in spite of their location and shabbiness.

His mother and Aurelia were already adding some touches: embroidery or a book left on a table, flowers, potpourri, laughter. Their first day in London, her ladyship made it plain over the breakfast table that Barlyon would be taking part in some of their plans.

"I know you will have many demands upon your time, but you may not have thought of certain things that must not be ignored. We must make some calls to introduce you to a few old friends and connections of mine."

He feared that "a few" meant a plethora, many of them with eligible daughters.

"I wish you will also arrange to sit for your portrait. Joseph Highmore, Thomas Hudson, or Allan Ramsay should all be acceptable. I wrote to friends immediately after Christmas, asking for recommendations."

"Ah…"

"The Long Gallery at the manor contains portraits of every Earl of Barlyon since the fourth or fifth. You should not be the exception, John."

He saw Aurelia lower her eyes to her plate, presumably to hide a smile.

"You will also need clothing suitable for the various events we will attend. Your country suits are all very well for the country, but in London one must dress with more…more…"

"Ostentation?" Aurelia inquired.

"Yes, I suppose in essence that was what I meant."

"I had hoped to avoid large social events." The statement sounded weaker than intended, but he could not actually hide, and if it were important to his mother to display him, he really had no choice. "I am particularly anxious not to be put on display for young ladies—"

"And their matchmaking mamas," Aurelia interjected.

"And their matchmaking mamas to inspect."

"I agree it would be daunting. The husband-hunt is often a source of discomfort for young ladies, too, although they are never warned in advance how it will be. Well!" she said cheerily as her eyes slid toward Aurelia. "Perhaps we can spare you from most of the balls, though I do not know what excuse we can use. I trust you will agree to attend the theater, the opera, Va—a few dinners, card parties, and musical evenings. Then, too, you will wish to make yourself known at the better coffee houses." She paused.

He did not miss the quick termination of the word "Vauxhall." The pleasure garden must hold some distasteful memory for Aurelia Kennet, for why else avoid it?

"Arranging my business affairs may take a good deal of time."

"You have a few days' grace, as Aurelia and I must visit a mantua-maker and do some shopping."

He cleared his throat. "I know of a silk warehouse that has a wide selection of goods. 'Tis cheaper to buy there than from your seamstress."

"Then we will make it our first errand. Thank you, John. What a sensible son you are."

****

After an exhausting morning of choosing lengths of silk and seeing a mantua-maker, they returned to Barlyon House to refresh themselves. Lady Barlyon passed the afternoon writing to all of her old friends and acquaintances who were in town, inviting them to call upon her and meet her young friend, Viscount Pennyroyal's daughter, up from the country with her.

"Making our presence known is our second priority, now we have ordered new gowns. My old friends will see to it we have invitations."

"Will any of them come, do you think?" Aurie longed to go out and see the sights she had missed on her last visit, but she had come to London in the hope of reentering society.

"Many of them will, I believe, if only because it would be unwise to scorn the mother of an eligible earl. If they wish to get Barlyon to an entertainment, they will have to invite me, which will entail inviting you as well. Those who are such sticklers that they will hold an ancient scandal against you will decline to visit us, and we wouldn't like them anyway. Would we?"

"Probably not, ma'am."

Lady Barlyon's transformation amazed Aurie. What a pity she had lost so many years married to the eleventh Lord Barlyon.

****

Lady Hortense Angwin and her daughter, Mary Rose, called the very next day. Lady Hortense, a bony female with a dry wit, if she remembered the scandal at all, did not care about it. Her old friend might populate her drawing room with Papists, heathens, or monkeys; it was all one to Lady Hortense.

Mary Rose was a sedate girl five or six years younger than Aurelia. Pretty and plump, and lacking her mother's liveliness, she seemed puzzled by Aurelia's being unmarried at such an advanced age. Evidently she had not heard the talk—she would have been in the schoolroom at the time—and her mother had not informed her.

"Now that you are in town, you will be busy night and day, as I am. We were in mourning almost continually for three years, first for my grandfather Angwin, then for my papa, and finally for my little brother. My mama meant to bring me to London several months after my papa's death, but then dear Randolph died and she could not contemplate attending social events," Mary Rose confided, thus explaining her own single state.

"I am sure you and your mother will be better able to enjoy town, now that you have had the opportunity to recover from your bereavements."

"Yes, and I mean to make the most of it. Mama says Lady Barlyon's youngest son is returned from the dead. I look forward to meeting him."

"Not literally from the dead, of course."

"No, but how exciting he should come back after being gone so long! Is he very handsome?"

"He is not precisely handsome. His looks are not in the common fashion, but he is very pleasant in manner." This extremely moderate praise was a little deceiving. However, Mary Rose likely favored the pale complexion and languid manner displayed by fashionable gentlemen. Lord Barlyon's sun-darkened face and hands and his suppressed energy would not appeal. Though his title might.

****

His host said, "Sorry it's not suitable for the nobility, Barlyon. I don't usually entertain here."

"Don't be an ass, Hawkins. I'm not suitable for the nobility, yet here I am." He accepted a glass of claret and gazed around Ambrose Hawkins's well-furnished rooms near St. James's Square. "I see nothing amiss with a bachelor establishment. Given why I asked to meet you, it's better. Less public." In fact, the several rooms would not disgrace any unmarried aristocrat. The furniture was expensive, upholstered in fashionable colors but saved from blandness by accent pieces in the vivid hues of hot, sunny climates: saffron yellow, turquoise, parrot green.

"A point." Hawkins cast himself into a chair. " 'Tis awkward, someone putting the bite on you, when you had no intention of coming back to town for some time. Though you look confounded different with the powder and the…the…"

"Country squire clothing, ay."

"Too bad you were known here by a name close to your own. Anyone who knew Barlicorn and then saw you as 'Barlyon' might guess the truth."

"I was a lad when I chose my nom de guerre. A lack of foresight on my part."

"Ay, a lad's cleverness." Hawkins grunted. "What do you want me to do?"

"If 'Otley' is expecting my reply at Simon's Coffee House, he must go in at times to see if it has come. If someone were set to watch for a man receiving a letter and followed him—"

"Two men would be better," Hawkins interrupted. "Sure as eggs, your prey would come in while a single watcher was answering a call of nature. And with two, one could ask the waiter if the fellow was his old friend, Otley, then tip his crony the wink to follow if it was."

Barlyon nodded. "You've done this before."

Color rose in Hawkins's face. "As it happens, I have and know the very men for the job. In fact, I used several, which I recommend. Best not to keep the same ones in place all day, every day. It's good if they don't always dress the same, too. How soon do you want them to begin?"

"At once." He shrugged. "At least, tomorrow morning. I sent off a letter the day we set out. It won't have travelled as fast as we did—you know what mail to and from country towns is like. But the sooner the fellow's caught, the better."

Having settled the business, they moved on to more personal news.

"How is it, being an earl?"

"A very mixed blessing. I've regained a mother on the one hand and a pile of responsibilities on the other. My steward can't understand why I know nothing about agriculture and little enough about farm animals. Apparently, he believes everyone, or every man, at least, is born knowing about hop vines and tenant rents. Also, every unmarried girl for miles around with any claim to gentility is dreaming of becoming my countess. I don't say it out of conceit: my mother assures me of it."

"You'll find it worse yet in London. An earl is a prize. Especially one who's plump in the pocket. You'll have to lie low." Hawkins toasted him ironically with his tumbler of rum.

"Yet one of my responsibilities is to get an heir. I will have to be careful not to die before I provide myself with one."

"Is there no male relative in line?"

"There is. I'm determined he shall not step into my shoes. He's cut from the same cloth as my father, I fear."

"Devil fly away with him, then. Shouldn't be hard to find a bride. A fortune and a title: you can take your pick."

Barlyon heard a bitter edge to his laugh and wondered if it had to do with Captain Easterday's marriage a few months since.

"As long as my former business doesn't come out."

"Ay. But that's in hand. I'll write when I've something to tell you."

****

Lady Grace Jordan was another old friend of his mother's, and while her husband was a mere commoner, she was the daughter of an earl, and her ballroom was as packed as a keg of salt cod. She and Lady Barlyon had made sure that all their friends and acquaintances heard that the lost heir, now reappeared, would make his first formal appearance in London at her ball.

One group present, however, patently found his marital state of greater interest than his personal history. He was stared at as if he were some exotic creature from Africa; he could feel the lions waiting. Nonsense. He was no one's prey…except perhaps match-making mothers and their daughters.

He led a countess into the first dance. Somehow that required courtesy led to his asking her daughter to dance. Then the pack was on him. He tried to request some of the married ladies to dance. They nearly all proved to have some young female nearby whose interests they wished to promote.

As he led a blushing maiden through the figures of a minuet, her shyness and his need to concentrate on the steps made even limited conversation impossible. While the informal dance at home had provided some practice, he could not perform the motions as effortlessly as men who had had years of practice. Just as well! He could not have conversed with this chit in any case; she could not be more than sixteen—her parents must have maggots in their brains, to think a tongue-tied child would make a suitable countess! Not that they knew the worst of him. His life in London during those lost years had been glossed over.

But perhaps he need not worry overmuch, if the girls presented to him were given a choice, as he had overheard a conversation between a girl and her mother when they had no idea he was near.

"I had hoped he would be handsome and not too old."

"It's true he is as brown as those Cherokee Indians I saw in town years ago. I suppose he must have been a sailor for a time, poor man: they commonly grow very weathered from the sun. But he is not old, Caroline, he is only thirty years of age. It is his complexion that misleads you. I am told he is nothing like his father or his brothers, and he is an earl and rich, my dear. I see nothing to dislike in those attributes!"

The current dance ending, he returned his partner

to her party and conversed for a few minutes before excusing himself. Avoiding Scylla and Charybdis—there a mama with a squab of a girl who giggled every time she saw him, here a matron with two daughters, one tall and thin and past her first bloom, the other pretty and dainty, with a supercilious expression—he made his way to where Aurelia stood conversing with two married ladies and an elderly gentleman. They greeted him with pleasure, and Aurelia smiled at him. After the exchange of greetings, he murmured, "The next set will not be for some minutes yet, Mistress Aurelia, but before anyone else can ask you to favor him with a dance, may I request the honor?"

She could not quite conceal her surprise. "Certainly, my lord."

They stood chatting with the ladies and gentleman, who evinced every evidence of enjoyment in his company. While he no longer felt as if he were masquerading as Barlyon, he did find it daunting that anyone would feel grateful for his condescension in talking to them. Rot him, who was Barlyon for folk to be so pleased with him? He understood why ladies in search of a titled, rich husband were flattering him, but the others?

It was the merest chance that his gaze fell upon a familiar face some distance away. Yet he might not have noticed if the man were not staring at him with a faint frown. He wore silver blue with silver lacing, restrained and elegant. Thank God for years of practice: Barlyon's gaze passed over him without pausing or changing expression. Viscount Ardrey was the last person he expected to see.

"Lady Grace has scored a triumph," Mr. Arthur

remarked. "I have never seen so many of the nobility at one of her entertainments, although she is a renowned hostess."

At least Ardrey had appeared puzzled. Perhaps he only found Barlyon's face vaguely familiar. Had he recalled their one meeting, his expression would be quite different. Then the next set was forming, and he could lead Aurelia onto the floor.

****

Papa had been correct. She had attracted no adverse attention. No one had shown any inclination to give her the cut or look at her askance. In fact, she had danced all of the sets, which boded well for her acceptance. One of her partners had been Ruthven, up from the country on some unspecified business...he probably intended to offer for her. Pshaw! It was perfectly obvious that he meant to feather his nest with her dowry, not for his own benefit but for his heir, his son by his first marriage, who was almost middle-aged.

Apart from the dancing partners arranged by Lady Grace and her friends, other men had requested introductions, and she had danced with them, too. And with Lord Barlyon, who was never at a loss for some amusing or perceptive remark. As Lady Barlyon's son, he might have felt constrained to dance with her, though he seemed to enjoy it, too. Even if he led her out only from courtesy, it was a benefit to her, for he was Polite Society's latest darling: an attractive unwed earl returned after a long absence.

Her previous visit had been daunting even before the visit to Vauxhall; probably every girl of eighteen found her maiden flight in society a source of anxiety. What if no gentleman asked one to dance? Or if one's face came all spotty, or one's hoop flew up or one spilled wine or food down one's décolletage? At her advanced age, she need no longer worry about such things, or not very much.

She and Mary Rose were standing with two admirers, recently down from university, who were vying for Mary Rose's attention. A pleasant baronet in his fifth decade had only just taken his leave of Aurie, after staying to converse for a few minutes after their set ended. He was a widower, well-informed and with a sense of humor. She thought he might have lingered longer, but for the presence of the young men, who were callow and a bit noisy, like puppies. Had she ever found boys of that age attractive? She must have done. Kit Hastings had been only a year or two older than this pair.

Perhaps Sir Randolph would seek her out again, when the lap dogs went away. Smiling more at her own thoughts than at the boys' witticisms, she failed to notice the approach of a gentleman in a handsome blue suit.

"Mistress Aurelia," he greeted her, ignoring Mary Rose and the boys. She glanced up at the sound of his voice. His face, attractive but austere, stirred in her recollection. Who—?

Mary Rose and her court were also taken by surprise. She gave a little squeak before making her curtsey, and the boys bowed, suddenly solemn.

Color rushed into Aurelia's cheeks as she recognized him. He had been slender as a young man, but in the intervening years, his body had filled out. Even then he had possessed an air of gravity; now he had the appearance as well. Perhaps it was more a matter of bearing than size. "Mr. Sedgewick," she murmured, managing not to stammer as she made her own curtsy.

"The Marquess of Furness now. My uncle was rewarded with a marquessate after the battle of Malplaquet. He died without a surviving son, making me his heir."

"Oh!" Aurelia hardly knew whether to offer congratulations or condolences, flustered by the unexpected encounter. She should have realized Robert Sedgewick might be in town. By the time she had gathered her wits, he was continuing.

"I confess I am surprised to see you in London. Have you a set free?"

Eight years ago, Robert's calm dignity had been a welcome contrast to Kit's ardor. Now it seemed rather chill, or did their last meeting cast a shadow over her perceptions? Surely he could not resent her refusal to marry, when his offer came only from some sense of duty. Try as she would, she could not recall his demeanor at their parting, or what her own emotions were. A fog of horror had surrounded her. She remembered only the conviction that she should not marry Robert. How uncomfortable that he should acknowledge her here when in such a crowd he could easily have ignored her presence.

No one had yet asked for the set, worse luck. To refuse would be unforgivably rude, when they were old acquaintances. Mary Rose and her swains maintained a respectful silence. Why would he want to dance with her when his memories could be no happier than hers?

"I do have the next set free. Thank you." Her response sounded cool even to her.

The marquess had ignored the presence of Mary Rose and the young men. Now he inclined his head in their direction, in bare acknowledgement of their existence, and offered Aurie his arm. She ought not to leave Mary Rose unchaperoned and started to say as much. The dance would not be forming for some minutes yet. Then Lady Barlyon, conversing with several other ladies, assessed the situation, spoke briefly, and approached, with a smile and nod to Aurie. Robert, Furness as she should think of him now, led her away. Heaven knew what Mary Rose and her young men thought.

"Conversation is not possible while dancing. May I suggest we sit so we may renew our acquaintance, Mistress Aurelia?"

"Certainly, if you wish." She wanted nothing less. But mayhap he meant to show that her refusal to marry him had not rankled—and why should it?—and that he did not intend to shun her.

He steered her to a settee in an alcove, a light spring rain making it unfeasible to sit on the terrace or stroll in the small garden. As she could not have agreed to do in any case, for fear of ruining herself further. The seat was partly sheltered by a pair of orange trees in pots, brought in from a glass house, giving them some privacy. The interval that followed was less painful than a public flogging, though not by much, despite the pain being mental rather than physical.

"My dear Aurelia, 'tis pleasant to see you again. How fortunate you have returned to London."

"Lady Barlyon invited me to accompany her. Our families have grown friendly, and she wanted a companion in town."

"Ah, of course. I do recall hearing you were staying at Barlyon House. I have never met the lady, although I became slightly acquainted with the previous Lord Barlyon through the House of Lords, you know. He was a man of sterling character, though not much given to society. I would have expected his widow still to be in mourning, but I suppose establishing the new earl takes precedence. Though I have not met him yet, her assistance in polishing him must be invaluable. 'Tis said he was in trade."

"His manners are those of a gentleman, however unaccustomed he may be to polite society. I believe Lady Barlyon was also reluctant to part with the son she had only recently rediscovered." One really could not say that Lady Barlyon felt more inclined to celebrate than mourn.

"He appears a bit rough around the edges, but one could not expect him to have acquired polish in trade. What was his business before he returned from the dead, do you know?"

"Not with any particularity, my lord. Something to do with buying and selling in wholesale lots, I believe." Which was more vague than Barlyon's explanation. She felt unaccountably reluctant to discuss Lord Barlyon with Furness.

"Then we must hope he has dissociated himself from such activities and means to comport himself like a gentleman."

No one would understand her discomfort. Furness did not upbraid her for her refusal to wed him, or mention the duel or anything else that might wound her. He inquired about her family and spoke of some of their former acquaintances: who had married, come into a title, or had children. Why did she burn with embarrassment? Did she feel guilty for not accepting his hand in marriage, when it spared him a wife with a tattered reputation? The scandal and her refusal to marry to redeem herself had harmed her family and she was sorry for it, but she could not have married Robert Sedgewick. It had not been noble self-sacrifice on her part. Something about him bothered her, though she had not been aware of it until their dreadful interview after Kit's death.

Since, she had often pondered her own motivations and those of others. Over the years, she had come to believe Robert's cool composure was not a sophisticated veneer but a coldness that went all the way to his heart. Now she puzzled over why he would wish to renew their friendship. Dancing or promenading around the room with her might indicate no more than a disinterested desire to assist in her restoration. Conversing with her at length showed some other intent. In another man, it might be graciousness or noblesse oblige. Somehow, those possibilities did not fit with what she believed of Robert.

She feared the consequences of their tête-à-tête. Her young friends had paid awed respect to the marquess, more even than they accorded other noblemen of similar age and titles. He bore himself like a duke and received similar deference from almost everyone as he strolled away after leaving her with Lady Barlyon. It was futile to hope their conversation had been unremarked.

Chapter 21

Lady Barlyon turned toward Aurie inside the coach. "Did you enjoy yourself, Aurie?"

"Very much, ma'am." Feeling this a rather tepid response, she added, "Everyone was most kind, and I was claimed for every dance." All of which was true if not the whole truth. Her sponsorship by the mother of the thrillingly reappeared new earl contributed to the ease with which she had been accepted. Though perhaps, as her papa claimed, memories were short in the beau monde. She hoped the darkness concealed her expression.

"The Marquess of Furness paid you very flattering attention. He is a stickler and considered a great catch now he is a widower. Or so I have heard from my friends. He must have been in the schoolroom the last time I was in town."

"We were acquainted during my previous visit to London."

" 'Twas a nine days' wonder, his inheriting the late Marquess of Furness's title. His uncle was from the cadet branch of the family but was made a marquess for some meritorious action at Malplaquet. Saving some royal personage's life, I think, although there may have been more to it than that, for one would think a knighthood or baronetcy would suffice as a reward. Furness died with only daughters, so the title passed to his nephew. He has renewed the acquaintance, has he? What a good thing! Few will hesitate to accept anyone in whom he shows an interest. Not that I had any doubts about your reception here," she added. "John, did you meet him?"

"No, I missed that pleasure." Furness, which would he have been? Barlyon recognized some of the male guests from seeing them at Vauxhall Gardens or public masquerades or less sedate entertainments. The only man he had noticed spending time in her company was Viscount Ardrey.

"He will be looking for a wife. According to Lady Hortense, he married very advantageously. The bride was a duke's daughter, had a good dowry and was excessively pretty. One of those slender, pale, sylph-like girls, you know. It's too bad Furness's mother was not alive to warn him about delicate young ladies."

"Warn him?"

"Men never take ladies' health and stamina into account. She miscarried late and died of it, poor thing. He needs a wife to secure the succession."

Barlyon rested his head against the back of the seat while his mother and Aurelia Kennet discussed the gowns other ladies had worn, the trees in tubs—even little orange trees—and the refreshments served. In truth, his mother talked, while Aurelia occasionally agreed or interposed a comment. She was a trifle subdued, or mayhap only tired, as he was. His first formal appearance had been taxing—very like a girl making her first appearance in the beau monde, or like Aurelia's reintroduction to society.

As a collection of London's most glittering inhabitants and jewelry literally worth a king's ransom, the ball had been impressive. Then Ardrey's name caught his attention, though he had missed the comment leading up to it, and failed to take in the balance of the exchange. If Aurelia Kennet knew the man, could he have been staring at her instead, rather than at the Earl of Barlyon who somewhat resembled John Barlicorn? They had been standing together, after all. He had seen Ardrey sitting out a dance with her and guessed it was an attempt to question her, but perhaps instead he hoped to resume his friendship with a young lady he remembered fondly. And she did have a very handsome dowry, too. Barlyon loathed the idea of Aurelia marrying Ardrey. She could do better for herself. Deserved better. She was wasted in spinsterhood. Marriage to a duke might be the highest ambition of most young ladies, but in the absence of a ducal suitor, surely an earl would be preferred over a viscount, though Aurelia showed no sign of interest in securing a titled husband. He would not like to see any woman fall into Ardrey's hands, and especially not Aurelia. Not given what he had learned of Ardrey at their one meeting two years previously.

****

Barlicorn chanced to be looking toward the door of Job's Coffee House when the finical fellow paused inside and gazed around the room. He tittupped over to the nearest waiter and spoke. The waiter replied, tilting his head toward Barlicorn's corner table. The stranger picked his way through the crowded room, weaving between scurrying servers, tables, and patrons who stood discussing the news, in the most direct path he could take. Another of the servers spoke to him and was dismissed curtly.

Billy Bly said, "Means to talk to you, seemin'ly. Don't see many like him."

"No." The Finical Fellow was plainly dressed, not out of place in Job's, but he failed to fit the pattern of those who came for Barlicorn rather than for the coffee. He had the bearing of an upper servant or perhaps a clerk or secretary.

"I'll shab off. We was done anyhow."

Barlicorn nodded absently. Bly took a different route away from the corner table to avoid passing the oncoming…whatever he was.

"John Barlicorn?" The man's nostrils pinched disdainfully.

An almost-gentleman, decently clad in brown cloth with a fawn waistcoat, might well sneer at coral silk and purple brocade.

"Ay."

"My employer wishes to speak with you. His coach waits outside."

"Fetch him in, then."

"You're to come out. His l—my employer is an important man. He does not frequent such places as this."

"If Job's baint good enough for him, we c'n meet at White's an' it be fine enough."

The Finical Fellow's mouth opened and closed.

"I cap I'll wear my best suit." Barlicorn smiled.

"Not in public! He'll speak with you in his coach."

"Nay. He can talk to me here."

"But, but…"

"Go tell him." Barlicorn sipped his coffee.

"You don't know who you are flouting!"

He regarded the fellow. "If it's His Majesty the

King, tell me. If it be anyone else, my answer's the same." He had no great respect for George II, who in any case did not speak English well, Barlicorn understood, so he was likely safe from a royal summons. He certainly would not get into a coach with someone unknown to him.

The Finical Fellow gaped at him for another few heartbeats, then turned and minced away slightly faster than dignity should permit, as if he needed the necessary house urgently. Barlicorn picked up the copy of the *London Gazette* he had laid aside when Bly arrived, looking for sales of the property of bankrupts or dead men. Their furniture and household gear was no use to him, but sometimes their stock in trade or land was a profitable investment.

The lively conversations hushed. This was sufficiently unusual that Barlicorn put down the paper. Standing near the door, the Finical Fellow at his shoulder, was the focus of every eye. The presence of the king himself could not cause a greater stir. The king, after all, was not so impressive a man as the one who gazed around the smoky, plainly furnished room. He wore a gray velvet suit with much silver embroidery down the front edges of the coat and around the cuffs and a formal wig, both too elaborate for a coffee house like Job's, with its wooden benches and mixed—very mixed!—clientele. Job's served men of rank and title occasionally, but they did not come dressed as if for a visit to court. Small wonder he wanted John to go to his carriage. But he did give him the choice of meeting elsewhere.

Barlicorn estimated his age at about thirty years, a little less or more, as he picked his way toward

Barlicorn's table. He was of moderate height, his features chiseled, and his expression cold. The Finical Fellow had not followed.

"Barlicorn." He stared at the bench contemptuously.

"Ye won't catch lice from it."

The look he received made him quite glad he was not this man's servant or dependent. The ice in his pale eyes, as gray as his suit—might be habitual. He seated himself gingerly and continued to scrutinize Barlicorn critically. The Gray Nobleman would be an appropriate sobriquet for him.

"Got business with me, do ye?" Ordinarily he would have added "sir" to the question. With this man, deference would be a mistake. To show fear would be fatal.

"A gentleman of my acquaintance tells me you are able to arrange…" His pause surprised both of them. This man would show hesitation as seldom as Barlicorn showed fear.

"I c'n arrange a mort o' matters." He saw his visitor's lips thin as they had every time he addressed him without any honorific. Nurse Reddy used to admonish the boys to keep a pleasant expression lest their faces freeze into a frown.

"A certain underbred dog annoys me."

Damnation! Not another request for a murder. "Can't help you with murder. I c'n tell you where to go to find a cutthroat." If you survive to get there.

"Death would be too quick. I want him crippled. Knees broken, blinded, hands broken, scarred, I leave it to your discretion, but it must be permanent and insure that he is undesirable."

"W'y?"

The nobleman's brows lifted. "The 'why' is my concern. Yours is what I am willing to pay you to do."

"Nay. 'Tis whether I be willing to do it."

"I was told—"

"I'm honest and reli'ble?" Barlicorn bared his teeth. His visitor might take it as a grin if he chose.

"I would not hire a man who was not."

"I don't take every job. Don't need to." He suppressed his grin, seeing the Gray Nobleman suppress his own incredulous thought, *Refuse money?*

They stared at each other, Barlicorn keeping his face bland in spite of the other's glare.

Finally: "He is a fortune hunter and has engaged the affections of a young lady of my family for whom I am currently negotiating an advantageous marriage. If he succeeds in seducing her or makes her the object of gossip, the match I intend for her will be impossible. Once he is marred, she will recover from her infatuation."

Barlicorn sat back. "I'll think on't. I'll be here Thursday. Send your cove to me with fifty pounds for if I take the job. The cully's name I'll have now."

"I will pay half in advance and give you the blackguard's name then, and pay the balance when I see the results."

"Once the job's done, 'tis mortal hard to get the rest o' the gelt."

"You impugn my honor as a gentleman." The fury in his voice was calculated to intimidate and as real as the man's "honor."

Barlicorn laughed out loud. "You want a rogue to cripple some cove and you claim honor? If I do it,

224

you'll pay afore or look for some other to do your work."

Like enough he'd never been spoken to in brutal honesty before. Barlicorn braced himself for an attack that did not come. The Gray Nobleman must want to hurt the fortune hunter more than he cared about his pride. "I'll send my servant to you on Thursday."

Barlicorn yawned. "And the name and direction?"

"Why do you want it now?"

"I won't ask a cove to work blind. If the fellow's a deadly hand with a smallsword or has a fond uncle who's a duke and'll make trouble, I want to know."

The man sitting across the table from him spat out a name and street before standing abruptly and turning to go without another word. Barlicorn watched him walk away, very much on his dignity, to join his minion. As soon as they were out the door, he beckoned the short, weedy man at the nearest table to approach.

"Ay?"

"You saw him, Peter. Try to follow and discover who he is and anything you can about him and his family, and about Jeremiah Fletcher, the Sign of the Cat, Sutton Street, by Soho Square."

A brief nod and Peter was gone.

Usually he knew by reputation the men who sought him out. Knew who sent them, who vouched for them. He knew nothing about the Gray Nobleman except that he disliked him, disliked the job he was offering, and did not trust him. All excellent reasons to turn it down. He didn't need the money, though he could always use it.

****

Two years ago, he could not have imagined his

225

path again crossing that of Viscount Ardrey any more than he could have imagined inheriting his father's earldom. Avoiding those who had known him in Little Barbary and at Job's should be easy. Ardrey would be another matter. The new Earl of Barlyon would appear at various social functions; inevitably he would encounter the viscount. Still, the haughty never noticed servants and underlings as individuals, unless they distinguished themselves for any reason—insolence, for example. He had given the viscount some cause to recollect his face. Thank God he'd not slipped in his coarse, low-bred speech! The flamboyantly clad, rough-spoken Barlicorn and the gentlemanly new earl in his subdued suits and powdered hair should not call each other to anyone's mind. Ardrey had evidently failed to recognize him tonight, mayhap had not even noticed him, if his attention had been fixed upon Aurelia. Next time he might not escape the man's notice.

Aurelia was sensible; she should not be deceived by him. However, Ardrey might present himself very differently to a lady than he had to a felon or a young man with pretensions to the hand of a female relation. Arrogance aside, someone willing to have crippling bodily injury done to another, merely to end an attachment he disapproved, was a ruthless man, a man without limits. Barlyon was used to such men among the dregs of society. Those who fought merely to survive every day, who had grown to manhood surrounded by criminals, could seldom afford scruples. To find a man born with every advantage was no better still took him aback, in spite of having known his father and older brothers.

Chapter 22

Lying in bed, Aurelia heard the ringing of a church bell and the watchman's cry of "Three of the morning and the rain's stopped." How fortunate that no one would expect her to rise early. Sleep eluded her after her encounter with the man she had known as Robert Sedgewick. What a fortunate escape she had had! Though she did not think she would have married him, even without the complication of Kit Hastings. His composure had only seemed attractive by comparison with Kit's fervid possessiveness and immaturity. The scalding memories roiled.

****

9 June 1732

While she lay on her bed, mind drifting aimlessly after drinking some soothing cordial pressed upon her by her mother, Kit Hastings breathed his last. She did not learn of his death until the next day, when whatever remained of her life came crashing down. She had risen, muzzy, separated from the world as by a wall of glass that deadened every sensation. Refusing to breakfast in her chamber, she made her way to the dining room to drink tea thirstily and try to nibble toast. Her mother had not come down. Her father lingered over his customary hearty breakfast until he saw that she would eat nothing more.

"Come to the library, Aurie."

She followed obediently, suspecting that he would tell her of Kit's death. The library in the townhouse they had rented for their stay was merely a room with a wall of bookshelves containing an odd assortment of books. She doubted anyone ever read them: collections of sermons, a few classical works in Latin and Greek, histories, poetry, plays, and novels, all old. For show rather than use, like the marriage Kit and his family had urged on her.

"Hastings is dead."

"I am sorry, Papa. But I'm not sorry I would not marry him." She found something deep inside, like one spark in tinder, and struggled to explain. "That gentleman from the East India Company who came to dinner…he talked about how Indian ladies are burned on their husband's funeral pyre. It would be like that."

He nodded absently. He probably did not take her meaning, and she could not have explained more clearly. It was simply the closest she could come to what she had felt in Kit's bedchamber.

"Whatever your reason for refusing, it was your right. I am very sorry for his parents, but I confess I had some doubts about his suitability even before his behavior at Vauxhall. He caused the scandal intentionally, meaning to force you into marriage, I apprehend. Otherwise, how would there have been a special license? I do not believe his father applied for it on his behalf while his son was expected to die at any moment."

His words were such balm to her soul that Aurelia failed to catch the next phrase or two.

"…cannot call upon us because of his injury, but his letter to me was very proper."

"What? I beg your pardon, Papa. Whatever was in the cordial Mama gave me must have been very strong."

"Ratafie and laudanum, most likely. I'll have Cook make you some coffee. Sedgewick was also wounded, though not, thank God, dangerously. He is expected to recover, barring the wound becoming putrid or a fever setting in. He requests your hand in marriage."

"He does? Why?" She had not taken his attentions seriously, seeing them as no more than flirtation. Though for some reason, when one gentleman distinguished a lady by his interest, it appeared to encourage others to do the same, whether out of a spirit of competition or because seeing one man attracted brought the lady's charms to the attention of others.

"He feels that since Hastings's actions have damaged your reputation, and Hastings is now dead, it falls upon him to, er, provide the remedy, as he challenged Hastings publicly, for which he apologizes. You may not be aware of it, but dueling over a lady's reputation harms her name as much the original insult. It should have been managed discreetly, on some pretext. He will call to make formal application to me as soon as his doctor releases him from his bed."

"He cannot wish to marry me. He never showed a real partiality for me. 'Twas only a mild flirtation."

"He is a younger son, however, and there is nothing wrong with your breeding or your dowry. He would be fortunate to secure you as a wife. His father must provide for his heir, his second son, and his two daughters. If Robert Sedgewick marries well, 'tis all to the good. Is he not acceptable to you?"

"I don't know. I never thought him truly interested

in me."

Her father sighed. "Well, it will be a week or more, I imagine, before he is able to call upon us. I will not urge you to accept, but you should realize that the scandal will damage you, though you are innocent."

During one of her few excursions out of the house, forced by need of fresh air and exercise, Aurie had heard a seller of broadside ballads crying the latest, a lurid account of the affair that made Kit a tragic hero and herself a monster of cruelty. Mama had hurried her past, but too late to escape the ballad singer's voice:

All in the merry month of May
When sweetly sings the linnet,
Young Hastings on his deathbed lay,
For love of Aurie Kennet.

Her one thought was *'Twas June, not May.*

An old friend of her mother's invited them to visit, sympathetic to their plight. She assured them society would forget, making Aurelia feel better momentarily. Then Lady Ketcham's daughters returned from visiting a friend. They came to sit by Aurelia when no one else was near, and the older one began, "I think you should know..." With barely concealed pleasure, she confided that the Hastings family made no secret of their resentment over Aurelia's having refused to grant their son's last request.

Some ten days later, Robert Sedgewick met with her father and subsequently was permitted to make his addresses to Aurelia. Until he was shown into the drawing room, she did not know how she would answer. Her mother had stressed the advantages of the marriage and, more to the point, the disadvantages of refusing.

When Robert entered the room, she knew she could not marry him. He had always been a pattern card of correct behavior. His cold eyes and firmly compressed lips told her all she needed to know. He believed she had been seduced by Kit Hastings. He did not want to marry her but meant to offer out of a sense of obligation, or pity, or because he believed it the correct thing to do. Marrying him would be as bad as marrying Kit would have been, though in a totally different way. She declined the favor.

Her family left for King's Penny two days later.

****

Now she feared it was all starting again. Robert—the marquess—might be an old acquaintance renewing a lapsed friendship, but surely he must realize it would revive the old scandal. Would he care? Considering the artificial manners of good society, she could not be certain. Very little of importance was discussed by young ladies and gentlemen in the intricate dance leading to courtship—or after, either. She did think he held to a high standard of behavior. Unlike many young men, he seemed unafraid of appearing different from others in his circle. She could recall with clarity how mortified her brother had been, once or twice, when something he had done or said set him apart from his friends. In fact, she was not sure Robert had close friends. She had seen boys of Philip's age clustering in ballrooms, working up their courage to approach a girl before the hostess forced them to partner some less-sought-after maiden. Robert had been several years older, of course, and might have outgrown the need for his comrades' support.

Or did he mean to revive her scandalous past to

avenge the injury to his pride from her refusal to marry him?

****

"John, have you noticed that Aurelia seems a little tense the past few days?" His mother had sought him out in his study and closed the door.

"I thought her only overwhelmed by the social life." Aurelia did appear nervous, but he would not let his mother know he had noted it. She might take it for interest in her protégée. Why give his fond parent ideas—even if he had those same ideas himself?

"It would be understandable if she were concerned about her reception in society, but this state of nerves began only recently. The talk about poor Aurelia has started up again."

"Do you know for certain there's gossip after so many years? Eight, is it not, since she was in London last? It's not merely that someone was unkind to her or raked up that old business?" He returned his quill to the ink stand and pushed to one side the sheet on which he had been making notes.

"Of course I know, I've heard it from several friends who have been helping me reintroduce her to society. They aren't malicious." Vertical lines appeared between her brows. "In fact, the talk, as it was described to me, is not actually malicious. It's more speculative."

"Is there a difference?"

"Indeed there is. 'Tis not a matter of sticklers cutting her acquaintance or referring to her as…well, by uncomplimentary terms. It is more the sort of prattle one hears when everyone is wondering about Lady E. and Lord W."

Whatever that signified. "Oh?"

His mother gave a tinkle of laughter. "You must know what I mean, my dear! The talk is titillating rather censorious."

"I do not quite comprehend—"

His mother stared at him, brows slightly contracted. "I keep forgetting you have lived in, mmm, commercial circles for half your life. Perhaps gossip is not as prevalent among the merchant class."

It was, judging by what he had heard from some of his more respectable former clients. It might not be as highly perfected an art as practiced among the idlers of the beau monde, and the topic was more likely to be business cheats or impending bankruptcy. In John Barlicorn's world, it would be who's been taken up, who's to be hanged or transported, or what deadly quarrel was playing out.

"The Marquess of Furness has been paying Aurelia marked attention, which naturally reminds everyone of the old scandal and leads them to wonder if she will be the next Marchioness of Furness."

He must be overlooking something. He had missed learning many of the subtle distinctions and rules that governed well-bred society. Fortunately, an ability to mimic the behavior of those around him had been a life-saving skill in his previous existence. "Why would his partiality for her reignite the scandal?"

"I suppose you had no reason to pay attention to the beau monde while you were away. Someday perhaps you will describe your life in London in more detail. Are we likely to meet any of your business connections and friends from that time? Are there any you wish to invite to call or dine?"

"One or two, but they are perfectly gentlemanly, ma'am. Younger sons of country gentlemen, you know, who had no taste for the military, law, or the church." Getting together with Sol would be more challenging, as in his neighborhood, someone might recognize the former John Barlicorn. And one really could not have a known moneylender, however gentlemanly, call at one's home. It would give rise to gossip. "You were going to explain why Mistress Aurelia's scandalous past is rising from its grave."

"Oh, of course. Furness was the suitor whose offer of marriage Aurelia refused after Hastings died as a result of dueling with Furness."

"I thought her other suitor was a fellow named Sedgewick, with no title."

"He was the Honorable Robert Sedgewick, only the younger son of Viscount Ardrey then. His uncle—who was created Marquess of Furness—died without a male heir."

"I see." Furness was Ardrey? Good God. "Then he is renewing his suit?"

"It is a little hard to believe," she replied. "Aurelia would have made a good match for him when he was a younger son, especially given her dowry. But his late wife was a duke's daughter, and he is said to be very wealthy now."

"Still, if he were attracted to her years ago…"

"I doubt it was a grand passion. My friends thought he offered for her only out of duty, because of the duel, and of course, because of her dowry. I heard, too, that he was quite bitter when she turned him down. Not that he talked of it, for that would have been ungentlemanly, and he has always had a reputation for pride and exceedingly correct behavior. Though perhaps he has mellowed and now means to make it clear he has forgiven her the slight." Her tone suggested she did not quite believe it.

"Which has the effect of reviving the talk."

"Well, yes. But Furness might snap his fingers at talk if he felt he were doing the right thing. Which is what he did when he offered for her after Kit Hastings died."

Life had been easier and more rational in Wapping.

"I will pay close attention whenever I am present, ma'am, and will make sure she suffers no insult. She is your guest, after all."

She gave him a searching look. "It would be a very good thing for her if they married, John. She may otherwise live out her life as a spinster."

"She is a very pleasant lady, Mother. I like her exceedingly and would hope she married a better man than Furness."

A tap at the door heralded their butler's arrival with the mail, preventing his mother from probing this remark. Most of the post consisted of invitations, many of them for his mother to deal with. One was directed to him. He did not recognize the hand, and it was sealed with a wafer rather than wax.

You have had near a fortnight to raise the sum, an easy task, the late earl's finances being healthy. In one week if the deposit has not been received, Society will hear of your history.

Otley

Unless Hawkins's watchers were asleep, he should now have information as to Otley's identity.

His mother's inquiry, "Is it an invitation, John?"

brought his attention back to the breakfast room.

"No, merely a note from an acquaintance, asking me to call upon him." He refolded the paper and stuffed it into his coat pocket. "I suppose you and Mistress Aurelia have plans for the morning?"

"We mean to go shopping. London social life is very hard on one's clothing. Gloves, in particular, I find. It's not only keeping them clean—I had forgotten how much soot and dirt there is in town—it's all the events one attends. I thought we might also see about replacing the draperies in the drawing room and dining room at least. I do not mind their being old, but the pea-green color in the dining room is very disagreeable, and the ones in the drawing room have faded almost to gray."

"You may replace the draperies and the furniture, ma'am. I wish you would. Everything is shabby, and the colors make me bilious."

"I have not liked to mention new furnishings because no doubt you will be marrying soon and it should be your bride's place to change things as she pleases."

"My bride, whoever she is, may make whatever changes she wishes. For the nonce, we may as well make ourselves comfortable."

"We will begin with the draperies. Visiting a furniture warehouse can wait a few days. Would you care to come to the warehouses, John?"

"I will spare myself that pleasure. I am sure Mistress Aurelia would enjoy going with you."

"Oh…yes, indeed," Lady Barlyon said thoughtfully. "It will take her mind off the gossip, too."

"An excellent idea. If you will excuse me, ma'am,

I must go out."

"Oh—will you want the coach?"

"No, it's at your disposal." Possibly most earls would go by coach. A coach emblazoned with a crest would have Cinnamon Street agog with curiosity.

Chapter 23

"He replied to my letter." Barlyon passed Hawkins the note. "What did your people learn?" It would be an unforgivably brusque greeting in polite circles, but as he and Hawkins inhabited the polite world only intermittently, his host was not offended.

Hawkins jerked his chin toward a chair in his office. "Nothing. No one's come to pick up mail. Well—barring several men well known by the waiters who come in frequently and receive all their mail there. The servers bring their letters with their coffee. It's not uncommon for men to use their favorite coffee house as their address."

"I know. None of them could be Otley?"

"My men contrived to learn a great deal about them. I don't think any one of them is a likely suspect. One's a lad just down from Oxford, one's a scandalmonger for a broadsheet—gets some of his mail at the printer's, I suppose, but has personal correspondence sent to Simon's as he's terrified of anyone learning his direction—and another's a would-be rake. Always getting love letters from ladies. The servers laugh about it behind his back. I'd been thinking your Otley was slack about managing his blackmail scheme. I wronged him." He poured healthy measures of a tawny liquor into tumblers and passed one to Barlyon.

"If your men did not somehow overlook him." Barlyon swirled his host's good cool-nantz in his glass. Run goods, probably, as much brandy was.

"The men I sent are not lacking in nous. If they missed Otley coming for it, they must have been cozened somehow."

"…then someone working in the coffee house is Otley."

"Or is an agent of Otley's. I'll send in a different man—I've been rotating them, but it will be best to use a new face—and have him get on friendly terms with the servers. In fact, I believe I have an idea."

****

Barlyon, sitting with his back to the greater part of the room, did not see the man enter Simon's Coffee House but was alerted by Hawkins's minuscule nod. Barlyon turned his head slightly. A man dressed and bewigged like a moderately prosperous tradesman stood a few paces from the door. In one hand, he held a dirty letter. It looked as if it had been dropped in the street, stepped on, and perhaps run over by a carriage wheel. The tradesman, a well-set-up fellow about Barlyon's age, glanced around the room until his gaze came to rest upon the comely widow brewing coffee behind the counter. He approached her and doffed his hat.

The proceedings were as good as a play: Hawkins's man smiled deprecatingly and displayed the letter. His inquiry was inaudible over the patrons' conversation and laughter. The owner's sister raised her eyebrows in surprise and replied, setting down the coffee pot to take the letter between forefinger and thumb. Timothy practiced his wiles. The woman possessed a pleasing face and a trim figure and should be easy meat for a man Hawkins claimed had a way about him. Presumably he made some comment about the state of the letter—hoped it had not been lost for very long, trusted the recipient was not fretting for it. The widow stooped to put it away under the counter, oblivious—probably—to Timothy's gaze on the vee of her fichu. Would it slip? Would he be treated to the sight of more creamy skin, possibly even a swell of bosom, over the top of her bodice?

Apparently not. But he continued to speak with her, and she continued to respond. One of the servers might have passed on Otley's letter or the owner of the coffee house might have done so, but he was not always present. His sister, currently laughing at one of Timothy's sallies, was in charge during her brother's absences and probably knew everything that went on in Simon's, anyway.

"You look different with your hair curled," Hawkins remarked.

It was difficult to act normally when their attention was focused on Timothy and the widow. They needed to appear to be conversing, like the patrons who were not simply reading the newssheets. It wouldn't do to be noticed staring; it might make the widow nervous. It wasn't even as if their presence was required; Hawkins trusted his man to pry out the necessary information. But Hawkins had intended to watch, to see if anyone showed an undue interest in the letter, and Barlyon could not resist.

"I feel ridiculous." His valet was happy to practice his new skills. The curled hair, white powder to give him a fashionably pale face, darkened brows, and rouge on cheeks and lips were not a style he meant to employ as a rule. Barlyon reluctantly admitted they gave him so different an appearance that no one would recognize him as the former John Barlicorn.

Hawkins set down his coffee bowl. "Perhaps I should take lessons from Timothy. His approach seems to be well received. No fulsome compliments, merely some banter to amuse the widow as she works."

Barlyon guessed he was speaking of his own blighted courtship of Olivia Cantarell. Who could have guessed that Ambrose Hawkins, known and often feared from the West Indies to China, would fall in love?

"More coffee, sirs?" the serving lad asked.

Timothy was moving toward the door, grinning.

"I'd best be on my way," Hawkins said.

"So had I." They rose in a leisurely manner and strolled out.

They found Timothy in the King's Head Tavern in Chancery Lane, around the corner from Fleet Street, at a table well away from the other patrons. No need to ask if he had succeeded.

After the barmaid served them, Timothy cut off his flow of banter as if with a knife. "Mr. Otley's a pleasant young fellow, quite the gentleman. Well dressed, well spoken. He doesn't come in for coffee and talk. The widow's only seen him once, when he came in to say he'd like to receive his mail there. He lives nearby. Didn't expect to get much mail but didn't want his family connections to know his lodgings are in a poor building and he's sharing with a friend. They'd worry and want him to move to better. He gave her a shilling to have one of the serving boys deliver anything that came for him and promised a tip to the boy for the favor."

"Clever." Barlyon approved. He would have arranged it the same way.

Outside the window, Chancery Lane bustled with messengers, attorneys, and gentlemen bound on who knew what legal business.

"Ay. And her son's one of the servers. He'll deliver the letter I turned in when he's done for the day. Before you ask, Hawk, I had the direction out of her. The house is in Crane Court, at the sign of the Heart and Hand."

"A trusting woman, to tell you."

"She didn't realize she was giving it away. I worked around to it. Said I was looking for a lodging in the area as I wanted to be near my work, and if Mr. Otley's suited him, his lodging house might be just what I wanted. I'm taking her to Marybone Gardens on her free day," he added smugly.

They went to Barlyon House after leaving Timothy to arrange for men to watch the Crane Court house. Barlyon waved Hawkins to one of the library's high-backed, thinly padded armchairs as he subsided into the other. Neither of them wanted anything more to drink.

"Once we have your hedge bird, what do you want to do with him?" Hawkins asked.

Barlyon had been wondering the same. Tracing the man had been relatively easy. What to do with him, however, was more difficult. And he wanted the business over as quickly as possible.

"That's the question, indeed. My excuse for not having paid him off should give us some time to decide: the slowness of country mail, legal formalities to be completed before I could get my hands on the gelt.

Everyone knows there's a mort of what Reeves calls red tape involved in any matter at law."

"You can prosecute him for blackmail with those letters as proof. The widow at Simon's wouldn't hesitate to testify about the delivery method. She won't want to be thought an accomplice."

"Charging him would lead to the notoriety I want to avoid."

"Let 'em talk and be damned to them."

"I wouldn't care, myself. But it would affect my mother and sister."

Hawkins shrugged. "Your mother doesn't plan to marry again, does she? She's been living in the wilds of Kent for years, never showing her nose in town. If she continues to rusticate, why would she care? The same's true of your sister, except she's already married. Talk won't affect your marrying."

"Strictly speaking, that's true…but they would be made unhappy. It doesn't feel like the right thing to do."

"Then make sure this viper can't spread his poison. It's easy enough to find a murderer—"

The door to the library opened, and a female peered in, saying, "My lord, your mother would—" The thick and tightly fitting doors in Barlyon House and a Turkey rug carpeting the corridor had muffled her approaching footsteps. Before Barlyon could speak, she hurried into further speech. "I beg your pardon. I didn't realize you had a guest with you. Excuse me." She began to pull the door shut.

"Wait, Mistress Aurelia!"

She froze.

"May I introduce my friend, Ambrose Hawkins?"

Hawkins sprang up and executed his best bow. Aurie cautiously entered and curtsied.

"This is Mistress Aurelia Kennet, Viscount Pennyroyal's daughter, who has come up to town to bear my mother company."

They exchanged pleasantries before she murmured, "I did not mean to intrude. Your mother only wished to know if you will dine at home tonight?"

Receiving an answer in the affirmative, she made her escape as quickly as possible.

Hawkins stared at the closed door. "Do you think she heard anything?"

"Almost certainly."

"Will she have hysterics or vapors and blab?"

"I don't think it. Mistress Aurelia's a sensible young lady, not like the heroine in some over-heated novel. She will think nothing of it. In any event, I can't countenance murder. Your cure is more trouble than the problem."

Hawkins tilted his head in acknowledgement. "You've the right of it, when there's no consequences for you except public embarrassment. Sometimes I forget England isn't the Spanish Main, though there are similarities. Never mind! Easy enough to have him pressed and less trouble. By the time he gets back from the Navy, if he does, you'll be dug in and he can say what he pleases."

"Ay, it's only that I'm recently come to the title that makes me vulnerable. Many who knew John Barlicorn might recognize me now if anyone claimed we were the same man. I'd hoped to stay home in Kent until talk about the missing heir returning had died down. I agree, pressing him is a possibility. The

Impress Office always wants men. But I want to know more about him first."

"Timothy's good at his work. He'll have him followed. He'll scrape acquaintance with the man if he can. Or make himself pleasant to the landlady or a maid. We'll soon know if your extortioner has a pimple on his arse. You find it irksome to have to rely on someone else, I'd wager."

Barlyon laughed wryly. "I do. My eyes, ears, and hands are all gone. I feel half crippled."

"Well, you've different advantages now. You'll become accustomed. How do you find your new life? Apart from not having your crew of spies and ruffians?"

"I'm not sure, Hawkins. In some ways, it's not as different as I expected. Instead, I have tenants, servants, a steward, and a green bag to do my bidding and guard my back. I'm learning to manage the estate. I find I enjoy it. And I've grown to pity my mother. The poor woman had to put up with my father far longer than I did."

****

Three days later, Barlyon read the letter from Hawkins and pondered.

...The pleasant young gentleman was followed to the residence of one Lady Madeline Hughes-Proctor on Golden Square, where he went to the kitchen entrance and waited outside until a man of middling years came out. They walked a distance from the house and spoke together for a few minutes. As they kept to areas away from buildings and people, my fellow could not approach near enough to hear what they said. The man was a little under average height, thin, a bit stooped,

with a pinched face, sour as a lemon, according to the description Jones provided. From his clothing, he thought Lemon Face might be either a secretary or valet. Do you want him watched or further inquiries made?

Barlyon took out a pencil and two sheets of paper and began to sketch. When he was finished, he wrote one line at the bottom of the second sheet and signed it. He should have a new seal engraved. He would order one in carnelian and put away his father's bloodstone signet ring. He hated using anything of his father's. Though he would retain the earl's bed at Barlyon Manor. It dated to Queen Elizabeth's time and had belonged to other, presumably better, men. His father and grandfather were no more than a deviation from a lineage which had served king and country and done their best by their lands, tenants, and the county.

He had spent several rainy days at Barlyon Manor examining the contents of the muniment room and only skipped over the surface of prior generations' legal documents, letters, commonplace books, and account books going back perhaps four hundred years. The most evocative find thus far was a great Bible with a tooled leather binding, gilt bosses to protect the corners, and gold clasps to hold the covers closed. On blank pages at the front, births, marriages, and deaths were recorded, beginning with the fifth earl. When those pages were filled, two additional sheets had been glued in. A number of the entries for male Barlyons bore notations by the date of death, "Newbury" and "Cheriton," among others. After some thought, Barlyon realized that they were all battles. The last entry was that of the ninth earl. Next to the date 6 July 1685 was inscribed in a wavering hand, "Sedgemoor. God save King James and damn the Duke of Monmouth."

In 1685, Barlyon's grandfather inherited the title and bought the Bible Barlyon recalled from his childhood.

Chapter 24

"A small, quiet gathering will be a respite from the balls, routs, and ridottos we have been attending. I knew it was the very thing when Lady Atherstone told me of her conversable literary evenings. I thought John would enjoy it, as I do not think he is partial to the other entertainments. I remembered Tate saying my son was fond of reading, you see. I wish you might have seen his face when I suggested it." Lady Barlyon laughed merrily as she led Aurie toward their hostess. "He rapped out a colorful oath, apologized, and told me that while he still liked to read, he doubted he had read the books we would be discussing."

The Countess of Atherstone's literary evening proved to be misnamed. While the stated objective was to discuss works of literature, accompanied by refreshments, many conversations inevitably veered into gossip and scandal. Fortunately, the countess and a number of her guests, more interested in books than tattle, clustered into groups debating the merits of various works.

Aurelia joined the one discussing Richardson's *Pamela*. Some regarded it as an uplifting moral tale of virtue overcoming vice; some condemned it as hypocritical.

"The chit is a scheming minx, cozening her master into marriage," one gentleman said, and one or two others agreed with him.

"And yet, if she had given in to his importunities, she would have been called a whore. If she bore a child, it would be a bastard. We condemn immorality around us—would any of you continue to employ a servant who became enceinte even if by a gentleman of the house who had taken advantage of her? Wouldn't you toss her out on the street without a reference? She would end as a common prostitute, and the baby would probably die. Is it decent to demand a serving girl gratify the unregulated lusts of a spoiled, arrogant young gentleman?"

After a few moments of dead silence, the gentleman who had called the heroine a minx protested, "Mistress Aurelia…he offered the girl excellent terms as his mistress. While such connections may not be right, men cannot be expected to live like monks. A gentleman would of course provide support for any child of the relationship."

One of the older women snorted in a markedly unladylike manner.

Oh, no. She had spent too many years in the country with plainspoken people. In for a penny, in for a pound. "Do you mean to say a maidservant or dairy maid or the like has less right to guard her virtue than a lady, sir?"

"Ahhh…" He made a quick recovery. "It's well known the lower classes practice a looser morality than ours."

Another lady stifled a laugh behind a handkerchief.

The second man murmured, "This is become a rather improper conversation for a group that includes ladies. Perhaps we should turn our attention to

249

Richardson's use of the epistolary form, as the current topic has stirred such strongly held opinions."

Aurelia thought she heard a feminine voice sigh, "Men!" just as a voice behind her spoke.

"I well remember Mistress Aurelia's strongly held opinions on virtue from her last visit to London, eight years since."

She did not need the ripple of greetings of "My lord" and "Lord Furness" to know the speaker. Turning, she dropped a curtsey and enunciated, "Lord Furness."

The lady standing next to her moved aside to allow the marquess to join the circle if he chose, and chubby Lord Bywater asked jovially, "What's your opinion of *Pamela*, my lord?"

"A hypocritical little miss, for all her pious prating about virtue."

"Surely that is a very harsh interpretation." Lady Mary, on the other side of Furness, had earlier admitted to finding the novel a fine romance.

"Her master was a fool to think she would make a suitable wife for a gentleman, and you may be sure she would have spared no further thought to him had she been able to come at a man of title. Had her true intent been to guard her virtue, she would have quitted his house at the first sign of his interest in her. If you have not yet read *An Apology for the Life of Mrs. Shamela Andrews*, you should do so. It came out a month or two since."

Somehow the marquess's presence cast a pall over the group, which soon dispersed to take part in other conversations. Before Aurelia could slip away, Furness engaged her in conversation. "And you, Aurelia, how are you going on since the Jordan ball? We did not have time enough to renew our friendship there. I assume, as you have come to town, you now intend to make a match? I understand your not having contracted a marriage in the country, where suitable men tend to be in short supply."

"I have no intentions, my lord."

He raised his eyebrows. "You should consider marrying. For a female, any marriage must be preferable to the single life."

"If some suitable man made me an offer, I would consider it. But I believe marriage to the wrong man would be worse than spinsterhood."

"I hardly like to broach this subject, and yet, a lady must consider her future. Being acquainted with your brother, I fear you cannot expect him to welcome your presence at home when he inherits."

"I am well aware of it, sir. On the sad occasion of my father's death, which I trust will not be for many years, I will remove myself from King's Penny."

"To be some elderly lady's companion or live in a tiny cottage or lodgings in town? A sad fate for a viscount's daughter."

"My father is well aware of my brother's feelings, and has made provision for me. You need not imagine me in dire straits."

"Even so, you would be well advised to seek marriage. Not all men would be reluctant to court you, even given the unfortunate events of your introduction to society and your age."

"It is kind of you to say so." In other words, the prospect of her dowry would attract some gentleman. How dared he presume upon past acquaintance to speak to her of such matters? And why would he?

"I remember you fondly and would be glad to know you were settled. I hope you consider me your friend."

As Lady Barlyon was approaching, she was spared the need to say anything beyond, "Certainly, my lord," before continuing, "My lady, may I present the Marquess of Furness?"

"Please do. I have not had the pleasure of meeting this Lord Furness. I remember the previous marquess, though he was still only a younger son at the time. A delightful young man."

The introductions completed, Lady Barlyon murmured, "Now—with apologies to Lord Furness—I fear we must go, Aurie. I am feeling a trifle fatigued and would like to leave now."

They thanked their hostess and were making their way toward the hall and blessed freedom. "My dear, much as I enjoy these evenings, some of the guests are rather tedious," Lady Barlyon admitted. "You did not appear to be enjoying your chat with Furness."

A plump little woman, half smile firmly in place, approached at an angle calculated to intercept them. The smile had not reached her eyes. Aurie distrusted her on sight.

"My dear Lady Barlyon," she trilled.

"Lady Axton, how nice to see you. May I present Mistress Aurelia Kennet, who has been staying with us?"

Lady Axton's eyes flickered with some emotion: surprise? Recollection of the scandal? The expression was too quickly gone to identify. "Of course I'd be delighted to meet your young friend."

Lady Axton showed every sign of wanting to

prolong the encounter. Aurelia's eyes slid longingly toward the door, knowing that escape would not be easy. Rowena Axton had not caught them by chance. "Perhaps Mistress Aurelia's presence makes my request a tiny bit less burdensome. I am in such perplexity."

"Whatever is the trouble, Rowena?"

"My oldest boy—Cornelius, you know—has been at Lea Court with a few friends from university and took a fall going over a fence. Riding like a fool, I'm sure, as these boys do. His most sensible friend sent a groom to town to let us know that although Cornelius has not broken any bones, thank God, he has lost his memory. The local doctor was summoned and says no harm was done, and he'll likely recover his memory eventually, but at the moment, there my son is, with no one but the staff and his light-minded friends to care for him. I must leave in the morning to attend him and make sure they aren't letting him drink brandy or ride or swim in the river or who knows what other folly, when he should be resting his poor head."

"Lud! Of course you must go. With proper care, I am sure the doctor is correct. It's a pity, for I know you prefer town life, but you could not stay under the circumstances."

"I couldn't enjoy myself with my first-born in such straits. Or my second- or third-born, either," she added, with the ghost of a smile. "But that brings me to my dilemma. I have been introducing my little Phoebe to society, and what am I to do with her? If I take her with me, she will be a year older the next time we are in town."

"I suppose Lord Axton remains in London?" Lady Barlyon sounded dubious.

"Of course, but what use is he? Or the younger boys? I cannot trust them to escort her everywhere, chaperon her, and make sure she dances only with suitable partners. The boys have no sense, and Axton will wander off to the cardroom." She sighed deeply. Her hands were clenched on her folded fan. She was going to damage it, if she did not relax her grip. "Edith, everyone I can think of who might take poor Phoebe in and be trusted to watch over her already has a daughter, niece, or goddaughter to bring out."

"I see." Lady Barlyon evidently suspected, as Aurie did, what Lady Axton intended.

"You might think it would be as easy to have charge of two girls as one, but it isn't. I don't necessarily mean to scramble to make Phoebe a marriage for she is still very young, but exposure to society this year will give her polish and confidence for next year. But she is so pretty and sweet that even my closest friends find themselves unable to take her in, lest she put their daughters in the shade. You are my last hope. Please, please let her stay with you. As you have Mistress Aurelia with you, it will be less of a burden, as she can help chaperon. Besides, Phoebe will benefit from having a friend who is older and can advise her how to go on." Lady Axton beamed a smile at Aurelia before turning an imploring gaze upon Lady Barlyon.

"Why, I suppose..." Lady Barlyon glanced at Aurelia. "It would be no trouble at all, Rowena."

"Thank you, thank you. I will deliver her on my way out of town in the morning. Such a pleasure to meet you, Mistress Aurelia. I'm sure you and Phoebe will have great fun together, almost like sisters."

When Lady Axton had flitted away, they made their escape. In the coach, Lady Barlyon was unwontedly silent. Aurelia asked, "Ma'am, was that not a very peculiar encounter?"

"It was. I am not quite sure what to make of it, although her reasons for wanting her daughter to stay in town with some lady to chaperon her are sound. I can understand, too, that Rowena's friends with daughters would decline the responsibility. I met her at Lady Grace's. Phoebe seems like a good, shy girl, unlikely to be troublesome, though she is tiresomely pretty. It all makes perfect sense, except...." Lady Barlyon lapsed into silence.

"One cannot but wonder why she would be willing to expose her ewe lamb to a female with such a reputation as mine." Aurelia knew precisely what Lady Barlyon's "except" meant.

"Oh, Aurelia...I could almost understand it if Rowena were a particular friend of mine. But she is a good ten years younger than I, and we only met a few times when the last earl brought me to London, and that was years ago, and of course a few times over the last weeks. Mayhap she is quite distracted with worry for her son."

Or perhaps she believed that if she introduced her daughter into the Barlyon residence, the girl would captivate the new earl. Aurelia sighed.

****

He was in his library in the evening when his mother came in. As he rose, he slipped Hawkins's letter under the book he had been reading earlier and pushed it aside.

"John..." Lady Barlyon's hands were clenched at

her waist, reminding him of those terrible half-hour visits to her when he was a child, which must have been as stressful for her as for him and his brothers.

"Is anything amiss, Mother?"

"I know you are engaged with business matters and did not mean to go about in society much or entertain, but something has come up and, oh, I am afraid you will not be pleased," she ended almost on a wail.

"Whatever it is, I promise I will not turn into the eleventh Lord Barlyon. Please sit down and tell me what has happened." He smiled at her.

She withdrew a handkerchief from her pocket and sank into a chair. "When Aurelia and I were leaving Lady Atherstone's, an acquaintance of mine begged me to take charge of her daughter for a time, while she herself must be out of town. Her son, Axton's heir, is injured at their estate, and she feels she must go to him to make sure he is cared for. I didn't want to agree, but she seemed so distraught and none of her friends would take the girl and I could not refuse. She means to bring Phoebe here in the morning, and I am sorry to inconvenience you, John, but what could I do, when she was so worried for her son and her husband and sons would be no use at all for chaperoning the poor child? And she will be company for Aurelia, who needs a young friend."

"No need to be in a pother, ma'am." Of course she was upset. If she had ever dared to agree to a houseguest without his father's consent, the eleventh earl would have flown into a rage. His mother had shown signs of kindliness since his return, and she had never developed the force of character necessary to refuse an appeal. Up to a point, he believed her story.

"If she is so young, however, she will probably not be much company for Mistress Aurelia, who is a lady of sense and intelligence."

She had managed to avoid meeting his eyes. Now she glanced up guiltily. "I know. John, I really am sorry, but though I did not think of it when Lady Axton was with us, afterwards I realized—well, Aurelia pointed out—there were certain inconsistencies in her request."

"Mistress Aurelia is a very perceptive young lady." As well as lovely and witty.

"I don't really doubt her son is injured but…it occurred to us to wonder why she would leave her daughter with us when we have Aurelia here. No one is unpleasant to Aurelia, but still, there's some talk about her. I cannot but wonder if it was a ploy to get Phoebe into your house so that you would become enamored of her. The chit is very sweet and bashful and everything gentlemen like in a young lady. "

"Then she has not the ghost of a chance with me, ma'am, so you need not worry on my account."

She dried her eyes, having teared up from sheer relief, but made no move to depart.

"Is there something else, Mother?"

She played with her handkerchief. "About Aurelia…"

"You mentioned there's talk." He did not want to think of Aurelia being shunned. Though he would like to know why she had refused both offers of marriage years ago, when accepting one or the other was the only thing that would have saved her reputation. She deserved so much better.

"Yes, but that's not precisely the problem. At the

257

literary salon, the Marquess of Furness talked with her at some length. He has paid her a great deal of attention. While he is a longtime acquaintance of hers and a former suitor, and it would be a great match for her, I am not easy about it. She did not appear comfortable with him, and naturally, his condescending to her only encourages the talk."

"You think he is courting her?"

"I do, and oh, John, she would be such a perfect match for you! You get on extremely well, and her family lives nearby. She is not as young as most, but she's young enough to have children and she would not have to grow into the role of countess. I did not mean to meddle or matchmake, but I am worried for her."

"We do not stand in loco parentis to her, and she is old enough to know her own mind. On the other hand, I am fond of her. If Furness is paying court to her, it is cause for concern. Furness is..." How to explain his objection to the marquess without revealing their past dealings? "He is too much like the eleventh earl."

His mother bit her lip. "If you are fond of her, I believe she would accept an offer from you..."

He sighed. "Mother, my first years in London were not easy. I know I must marry to secure the succession, though you will be provided for in any case, but I do not feel worthy of any decent lady."

"My dear, I cannot believe you did anything so very bad."

"I would have to explain my history to any lady I courted. I will not marry under false pretenses."

"You are not already married?—to some unsuitable female?"

"Good God, no!"

"Then a sensible lady will not hold your past against you. Females find it easy to overlook past errors in a man who is kind, as you are."

If only it were true. "I will mention my suspicions about Furness to Aurelia. That is all I can promise."

She beamed at him, evidently taking it as children interpret a parent's cautious provisional agreement to permit sweets or the acquisition of a kitten, and departed to order a room prepared for her guest. So his mother would be happy for him to marry Aurie Kennet. He wondered if she were correct about ladies' forgiving nature. He must think about Aurie and Furness, but first he must return to his correspondence. The third letter he opened proved to be from Sol.

Lord Barlyon,

One of my clients having informed me this afternoon that he expects to be able to pay me the balance and interest due on his account by means of a very clever scheme (as he deems it) which involves you, I write to give you warning. Oliver Stanwood, Baron Axton, means to insinuate his daughter into your household, where the girl will be compromised by you. He believes you sufficiently ignorant of law and Polite Society (as it is called) that he will be able to arrange the marriage settlements in such wise that you will part with enough money to cover his debt to me, which is large and pressing.

Even to clear my books of his debt, I am not willing he should victimize you.

Your Most Ob'nt,
Solomon

Chapter 25

Sol! Barlyon grinned. For all the hunger, fear, dirt, and brutality he had experienced from his first arrival in London until the day he had left, he did have some good memories. Acts of kindness done to him, bloody retribution he had prevented, the few friendships he had made. He had been surrounded by men who did his bidding without being one of them, because he had not been born among them or among people like them. Some called him "y'r lordship," only half mocking. His friends, or those who were almost friends, were like him, men who stood alone or were outcasts.

Lem Grigson, his lame, silent valet/butler and all-around servant.

Hawkins, with his reputation for ruthlessness and history of supposed piracy, which he did not discourage. Captain Easterday, who was not quite a friend, but might become one. Outwardly conventional, he had married a gentlewoman with her own shipping agency, a profound breach of the normal order. Did they pay for delivery of two copies of the shipping bulletin *Lloyd's List*, and read them at the breakfast table? And Solomon, a Jew, was certainly outside the class of English gentlemen and nobility who borrowed from him.

He'd met Sol dodging through an alley to escape a gang of larger boys.

John had stolen a pair of apples off a barrow. For once, no one gave chase—not many people were about and the apple seller was unlikely to leave his stock unattended. Well away, he paused in an alley to catch his breath. Then he heard shouting, and a boy pelted into the alley. Half a dozen older boys came baying after.

He had survived London for several months by then and took to his heels. Even with a head start, the little boy—he looked several years younger than John—caught up and passed him. Adzooks, he was fast! But mayhap he was not already blown from running far. Or was better fed. And he was running from trouble, not leading trouble to John, as he'd thought at first. He sprinted after. At the first opportunity, he would take a different turning to get away from the pursuit.

The area east of Tower Hill was a maze of courts and alleys, unfamiliar because it was outside his usual range. This alley was lined on either side by the backs of houses. He did not need to try the doors to know they would be locked. Ahead, a girl was shaking dust from a rag. As soon as she caught sight of them, she ran inside and slammed the door.

Almost the first thing he had learned in London was the wisdom of running whenever someone ran toward him. Please, he didn't want to be beaten…or die…or be caught…He'd seen gangs like the young ruffians behind him. If he attracted their attention, they'd be on him like dogs on a rabbit.

In spite of his exhaustion and hunger, fear gave him a burst of speed, and he passed the little lad. Ahead on the left he spied a narrow gap between two buildings, closed off by a wall. By some mercy, there was a barrel at the corner of one of the houses. He tossed his apples away and scrambled up on it. Leaping for the top of the wall, he succeeded in sprawling across it. Behind him he heard the boy give a gasp. Getting astride the top, he saw the child was on the barrel but was too short to reach the top even by jumping.

"Arter 'im!"

It was too late for the boy to run. John leaned down to grab the thin wrists. As he hauled him up awkwardly, he lost his balance and they both fell over. He heard the barrel fall and roll—the boy must have given it a kick as he was pulled up. John landed jarringly on hands and knees. He hoped the boy hadn't fallen badly. Apparently not, for he was already running through the little yard where a brawny man was sawing a timber.

The little boy made a sharp detour around him as the man stopped work. "What's this?"

John stammered out, "Press gang, sir. My little brother's afraid. So am I," he added. He could hear voices and scrabbling on the other side of the wall.

"A press gang, you say." The man grinned skeptically, showing a missing front tooth. "Out that way with you, then," with a jerk of the head at the heavy gate in the wall that blocked the other end of the yard. He set down the saw, picked up the biggest hammer John had ever seen, and turned to face the far wall. Then John ran after the boy, who had paused, hand on the gate latch.

They emerged into a street John did not recognize, busy with people passing by and street sellers. He glanced both ways, wondering which way to go. He didn't want to find himself doubling back and meeting the gang again.

The boy said, "This way."

Having no better idea himself, he followed the boy to a short street lined with shops, and into a narrow passage between a greengrocer and an apothecary. It ended in a little cobbled court surrounded by small, decent houses.

The boy stopped and faced John. Now he had time to look, he saw the bantling was likely ten or eleven. Being undergrown himself, he found it difficult to assess others' age.

"Thank you for helping me."

He resembled some of the foreigners from the docks and quays, Spaniards or Portuguese or Italians. But he spoke educated English. He was dressed neatly except for some streaks of dirt and soot and a missing button on his jacket. He must have a home and a family.

John shrugged. "It was no trouble."

The boy dug into his pocket and brought out a sixpence. "It was some trouble. You lost your apples."

John shrugged again. He wanted that coin badly. At the same time, it seemed wrong to take it for trying to save a little boy from…who knew what? And he hadn't paid for those apples so it wasn't money out of his pocket.

"Please. My father says a man pays his debts. I am very grateful for your help."

"If you won't be punished for losing it…"

"My father will not care. He'll be glad for my escape."

John nodded gravely and accepted the coin. He could eat for days on that amount, if no one stole it from him.

The boy toed a loose cobble. "I think the greengrocer there needs some help sweeping the shop and doing errands and the like. He's old. If you wish, I'll introduce you."

"I'd like work. My name is John…Barlicorn."

"Mine is Solomon de Toledo."

"You're a Spaniard." At least, Toledo was in Spain so it couldn't be a bad guess.

"…not exactly. Our name used to be Toledano, but that's difficult for the English to pronounce correctly. De Toledo means the same thing and is easier to say. My family's been here since the Commonwealth, so I'm English. Except that I'm a Hebrew."

"Oh." Which is like saying something is an apple except it's a pear. In spite of canings, he had considered it a point of honor not to listen to Bible readings. Even so, a few points stuck in his memory. There were Hebrews in the Bible, and they weren't English. Hebrews were Jews, weren't they? There was considerable prejudice against them, he thought. But they'd been hunted together, which made a bond. He did not give a fig about Solomon's religion—why should he, when his own father had taught him to hate religion?

The greengrocer did need a boy to help and let John sleep in a storeroom. His niece provided meals for both of them. Odd how a single, impulsive action could lead to a string of consequences. He and Sol had been friends from that day. Now he had advance warning of an attempt to trap him into marriage.

****

They had not yet risen from the breakfast table

when Lady Axton arrived, bringing her daughter, a fair, flaxen-haired girl, insipidly pretty. Aurelia smiled at the chit; Lord Barlyon did not. His manner was cool and formal, enough to daunt a girl making her first appearance in society. Not that it would be difficult to daunt Phoebe Stanwood, judging by the way she kept her eyes on the floor and started when Barlyon addressed her.

"I understand you will be keeping Lady Barlyon and Mistress Aurelia company. I trust you will enjoy yourself while you are with us."

"Yes, my lord. Thank you."

"My Phoebe is such a timid little goose. You must be gentle with her, Barlyon." Her fond mama's admonishment caused her to blush unattractively.

"I am sure my mother and her friend will be all that is kind. Now if you will excuse me, I have business to attend to."

His unusual brusqueness suggested he was not pleased to have them imposed upon. Aurelia could not blame him; Barlyon was intelligent enough to realize the girl had been foisted upon them in the hope he would be induced to offer marriage. Phoebe Stanwood would be considered a suitable choice in many ways: pretty, biddable, and young. In other ways, she might not suit Barlyon, who had little patience with foolishness—if she were not mistaken, the girl had not two thoughts in her head. Lady Barlyon had made it clear that such a match would not have her approval, so Aurelia's clear duty was to act as a buffer between Barlyon and Phoebe. Or a chaperon.

Aurelia tapped on the library door and received no answer, then tapped again. Still no response. She had grown wary since intruding upon the earl and his guest. Mr. Hawkins, was it? He had looked dangerous. Clearly, no one was in the library now, making it safe to go in and see if she could find a book to read on this rainy afternoon while Phoebe sat embroidering in the parlor. Lady Barlyon meant to take a nap as she had confessed with some embarrassment that such weather made her sleepy. Tomorrow, they would visit furniture warehouses.

The novels, such as they were, could be found on shelves to the left of the desk. Passing its corner, the skirt of her gown caught on something—the corner of a book, she realized as it hit the floor—that had protruded over the edge of the desk. It lay open, face down. She stooped to retrieve it, hoping no damage had been done to its spine or pages, her governess having held that a dog-eared page was an abomination. As she set it down, she noticed something white sticking out from under the desk. How vexatious! The earl must have marked his place with a scrap of paper and now she had no way of replacing it and Barlyon would know someone had moved it. She would have to apologize, which she did not mind, and admit to her clumsiness, which she did.

Taking the paper by its protruding corner, she discovered it was a folded and refolded rectangle of writing paper, a broken wax seal on the uppermost side: a letter. Lud! Had the letter been in the book as a place marker or simply fallen on its own? What difference whether she had picked up a scrap or a letter?

Barlyon would wonder if she had read the letter. Anyone would; how could he not suspect it? Or had her own experiences led her to suspect the worst of anyone she did not know well? Any man, at least; she felt no doubts about Lady Barlyon.

For months after her humiliating flight from London, she wondered how she had misjudged Kit. Were there really no indications he was unbalanced? Her mama and papa assured her that it was understandable. A trusting nature and inexperience were why girls were to depend upon their parents to shield them from inappropriate suitors and unwise actions. They never discussed how they had failed to notice Kit's instability in time.

If trust and lack of experience led to errors of judgement, the only way to be safe must be to distrust everyone. Or at least to analyze their motives and try to get independent confirmation of their statements and to observe them closely. She had known early in her acquaintance with Kit Hastings that he was somewhat spoiled and liked to get his own way. She had seen that his parents doted on him uncritically. Yet she had believed Kit when he told her that some of the boys and masters at Harrow had treated him unfairly. A few of the gentlemen in their circle seemed not to like him, but he called them arrogant or explained he had bested them at some sport, for which they had never forgiven him.

No one she knew thought that Kit Hastings was anything more than a likable, slightly indulged young man. Even when she began to find his possessiveness worrisome, she had ascribed it to simple jealousy. But appearances could be deceiving, as she realized after Kit's death.

She had begun to watch her family's friends and tenants, focusing on every word and action as Robert Hooke had studied fleas and other common objects under magnifying lenses. It did not increase her happiness, but it was the only way to be safe. Luckily, except for Dr. Simmons and her papa, no one noticed.

Almost without further thought, she unfolded the sheet. The two lines and signature were bold and sprawling.

Jones identifies your first drawing as the fellow he followed and the second as the sheepbiter he met with. I conclude you suspected who they are. Plans?

A. Hawkins

She would confess to having knocked the book off the table and say she had found the letter on the floor, and do it in so casual a manner he would not guess she had committed the gross impropriety of reading it, which would be bad enough. What made it worse was the content that obviously referred to some private matter. Some dangerous private matter, for what else calls for following someone?

She was still standing, letter in hand, when she recalled the odd snippet of speech uttered by the earl's guest. "…make sure this viper can't spread his poison. It's easy enough to find a murderer—" Probably Mr. Hawkins was only recounting some tidbit of gossip. At the time, Aurelia had been too embarrassed about her intrusion to form an opinion of him, though she had not failed to observe certain details. He had a not-quite-gentlemanly air about him, even an aura of danger. She could believe anything of him.

But she liked the Earl of Barlyon: the amusement lurking in his hooded eyes, his kindliness, his attempt to overcome his estrangement from his mother, his determination to work at his new position. That he and Hawkins had been talking about murder was disquieting. Given her past, she could not overlook it.

She refolded the letter with nerveless fingers and set it beside the book before turning to the shelves and grabbing a novel at random. She wanted to escape the library before Barlyon or anyone else came in and wondered at her agitated manner. It was not until considerably later, after she had composed herself while listening to a string of inanities from Phoebe, that she found the book to be a copy of *The Fortunes and Misfortunes of the Famous Moll Flanders Who was born in Newgate, and during a life of continu'd Variety for Threescore Years, besides her Childhood, was Twelve Years a Whore, five times a Wife (whereof once to her brother) Twelve Years a Thief, Eight Years a Transported Felon in Virginia, at last grew Rich, liv'd Honest and died a Penitent*, inscribed with Matthew Cornell's name. From the title, it was exactly the sort of book Matthew would have read. A lady should probably not admit to reading it.

Whatever was she to think about the Earl of Barlyon now? What sort of life had he been leading during those lost years? And what was she to do? The note might be innocent and unrelated to a few words heard out of context. Certainly she could not accuse him of plotting murder on so frail a foundation. She would have to actually witness him killing someone, and it was not clear from Mr. Hawkins's words who would want to find a murderer. He might have been speaking of someone else or even of some event mentioned in a newssheet. Even if she saw the earl committing a murder, an accusation would bring more trouble upon her and her family than upon him. He would be tried in the House of Lords, and her testimony would be impugned by her scandalous past (if indeed the matter ever went to trial). Nothing would be accomplished but more notoriety and humiliation for her family. And why was she thinking the worst of a man she liked, except that she had been deceived before?

She could do nothing but guard her heart, as she should have done anyway. The earl had to marry a lady of unblemished reputation, given that he had few connections to Society because of his long absence. No matter how kind he and his mother had been, they would want to forge an alliance with some great family. While the Kennets came of old stock, they had never belonged to court circles or bothered with dynastic marriages.

Phoebe Stanwood, at least, would not be his countess, which was an encouraging thought.

Chapter 26

He had gone out early to ride in the park, thereby avoiding the ladies at breakfast, then to meet Hawkins by appointment at his lodgings.

"It was your man's description of the young would-be gentleman and the sheepbiter made me think of Huggins and his nephew." He savored the aroma of the tea. Hawkins was a connoisseur of the beverage, as he was of Chinese art. "It was no more than a feeling that such a pair sounded similar to Beau Cornell and my father's valet."

Hawkins said, "It does make everything easy. You'll prosecute them for the imposture at least, I suppose? Or the blackmail?"

"I am not sure I dare do so. A new factor has arisen."

"Hellfire! What else?"

"There is a man whose attention I would rather not attract. He might remember where he'd seen me before. A prosecution for the imposture would certainly garner much attention, and any mention of the reason for the blackmail would surely come to his ears."

"Who cares what the fellow thinks," Hawkins grunted. "You're an earl."

"He's a marquess." The words hung in the air.

"Mayhap you'd better tell me more, Barlyon."

"Two years ago, he was still Viscount Ardrey. He

sought me out to have violence done…"

Hawkins listened without comment until the end. "Do you think he took enough notice of you to recognize your face? He sounds the sort who never sees servants or tradesmen. I see John Barlicorn in you only because I've known you for years. You dress, speak, and carry yourself differently now."

"I believed those changes would be enough. But he had cause to remember me, and he is courting my mother's guest, making it likely we'll meet occasionally. As I am not attending many entertainments and will return to Barlyon as soon as I can, I still might escape his attention if no one alleges I am a felon, and if I do not otherwise make myself conspicuous."

Hawkins expelled a breath: "Huh!" He contemplated the simple blue design decorating his tea bowl. "If you can't ignore their demands or prosecute them, your choices are limited to paying them, which is an invitation to be bled regularly, or…"

"If someone tried such a game with you?" Hawkins owned a streak of violence, perhaps the result of his years as a sailor and his brief stint as a pirate. Barlyon suspected their boyhoods had otherwise shared certain similarities. If true, his suppressed anger went deeper than Barlyon's.

"It would depend on who it was. Your claimant is a cardsharper. A man like that courts a bad end. Who thinks twice if he's murdered in the street? Or he might fall into the Impress's net even if he's not a man 'of seafaring habits.' The press gangs don't worry much about inexperience. A valet is another matter. He's too old and too respectable to be the Impress's meat. It wouldn't be hard to ship him to the Colonies, but that works better with scum no magistrate will believe. He might convince someone he'd been abducted."

"I don't want anyone murdered. My own past hasn't been spotless. I'd hate to have been put down like a rabid dog before I had a chance to change."

Hawkins shrugged. "What are the chances he'd change? But if you're set against murder, there's no more to be said. I don't like it, myself...except in the direst circumstances. What I would like to know is how your precious pair came to know what you were doing in London."

"I wondered myself though it's not important. A cardsharper mixes in all sorts of company. It might be no more than hearing from some rogue that John Barlicorn, well known among the canting crew, vanished a few months ago, and then noticing that John Cornell, Earl of Barlyon, appeared around the same time, after a long absence."

"Then what will you do?"

"I think I will do nothing."

"Ignore them? Let them get away with trying to extort money from you?" Hawkins demanded.

"Ay, it goes against your grain, but I think it's the best way to avoid scandal. Now that we've talked it through, I'm less concerned. Huggins and his nephew are welcome to cause talk if they can. You were correct, Hawkins, a little gossip will have no real effect on my mother and sister. It won't affect my chances of marrying. The most damaging gossip spreads in the circle in which its victim moves, to which neither of this precious pair has access. How much damage can they do?—one lives by cheating squires and yokels at cards, the other is a valet, and not even to a member of the beau monde. My greatest concern was that Ardrey—Furness—had recognized me, but he may have been watching Mistress Aurelia, who chanced to be standing beside me, instead. Even if he did hear talk linking me to John Barlicorn and recognized me, what could he do about it, but spread more talk? He could not bring a criminal charge against me without revealing how he knew Barlicorn."

"Do you have no former associates who might peach to bring the law down on you?"

"There's men resented me. I don't fear it. Consider: the law is lazy. If you want a pickpocket or burglar caught, you must apprehend him yourself or hire a thieftaker to do so or advertise for witnesses. The watch seldom captures anyone. A magistrate might send a constable to question some of my former associates, based on some allegation against me, and indeed a few might confirm my identity. What of it?"

"Trial? The nubbing cheat? Doesn't take much to hang a man."

"I've studied on the matter and am reassured. Trial would be in the House of Lords. Even if I were found guilty, the legal consequences would be inconsequential. No one can accuse me of treason, which is the only charge likely to carry the death penalty for a peer of the realm. In a century and a half, eight peers have been tried for murder and either been found not guilty or been pardoned. In certain cases, one can plead one's privilege as a peer and escape punishment. The only nobleman executed for a crime less than treason was found guilty of rape and sodomy. I suppose we can guess which was thought the greater offense! No need to worry about my transgressions of the law. Ostracism by the beau monde is the worst I would face. I will probably emulate my father this far: I'll come up to town to do my duty in the House of Lords and the rest of my year will be spent in the country."

Hawkins slapped his knee and guffawed. "I always suspected a poxy peer could get away with murder."

Meditatively: "I do think I will write one last letter to 'Otley' to inform him that his and his uncle's identity is known. It should discourage them from even attempting to spread talk."

"Not the less because knowing of John Barlicorn, they may be aware some of his friends would be fierce in his defense. Even if he is now a curst earl. Damn my eyes, they'd call you the new Robin Hood. Somebody would pen a broadside ballad in your honor."

"May I be spared such a fate!"

Hawkins grinned piratically. "Too bad all our problems are not so easily resolved."

"Indeed. To put it in perspective, I am now more in danger of finding myself betrothed to a girl straight out of the schoolroom, who is staying with us and whose father hopes to milk me to repay his debts."

"Ha!"

"Just so. Sol warned me, and I must therefore stay out of the house as much as possible, except when I escort my mother and the young ladies to some event and am therefore chaperoned."

"Shall I expect you to inhabit my bookroom until the chit goes home?"

"No, although it's a handsome bookroom. Your collection of jade and ivory is impressive. I like the

Chinese paintings, too."

"You'll be taking up residence at a coffee house like any idle gentleman?"

"No, my man of business—not the one who deals with Barlyon family business, the other one, who handles my personal business—has a room available for my use in his offices. I'll talk to him about the Barlyon investments to see if they can be improved, spend some time reading, ask Sol to visit me there…it will be my lair until it's safe to go home."

"Does your business agent know who you are?"

"There was no way to avoid it when I knew I had to return to Barlyon and claim the title. He's safe. Sol recommended him, and Sol has never given me bad advice. The fellow handles Sol's investments, too."

"Good. Can't be too careful."

****

To Alfred Huggins and Sebastian Huggins:

Alfred Huggins would find his livelihood affected if word of his cheating at cards got around. Lady Madeline Hughes-Proctor, the employer of Sebastian Huggins, would not be well pleased to discover her son is valeted by one who attempted to pass off his nephew, a cardsharper, as the heir to an earldom and subsequently attempted extortion. "Mr. Charles Wilmott" need not expect any increase to his account at Hoare's Bank.

Barlyon

Chapter 27

"I used to be not unlike poor Phoebe when I was a girl." Lady Barlyon sighed. They were alone in Lady Barlyon's boudoir for once, a party of Phoebe's particular friends having collected her to go shopping. They were chaperoned by two of the mothers and a pair of maids, allowing Lady Barlyon to stay home.

"I cannot believe it, ma'am."

"Thank you, Aurie. I do think I was more intelligent than Phoebe seems to be, but I had no more character or resolve. In proof of which, I allowed my papa to marry me to a man I had never met. Can you believe it? No one would now think it appropriate; even very strict fathers would expect the couple to meet a few times before the formal offer and acceptance."

"It's easy to make mistakes from inexperience, my lady."

"Aurie…"

"Ma'am?"

"You were of great assistance in sorting out which of the two claimants was my son. I don't know quite how you did it, but Dr. Simmons recommended you to Attorney Reeves for your good sense and powers of observation."

"I don't believe I did very much."

"Be that as it may, I wish you will turn your eye upon Phoebe and tell me if you think there is something wrong. We thought she had been planted with us to give her a chance to snare my son, which still seems likely. But he has gone to earth like any fox, and she doesn't seem—" She shrugged delicately.

"She doesn't seem to have enough confidence to attach a gentleman. At least, not one who is not either callow or shallow. I can't imagine Lord Barlyon being smitten by blushes and fluttering eyelashes and no conversation."

"In a nutshell, Aurie! She's shy around him, as well—more even than she is around us—and doesn't seem bereft when he vanishes all day and only comes back in time to dress for dinner or whatever rout we are to attend."

"I wonder if she has a secret beau and would rather not receive an offer from Lord Barlyon?" Please, let it be true. Not that she thought there was any chance of Barlyon offering for the child. Or for her own ruined, aged self.

"I suppose she could. She's at the age to form some impossible tendre. It would be unfortunate if she contrived to run away with a cit or a fourth son of some impoverished baron. It would reflect badly on my chaperonage."

Though not as unfortunate as Phoebe snaring poor Barlyon. She resolved to watch the girl.

****

Waiting for their coach to be brought up outside the Theatre Royal, Covent Garden, Mistress Aurelia remarked, "I have read *The Merchant of Venice*, and it seems to me tonight's performance deviated somewhat from it."

Barlyon, escorting his mother, grinned. "The

managers and actors do not always feel bound by Shakespeare. I have seen a performance of King Lear in which both Lear and Cordelia survived. The original ending was thought too melancholy to appeal to the audience."

Hawkins, at Aurelia's side, laughed. "They must make money, and therefore must pander to their customers."

Phoebe Stanwood was partnered by a callow young man who was a nephew of Lady Grace Jordan, well matched to the girl by shyness and lack of conversation. Barlyon gave his mother credit for managing it and for arranging them all in the box so the Stanwood girl had the Jordan nephew on one side and herself on the other. Somehow, she positioned Aurelia between himself and Hawkins. A very pleasant evening, on the whole.

"I do not think I would care greatly for a play that did not end happily," the girl said. She could never have seen Hamlet. "I am sure I will have nightmares about that dreadful Shylock."

He smiled at the memory of Sol's pithy comments on the play, rather than at Phoebe Stanwood.

A passing female stared boldly at an unaccompanied gentleman who gave her a sharp glance and shook his head. Turning away—in search of other prey—she lost her balance. Barlyon shot out his arm to steady her before she fell.

"Thank 'ee, sir. I'd be frechet if I'd dommocked my gownd in falling."

The Herefordshire accent warned him. He froze, hand still on her arm. He had noted her only as a brightly clad woman of the town. Then she glanced up at him. Polly. She recognized him, too: her eyes widened. He said coolly, "I trust you are steady on your feet now," and released her arm.

"Ay, sir, and that glad for your help. No need to consarn yourself." Polly gave him a genuine smile, not her practiced harlot's smile, before she sauntered away.

Their coach drew up then, thank God, and he assisted the ladies to mount the steps. Hawkins and young Jordan had arrived separately. The latter thanked them for inviting him and bade the ladies good evening. Lady Barlyon asked if he should not take a hackney or a chair to his destination. He blushingly assured her that, as he had rooms by Lincoln's Inn, he could easily walk home. Was John himself ever that young? What had he been doing at twenty?

He had left the printer's employ several years earlier when the shop was shut down for Holt's printing of books and pamphlets said to be seditious. Luckily, one of his customers having given him the office, they had time to move part of the stock before Holt left the country. Barlyon had been paid well by his employer's friends to whom he delivered packages of the banned books.

"I can't take them all with me, John me lad. You can sell them—you know who'll buy 'em—but for God's sake, don't get taken up with them." Barlyon hoped Holt was still in the printing business. Mayhap enforcement was looser in the American colonies.

By young Jordan's age, he had already been buying and selling small lots of goods for several years. He'd steered men to a certain bordello and gambling house—though in his own defense the games there were as honest as one could expect—and then referred those who had lost too heavily to Sol's family business. He had begun to mediate disputes: his time with the printer had been almost as good as studying at university. Old Holt had encouraged him to read—not that he'd needed urging—and many of the books they printed dealt with law and natural philosophy. He'd always had a cool head, fortunately.

Hawkins made his farewells. He meant to go in search of further entertainment. But he gave Barlyon a significant glance. He had noticed what had passed between him and Polly. The ladies, of course, would have been willfully blind to his brief exchange with a whore. Except perhaps for Aurelia, who had a very noticing way about her.

****

She awoke in darkness with the conviction she had heard something. Not the watch, calling the hour and weather. She lay cocooned in bedclothes and the dark, straining to recall what she had heard. Not a night-soil cart or roistering young gentlemen on their way home. She had grown accustomed to those expected London night sounds. Not wind rattling the windows. It was something inside the house. She had heard it as she was getting ready for bed: the creak of a floor board outside her door. It had woken her moments ago.

Who would be walking around in the middle of the night? They had come home from the theater, and the ladies had retired after discussing the evening's entertainment. Barlyon had excused himself to go to his library, pleading correspondence left unread earlier. He might be on his way to bed, but surely he would not have stayed up so late over his letters. The other possibilities were Lady Barlyon and Phoebe Stanwood.

Aurie could not imagine Lady Barlyon or Phoebe

getting up to make a raid on the kitchen or seek a book in the wee hours. Lud! She would never get back to sleep if she failed to satisfy her curiosity. Disdaining both slippers and dressing gown, she padded to the door and pulled it open. To her right, the corridor was empty as far as its turn. To the left, the petite white-gowned figure outside the last door was clearly no ghost.

Without pausing to think, Aurie left her door open behind her and all but ran toward Phoebe Stanwood, whose hand was on the door handle.

"What are you doing?" she hissed. The chit jumped and squeaked.

Aurie grabbed her by the wrist and dragged her back down the passage and into her own room. She pushed Phoebe into the chair by the window, where faint moonlight shone in, making it unnecessary to attempt to light a candle. The girl sat hunched over, whimpering and cradling her wrist.

"You hurt me." She sniffled. Aurie snatched up her spare handkerchief from the bedside table and passed it to Phoebe, who proceeded to sob into it far longer than necessary. Finally, she stopped and began to wipe her eyes and nose.

"What were you doing outside Lord Barlyon's bedchamber?"

Phoebe bit her lower lip, held the handkerchief to her eyes again and mumbled, "I don't know."

"How can you not know? You were there. If I'd been a minute later, you would have been in Barlyon's bedchamber, and what a scandal that would have made. Your reputation would have been destroyed. And—" Barlyon might have felt he had to marry the little baggage.

"Please don't scold me! I can't endure it when people raise their voices and rail at me." She snuffled dolefully. "I must have been sleepwalking and mistook my way."

"You had best make it a habit to lock your door, then, and tie a cord around one wrist and then to a bedpost. You will not like being the object of scandal. Scorned at parties—if you are even invited—called a slut, deemed unmarriageable unless your dowry is large enough—"

"It isn't."

"And even if it is, courted only by men who already have heirs, for the others do not care to risk marrying a loose woman—"

"I'm not, I'm not!"

Another bout of weeping ensued, this one genuine. The first, which had given the minx a chance to gather her wits—such as they were!—had not been productive of the puffy eyelids or the gasping that resulted from real tears. Controlling her impatience with difficulty, Aurie waited until the sobbing subsided before walking the girl back to her own room. Thank God, the girl had kept her voice low and not wailed out her misery. Lady Barlyon, whose chamber was next door, was a sound sleeper. Her rest was assured by a nightly cup of warmed milk with a composing draught added to it. At least, it was referred to as such. Aurelia had once been in the passage when Lady Barlyon's maid was taking the cup to her and thought she detected the scent of brandy.

****

He had been in two minds about speaking with Aurelia. As luck would have it, however, he found himself breakfasting alone with her, Lady Barlyon preferring to eat later, after a restorative cup of chocolate in her room. Phoebe Stanwood had requested a tray in her bedchamber.

His father would have had at least one footman on duty to serve them. It was a formality he and his mother had dispensed with soon after his recognition as earl. They served themselves, though mayhap if there had been a number of guests at breakfast, it would have been convenient to have servants preparing the plates.

"Did you sleep well last night, my lord?" Her voice was hesitant. Aha!

Barlyon seized the opportunity. "I wake at night to any strange sound or change in the weather." Coming alert to such things could be the difference between life and death when one slept in the open or in poor lodgings. Though it was an ability he had learned as a child rather than in London; he had never known when Matthew or sometimes Matthew and Mark would creep in to his chamber to tip him out of bed, or douse him with cold water, or leave a dead animal tucked into bed with him.

"Oh…Do you? That must be inconvenient."

"No, not really. Last night, very late, someone tried to open my door."

Aurelia Kennet colored up and appeared to have trouble chewing.

"I heard two voices, then it grew mercifully silent and I was able to doze off again."

She swallowed with difficulty and drank tea. Embarrassed. Did she think he thought it was she who had tried his door? Would that it had been!

"Phoebe is given to sleepwalking."

"That is the discreet explanation. As it happens, I feared some such violation of my privacy and had locked the door. Braced a chair under the handle, too," he added, "in case it occurred to her that any of the door keys would work in any lock in the house. Thank you for intervening. It may discourage her from trying any further ploy."

"You guessed she would attempt such a scandalous, wicked thing?"

"Someone warned me she might."

"Thank goodness. Lady Barlyon and I worried she might try to compromise herself—"

"It generally requires a man to compromise a lady. For a lady to compromise herself would seem unnatural." Not something he should have said. Not to a rum-mort anyway.

Before he could apologize, she responded, "Like a lady impregnating herself?"

She did not titter or smile and her gaze met his levelly, but he could see the laughter lurking in her eyes. Her humor and intelligence drew his interest more than her beauty. She was kind, too. Aurelia Kennet was everything he could want in a countess. It would appear to the world to be an acceptable match, if not a brilliant one. Yet how could he offer her marriage, given his past? How could anyone love him, even without his past? Realizing he wanted his bride to love him came as a shock and an embarrassment. Love was not required in marriage among their sort, and still he wanted it.

She nibbled a sweet bun, their cook's attempt to duplicate the rolls sold at the Chelsea Bun House: bread dough, butter, sugar, currants, and mixed spice.

How could he approach the matter? What if she

285

were appalled? She would not spread talk of his criminal associations, but his past must give her a disgust of him. He would swear he could hear Sol's response. "What of her own past? Has it made you think the worse of her? Men are allowed behavior which would ruin a woman."

"Mistress Aurelia...I believe you noticed the female who stumbled near us last night outside Covent Garden."

"She would have fallen if you had not helped her."

He could not read her expression or tone. She might be commenting on the weather. He suspected that most ladies would have replied, "I do not notice such creatures," or "I do not care to discuss the subject."

She spoke again before he could go on. "She knew you, didn't she?"

"Not in the biblical sense. I was slightly acquainted with her."

"I thought as much."

"I had a number of disreputable friends, or at least, men and women who did not move in decent society." The morning was advancing. Sooner rather than later, a footman would come to see if they wanted anything else and to take away empty serving dishes and clear the table if they had finished their meal.

"You arrived in London as a boy and without money or friends. Survival cannot have been easy. You mentioned some of the shifts you were put to, in order not to starve."

"Thank you for understanding. And for dealing with the awkwardness last night."

When he rose, he bowed over her hand, stopping just short of kissing it. Too familiar and too formal for the occasion, but he did not know how else to signify his appreciation. A scent of spice and butter lingered on her fingers from the bun, tempting him to suck them. Not something he could do at present, alas.

He wanted Aurelia for his countess. But before he could approach that subject, he must decide how much to tell her about his past. He knew only three men who might advise him.

Hawkins would say, "Damn your past! You're an earl, she's a viscount's daughter, and you admire her. Your past is dead as yesterday's fish."

Based on Captain Easterday's two failed betrothals and subsequent marriage to a very unconventional lady, Barlyon wasn't sure he would have any advice to offer.

Sol would look at him with his inscrutable dark eyes and say, "She sounds very suitable. Would she object to the life you led as John Barlicorn?"

That was the question, wasn't it?

Chapter 28

How he came to think of Clement he could not imagine, unless it sprang from having spoken of knowing Polly in the biblical sense. Or rather, not knowing Polly that way. He could talk to Clement, if he could find him. Clement was the lecturer in St. Clement Danes parish, but from his account of his work there, it was as likely he would be calling upon parishioners or reading scriptural passages and commenting on them or lecturing in a neighboring parish. As luck would have it, he caught Clement at the end of the morning service and murmured that he needed some guidance.

"Come to my lodgings. We can talk there without interruption."

Clement Pettigrew inhabited pleasant rooms in a house nearby, putting to rest Barlyon's fear that he lived in squalor. The parish included poor areas, like the Backside of St. Clements, Butchers Row, and the Clare Market, as well as the better-behaved population of the New Inn. While the law students of the latter might not be angels, they were at least nominally gentlemen.

Ensconced in a comfortable if threadbare armchair, probably a castoff of Clement's mother's, as it was upholstered in pink, and of too good quality to have come with the lodgings, he began, "I have a dilemma, and I could think of no better man to ask for advice."

"I try not to give advice, John. So few actually want it. But I am here to listen. Some find clarity in expressing a problem." He busied himself pouring out glasses of claret, and passed one to Barlyon before seating himself.

"It's hard to know where to begin."

"There is no hurry."

"I must marry to prevent my mother becoming dependent upon my heir presumptive if I should die before her. He's a Dissenter…"

"Which does not mean he is not a good man, even if he is not a member of the Church of England. I greatly admire John Wesley, who has now wandered a distance from the Church, yet some of his ideas are worthy."

"I fear my heir is too similar to my father. I have settled a sum on my mother to support her, but Barlyon Manor has been her home since she married. She might find it difficult to uproot herself. If my relation became the thirteenth earl, his wife, for I assume he has one or would soon get one, would take my mother's place as lady of the house. I do not think she would be comfortable in such circumstances. Otherwise, my dying without male issue would make no difference."

"Would it not? If he is like your late father, would he treat your tenants well?"

Rot him. "No, I suppose not. You mean I have a duty to them, too."

"Do you not think so?"

"I am not yet used to my position. I had forgotten them."

"You were never taught how to go on as landowner and earl."

Barlyon regarded an arrangement of half a dozen small pictures on the opposite wall. The work of one of Clement's sisters, probably, for while they were well done and good likenesses of his parents and siblings, they had not the appearance of professional portraits. What would it be like, to have family whose faces one wished to see on one's walls? "If I had been his first son, I doubt I would know much more. My father had very little care for his tenants, apart from their souls. Which I prefer to leave to their own consciences."

Pettigrew steepled his fingers. "He has now answered for or is answering for his actions. I do not suppose he escaped all punishment in this life, either. Would you say your father was a happy man?"

"When he was beating us, perhaps." Remembering his father was the last thing he wanted to do. He had spent seventeen years forgetting him. "No, in fact, I can't recall him ever smiling or showing pleasure at anything."

"In my experience, those who are…mmm…committing grave spiritual errors are seldom happy or even content."

"Clement, I can't forgive him. He made my mother and sister unhappy, and I think made my brothers what they were."

"I don't ask you to forgive him. But recall he may have learned his ways from his own father and not been strong enough to resist them. I do think you should put him behind you, as there's nothing more he can do to you except taint your own happiness."

He could not answer at once for the tightness in his throat. "You must be very good at your calling."

Clement smiled wryly. "I hope I'm of some use to

my parish. You said you wanted advice. I doubt you wished to talk about your father."

"No, I didn't. Sorry we wandered so far from the point." He savored a mouthful of claret while he collected himself, banishing memories. "I need to marry. But my past makes it difficult."

Clement waited. In the street, a female voice caroled "A Fox May Steal Your Hens, Sir" to the accompaniment of passing vehicles and street cries.

"You know how I described my life in London at the house party."

"I do. It sounded fairly innocent. Too innocent, knowing what I do of the London poor and children who have no family to support them."

"I did not precisely lie. The truth was a little more brutal than I admitted. I could not divulge everything I had done, because if someone at the house party had reported my activities to a magistrate…"

"You might have been hanged or transported? I don't suppose John I would have hesitated to lay an information against you."

"No."

"Go on."

"Before I was lucky enough to find some honest work, my crimes were limited to stealing food. I worked for a greengrocer until he died. I stayed out of trouble for two years while I worked for the printer, until he had to close because of some of his pamphlets and books. Later, I acted as a lookout for gaming hells and other, er, businesses that would pay to be warned of raids."

An encouraging nod though his old friend undoubtedly knew what he meant.

"I suppose I broke some law by selling the printer's seditious works. But afterwards…" A patch of sunlight lay across the Turkish rug, brightening colors dimmed by years and wear, like his memories. Talking of those days brought them back to vivid life. Very little of what he had done seemed reprehensible at the time. Now the prospect of confessing it to an old friend loomed appallingly. "I bought and sold anything that came my way. Some of it was stolen. Most of it, maybe. Wrote out French or Latin sometimes for a man who forged documents and letters. I forged letters of reference for servants who'd been discharged without a character. When I could afford to buy at the sales of bankrupts' goods, I became an honest trader. For the most part." He took a last, fortifying sip of claret.

"All very discreditable, John, but understandable. However, I sense you have not quite finished unburdening your soul." Clement refilled Barlyon's glass. "Some of those activities might have got you hanged or transported, but given the choice between starving or committing them, I would be surprised if you bitterly regretted them. Did you commit robbery or murder? You cannot have committed highway robbery, for I saw you sit a horse at Barlyon."

Barlyon laughed. "I was seldom aboard a nag after I ran away." He took a deep breath. "I beat a man nearly to death."

"Why?"

"He was the son of a nobleman who is—was, at the time—active in court circles. He forced the daughter of a small tradesman I knew. Her father told me, when he asked if I could write a reference to get her a place as a maid somewhere away from London. She could not bear to remain in the neighborhood where people might know what had happened, and she did not want to risk seeing the fellow again. I wrote the letter for her. But it bothered me. He had committed a heinous crime, and the law would never punish him for it, given his family connections. She had been decent, and now she was ruined. The young sprig of nobility wasn't. I hunted him until I caught him leaving a brothel one night and left him with his face well smashed and two broken legs." He shifted uncomfortably. This was the hardest of his crimes to admit, despite being the most justifiable in his own opinion.

"So if it became known, you might well be charged with the crime."

"No one knows, except you. The girl and her father never knew or even suspected. I'd never made a reputation for violence. I suffered too much of it at home. He never saw my face, and I robbed the scum. Robbery with violence is common enough to pass unremarked."

His hearer frowned. "It doesn't sound as if you regret doing it. It was a crime, of course, but…If I were a Roman Catholic, I'd prescribe Hail Marys. As I'm not, I'll ask if you have done anything to expiate your sins. Or if not, what you intend to do."

"Clement, you are changing my opinion of religion. I put the money and jewelry toward hiring a house where homeless children could eat and sleep safely and learn to read and write. A sort of private orphanage. As many of the attendants as possible are women who lost their characters through no fault of their own or male servants discharged because of age or infirmity."

"That was a good work. If your conscience does not need unburdening, why are you here?"

"How can I marry a decent woman?" How could a decent woman ever have any regard for him?

"First, find one you like or, better still, love. Then the accepted practice is to ask her papa for permission and when he gives it, you go down on one knee, possess yourself of her hand—if one is available—and—"

"Stop, stop!" Barlyon laughed. "I should have said, how can I expect a decent woman to marry me?"

"That depends on whether she knows of your past or not. If she does not, why would she hesitate?— because you survived in London on your own by buying and selling odd lots of merchandise? Nonsense. You have a title and fortune, and you present a good appearance. That you returned from your adventures to claim the title only adds a touch of the romantical. Apart from those attractions, you are also good-tempered and a good man."

"Are you so certain, Clement?"

"You were a good lad, and I observed you closely at Barlyon. You have not changed much."

"How could I not tell her the truth?"

"That depends upon the lady. Sometimes it is kinder not to burden someone with knowledge which will only cause distress, if it has no bearing upon the present and future. For example," he said, leaning forward and fixing his gaze on Barlyon, "if you had acquired a habit of playing deep at basset or hazard, honor and honesty both would require you disclose it to your intended bride and her papa. The details of how you earned a living before you came into the title need not concern the lady. Gentlemen who have never had to steal in order to eat do not tell the ladies they mean to marry about their less reputable connections with women or about their by-blows. This is not much different."

"Unless I am accused of the crimes."

"Hmmm. Is someone like to come forward?"

Then he had to explain about Huggins and the blackmail.

"Sour grapes at his nephew's failure, and why would they speak when it meant their crime would come out?"

"Such is my reasoning, too, but there is an added complication."

"Ah." Clement sat back in his shabby armchair and waited.

"After I'd been in town for some time and was no longer struggling to get enough to eat, I discovered I had a talent for negotiating." He should have mentioned this earlier. Now it sounded as if he had held it back, when he had omitted it because it did not seem important. "More to the point, others noticed I could persuade men to make up their differences, which led to my being sought as a mediator. Or a sort of informal magistrate."

"Blessed are the peacemakers."

"Because they trusted my judgment, some began to ask me to find someone reliable who could perform this or that service for them, and who would accept my decision if there were a dispute about the matter later."

"I see. Some of the services were criminal?"

"Indeed. I never arranged for murder or fire-setting. I did provide temporary employment for a variety of other criminals. On one occasion, I negotiated the terms between a man and the young woman he wished to employ as his mistress. I think I generally assured that those who needed a mill-ken to break into a house—to retrieve incriminating letters, say—got one who was competent and would not bungle it or panic if confronted by the householder. Or make use of the letters himself."

"You provided a sort of ongoing hiring fair for felons, in fact."

"Well…yes." Put thus, it was almost laughable, like something from *The Beggar's Opera*.

"Reprehensible, but no worse than what you've already told me."

"This was merely the background. I used to keep regular hours at a certain coffee house in St. Clement's Lane, Lombard Street. Two years ago or a little more, a nobleman sought me out. He wanted a man maimed for daring to court a certain young lady. It was not a commission I cared to accept, but I led him to believe I needed to think it over."

"Dear Lord," Clement muttered.

"Not so dear a lord, in my opinion. I pried the victim's name out of him and…er, gave him the office. I wrote, explaining that Lord What-have-ye meant to have him crippled or scarred and suggesting in the strongest language that he should flee. You see, Clement, if I simply turned down the request, the Gray Nobleman—as I called him—would have found someone else, probably someone worse, and the aspiring suitor might easily have been killed." He thought the incident had turned out well, until the Gray Nobleman's minion had come to Job's on the appointed day.

"The suitor had taken my advice to heart and fled and took the young lady with him to Scotland. My would-be client was furious and blamed me for not arranging the attack immediately, for by the time I'd set for giving my answer, the couple was away. The suitor arranged it quickly and avoided the Great North Road, where of course they were sought for.

"After they wed, they sent notice of the marriage to the papers and rusticated at his family's country estate for a time. There was nothing the Gray Nobleman could do. The marriage was consummated; the girl wasn't even under age."

"He didn't guess it was your doing?"

"He saw a common felon dressed in tawdry finery—you would not believe the colors, Clement! Garish clothing makes an excellent disguise—who spoke the patois of the gutter and arranged crimes. It cannot have occurred to him I would forego fifty pounds and warn his prey. But he thought me insolent, which may have caused him to remember me."

"And now you are moving in circles where you may encounter your Gray Nobleman, he might recognize you." Clement stared into his wine. It glowed like a ruby in a beam of sunlight from the window. His shrewdness was undoubtedly useful in his parish.

"Ay, and there's worse. He is courting Mistress Aurelia Kennet."

"That cannot be permitted. Such a man would be no fit husband." Pettigrew frowned thoughtfully. "At Barlyon, I thought you were attracted to the young lady."

"I was. I am. Which is another horn of my

dilemma."

"How many horns does your dilemma have?"

"Three? Four? I've lost count."

"Still fewer than the beast in Revelation."

"I fear I have forgotten all the religion my father beat into me."

"Revelation 13.1. A beast having seven heads and ten horns."

"Oh, well, in that case, I scarcely have a problem." Which was actually true, as he had no fear of being convicted or even charged with any crime.

"In order to warn Mistress Aurelia, however, you must tell her what you know about the fellow."

"I could simply offer for her myself. I need a wife, and she appears to enjoy my company. I think we would deal together well."

"Without telling her about your past?"

"You did say the details need not concern her."

"I also said 'if it has no bearing upon the present and future.' You may not run any risk of punishment—it's rather appalling, really, that a plain man can be hanged or transported for a crime for which a lord would escape scot-free—but your extortioners and Gray Nobleman could certainly cause talk. How would your bride feel about being the wife of a notorious noble accused felon?"

"I must confess to her, then." As he had feared.

"You must look to your own conscience, but I generally feel that honesty between spouses is best, when any chance of current consequences exists. Those who do not practice it are apt to feel guilty, which is a canker on the soul. This situation is similar in some ways to that of a young woman who grants her favors, even only once, to a man other than her intended husband. Can she marry him without telling him she may have conceived by the other man?"

"It would cause some awkwardness, I imagine."

"Do you not trust her enough to confide in her? Will she advertise your past?"

"No."

"You are sure?"

"Yes."

"Though I suspect she has not trusted you with her own past?"

"Even so." Barlyon shrugged.

"Then why hesitate?"

"Shame. I don't want her to think badly of me."

"Mayhap she will think the better of you for owning up to your past. She may also be ashamed to confide her past to you."

Clement was correct. Much as he dreaded such a disclosure, if he accomplished nothing else, at least he would have opened Aurelia's eyes to Furness's character. He nodded and rose to take his leave. And if Aurie should feel impelled to talk about her secret, so much the better.

"John."

"Ay, Clement?"

"You declined to pay for those rascals' silence, but they might still start rumors. The Gray Nobleman might perchance recognize you and make inquiries. I agree it's unlikely you would suffer any legal consequences. However, you should consider the effect upon your mother and sister if your less respectable doings are bruited about."

Telling Lady Barlyon—his mother!—and Tamar

would be easier than telling Aurelia. Tamar would not condemn him; she understood why he had had to leave. As for his mother, he understood why she had been unable to protect him or even show any affection. She wanted to make up for her seeming indifference in his early life, and he understood that, as well. They were still uneasy with each other. While she showed every sign of doting on him, all he felt for her was some liking and pity. Eventually, he might warm toward her. But at the moment, he still did not greatly care what she thought of him.

"I must tell them, then."

"I would, in your place." Clement clapped him on the shoulder, an action as warming in its way as the April sun streaming in through the window.

Telling his mother would present no difficulty, as he could speak with her alone in her boudoir or in the library. Tamar would be more difficult, as he would either have to entrust his confidences to a letter or travel to Rutland. However, if there were gossip, it would travel but slowly to the country. Telling Tamar could wait a while. He must tell Aurelia first, which would require some ingenuity. What he had to say could not be divulged in front of a chaperon.

Chapter 29

After seeing Clement, he sought refuge at the offices of his man of business. There had been a lease and accounts to review and some matters relating to the homeless children's charity. Being out of Phoebe's reach was not the only benefit. His presence in the office eliminated the need for correspondence back and forth. What could be resolved in a few minutes' discussion with Simon Hayes might otherwise require several exchanges of letters, with the risk that any given letter might be lost if it went by post to Barlyon Manor. Hayes assured him that anything important traveled by special messenger, but even then there was the danger of the man being robbed by a pad or delayed by foul weather.

He wished he might visit the children's home in person, but too many knew it had been founded by John Barlicorn. Now that Barlicorn was gone—and some said, dead, a rumor set about by Hayes and Solomon— the charity was thought to be supported by contributions. The scheme was intended to explain the source of funds over and above the original outlay for the building and the amounts allocated for the staff, food, and clothing. He and Hayes had foreseen the need for additional monies over the long term: for major repairs, possible medical expenses for the children, apprenticeships.

****

He entered his mother's boudoir, the butler having told him the ladies were in conference there, smiling at Hayes's revelation that the charity had actually received a number of contributions, both in coin and in kind. According to his agent, they came from unusual sources: subscriptions at a coffee house or tavern, sellers of fish or vegetables, a printer who donated primers for the children's education, men of no stated occupation who slunk in with a shilling or a crown or even, once, a guinea. "You had—have—friends," Hayes said.

Smiling turned out to be a mistake. The ladies looked up from the settee where they had been peering at a collection of fabric samples and several pen and ink drawings of ladies' accoutrements. His mother and Aurelia smiled in reply. Phoebe Stanwood, encouraged, jumped up and hurried to meet him.

"Oh, my lord, there is to be a masquerade at Vauxhall Gardens! Do say we may go. I have never been to a masquerade before, except at the home of friends, and that was sadly flat for no one or scarcely anyone, at least, dressed in costume, only in dominos. Please?" At the end of this breathless speech, the longest he had ever heard from her, she gazed up at him beseechingly, a kitten hoping for a tidbit of chicken. A rather nervous kitten, possibly because he recoiled slightly at her onslaught.

He escorted her back to the settee and took a side chair himself, pausing to arrange his coat skirts so as not to crush them. "If my mother and Mistress Aurelia agree to this…er, treat, I will escort you."

His mother cast him an apologetic glance. Aurelia,

expression carefully bland, added, "Phoebe's brother mentioned it when he took her visiting earlier." She evidently did not favor the expedition.

He gave Aurelia a slight smile, hoping she would understand he was acknowledging her message. No better place existed in London for a lady who wanted to be compromised, as Phoebe did.

Lady Barlyon murmured, "I know it is very popular, but I have heard some shocking things about what goes on in the Spring Gardens." Lady Barlyon used the older name.

Anyone who could afford the shilling admission price went to the Gardens: decent folk of the middling sort with their children, apprentices on a spree, gentlemen young and old looking for amatory adventures, courtesans and women of the town, men in search of loot or prey. Men like John Barlicorn.

The idea sprang full blown in his brain. "It is perfectly safe for ladies who are appropriately escorted. The tone of the place becomes less wholesome after the entertainment ends, and we need not stay later. We must think of two more gentlemen to make our numbers even."

"My brother, Bartholomew, who told me of it, would be happy to make one of the party, my lord."

"I believe your brother is a lively young man who will not wish to be partnered with his sister, and if I know anything of boys of his age, cannot be relied upon as an escort. No, my dear Mistress Phoebe, he would be off at the first opportunity to join his friends."

The girl could not deny it without lying. She sighed. "I fear you are correct, my lord."

"However, I know gentlemen who would enjoy

such an entertainment and be reliable escorts.

"Thank you, my lord. I look forward to it so much."

He stole a glance at Aurelia, raising one brow interrogatively.

"I have no doubt it will be most entertaining, Lord Barlyon." A certain lift in her voice suggested she understood he was planning something. He had plenty of time to go out before dinner to set things in motion.

****

The heavily muscled clerk instructed him to wait in one of the little side offices meant to keep clients from encountering each other. Barlyon did so impatiently, though there was a comfortable chair and a few books. He looked them over to see what his old friend thought might entertain a man waiting to see a moneylender. *The Compleat Gamester*, *The Court-Gamester*, *Moll Flanders*, *A Dictionary of Husbandry, Trade, Commerce, and All Sorts of Country Affairs*, and the *Dictionarium Rusticum and Urbanicum* seemed to cover the range of topics likely to be of interest. He spent an amusing half hour dipping into the latter two volumes in search of useful knowledge until he was shown into Sol's office.

"If someone comes, suggest they return tomorrow, unless they are willing to wait," Solomon told his Cerberus. "This may take some time." He would have guessed Barlyon would not visit him at his place of business without a pressing reason, for only the second or third time in eight years.

It would be easy to forget the nature of that business from the furnishings, which might have been found in a simple country gentleman's home or a moderately successful lawyer's office. When they sat with glasses of sherry in the armchairs in front of the desk, Barlyon ventured, "Sol, do you know anyone who wants to marry the daughter of a nobleman?"

"A good many. Can you narrow your question somewhat?"

"The father is a baron, the girl is pretty and, mmmm, biddable—"

"Rather than beddable?"

"She's very pretty."

"John, I sense an evasion."

"She is shy and silly and hopes to become my countess by hook or by crook, put up to it by her family. She is seventeen, I think, so she may get over the silliness."

"Or she may be stupid, which is a thing one does not get over. Dowry?"

"You would know better than I. It's Axton's chit."

"The one I warned you against." Sol's expressive eyebrows rose.

"The very same. Lady Axton managed to get her invited to stay at Barlyon House by playing on my mother's sympathy. Claimed she had to go to their seat to care for the oldest son who had injured himself and wanted to leave the girl with someone who could chaperon her. My mother and Aurelia Kennet, who's staying with us, both know what's going forward, and it's been easy to thwart Axton's plans thus far. Now Phoebe wants to attend the Vauxhall masquerade."

"You could not bring yourself to overrule your mother's agreement to chaperon her, and now you can't refuse her desire to go to a public assembly at a place known for assignations." The eyebrows commented.

"I will not behave as my father would, Sol, in spite of suspecting her middle brother will be lurking nearby, ready to pounce as soon as she succeeds in luring me away from the others."

"Is it your idea to offer up some man who's willing to marry her in the hope she'll fasten on him instead? If she's biddable, she won't go against her papa's orders. On the other hand, if she's silly and he takes her fancy, she might, and if the brother catches them together..." Solomon meditated, resting his chin upon his steepled fingers. "The fellow would have to be acceptable to her family, which I judge would mean having enough money to be bled, whether he's a cit or a gentleman. But a gentleman rich enough to rescue Axton from his embarrassments wouldn't need my help to find a bride. Except...Well, there is one. A viscount, money enough to satisfy Axton, but not a family with whom most would want an alliance."

"I wouldn't want to marry into Axton's family, so it's six of one, half a dozen of the other, surely?"

"Axton's a spendthrift and so are the boys, I think, but no worse. Not that prodigality is a minor fault. Viscount Thus-and-Such is worse, to most of society's way of thinking. His mother could not have told which of several men fathered him, though it's believed extremely unlikely to have been the previous viscount. He did not disavow him, but he also did not acknowledge him until he knew he was dying. Then he did so mostly to make sure his brother didn't get the title, or so I hear. The new viscount himself is not a bad fellow. That is, he has no remarkable vices.

"Then, I know of one or two City men who would like to marry into a noble family and are rich enough to be fine catches, although neither could pass as a gentleman. One's a bit old to appeal to a very young lady, unless she is drawn to the avuncular sort."

"There is one other qualification. He must be similar to me in height and weight."

Solomon contemplated him, frowning slightly. "You are not merely offering the girl a choice in the hope of distracting her."

"No."

"Tell me."

Some minutes later, Barlyon concluded, "…and that's why I need someone who can be mistaken for me when clad in mask and domino."

"Two of the men I suggested are not tall enough to be mistaken for you, I fear, and the one who is almost your height is too portly." Solomon blew out a breath. "How important is it that she marry one or the other of your imposters?"

"Not at all. I'm not setting up as a matchmaker. I also don't want her ruined, which is why I want to provide her a possible match. If she does find herself marrying one or the other, she will at least be better off than she is with her family, who might well sell her to someone worse."

"Ah, but would the groom be better off?"

Barlyon shrugged. "As I said, pretty and submissive. Many men are happy with those qualities."

"You realize the girl may be ruined if she is discovered alone with a man who is not acceptable to her father."

"I do. I pity her for having a family who have put her up to entrapping a man into marriage but not enough to sacrifice myself. Even if I intended to make a loveless match, I would insist on a lady capable of fulfilling the duties of a countess. Nor am I willing to be squeezed by her father."

"I am glad you have not put away John Barlicorn's good sense with his appalling wardrobe. I have seen men make ill-advised matches out of foolish scruples or because their family wished for the alliance. One owes a good deal to one's family, of course, but there is no reason to sacrifice one's own happiness."

Barlyon was not surprised: Sol, close as he was to his family, had chosen to pursue a career none of his relatives approved of.

Sol ran a finger around the band of blue glass circling the Murano goblet. "Very well. I'm your man."

"What?"

"I am not quite as tall as you, but it should not be a noticeable difference. We are both lean." Wryly: "I can be mistaken for a gentleman by my speech and manners. Will you provide the dominoes and masks?"

"Sol, have you considered the risk of ending up married to Phoebe Stanwood? It's not like you to be impulsive."

"I have almost always done as I ought to do and worked hard. I enjoy my life, but sometimes I have thought it could use a little seasoning. A touch of daring, a dash of dash. When we were boys, I wanted to be like you."

"Homeless? With no family? Doing whatever you could to survive?"

"Free to be whatever I could make of myself." His twitch of a smile mocked his reply. "Ridiculous, I know. Very few people are free in any real way."

"What would you have made of yourself?" It was a

topic they had never discussed. As a boy, Barlicorn had the choice of surviving or not. It should have been easy for Sol, who could have become a banker or importer like several of his uncles and cousins or a doctor, like his father and paternal grandfather, who had studied medicine at Leiden and Padua.

"I would have studied law at Oxford and been admitted to the Bar of the Court of Chancery. Impossible, of course, without converting. Someday, I may set up as a landowner. That became possible by act of Parliament about twenty years since. I don't suppose I'd be acceptable as a magistrate even then." After a long, contemplative pause, he added, "Particularly after I'd rendered a decision or two in poaching matters. I quite understand why a landowner might wish to preserve his deer and pheasants, but rabbits? If the tenants and villagers are unable to afford meat, let them snare the bunnies."

Barlyon shook his head sadly, "Sol, I fear you are a Leveller. Mind you are not clapped up for sedition. Before you set up as a country gentleman, be aware 'tis a surprising amount of work. You'd have to take an interest in cattle and sheep and crops. I can't imagine a manor without pigs, either. Still, you could add some excitement to your life without risking your future happiness."

Solomon laughed. "There is no chance of my ending up married to Mistress Phoebe. Only consider: say her brother finds us in some secluded nook and cries out, 'Seducer! You'll marry my dear little sister for ruining her!' Then when I am revealed not to be you, and yet worse, am discovered to be neither titled nor wealthy, never mind the religious problem and my profession, will Axton insist on a wedding or will he hush it up?" He smiled cynically.

"The brother might call you out. Have you ever even handled a smallsword?"

"Only if I was valuing it for security against a loan. No, he won't challenge me. He is a gentleman—even if he is willing to help his sister compromise herself into a rich marriage. He would no more consider it than he would challenge a servant or a chimney sweep."

"He might thrash you."

"He might try." Sol grinned. "You taught me how to fight. I haven't forgotten."

Sol found the scheme feasible. Barlyon began to look forward to foiling Axton's stratagems. The prospect of having a friend with him made the difference. What could go wrong?

"Then I'll see to the masks and dominoes."

"John, is this meant to be like the thimble cheat?"

"In essence, yes."

"That game works well with three thimbles, but...I suppose it will work with only two," Solomon ended doubtfully.

"There will be three of us. I'm on my way to enlist the third now. And he may even wish to marry the girl. He's been looking for a wife."

Chapter 30

The Barlyon coach carried them to the White Fryars Stairs, where a shallop awaited to carry them upriver to Vauxhall Gardens, Barlyon having said he did not care for them to go by wherry, which might pick up any sort of passenger along the way.

"How pretty!" Phoebe exclaimed when they saw it.

Aurie agreed. Many noblemen owned their own pleasure barges, travel by river being easier and faster than going by coach, if one were going from one riverside location to another. It might theoretically be possible to go by coach, crossing London Bridge and then threading one's way through a maze of roads and lanes. No one Aurie had ever heard of did so when going by boat was so easy and enjoyable, and there was no danger of becoming lost in the dark on the way home.

This boat with its high prow displaying a painted and gilded dolphin, eight liveried oarsmen, and handsomely canopied passenger area in the stern, would not have disgraced a duke.

As Lord Barlyon assisted his mother into the shallop, Lady Barlyon asked, "What of the two gentlemen you invited?"

"It was more convenient for them to meet us there. Have no fear; you ladies will not lack for partners."

Fear. She could not say she was afraid, though she

was nervous, partly because her memories of the Gardens were not pleasant and partly because she dreaded the possibility of encountering the Marquess of Furness. The way he appeared at every event she attended and engaged her in conversation or danced with her had begun to remind her of Kit Hastings's courtship. Other men who had shown some interest in her had begun to sheer off. Still, how could he be aware she would attend the masquerade? It hardly seemed the sort of entertainment to appeal to him now that he was grown so serious.

The tremor in Lady Barlyon's voice told her she, too, was nervous, probably out of concern at being responsible for Phoebe Stanwood. Her hostess, immured so long in the country, could not have been any girl's chaperon recently. Her daughter had not been introduced to society in London before her marriage. She might also worry that Phoebe would succeed in entrapping Barlyon. Imagine that insipid child as a countess! If not for her past, Aurie would have a mind to try if she could engage the earl's affections.

How could she endure until Lady Barlyon decided to go home to the country? Aurelia had agreed to lend her company until then, but she had been persuaded—and persuaded herself—that her past had been forgotten. What a goose she was! A reputation like hers was impossible to live down, though it was not until Robert—Furness—began paying attention to her that she heard whispers and low-voiced conversations that broke off when she approached. It was all too familiar from the end of her last London season. Why on earth was he courting her again? His singling her out was blatant enough that several acquaintances had commented upon it.

"He is very proud and seldom distinguishes any lady beyond a dance. He must be interested in you," Mary Rose Angwin had whispered to her at an evening party two nights earlier.

Her forthright mother had taken Aurie aside. "It is no place of mine to speak, and you are old enough to know your own mind, but do you like Furness? To me he seems rather a cold man, and I believe his poor wife was not happy in the marriage. I know her family well and have heard things from her mama which would make me unwilling to let Mary Rose wed the marquess. Not that he would be interested in my girl," she added. "Still, it is flattering and you would be a marchioness, and his late wife was much like Mary Rose, so very likely you would be better able to deal with him, having sense and maturity. And I hope you will forgive me for mentioning this, but he seems to care nothing about that nonsense with the Hastings boy, which is encouraging."

Lady Barlyon had also noticed. "My dear, I cannot help hoping some other gentleman will take your fancy, even if he is of lower rank than Furness. Though not much lower, of course."

Looking back, it seemed an odd remark if Edith Barlyon considered her unmarriageable. It might even be regarded as hopeful, as an earl was "not much lower" than a marquess, and she knew Lady Barlyon liked her. On that cheering thought, she found herself able to enjoy the pleasant breeze, the sight of many other craft on the river, and the witty and profane banter of the wherrymen. Oh, she recalled that from her previous visit to Vauxhall! She smothered a smile.

It died a natural death as she heard Phoebe ask,

"How long until we reach the Gardens, my lord?"

"Half an hour, mayhap."

They had set out a little later than planned. By the time they arrived, twilight would be approaching.

Phoebe had fluttered and fussed all day, preparing for the masquerade. No, "fussed" was unfair, for she had not been unpleasant about it, merely anxious to look her best. To be perfect, in fact, like any other girl preparing for a major event. But her anxiety over her gown, domino, mask, and hair seemed underlain by something more than nerves. Did she mean to lure Barlyon away from others and seduce him? She could not quite imagine Phoebe doing anything as daring as seduction—outdoors, too, where her gown might be damaged!—or Barlyon being foolish enough to permit himself to be compromised. Could one compromise a gentleman's honor? It would be a delicious thought, if only one's own honor permitted it.

The chit was looking her best, in pink silk. Her lips were tinted to the same color. Her domino, oddly, was white, sewn with silver spangles. Aurie would have chosen a leaf-green domino, to make the pink gown resemble a giant rosebud, to tempt an otherwise sensible man to see the petals unfurled. What a pity there had not been time to devise real costumes. She feared her own deep-yellow robe volante and domino would bring to mind a pile of wheat.

Well, she would watch Phoebe to prevent any hoydenish tricks. Lady Barlyon was taking her duties as chaperon seriously, but she did not know of the girl's attempt to visit Barlyon's bedchamber. Aurie had not told her for fear of sending her into a nervous collapse. Barlyon might have done so, but if he had, his mother would be even more concerned about Phoebe Stanwood. Very likely she would have discussed it with Aurie.

How much of a nuisance would the other two gentlemen be? Barlyon had said nothing more about them. They could not be well known to him as he must have met them only recently. One would probably be of his mother's age. Would the other be of assistance in diverting Phoebe's attention?

Barlyon sat at ease on the upholstered bench across from them, back to the shallop's prow. No one made conversation. After Lady Barlyon's question about the other gentlemen, Aurie had ventured a comment about the pleasure of travel on the river. It sounded awkward even to her ears. No one else made any remark until Phoebe's inquiry about their arrival. Voices from other barges and wherries drifted across the water, the laughter and light-hearted banter of people looking forward to an evening of enjoyment.

Their own party was not in spirits. Aurie glanced toward a particularly loud burst of hilarity from another boat. Her gaze met John Barlyon's, and the mischief she read in his hazel eyes arrested her own. Could he be unaware of the danger posed by Vauxhall's romantic walks and secluded groves?

"Have you visited Vauxhall Gardens before, Lord Barlyon?" she asked. Perhaps he was ignorant of its risks. He seemed to have been successful as a tradesman or merchant or whatever it was he'd been, and all classes went to the Gardens, but he might have been the exception.

"Oh, yes. But I vow tonight will be an exceptional occasion, Mistress Aurelia."

Whatever did he have planned?

Phoebe chirped, "I am sure you are correct, my lord. I look forward to it with the greatest—" She stopped, lost for the right word.

One of the rowers cried out, "Vauxhall Stairs ahead!" and Phoebe leaned out for her first glimpse at London's favorite pleasure garden, the end of her sentence forgotten. What had she meant to say? Pleasure? Satisfaction? Misgiving? "Misgiving" certainly summed up Aurie's feelings.

Setting foot on the Vauxhall water stairs once more, her heart thumped unpleasantly. She must shake off her apprehension. This time there was no Kit Hastings to attempt to force a marriage, no Robert Sedgewick to make the situation worse. Tonight, she must help Lady Barlyon chaperon Phoebe.

They donned their masks as they approached the entrance. Lady Barlyon's mask matched her gown and was meant to be held before the face by its stick, rather than tied on. Phoebe had chosen a half-face mask the color of her robe à la Française and had added green silk leaves around its edges and green ribbons to tie it on, enhancing her resemblance to a rose. Aurie had chosen one at random from the shop's stock. The proprietor claimed it represented the Venetian carnival character Columbina. Lord Barlyon, the hood of his black domino pulled up, black tricorn atop it, wore a stark white mask which entirely covered his features, though it angled outward at the bottom, presumably to allow him to breathe and converse, as it had no mouth. It was also Venetian, she understood, and represented the bautta character.

They arrived at their supper box to find two

gentlemen already present. Like the earl, they wore black dominoes with hoods, hats, and the same full face masks.

"As this is a masquerade and one should not know the identity of other masqueraders, I shall not introduce my friends to you, ladies, except as Bautta I—" The figure indicated bowed slightly, affording them a glimpse of the black suit under the silk cloak. The effect was quite sinister.

"And this is Bautta II." The second white-faced figure clad in black also bowed.

"But you are all disguised alike," Phoebe protested.

"I thought it would be amusing as a sort of game," he murmured. "Like my attorney's determination of whether I or the other claimant to my title was the real Earl of Barlyon."

It might make it harder for Phoebe to entice Lord Barlyon to his downfall.

She appeared to be perplexed. Aurelia wondered if the chit had not heard the gossip about the two claimants, which had made its way around the beau monde, though not until the question of Barlyon's identity had been settled.

"But three makes it much more difficult. There cannot have been any real challenge in choosing between you and some other fellow. My papa says you can always recognize a nobleman, and I do not suppose the impostor was noble, was he?"

Aurie's mood lightened at Phoebe's disappointed expression.

"Not in the least. But I am sure you can determine which of us is which by adroit questioning."

How clever the ploy had been soon became clear.

The masquerade had drawn throngs, some in elaborate costumes, others with only a domino and half mask, all of them talking and laughing and seeming to be in endless motion. The three male members of the Barlyon party were not the only ones wearing the bautta mask, though none of the others she saw wore black suits.

Someone suggested they should stroll until it was time for supper. With the orchestra playing some lively piece, Aurie could not be certain whether the voice belonged to Barlyon or one of the other men. In the confusion, she was not quite sure whose arm she was offered. Not Barlyon, she thought. Bautta I? Bautta II? Whoever it was, he inquired if she were enjoying her stay in London.

"Yes, indeed." Her reply was only partly mendacious, as she found the earl's company very pleasant. "Have you known Lord Barlyon long?"

"For some time."

They paused to admire the statue of Handel, which none of the ladies had previously seen, it having been in place only two or three years. It was startlingly modern in style, depicting the composer in dishabille, playing a lyre, with no wig and one slipper on, the other off. She found it delightful. He might almost be in his own chamber, though she doubted he composed his music on a lyre, which was the only classical thing about it, excepting the cherub sitting at his feet, writing down the notes.

The three couples did not separate, though Aurelia thought she heard Phoebe, who was last in the line with her escort, asking if they could not go to the right.

"I have heard there is a walk over which the boughs meet. It is said to be delightful."

318

The Druid's Walk, favored by lovers for its dimness even in the early evening—and its lack of lamps after dark. She had heard of it but could not recall it from her own visit. The presence of Frederick, Prince of Wales, was one of few details she remembered clearly from eight years before, apart from the horrid scene with Hastings and Sedgewick. Even now she smiled a little at the memory of the prince, who was neither handsome nor as regal as one expected of a prince but appeared to be an affable man. A far more important consideration than rank or appearance, if one were thinking of a husband. Which one was not, except in the abstract.

Phoebe must believe she was with the earl, to be suggesting a stroll in such a place. The man's low-voiced reply was lost among the music from the rotunda where the orchestra played, but Aurie, glancing over her shoulder, saw that Phoebe and her partner were following sedately. Then Aurie's escort courteously steered her to one side, and they fell in at the back of their little procession. Had her own bautta also heard Phoebe and taken steps to ensure it would be impossible for her to lead her cavalier away for a tête-à-tête?

They proceeded along the Grand Walk to view the statue of Aurora at the eastern end of the Gardens. There, Phoebe's escort pointed out interesting features of the work, distracting her attention. Then one of the other two gentlemen called out, "Look—a mama rabbit and her babies!" Aurelia's own partner had moved off a little way to get a different perspective.

"Oh, where?"

"Just over there, Mistress Phoebe, under that

shrub."

Aurelia also turned to look, even as she realized that the men were moving.

"I don't see them."

"She must have shepherded her little ones into the shrubbery as soon as she realized we saw her. The sight of such Brobdingnagian creatures as we would naturally terrify the poor things."

His voice or the humor in it called to mind Aurelia's bautta, who was no longer beside her. The bautta nearest her offered his arm.

"Oh, of course," Phoebe said vaguely.

Aurelia had seen no indication during the girl's stay at Barlyon House that she enjoyed reading. No doubt she had missed the reference to *Gulliver's Travels*.

"Shall we go right or left?" one of the gentlemen inquired.

The men never seemed to stand side by side or even near each other; if they had, the slight differences in their heights would be easier to see. They all spoke softly, and the peculiar masks disguised their voices as much as their features. Yet Aurie was sure one of them had a deeper voice and moved with an air of authority, his gestures rather abrupt, while the one who had drawn their attention to the mythical rabbits was almost cat-like in his movements. The third fell between the two in his voice and carriage.

They were on the Dark Walk at the eastern end of the grounds and the northern side was bordered by another Dark Walk, though they were still only dim. To the south—

"Let us go to the right." Phoebe was determined to

visit the Druid's Walk, the minx, perhaps not realizing that while it would be quite dim, it would not be as dark yet as it would later become. Or it might be she was scouting for a suitable place to waylay her escort later.

The music ceased then. The interval before the orchestra struck up again lasted while they traversed the romantic walk with its arched canopy of branches and came out into the central Grove. Phoebe prattled artlessly to her gentleman, which should keep her from noticing in his brief replies that his voice was lighter than it had been. Her own gallant now had a deeper voice. They had nearly reached their supper box at the far edge of the Grove when, at a shrill whistle, all the lamps in the Gardens (except on the Dark Walks) lit at once, causing Phoebe to exclaim and clap her hands in delight. Only the most jaded could fail to be thrilled at the seemingly magical instantaneous illumination, one of the wonders of Vauxhall Gardens. The orchestra commenced to play Handel's "Sailor's Complaint" as they entered their supper box.

The back wall of each supper box featured a painting of some amusement. Later, Aurelia regretted not having paid more attention to them as they were said to be admirable, but she was too much absorbed in wondering what scheme was afoot to take notice. Phoebe seemed not to be aware that her partner at table was not the same one who had accompanied her in the Druid's Walk.

Lady Barlyon's expression reminded Aurie of her brother's face when his tutor set him a proof in geometry. What was that thing about a line intersecting two parallel lines?

The masks, of course, had no expression. How

fortunate they had been designed to allow their wearers to eat and drink.

Conversation was somewhat limited during supper between the necessity of eating and her own and Lady Barlyon's certainty that something peculiar was going on. The music and the sounds of merriment from the other boxes masked voices nearly as well as the stark white masks covered the men's faces. Phoebe, beside the bautta who Aurie was almost certain was the earl, chattered on in answer to his murmured questions about the things she enjoyed most in London, in the country, and at Vauxhall. On her other side was the deeper-voiced bautta who asked Aurie her opinion of the painting forming the back wall of their box and listened attentively to her answer. She suspected he knew far more of art than she did: he knew the name of the artist and that eventually there would be paintings in all fifty supper boxes. "This is only the latest notion of the owner. I look forward to whatever else he may think of in the next year or two."

At one point, he exchanged a glance with the man on Phoebe's right and gave a tiny shake of his head.

The third bautta, on her left, devoted himself to drawing out Lady Barlyon. He ignored the paper-thin slices of ham in favor of the chicken.

At the end of the meal despite her best efforts, she found herself unable to tell which man was which, until they spoke. She was sure Lady Barlyon's supper partner had walked with her earlier, but he must have deliberately spoken in a deeper voice, for now he seemed to be a tenor. The men shifted position as fluidly as water.

"We have not yet taken the walk on the north side

of the grounds," someone said.

The other Dark Walk.

"Ma'am," one of the men said to Lady Barlyon, who linked her arm with his. Was it the deep-voiced gentleman?

Phoebe stood by the entrance to the box, staring toward a table in the open area before the orchestra building, where a young man was lounging. Although he was wearing a black domino like so many others, he had thrown it back over his shoulders, revealing a coral-colored suit. It seemed familiar to Aurie; had she noticed it earlier? Then one of the bauttas bowed to Phoebe and led her after Lady Barlyon and Deep Voice, and the last bautta claimed Aurie. Making their way up the Grand Walk to the first intersecting walk, they turned left and soon found themselves on the narrower way bordering the north side of the Gardens. No lamps illuminated it, though lights on the Grand Walk twinkled through the trees.

As they walked, Aurelia was tolerably sure that the man beside her was the Earl of Barlyon. His pace slowed, and they fell a little behind Phoebe and her beau, which she thought reckless. However, the pair were not far behind Lady Barlyon and her escort.

"My dear Aurelia, or may I call you Aurie?"

The moon had risen. Being at the full, it flooded the way with light. So much for the Dark Walk! Romantic as that cool nacreous illumination was, those wanting more privacy for their courting (or dalliance) had slipped away, probably to the Druid's Walk. Aurie rather wished they had returned to it. But given that they had this path almost to themselves but for an unaccompanied gentleman sauntering toward them and the rest of their party some distance ahead, it would do. The moonlight was a charming accompaniment to a ramble with a man she found too attractive for her own good. If indeed he was Barlyon and not one of the others. She stifled a sigh.

The oncoming walker exclaimed, "Aurelia?"

She stopped. The man's back was to the moon, leaving his face invisible, but his form and his tone were all the clue she needed. "My lord marquess?" Her voice raised in pitch almost to a squeak.

"Who is this fellow and what pretensions does he have, that you are alone with him?" Furness uttered the demand in a voice thunderous enough to frighten the bunnies in the undergrowth or any couples dallying there. Nine years vanished in a blink as she was catapulted back to the seventh of June, 1732.

Chapter 31

Ahead of them, Barlyon saw Hawkins wheel around at the sound of Furness's raised voice, inadvertently pulling Lady Barlyon with him. Then a slight man pelted past, startling Barlyon, who had not heard his thudding footfalls approaching, so intent had he been upon Furness. Who the devil—?

In the silence as he and Aurelia and Furness stared after him, the sounds of hasty passage through shrubbery were audible. Before he reached Lady Barlyon and Hawkins, the runner cut into the thicket at an oblique angle.

Aurelia breathed in sharply. "Where have they gone?"

His mother and Hawkins had been first in their procession, and he and Aurelia had been third. Now there was no one between them.

The girl must have bolted into the trees; Sol would be following her, as areas off the walks sometimes harbored robbers or men who molested women. While guards were posted at the ends of the walks to prevent assaults, they could not be everywhere.

Not that lurking ruffians were the chief danger. That distinction belonged to Phoebe and her brother, if it were he. Damnation! He had expected some member of the Stanwood chit's family to be lying in wait for her to decoy him into a compromising situation. The attempt would have to come now, just when Furness had created a crisis.

Barlyon would have to follow. Hawkins could not pursue the fellow because he could not drag Barlyon's mother through the trees and brush, certainly not fast enough to do any good. Instead he was ambling back toward Barlyon with Lady Barlyon, who could not walk swiftly in her delicate, heeled shoes. The presence of two more people might calm the waters, leaving Barlyon free to deal with the girl and her defender.

Furness, ignorant of what Barlyon and Aurelia were all too aware, spat out, "If you are no seducer, unmask and give me your name."

Lady Barlyon withdrew her arm hurriedly as she and Hawkins reached them and tripped to Aurelia, who looked nigh to swooning. Drawing her aside, she put her arm around Aurie and whispered reassurances.

Barlyon pulled off his mask. "Barlyon. *À votre service.*"

The icy, drawled words and French phrase were as unlike John Barlicorn's careless, cant-filled diction as he could make them.

"Barlyon..." The man's face was in shadow, masking his expression, but something in his pensive tone prompted Hawkins to interrupt.

"Sir, your words and manner distress the ladies. What cause have you to accost my friend?" Hawkins had left home at an early age—like himself, come to think of it—but he too could mimic the beau monde's speech, even if in Wapping he often sounded like the veriest Jack Tar.

"Earl or no, he has separated Mistress Aurelia from her party, enticing her into indiscretion. My dear, let me help you out of your difficulty."

Aurelia, to whom this was addressed, had recovered from her momentary alarm rather than being plunged into a fit of vapors. Barlyon liked a woman with courage.

"My lord, I was in no difficulty whatsoever until you approached and accused me of impropriety. May I present the Earl of Barlyon and…" She hesitated. He had not introduced the two other men by name.

"Hawkins," Barlyon interpolated.

"Mr. Hawkins. Robert Sedgewick, Marquess of Furness."

Hawkins gave a curt nod.

To Barlyon's surprise, his mother entered the fray. "Lord Furness. Mistress Aurelia was not separated from her party. I and another lady, accompanied by Mr. Hawkins and another gentleman, were a few steps ahead, close enough to hear your outburst."

"Which seems to have terrified Mistress Phoebe Stanwood, Baron Axton's daughter, into precipitate flight into the woods," Barlyon added.

"Lord Barlyon, should we not attempt to find her?" He knew Aurelia well enough now to recognize her unease. She had not mentioned that Sol must have gone after the girl, which was probably as well.

"I mean to do so at once, now that Hawkins and my mother are with you. If you will excuse me, Furness?"

"Go, by all means." He turned to face Aurelia. "My dear, we had an understanding." Furness caught her by the wrist before she could move away.

Barlyon rapped out, "You take liberties with a lady, my lord." For several interminable seconds, he

327

thought the marquess meant to ignore him.

"Remove your hand, Furness." The fury in Aurelia's voice cut through the moment like a blade.

The marquess dropped his hand to his side. "I believe I have some right. Barlyon, I have been courting this lady since her return to London, as she will tell you, and I have every expectation she and her father will accept my proposal."

"Were you courting me? I was not aware of it." The words dripped icicles.

"I have spoken and danced with you at every ball you have attended. I have accepted invitations I would decline but for the hope of furthering our relationship. My love, why did you think I was drawn to you as the tides are drawn by the moon? I had hoped for more romantic circumstances to ask you to be my marchioness, but I must make do, I suppose."

"I know you sought me out, in spite of my giving you no encouragement. My father did not force me to accept you nine years ago when I was under age. He has nothing to say in the matter now."

"If I went about this wrongly, I beg your pardon, but surely you will not refuse me. Be mine and let us put right what went wrong in the past, Aurelia."

Reading simmering anger in Aurie's expression, Barlyon said, "I think the lady has already refused you."

Furness ignored this. "Aurelia?"

"Lord Barlyon understood me, if you did not. I will not marry you. Should we not go to find Phoebe, Lord Barlyon?"

The marquess having turned as she moved, Barlyon saw rage in his thinned lips and narrowed eyes.

Not a bad thing, in its way: if he were dwelling on his offended pride, he would not be wondering if Barlyon reminded him of someone else.

"I will go. Hawkins, you'll stay with my mother and Mistress Aurelia? Goodnight, Furness." He kept his voice light. He fancied he could hear the marquess's teeth grinding.

Lady Barlyon murmured, "Surely she cannot have come to harm. The other gentleman must be with her, or in pursuit of her, at least."

"I will give myself the pleasure of accompanying you, Barlyon, in case there should be malefactors lurking. Or if you prefer, I will remain with the ladies while you and…Hawkins?…deal with the problem."

"Come, if you will." How the devil were they to get rid of Furness? Curse the girl for using the situation to compromise herself. The marquess's presence would be awkward.

****

Barlyon and Furness emerged into the clearing to hear Sol declare, "I can support a wife decently though not in great state. She would have to convert, of course. My family would insist upon it."

"Good God, you're a Papist?" The appalled demand was uttered in a youth's voice. Phoebe's brother, Barlyon supposed.

"I am a Jew. I have a small business lending money. I believe I could manage to give your sister as much as five pounds a quarter for pin money."

The slight young man confronting Sol blurted out, "A moneylender?"

"A moneylender is a member of your party?" A poisonous pleasure tinged the marquess's question.

"A longtime friend of mine." He had asked Hawkins to stay with the ladies because he did not quite trust Furness not to drag Aurelia into the trees and compromise her. The fact that the marquess had angled for the opportunity to remain behind suggested he had had some such notion in mind. In retrospect, it would have been better to leave both the marquess and Hawkins behind.

Phoebe Stanwood's witness, most probably her brother, Bart, whipped around. Evidently he had not taken note of their approach.

"Lord Barlyon," Sol greeted him pleasantly. "Mistress Phoebe was distraught at the sound of a raised voice and fled, fearing violence."

"How fortunate you were able to succor her."

Bart, if it were he, whispered urgently to the girl, "Feeb, what were you about going off with this fellow?"

"I—I thought it was the earl! He sat with me at supper, and I was sure…" Her voice trailed off as she realized the other three had gone silent.

Her brother, less perceptive, failed to notice their audience. "You've ruined yourself for nothing, then. Papa will be beside himself."

"Oh, don't say so, Bart. I know he will be in a rage, and I can't…can't bear it." At this she went off in a fit of hysterical wailing and sobbing.

"Hush, Feeb." Her brother patted her shoulder ineffectively and pressed his handkerchief into her hand. "Pray, do be quiet, Feeb. You don't want to attract any more attention. The more notice is taken, the more he'll rant."

It hardly seemed the way to reassure a timid chit

already in fear of her father's wrath, but after a gasping whoop, she took a deep breath, removed her mask, and began to mop her eyes. At this sign of the abating storm, even Furness seemed relieved.

"I am sure none of us will mention this matter, and if we do not speak of it, it never happened. Furness? Sol?"

"Certainly not, as nothing occurred but a lady taking fright and seeking to hide," Sol agreed.

Furness laughed. "I won't embarrass the young lady and her family. But you, Barlyon, you are a disgrace, consorting with such disreputable company. You should have left your sordid commercial associates behind when you claimed your title. It will do Aurelia Kennet no good to be known to mingle with your 'friends.' "

Solomon de Toledo remarked languidly, "Almost everyone has something to his discredit, my lord. For Lord Barlyon, it is some of his friends. For you, it is your want of money, which you try to conceal. Many noblemen are in similar straits." He shrugged. "The time-honored solution is to marry a lady with a large dowry."

After an instant's frozen silence, Furness retorted, "I have no need to marry for money. My late wife was exceptionally well dowered."

"Which dowry you have spent on maintaining a style of living equal to that of many dukes. Your marquessate consists of little more than the title and a small estate, as your uncle, the first marquess, was only a second son, and the viscountcy you inherited from your father is not a wealthy one."

"How—" The rest of the sentence was bitten off.

"How do I know your financial circumstances? A moneylender must be familiar with the finances of those most likely to be borrowers, as a horse-coper must know horses."

A long, thoughtful pause ensued.

Barlyon ended it finally. "Do any of you see a reason to share tonight's revelations with the vulgarly curious?"

"A moneylender must be discreet. I have no interest in speaking of anything I know or have heard tonight about anyone, assuming everyone else agrees."

A throat-clearing from one side reminded them of the presence of Stanwood and his sister, who was hiding her face against his shoulder. "If you would all be so good as to overlook my sister's presence here, we would be glad to forget tonight and everything about it."

The marquess did not respond.

"Furness?"

"I suppose I have no choice but to agree. Do you swear not to speak, Barlyon?"

"I do."

"Then let us get out of this curst wood and go our ways." Furness turned abruptly and strode back the way they had come.

****

When they emerged onto the Dark Walk, his mother, Aurelia, and Hawkins stared at them apprehensively.

"All's well," he said briefly. Though they must be curious, particularly at the acquisition of another, and unknown, member of the party, this was too public a place for explanations. Before they left the glade, the

332

Stanwood boy had given Phoebe a shake and ordered her to compose herself, lest she set their efforts to naught. Solomon had replaced his bautta mask. Barlyon gathered he had taken it off to prove to Bart Stanwood he was not the Earl of Barlyon.

"Any number of my clients may be here, and as Furness has pointed out, my acquaintance would not reflect well upon you. Any of you," he added as an afterthought.

Aurelia said, "When the Marquess of Furness came storming out of the trees with no sign of any of you, we were concerned. He did stop to speak to us and…er…assure us there was no cause for alarm."

His mother cast a troubled glance at Aurelia.

"Pray forgive him if he was curt. He was in a bad mood. I suspect he is a stickler for correct conduct, like my late father. Speaking of which, ladies, may I present Bartholomew Stanwood, Mistress Phoebe's brother?"

Aurelia curtsied and murmured a greeting.

"How nice to meet you, Mr. Stanwood. I hope your brother Cornelius is recovering?" his mother inquired delicately.

"Oh, ay, he's fine, ma'am. Enjoying the country sports."

"Bart, you know Mama was worried about his head. 'Tis why she left town," Phoebe hissed.

After a moment, her brother picked up the hint. "Oh, she worries too much. Corny's got a hard head. He'll be fine, if he isn't already."

Barlyon knew Aurelia was fighting not to laugh, as he was, because she was careful not to look at him. His mother, however, showed the tact of the natural hostess.

"Would you care to join our party? Though I

suppose you are with a group of your young friends and would find us very sedate."

"As it happens, my lady, I am here on my own, the friend I was expecting to meet having failed me. I'd be pleased to join you."

"I fear we mean to leave soon, as the ladies have had an upsetting experience, but we have room in our barge for you."

"Thank you, my lord. Phoebe's easily overset by loud voices—zounds, you should hear Papa roar!—and the marquess was near as bad. My mother would send Feeb to bed with a cup of warm milk."

"Bart, please do not speak of our Papa." She dabbed at her eyes again.

"There, there, Feeb."

Hawkins spoke. "Now there's another man, I'll go on ahead and whistle up our barge, so the ladies will not be waiting at the water stairs."

And so Phoebe's and the men's disarrayed hair and clothing would not be exposed to public view longer than necessary. Barlyon had lost his hat and the ribbon that had tied back his hair; his hood had fallen back. Running a hand over his head, he found several leaves and a twig.

Stanwood asked hesitantly, "If it is brought up before we are there, will others not board it? Corny and his friends once got into a brawl over possession of a wherry."

"The oarsmen will stand off any boarders but ourselves." Hawkins grinned, an intimidating sight in itself, now he had removed his mask. "Any such river pirates will find themselves swimming home."

"It's a privately owned shallop," Barlyon said.

Hawkins's preferred mode of river travel, in fact.

They sorted themselves into couples, Sol with Lady Barlyon, Phoebe with her brother, and Aurelia with him at the tail, as they had been when the evening went awry.

"I was hoping for a few private words with you when Furness intervened." He spoke softly near her ear. "Now it will have to wait for tomorrow, I think. Mayhap you will wish to walk in the morning before breakfast? I misdoubt Phoebe or my mother will be up early." Furness's agreement not to speak of the events in the wood might not prevent his mentioning Barlyon's past, if he remembered it, although it seemed likely he had not recognized Barlicorn in the earl. Nevertheless, it was time and past time he spoke to Aurelia.

Furness would not violate their compact regarding Phoebe and Solomon, as he himself had much to lose by doing so. One loophole remained. He could not attempt to force Aurelia into marriage, but he might still continue to pay her attentions, trying to wear down her resistance. Furness might write to her father, expecting him to use his influence on Aurelia. She had the strength of character to resist, but he wanted to spare her the discomfort of the marquess's continued courtship.

"I almost always rise early, no matter how late I have been up. And this will be an early night, and I for one am glad of it."

"Ay, the music ended some time ago, so it's gone ten o'clock. Families and such folk as do not care for carousing or for men who are cup-shot have gone or soon will. It can hardly be much later than eleven, however."

By the time they reached Vauxhall Stairs, the ladies' progress being slow in their heeled shoes, the shallop waited. Hawkins stood before it, looking like bull-beef, arms crossed on his chest, domino flung back. Some dress swords were more for show than for use. Hawkins's was not. It would take a bold young buck to try to board. Besides, the oarsmen looked like proper tars, possibly some of Hawkins's former shipmates turned watermen.

Barlyon managed to sit beside Aurelia, but Phoebe ended up by his mother, who put her arm around the girl protectively. Bart Stanwood was seated next to Sol, nodding occasionally as Sol spoke to him. Barlyon caught a few phrases: "...viscount...rich and looking for a girl of good family..." Hawkins, on Aurelia's other side, leaned back without speaking, watching Sol and Stanwood with veiled amusement.

He and Aurelia did not speak, but one hand found its way to where Aurelia's rested on the upholstered bench and covered it.

Chapter 32

When Aurie entered the dining room, she found Barlyon already present.

He sprang to his feet and stood while she filled her plate and poured out a cup of chocolate, then pulled out her chair and seated her. "Are we to take some exercise this morning, Aurelia? If I may presume upon our acquaintance to address you informally?"

"Yes to both questions, my lord."

"Good. But I think you might use my given name, as my oldest friends do."

She lowered her eyes to her plate. "It seems presumptuous, sir."

"Perhaps it will seem less so after our walk. I would like to talk to you at some length when there's no chance of interruption. Where shall we go?"

"I meant to visit a milliner in Middle Row, Holborn, to buy a new fan and some lace. We might stroll in Lincoln's Inn Fields after. We could talk there, and in such an open, public place no one could object."

"Nor could anyone overhear."

They spoke only of trivialities on the walk to Holborn. Aurelia chose the first lace she saw of the correct width and selected a fan almost at random, the quicker to get to the important part of their errand.

"It seemed to me that a great deal was going on under the surface last night," she ventured after they continued up Holborn. "We were quite alarmed, too, by the marquess's manner when he preceded you out of the wood."

"Did he give offense?"

She shook her head. "No. It's only that I felt he was concealing annoyance. Whatever passed with Phoebe and her brother?"

Barlyon would not speak of it until they reached the broad expanse of Lincoln's Inn Fields. "It's easiest, perhaps, if I begin with last night's events. As we knew the Stanwood girl intended to maneuver me into having to offer for her, I arranged the thimble cheat with my old friends."

"Thimble cheat?"

"It's a sort of game in which the fellow running it puts a dried pea or the like under one of three thimbles, and the onlookers wager they can guess which thimble conceals it after he moves them around. He very seldom has to pay out."

"You and your friends kept switching places, like the thimbles. It was cleverly done, but it does explain why they had so little conversation, for they did not sound alike when they forgot to alter their voices. It seems to have worked, however."

"It did, and one of them has been considering marriage and might have been interested in courting Mistress Phoebe."

"Thus preserving you. I gather, on acquaintance, he decided against it." Explaining Deep Voice's slight headshake in the supper box.

"You met Ambrose Hawkins once when he visited me. Hawkins is not a man to enjoy a steady stream of tattle. I didn't know she chattered like a magpie. She never has in my company."

"She finds you intimidating."

"Compared to Hawkins, I'm a lap dog." He did not continue until a young man carrying a stack of several thick tomes scuttled past, his expression harried. "We had hoped to prevent the girl putting her plan into effect—unless of course Hawkins was willing to marry her—and I think we might have succeeded, if not for Furness creating a scene. I don't know whether she really was startled into running off into the trees or whether she saw her chance and grabbed it."

A little of both, perhaps. One's motives were seldom unmixed.

"Solomon de Toledo had no choice but to follow her—"

"A Spaniard? I would never have guessed, from his speech."

"His people came from Spain originally, but he's London born and bred. My first friend in London. He has no interest in marrying at the moment, or at least not in marrying Phoebe, but he volunteered to be my second decoy."

"Then her brother arrived? It must have been like a farce."

"Very like. Still, we were prepared for it. Solomon is ineligible by her family's standards. There was no danger of his being forced to offer for her."

"Thank goodness. I liked him. I suppose Lady Axton has set her heart on snaring a title for Phoebe."

"It's rather a question of Lord Axton needing a rich son-in-law, but the greater objection would be that Sol's a Jew and a moneylender. Though if he possessed enough wealth and were not in business, or at least not in the moneylending business, Axton might be willing to overlook the religious aspect."

"Well, I'm glad Mr. de Toledo wasn't sacrificed on the altar of matrimony. But then, what threw Furness into a temper?"

"That explanation brings us indirectly to the reason I wanted to talk to you. You had shortly before rejected Furness's offer of marriage."

"Was I meant to feel grateful that he is willing to marry me to restore my reputation?" Pointless, angry tears sprang to her eyes, and she drew her handkerchief out of her pocket.

"Pretend to stifle a sneeze."

She nodded, surreptitiously dabbing her eyes while seeming to cover her nose. She stifled her outrage along with her tears. "How can he think to resume his suit after all these years? Especially when I do not think he was seriously courting me and only offered for me—" But Lord Barlyon did not know she had been ruined. Did he? "I would not marry that man for any title or wealth he could offer."

"I rejoice to hear it, though I am not surprised. You are a woman of superior sense and discrimination."

"Why would he pursue me, anyway, unless to satisfy a desire to condescend to me, like King Cophetua to his Beggar Maid?"

"But you are not a beggar maid, Aurie." He paused, frowning. "I beg your pardon, I've heard my mother call you Aurie, and it is a much more approachable name than Aurelia, which makes me think of a stern Roman lady."

"With a frown and a Roman nose. And an imposing—" An imposing bosom. She really must mind her tongue. She might say such a thing to a female friend but never to a man. It sounded flirtatious.

He grinned down at her. He must have read her mind. The grin faded. "You are lovely, intelligent, witty, practical, everything a sensible man could ask in a wife."

"My lord, I fear you flatter me." If only she were all he wanted in a wife. But it hurt too much to wish he might court her, when it was impossible. "I do not enjoy the marquess's attentions. He wasn't as haughty when I first knew him." Realizing she had been diverted from her earlier question, she forged ahead. "In any case, it seemed to me he left the spinney more irate than he entered it with you, despite trying to conceal it."

"He is always on his dignity, and things were said that offended him. I can't repeat them, as we all agreed not to speak of them, to safeguard Phoebe's reputation."

"I see."

"That brings me to my confession."

"Confession?" Her heart, which had lifted somewhat at Barlyon's compliments, plummeted. His confession that he was already married? Or would have married her if her reputation were spotless?

"We've walked all the way around and come back to our starting point."

Barlyon's remark came as a surprise. Strolling along, she had paid no attention to their surroundings at all, only to the warmth and strength of his arm and the sound of his voice.

"Shall we make another circuit? Or we could walk back down this side and follow the street past the Lincoln's Inn buildings to Chancery Lane and thence to Holborn."

"The latter, I think, if it is possible to talk on the way."

They turned to retrace their steps to the southeast corner of the square and the beginning of Searle Street.

"You were saying you had something to confess?"

He sighed. "The account I gave of my life in London was considerably edited. I think only Clement Pettigrew understood how unlikely it was I could have survived without committing more serious crimes than snatching the occasional apple from a barrow. I was extremely lucky in meeting Sol soon after I arrived. Through him I found work that paid little but provided food and a safe place to sleep. Mayhap some other time I will give you a fuller account of my career, but the fact is, I dealt with the criminal class and aided and abetted criminal acts."

"How criminal?" she asked reluctantly.

"Say someone wanted to hire a mill-ken—that's a housebreaker—I would arrange it for a small fee."

"No worse than that? Not that that's not bad enough," she added.

"I did not deal in murder or fire-setting or counterfeiting. I arranged for things or men to be smuggled, and for stolen goods to be sold profitably. "

"I believe smuggling is almost a way of life in some parts."

"Ay, but it's still against the law."

She did not speak until they turned into Carey Street. "I suppose most of us would be willing to commit those crimes or worse, in order not to starve or freeze. I have spent enough time in London to see people, even young children, who are so thin and poorly clad that I ache for them. I know a servant girl who is turned off with no character must almost certainly turn to prostitution if she has no family to aid her. I won't cast the first stone, even if none of my sins are hanging offenses."

"I hoped you would understand. There can be no real legal consequences from my discreditable career. The House of Lords is notoriously reluctant to punish one of their own. However, if my past comes out, there would be social consequences. Someone might recognize me and mention it to someone who would mention it to others."

She felt his arm move ever so slightly, in some motion too small to be called a shrug. His face was tense.

"Like the woman in Covent Garden?"

"She won't say anything, but others might, if they knew me. They would likely not be heeded."

She detected an emphasis on the word "they" and looked up at him.

"It may come out, if Furness remembers where he first met me."

"He knew you before you came home?"

"We spoke once. He was still Viscount Ardrey then. He wanted to find someone to cripple a man who was paying court to his sister. She was inclined to favor a man who came of decent county gentry, therefore from Ardrey's perspective, he was a threat and had to be removed."

"He did that?" It came as a shock, no matter that she now realized Robert Sedgewick had always been swollen with pride, although as the son of a mere viscount, he lacked even a courtesy title. His family had been comfortable rather than wealthy. He had boasted that all their income derived from their lands: "We think it unbecoming our dignity to engage in commerce." He spoke as if investment in imports or mining or manufactories was the same as selling hot cross buns. Her own father owned shares in a shipbuilding business.

She had supposed that he had courted her only from a spirit of competition with Kit Hastings, never having believed he was deeply attached to her. Had he instead thought to make a rich marriage? Her dowry would have gained him no title but could have bought him a good manor and allowed him to live in more state than his father. Robert would have relished his improved status. Did the unexpected inheritance of his father's title and becoming heir to his uncle's marquessate feed his pride and self-importance to monstrous dimensions? It ought to have been unthinkable.

"I'm sorry. You have known and liked him for years. I understand how reluctant you must be to think ill of him."

"I was flattered by his attentions when I was eighteen, my lord. I am not sure I ever liked him. When he offered to marry me to save my reputation, I refused. Marriage to him would have been sensible, yet I could not do it. I acted from instinct rather than a reasoned decision, I fear."

"Instinct can be a valuable ally."

"What happened with his sister and her admirer?"

"I delayed, claiming I needed time to find a bravo, a man who would do harm for pay. Then I warned the suitor of Ardrey's intentions. The sister and her inamorato eloped. Ardrey's lackey conveyed his displeasure at my failure to act in time." A wry smile. "I had already offended Ardrey by my failure to grovel enough."

"Thank you for telling me. It makes me thankful I did not agree to marry him years ago and have discouraged his advances since returning to London." Carey Street ended at Chancery Lane, opposite the Rolls Buildings. She said no more until they had passed a group of three gentlemen of the legal persuasion who had stopped on the pavement to discuss some point of law. There would never be a better time to make her own confession.

"Ruined as I am, marriage to a man like that would be worse than living my life as an old maid. I suppose you are aware of my scandalous past." Someone must have informed him.

"I did hear of your unfortunate experience, at least as much as has been talked of. It appears obvious there are facts not generally known that made it impossible for you to wed either man."

She swallowed a lump in her throat. She really could not burst into tears on the street. To fight down the temptation both to weep and to throw herself into his arms, she thought of the home farm pigsty: the smell, the way the pigs snorted and gobbled the food scraps in their trough, the darling piglets that would eventually be flitches of bacon and hams, pork pies and sausages. It was a trick she had perfected years ago to keep countenance in difficult circumstances.

And then she felt able to explain her reasons for failing to redeem herself by marriage. "I refused to marry either Kit Hastings or Robert Sedgewick, who is now the Marquess of Furness, because to do so would have been to admit I had been compromised. Perhaps I might have blundered into marriage with Kit but for the shrine in his bedroom. I don't know if you can understand how unsettling I found that monument to his fascination with me. Some might think it mere sentiment. It terrified me. And he already had the special license. It was obvious he had planned to force me into marriage. Then even though he was dying, he would not give it up. I wouldn't marry Robert because I believed he offered out of duty rather than affection. I would have been trapped in a spiderweb of deceit and pretense whichever one I married." When she was done, Aurie wondered what he would think. What he would say.

"Hastings must have been a Bedlamite. Thank God you didn't marry either one."

She stopped and stared at him. "You are the only one to say so. Apart from myself. You don't agree with almost everyone that I should have married Kit and been a widow soon after?"

"No, because when you were out of mourning, some lucky man would have snapped you up, and I would never have met you except as a married lady."

She could not bear to think about what his words suggested. She must be mistaken. Think of the dear little pigs and Cook's receipt for pork pie.

They passed Holborn Bars. Barlyon said, "We have not much more time before we reach Barlyon House, and I have not yet finished my confession."

"Is there more?"

"I have not told you the worst thing I have done, which makes me little better than Furness. I beat a man very severely, leaving him permanently lame."

"Why did you do it?"

"He raped a tradesman's daughter. His family was noble. As a practical matter, the law offers no real remedy in any dispute between a member of the aristocracy and a commoner. The word of a gentleman weighs more heavily than that of a baker or costermonger or seamstress."

"You avenged her."

"Yes. Not much different from what Furness intended for his sister's suitor. I would plead that there is some difference, but you may not agree. I swear I am not violent by nature or inclination."

She gazed up at him, meeting his eyes. She understood how he had come to do such a thing: she possessed her own depths of anger. Still, she could hardly admit that she was actually glad one man had paid a price for his cruelty to a female.

"There is a world of difference. When the crimes of gentlemen are treated as sternly as those of the poor, I will take the church's condemnation of vengeance more seriously."

He smiled crookedly. "I hardly know how we can expect a man of the cloth who relies upon a nobleman for his living and for donations to the parish church to bite the hand that feeds him." After they strolled on for a few more steps, he began, "I could not speak until—"

A boy of eight or nine erupted out of Fetter Lane in front of them and turned east, running as fast as his short legs would carry him. Aurie stopped short to stare after him, only to find herself unceremoniously hurried forward a few steps. Barlyon's arm brought her to a halt where Fetter Lane met Holborn as a tradesman of the poorer sort tried to pass the earl. Instead, it was not quite clear how, the fellow jostled Barlyon, who released Aurie's arm and caught the man by the shoulders.

"Here, you must not thrust aside other passersby. Apart from being churlish, you might have injured the lady."

"I—I'm very sorry, sir," he stammered when he was able to catch his breath. "I never meant to—don't know how it happened. I was chasing a little limb of Satan that tried to snatch a bun I'd bought and set down on my workbench. Begging your pardon again, I'll be on my way, if I've not already lost him," he ended glumly.

"You've a paunch to slow you. You must have some success in your trade. You're winded now and in no condition to run farther unless you want to bring on an apoplexy. Did the brat get your bun, then?"

"No, sir, my son saw him and cried out to warn me."

"Your son should have pursued him."

"My boy's lame. I left him to guard my shop."

"Well, here's a coin to buy an ale to cool you and restore your humors."

The man babbled his thanks for his lordship's kindness, perhaps less for the coin than for overlooking his clumsiness in shouldering the earl aside.

Neither spoke until they had continued on and turned into Hatton Garden. "You meant that child to escape."

"I did. I was a few years older than that poor little rat when I came to town, and surviving was hard enough for me."

"I'm glad you let him get away." A few gentlemen

would have tried to stop the boy. Barlyon had contrived to get into his pursuer's way and stop the chase. Understandable, given his account of his life before he returned to his home.

She cast her mind back over their earlier conversation. He had told her of the more discreditable parts of his past. He had listened sympathetically when she explained why she could not marry either Kit or Robert, and he had understood her reasons. He had revealed the one incident about which he evidently felt guilt. Unnecessarily, in her opinion. The earl had said, I could not speak until—Until what? Speak of what? Why had he confided in her?

She wracked her brain for a way to resume that interesting conversation, but Barlyon House was in sight and it was too late.

Chapter 33

"...amazing vocal range and ability to hold a note...Senesino!...did you hear the aria by Handel... Farinelli...heavenly..."

Barlyon stole a glance at Aurie, who listened with well-feigned interest to his mother and her elderly cavalier's discussion of the finer points of Italian opera. Barlyon would rather have stayed home, if he could have done so with Aurie. He had been forestalled in completing their exchange two days ago both because there had been a great deal to say on either side and by the interlude with the ragamuffin and his pursuer. No opportunity had occurred since to address her privately. Perhaps if she could be persuaded to come down early for breakfast...Phoebe would be staying at her own home overnight, as her papa had—surprisingly— insisted that she dine there tonight. Mayhap it was the result of the fragments of conversation between Sol and the girl's brother overheard in the shallop.

Standing in Lady Grace Jordan's salon, his mind drifted. The swirl of bright colors reminded him of his Barlicorn wardrobe: crimson, saffron yellow, pink, sky blue, green, and puce, with glinting accents provided by gold or silver embroidery. The gathering was small compared to her ball but even more exclusive. Lady Grace had hired a soprano, the opera's latest darling, to entertain her music-fancying friends. They were also to be treated to performances by a harpsichordist and a violinist. Attendance in the ballroom would not be mandatory, Lady Grace being well aware that some who were present as escorts would prefer conversation in the salon or whist or loo or ombre in the library.

He would accompany his mother and Aurie when the beginning of the performance was announced. It would be the courteous thing to do, although his previous experience of opera, soon after they came to town, left him unimpressed. The word "caterwauling" sprang to mind. He much preferred country tunes and the current popular airs. On the other hand, it would give him the opportunity to sit beside Aurie. For that alone he would make the effort, especially as Sir Evelyn, having laid claim to Lady Barlyon almost from her arrival, appeared unlikely to move from her side.

Lady Grace was approaching their group, a young couple in her wake.

"May I present my dear Theo's nephew, Mr. Jeremiah Fletcher, and his wife, Mrs. Fletcher? They are visiting from Shropshire."

Jeremiah Fletcher. The name sparked a memory of Job's Coffee House, with its scents of coffee, chocolate, and tobacco. In the ensuing flurry of greetings, questions, and exclamations over the musical delights in store for them, Barlyon teased at the tendril of recollection.

Not only the coffee house, but Peter, Barlicorn's human bloodhound, as well: "The cove's Viscount Ardrey. He's his sister's guardian. He's a widower, as his whither-go-ye died some time ago. He's been in no hurry to marry again, having already got two sons. Recent-like, he's in the market for family connections."

"Did you hear anything about the sister?"

"She's a rum-mort, pretty and pleasant, they say, with a dowry fit to buy a small county. She don't much care for the idea of marrying the man her brother's set on, some old earl that's promised Ardrey his daughter. A trade, like."

"And the undesirable suitor?"

"Hasn't got a title nor much in his pockets. The ones as has to do with him like him. Pleasant-spoke, like the girl."

Barlyon forced his mind back to the present. Lady Grace moved on, leaving the Fletchers behind. Neither had been in town since their marriage. A relative's wedding gave them the opportunity to visit and see old friends and family connections. They gave every evidence of enjoying each other's company.

"I vow I will be glad to go home again," Mrs. Fletcher admitted. "We left our daughter there." She blushed prettily, causing Barlyon to suspect that she was breeding and had colored up at the thought of the daughter's eventual brother or sister.

Her cream taffeta mantua was not new. Familiar with the tricks a tailor could perform, he noted that the sleeves had been altered and the trimmings changed in an attempt to follow the latest fashion. Or what was believed to be the latest fashion in whatever town was nearest the Fletchers' manor.

Ardrey's sister had been said to have a good dowry. Surely she could afford a new gown? From casual references he gathered they lived very modestly on their property, a wedding gift from Uncle Theo Jordan.

Fletcher had been describing his efforts to help

with the sheep shearing their first year at the manor. "We were short by two laborers as one had taken ill and the other fell off a ladder and broke his arm. It looked simple enough…"

Barlyon noticed that Aurelia's voice broke off in mid-sentence in the other group, because he tended to notice everything pertaining to Aurelia.

Fletcher ended, "…and the next thing I knew, I was on the ground, the blasted sheep was on top of me, her hoof was on the shears, and her expression was thoughtful, if you take my meaning."

Barlyon laughed aloud, even as he saw Aurie and Fletcher's wife gazing past his shoulder with very different expressions. Aurie looked angry, while Mrs. Fletcher looked apprehensive.

"Lord Furness." Aurie's tone was cold. Barlyon turned.

"B-brother," Mrs. Fletcher stammered.

"Barlicorn!"

The exclamation turned heads though Furness had not shouted. The chamber, previously spacious, seemed to have shrunk. Conversations in their immediate vicinity died.

Oh, hell. Barlyon faced him, raising his eyebrows. "I beg your pardon?"

"I know you." The marquess spoke in a low, furious voice. Silence spread like a ripple in still water. Evidently realizing he now had an audience, Furness swiveled to address the greater part of the room.

"The noble Earl of Barlyon is a common criminal. He was known as John Barlicorn at a mean little coffee house he frequented to transact his felonious business. It was called Job's, in St. Clement's Lane, off Lombard

Street."

"I used Barlicorn as my nom de guerre from the time I ran away as a boy to make it harder for my father to find me." If his father had bothered to search for him. "I did visit Job's Coffee House occasionally." He would not deny the charge he'd been a criminal because a criminal would deny it. Would those listening take his refusal to reply to Furness's allegation as proof he had been a rogue or as contemptuous dismissal of it? He hoped for the latter.

Sir Evelyn spoke, startling them all. "How do you know this, Lord Furness?"

"I saw him there, of course!"

"At the…ah…'mean little coffee house'?" Sir Evelyn's brows arched delicately. His mild inquiry was impossible to take for either disbelief or irony. Almost.

"Yes."

"I would hardly have thought to find you in such a place, my lord."

The marquess made a quick recovery, almost quick enough for his hearers not to notice his reply came a breath too slow. "I had heard the place was as remarkable for its collection of felons as the Royal Menagerie is for its exotic beasts or Bedlam for its lunatics."

"How interesting. From whom did you hear of it?"

"Why, how should I recall now? 'Tis several years since I viewed the place. I suppose I heard of it in some other coffee house or in a group of acquaintances."

Their group was now surrounded by a ring of onlookers too fascinated by the show to pretend to ignore it.

Sir Evelyn Barstow's gaze passed over the circle

and stopped at the Duke of Guysbridge. "Your Grace, you were tolerable familiar with the amusements to be had in London, I think. Were you aware of a den of felons to be found at—what was the name of the place? Oh, Job's, that was it, I think?—at the coffee house known as Job's?"

Barlyon kept his countenance bland. The duke was well known to have been poor as a church mouse until he came into his late brother's title and sure to be aware of any inexpensive source of entertainment.

Guysbridge possessed the sangfroid and hauteur of the Spaniard from whom he was descended. He raised his eyebrows. "I never heard of the place." He smiled charmingly. "If I had, I would certainly have visited it."

Barstow's sharp eyes went next to a middle-aged man who was well but quietly dressed. "Markham. You have connections in all parts of London. Do you know of Job's?"

Barlyon had heard of Roger Markham. The man was an importer of various goods, recently retired from the business. At least as of the time Barlicorn disappeared from London, he had still been buying and selling information, as Barlicorn had done with a less exalted clientele. The beau monde in general might not know of it, but gentlemen who needed Markham's services would. From Furness's expression, he was aware of Markham's reputation.

Markham said, "I have heard of Job's, as it happens. A small place, not fashionable, and perfectly undiscriminating. Men of all stations resort there, rather than one sort only. In my youth, one might see a gentleman, a duke, a haberdasher, a student, a carter, and a printer all at the same table, exchanging views on politics or natural philosophy. 'Penny universities,' they called coffee houses then. Job's has seemingly kept that tradition while other coffee houses have taken to catering to one group or another: lawyers or Whigs or scribblers. Upon my soul, I suspect you might find a felon or two even at the most exclusive coffee houses. I am not aware Job's is noted for criminals."

Several men around them nodded or muttered agreement. A lady protested, "I cannot believe you would find a criminal in the better sort, sir. Our husbands and sons would not consort with a felon."

Markham inclined his head fractionally before meeting her eyes. "Mayhap not if they were aware of it."

Barlyon knew nothing of the woman beyond the fact that she was Mistress Tyne-Wilkes, but Markham's bland remark struck home. While her face, neck, and bosom were too heavily painted to reveal a blush, her body reacted to it. Her grip on her fan tightened, and she looked away.

"After all, even in the best society, crimes are sometimes committed: a death aided for the sake of convenience, a dowry embezzled or wrongly withheld, a theft." Markham's genial smile should have robbed the words of offense.

Mrs. Fletcher tightened her hold on her husband's arm. He smiled down at her and gave an almost imperceptible shrug.

White with fury, the marquess snapped, "I resent your suggestion that any gentleman would commit a crime. I bid you good evening."

They watched in silence as Furness strode toward the front hall. Markham, Barlyon concluded, was a dangerous man and far more subtle than the marquess. The spectacle having ended, the bystanders moved off, leaving Barlyon's party, the Fletchers, and Markham.

"It's passing strange Lord Furness should take such violent exception to an innocent comment," Aurie observed. "It is really not unthinkable that a gentleman should commit a crime, after all. Was it not about a year ago that an attorney in Suffolk was murdered by his son? It was spoken of as very fine work on the part of Colonel de Veil, the magistrate."

"I suppose it was for the sake of an inheritance." His mother fingered the ruched silk edging the front of her gown, a sure sign of either embarrassment or nerves. At a guess, she thought it unfeminine for a young lady to speak of crime. The restrictions on what proper young ladies could speak of made many of them very boring conversationalists.

Sir Evelyn requested permission to present Markham. In the spate of social trivialities, the Fletchers exchanged glances. They came to some agreement, as Markham excused himself.

Mrs. Fletcher coughed delicately. It was Fletcher who spoke.

"Sir Evelyn, Mr. Markham, we feel you should be warned that Furness is dangerous. He is my wife's brother, and we have cause to know."

He did not immediately continue. Mrs. Fletcher said hesitantly, "My husband is reluctant to say more. I am not. Robert was already at Harrow when I was born, and so we never became close. He inherited the title unexpectedly. I'm sorry to say he became increasingly arbitrary and resented any thwarting of his will."

"Perhaps it is not necessary to go into more detail,

Henriette."

"I think it is, no matter how embarrassing it is for us. I have been fearful ever since you received the letter that warned you of my brother's intentions." She gazed first at Sir Evelyn, then at Markham. "He meant to have Jeremiah grievously harmed in order to force me to marry a man of my brother's choosing. We eloped instead. I do not regret it, and I do not care that," she snapped her fingers, "for the scandal. You both made Robert look foolish, as he would see it. We could not let you go in ignorance of the risk."

"Thank you, Mistress Fletcher. Forewarned is forearmed."

"No wonder he was furious." Barstow's tone was soft and dry as dust. "The suggestion that a gentleman could commit a crime pricked him."

"I may have pricked him in another place as well," Markham murmured.

"Was your allusion to embezzlement of a dowry an arrow shot at random?" Barlyon asked.

Markham made an apologetic grimace. "I mentioned it based only on circumstantial evidence."

"Circumstantial evidence has hanged a good many men," Barstow remarked. "I read law as a young man, ay, and practiced it until my father died. Fletcher, may one commit the vulgarity of inquiring…?"

Fletcher laughed ironically. "Sir Evelyn, we left London posthaste for Scotland, and then went to earth in my family's manor. Under the circumstances, it seemed unwise to raise the issue of marriage settlements."

Lady Grace's husband announced that the musical entertainment would commence in a few minutes. The

Fletchers excused themselves, and Sir Evelyn offered his arm to Lady Barlyon.

"My thanks to you, Sir Evelyn and to you, Mr. Markham, for smoothing over an awkward situation. To refute his accusation would have made me sound guilty." More guilty than he was.

"Markham and I did very little, my lord."

"You cast doubt on the truth of his accusation."

"I merely posed a few of the questions he would be asked at trial by any competent barrister. He could not prove you had committed any crime. He might bribe someone to testify, but the perjured witness would have to admit to knowledge of a crime. You will rarely find a man willing to incriminate himself to testify against another unless he's already promised immunity in return. I believe Furness has now realized his mistake."

He shot without aiming. John had laughed at him in Job's. Seeing his sister and Fletcher and John and perhaps recognizing his laugh, all kindled his memory of Barlicorn.

"Still, this affair will be talked of, and the talk will last longer than on-dits about Mr. X and Lady Y," Markham said.

"I refuse to worry overmuch about talk. Heed Mistress Fletcher's warning. Furness is dangerous."

"I have no doubt of it." The baronet traded glances with Markham. "We are wily old foxes."

With the flash of a grin hinting at the rakish, go-to-hell fellow Markham might once have been, he added, "Furness is not."

Someone hailed Markham then and bore him off to the cardroom.

"Shall we make our way to the ballroom to find

seats?" Sir Evelyn inquired. Barlyon and Aurelia followed them, pursued by a hum of speculation. Damn Furness.

Barlyon bent his head to speak into Aurie's ear. "I hoped to take you aside for a few private words tonight as we were prevented on our walk the other day."

"Do you not still hope to speak with me, my lord?" Her eyes lowered and only her profile was visible, making her expression impossible to read.

"Circumstances have changed. You may not want to hear what I have to say."

"Nevertheless, it must be said."

They entered the ballroom to find Sir Evelyn and his mother had paused to talk with the Duke of Guysbridge and his duchess.

"Barlyon, we have been asking Lady Barlyon if we may join your party. Last year's two unexpected heirs should flock together."

The merger of the two groups made them the focus of all eyes and subdued conversation around them proved that scandal was under discussion. In some way, however, the effect was diluted, whether because the other guests were dividing their attention between two scandalous peers or because the duke's evident approval conferred a cachet. His mother and Sir Evelyn showed no discomfort, nor did Guysbridge or his lady, who was telling Lady Barlyon about a recent Italian musical invention, the *gravicembalo col piano e forte*, which, she said, "I understand to mean it resembles a harpsichord but plays both loudly and softly." Aurie seemed downcast though she paid superficial attention. Then the soprano was announced, and conversation ended.

As Sir Evelyn had arrived by chair, they took him up in the Barlyon coach to deliver him to his lodgings. At Barlyon House, his mother tactfully went up to bed, after kissing his cheek and patting Aurie's hand. This unusually demonstrative behavior he took as encouragement. Thank God he had told her days ago about his past so Furness's revelation had not come as a shock.

Barlyon dismissed the footman who had admitted them and taken the ladies' cloaks.

"Will you come to the library with me for a few minutes, Aurie? It's not proper, but I must talk with you. Tomorrow there will be servants bustling about, and while my mother can be relied upon to ease the way, there's Phoebe as well."

She smiled sadly. "I've been ruined for years. I believe I need not worry too much about the proprieties."

He lit all the candles in the library, bathing them in a golden glow, while Aurie seated herself in one of the comfortable chairs by the fireplace. He should have remembered the room lacked a settee. They could have gone to the drawing room instead. Though doing so would not have guaranteed she would choose the settee. No, this matter called for the coziness of dark oak paneling, books, and the cheerful red and blue Turkish carpet.

How to do it? She was staring at her hands clasped in her lap, not the posture of a lady expecting good news. What good news was she not expecting? People, including females, were far more forthright in his old neighborhood. "Now, then, Barlicorn, what's all this?" Gwen would have demanded. All this genteel propriety was a great mistake. Still, he should do it in style. He went down on one knee before her chair.

"Aurie, I love you. Will you marry me, in spite of the talk?" Which might last for decades.

"M-marry you?" She sounded astonished almost to speechlessness.

"I've wanted to ask you for weeks, and I meant to ask you before that young imp crossed our path and then the opportunity was lost."

"Earlier this evening you said circumstances had changed, that I would not want to hear what you had to say."

He reviewed his words. "I expressed myself badly. I had been conceited enough to believe you might be willing to marry me. With tonight's events, I feared you would have changed your mind. If you'd been willing before, that is. I never took for granted that you might feel some regard for me."

"Are you saying you still want to marry me? There are dozens of ladies who would be glad to wed you."

"In spite of my reputation?"

"You are an earl. If you had two heads, you would still be accounted a prize, whatever Furness said."

"But they would want me for my title, whereas I hoped you liked the man, even after my confession to you."

"Were you to marry some lady of a family with good social connections, Furness's denunciation would soon be forgotten. I sensed his claim was already being dismissed, probably because of Sir Evelyn and Mr. Markham and the duke. I am an expert in evaluating gossip, my lord."

"I would rather have a wife who felt warmly

toward me than one with social connections. Aurie, will you marry me? Please?"

"You mean it."

Was it a statement or a question? He could not tell, as the last word ended in a gasp. Candlelight reflected on the tears in her eyes.

"Yes." Awkward to embrace a lady sitting in a chair when one was kneeling. Then she threw her arms around his neck and fell forward into his arms. This would have been delightful, except that he was now lying on the floor, one leg bent uncomfortably to the side, under a warm bundle of curves, scented with violet. He ran his hands over her firmly corseted waist and back. On second thought, the leg was no problem at all.

"I take it that you accept?" he murmured into her hair.

Her "Mmmm," was muttered into his shoulder. Her fingers kneaded the back of his neck.

He kissed the top of her head, getting a few stray hairs in his mouth. She twisted her head and kissed the side of his neck.

"I love your enthusiasm, Aurie, my sweet."

"John…"

The library door opened. "John, are you still up?" his mother inquired. "I wanted to—oh!"

Aurie squeaked and tried to disengage herself, no easy or graceful task with her upper body confined in a rigid corset and yards of petticoats and gown hampering her lower limbs. Her lovely lower limbs, which lay on either side of his leg, the one that was not bent awkwardly.

"I am indeed up. Forgive me for not rising

immediately, Mother. It's my pleasure to inform you that Aurie has consented to marry me."

And as she struggled to rise, her rump did twitch.

Aurie scrambled to her feet and curtsied. "Lady Barlyon…"

"My dear! This is excellent news." His mother swept her into an embrace.

Barlyon succeeded in standing and made her the court bow he had practiced against presentation to the king, who, mercifully, was currently in Hanover. By the time he returned, Barlyon hoped to have perfected all the pettifogging rules of court politesse.

"Now, Aurie, I think it is time you went to bed."

Aurie curtsied again. "I'm sure you are correct, ma'am." Her face still rosy with embarrassment and—dare he hope?—desire, she turned to smile at him before tripping out the door, delightfully rumpled.

"I trust you will be sending a notice to the paper tomorrow, John."

"Perhaps I had better send a groom with a letter to Lord Pennyroyal first."

"Yes, dear, perhaps you had best get the proprieties out of the way now that you have taken care of the important matter."

"It was not quite what it looked like, ma'am. May I ask what brought you down to speak to me—now that we have taken care of the important matter?"

"Why, I was hoping to catch you in a compromising situation with Aurie, of course. I knew she had not yet come upstairs. I couldn't think what was keeping you from making an offer when you were so clearly *épris*."

"Mother, have I mentioned that I love you?"

"No, but I never told you, either, did I? Am I forgiven for not doing so?"

"Oh, yes." He hugged his mother, possibly for the first time in his life. John Barlicorn was home at last.

A word about the author…

When she was three years old, Kathleen Buckley's father bought a set of the Encyclopaedia Britannica. Big books! With all kinds of words (and pictures) in them!

By the age of twelve, she knew she wanted to write fiction. (She also wanted to be a journalist, a spy, and a spaceperson—but NASA wasn't accepting female spacepersons then.) She never became a journalist because she hates asking pushy questions, nor a spy, because she's not good with foreign languages, has bad eyes, and is not athletic. But along the way, she worked in a hospital billing department, as a bookkeeper in a print shop, as a paralegal, and as a security officer.

In semi-retirement, she began to write full-time, at least when not pursuing her other hobbies: reading, cats, cooking, costume projects, and spinning wheel repair. And no, she can't spin. That will have to come after the spinning wheel repair.

Thank you for purchasing
this publication of The Wild Rose Press, Inc.

For questions or more information
contact us at
info@thewildrosepress.com.

The Wild Rose Press, Inc.
www.thewildrosepress.com

To visit with authors of
The Wild Rose Press, Inc.
join our yahoo loop at
http://groups.yahoo.com/group/thewildrosepress/

www.ingramcontent.com/pod-product-compliance
Lightning Source LLC
Chambersburg PA
CBHW051128030726
47504CB00004B/761